KU-571-418

A NURSE TO CLAIM HIS HEART

JULIETTE HYLAND

NEONATAL DOC ON HER DOORSTEP

SCARLET WILSON

MILLS & BOON

All rights reserved including the right of reproduction
in whole or in part in any form. This edition is published
by arrangement with Harlequin Enterprises ULC.

This is a work of fiction. Names, characters, places, locations
and incidents are purely fictional and bear no relationship to
any real life individuals, living or dead, or to any actual places,
business establishments, locations, events or incidents.
Any resemblance is entirely coincidental.

This book is sold subject to the condition that it shall not,
by way of trade or otherwise, be lent, resold, hired out
or otherwise circulated without the prior consent of the publisher
in any form of binding or cover other than that in which it is published
and without a similar condition including this condition
being imposed on the subsequent purchaser.

® and TM are trademarks owned and used by the trademark owner
and/or its licensee. Trademarks marked with ® are registered with the
United Kingdom Patent Office and/or the Office for Harmonisation
in the Internal Market and in other countries.

First Published in Great Britain 2022
by Mills & Boon, an imprint of HarperCollins*Publishers* Ltd,
1 London Bridge Street, London, SE1 9GF

www.harpercollins.co.uk

HarperCollins*Publishers*
1st Floor, Watermarque Building,
Ringsend Road, Dublin 4, Ireland

A Nurse to Claim His Heart © 2022 by Juliette Hyland

Neonatal Doc on Her Doorstep © 2022 by Scarlet Wilson

ISBN: 978-0-263-30119-9

03/22

MIX
Paper from
responsible sources
FSC® C007454

This book is produced from independently certified FSC™ paper
to ensure responsible forest management.
For more information visit www.harpercollins.co.uk/green.

Printed and Bound in Spain using 100% Renewable Electricity
at CPI Black Print, Barcelona

A NURSE TO CLAIM HIS HEART

JULIETTE HYLAND

MILLS & BOON

For Dad, whose bookshelf I longed to join as a kid.
Thanks for all the support and love.

CHAPTER ONE

CROSSING HIS ARMS, Dr. Benedict Denbar played the "can I get comfortable in the small metro seat?" game. He considered standing, but it was early in the morning, and he was going to be on his feet all day while working at Wald Children's Hospital. At least the uncomfortable plastic let him avoid the crush of people pressed into the metro car. It wasn't much in the way of quiet time before his shift started, but it let him clear his head before starting the day as the attending physician in the level four neonatal intensive care unit.

The NICU was quiet. In fact the doctors and nurses did their best to keep the noise level below forty-five decibels as recommended by the American Academy of Pediatrics to protect the tiny babies in the unit. But the quiet wasn't restorative and the stress of the environment, where patients shifted from stable to critical in hours, sometimes minutes, wore on many of his colleagues. He'd seen dozens of doctors and nurses seek different specialties.

And he didn't blame them. But the NICU was his calling. His place to make a difference. His place to make amends.

He closed his eyes as his thoughts wandered to Olivia. They'd traveled there so often lately, as his dream of a high-risk maternity unit in the children's hospital was finally becoming a reality. Assuming Wald's Children's Hospital could fund the multimillion-dollar investment.

He'd been on the committee suggesting fundraising ideas, and there were several high-profile fundraisers planned. But was it enough?

He blew out a breath. This was his dream. Benedict needed the unit funded. Needed to find a way to support the mothers of the babies in his unit.

Medical care for NICU patients had come a long way since he'd stood over Olivia's incubator, not knowing that the heated crib was actually called an isolette. But too many mothers were separated from their children while they received care and their children were treated in the high-risk nursery.

If only she'd been born a few weeks later…a few days even. If the world were fair, he'd be helping plan her eighteenth birthday now. But life wasn't fair.

And if she'd lived, he wouldn't be sitting on an uncomfortable chair in DC. Hell, he probably wouldn't have become a physician…at least not a pediatrician specializing in neonatal care. His life would look completely different.

All sacrifices he'd have gladly made to raise Isiah's daughter. His brother had been gone for nineteen years this month. Nineteen years… A lifetime.

He'd now lived more of his life without his baby brother than with him, but Benedict still found himself searching for him. Still longed to call him at the end of the day. It was a funny feeling to miss part of yourself.

Benedict shook himself and straightened in his seat. He'd thought of Isiah a lot over the last few months. And Olivia, and her mother, Amber—his wife.

At least his wife according to legal documents. A connection bonded by a vow he'd made to Isiah, but never even sealed with a kiss. A vow that shouldn't have been necessary, if Isiah had only listened to Benedict's arguments about his shift from certified drag racing to illegal street racing for cash.

Amber had arrived at his door less than two weeks after Isiah's funeral. Tears streaking across her face as she protectively cradled her belly. He'd known her predicament and that her mother would disown her for getting pregnant at eighteen. An unwed mother would not be welcome in her home. It might have been the twenty-first century, but that didn't matter.

Isiah had planned to use the winnings of his last illegal street race to run away with her. If only he'd told Benedict, they'd have found a different way.

There was almost always a different way. Something else you could try. But that was a lesson that came with age and experience. And blinded by love, his brother hadn't been able to think clearly.

His phone dinged, and he pulled it from his pocket. His mother's face with a new ring held in front of her face and giant smile with a guy he did not recognize flashed on his screen. He couldn't stop his eyes from rolling to the ceiling. If she made it to the altar, this would be her sixth husband, and he'd lost count of the number of fiancé's she'd dumped or been dumped by. Yet, with each new relationship, she sent him a text… that he never answered.

Love.

Benedict scoffed and ignored the stare from the elderly woman sitting next to him. He hadn't meant to let noise out, but love or the feeling that people claimed was love really was too fallible to be trusted. It either turned to hate or destroyed.

Responsibility, friendship, even honor, last longer than love. Which was why he'd stepped in where his brother could not. Accepting a platonic union as they'd helped each other mourn the loss of his brother and then the loss of Olivia when she was born too early.

So tiny.

And with that, his connection to Amber should have ended, and in many ways it had. They'd married when he was nineteen, and separated three days before he'd turned twenty-one, just after he'd enrolled at Oregon State University, determined to help babies like Olivia.

But Amber hadn't wanted the shame of a divorce. Her family, difficult though they were, were all she had left now that Isiah and Olivia were gone. She'd asked him to stay married, at least on paper. And he'd agreed, after all he'd promised till death, and Benedict hadn't wanted to follow down his parents' path of broken vows. He'd meant the words when he said them—vows were not to be made lightly no matter what his mother and father thought of their promises.

So they'd stayed married. Amber got to keep the illusion that she was married for her mother and Benedict got to do right by the woman his brother had loved. It wasn't as though he'd ever planned to marry for love anyway. He'd seen how dangerous that was, so what did it matter if he remained married to Amber for duty's sake?

A young couple entered the metro with a newborn. The young man wrapped his arms around the mother. They looked exhausted, but most parents at that stage wore exhaustion well, almost basked in it as they loved on their baby. The woman laid her head against her partner's shoulder while cradling the infant wrapped against her chest. It was picture perfect, but one never knew what went on in other people's homes.

He deleted the text from his mother, then looked at the message he'd sent Amber yesterday about starting their divorce procedures. She'd left it on Read. He shook his head as he added following up with her to his mental to-do list. A few weeks ago, she'd asked to wait a bit longer while she dealt with her mother's illness.

But how long?

The metro slowed, and Benedict leaned forward as the door to the Foggy Bottom Station opened. Penelope Greene, Penny, stepped onto the train. She met his gaze, nodded and quickly shuffled to the other side of the car.

He tried not to let that hurt.

He and Penny were colleagues. Nothing more. Though seven years ago, they'd been as close as work colleagues could be. Coffee breaks, laughter and support as she found her way as a junior nurse, and he navigated the last days of his residency. He'd been attracted to her, desperately so. Their friendship nested on the edge of so much more. He'd dreamed of kissing her more often than he cared to remember.

But Penny had made no secret of the fact that she wanted a family. A re-creation of the happy home that she and her little sister, Alice, had grown up in.

For a brief second all those years ago, Benedict had wished he could give her those things. Wished that he believed a happily-ever-after was possible. Wished he were free to promise things that no one could really promise. Life shifted too unpredictably for anyone to truly promise for better or worse and forever.

And love eventually faded...if you were lucky. If you weren't, it destroyed you, body and soul.

And Penny was an unfortunate exhibit in that truth. She'd been engaged when she left Wald Children's Hospital three years ago. He'd tried to be happy for her. Tried to ignore the tingle of jealousy that crested through him. And he'd tried not to be happy when she'd returned last year.

She'd moved back in with her sister, another nurse in the NICU. The fancy ring on her left hand gone, though the tan line had been visible through most of the winter. She didn't smile as much as she had before. There were no flirtatious jokes or coffee runs anymore. But it wasn't Benedict's place to ask what had happened.

It was selfish to wish they could go back to their friendly talks. Selfish to be glad she was back…without a wedding band. But he was glad, so glad.

The metro car jerked and halted as the lights turned off. A few cries of alarm echoed in the car before the emergency lights flipped on.

"You've got to be kidding me." The words of the passenger next to him floated into the metro car, and Benedict involuntarily nodded.

The DC metro usually ran without a hitch. But with over six hundred thousand daily commuters and tourists, when slowdowns occurred they affected nearly every sector of the city, from government and military employees to private-sector employees and medical providers to the tourists who crammed in each day to see the National Mall and free museums.

"No!" the young mother he'd seen earlier shouted as she gripped her baby. "Is there a doctor, please?"

Benedict stood and moved toward the couple, and he saw Penny start toward them too.

"What's wrong?" Benedict couldn't see anything

immediately wrong with the child, but the lighting wasn't great.

Penny grabbed her cell phone and turned on the flashlight function.

Benedict nodded to her and redirected his attention to the mother. "I'm Dr. Denbar, a neonatal pediatrician, and this is Penny Greene, one of the finest NICU nurses you will ever meet. What is going on?"

"My brother has seizures." She choked out as her partner patted her knee. "Last night Cole jerked forward. I remember my brother doing that. But it was over so quick. I thought. But just now he stiffened again. Our pediatrician recommended we go to Wald Children's this morning, to be evaluated in the ER."

"Can we get a little more light in here, please?" Penny called as she looked to the four closest riders. "You can stay where you are, but if you have a cell phone and could turn on the flashlight, that would be helpful."

A few passengers followed her instructions, but he saw several others hold up their cells without adding their flashlight. No doubt filming the encounter.

Why was everything a social media post?

"Does anybody have a towel?" Benedict asked, not really expecting an answer. The Blue Line that they were on was usually trafficked by commuters at this hour. When no one immediately volunteered, Benedict racked his brain, trying to think of something the train full of commuters would have.

"Can I please have your BDU shirt?" Penny's question sounded more like an order as she addressed the military member to her right. "It will provide the baby some safety as we evaluate him. The floor here is the definition of unsanitary."

The military sergeant quickly unbuttoned the outer layer of his battle uniform and handed it to Penny. She handed him her phone, and he stood with the light over the area. She was a commanding presence in the NICU and out.

Laying the uniform on the floor, she looked at the mom. "Can we take a look at your son?"

The mother carefully unwrapped the child and gingerly handed him to Benedict. The baby looked to be about six weeks old. Given the size of the newborns Benedict routinely worked with, this guy was hefty—which was perfect.

Until the left side of his body tightened. He saw Penny look to the watch on her wrist as she timed the muscle group tensing. It was classic myoclonic seizure presentation in an infant. Something most parents wouldn't recognize, unless they had a family member that experienced seizures.

"Forty-three seconds," Penny stated as the muscles released.

"Call the train operator. Then alert the NICU that we have a patient inbound and ask to have the neurologist on call notified."

Penny nodded as she moved toward the call station behind him.

"You were right to head to Wald Children's this morning. And I think your son is having myoclonic seizures."

The boy's limbs seized again, and Benedict felt his insides twist. So little and three seizures in less than five minutes. Seizure clusters were not uncommon, but he wanted this little guy somewhere where he had access to medical equipment.

"The cars separated behind us. The metro may be stuck for at least an hour—"

"We can't wait that long. He seized again while you were talking to the conductor." Benedict felt bad for interrupting, but at least an hour likely meant at least three to get them back on their way. And there were still three additional stops before they reached theirs, then Wald's was another ten-minute walk. A very pleasant commute, when you didn't have an ill child.

"I know." Penny turned her attention to the parents. "I already worked out with the conductor for Dr. Denbar and I, and one of you to walk along the emergency route back to Foggy Bottom Station. An ambulance will meet us there to transport us to Wald's."

Of course she'd worked it out. Penny and her sister, Alice, had grown up all over the place as their parents, both active duty military, had moved around the world. The girls were two of the most resourceful women he'd ever met. And bound tightly together after a childhood of picking up and leaving everything but family behind.

Alice still kept her distance from him. She was professional in the hospital but reserved. If he'd had more than a workplace friendship with Penny, he might have suspected Alice hated him for breaking her sister's heart. But their connection hadn't been that deep—though it had felt like it could be. *So easily.*

Shifts where one or both Greene sisters were on duty ran smoother than any he'd ever experienced.

"It has to be me." The mom pursed her lips as she looked at her partner. "I'm breastfeeding and..."

"I know." Her partner leaned his head against hers before kissing it. "I'll be there as soon as I can. Promise." Then he met Benedict's gaze. "My heart and soul are going with you. Take care of them."

"Of course," Benedict answered, trying to ignore the push of emotions deep in his soul. Emotions that he'd been able to ignore until recently.

Until Penny returned, if he were honest.

The look of love between the two sent a pang of jealousy through him. No one had ever looked at him that way, and he never expected anyone to. But a tiny ache in his heart pressed against him.

"I think it will be best if you wrap him next to you again. The emergency evacuation route is tight." Penny gently bent to pick up Cole. She cradled him while his mother readjusted the wrap, then smiled as she handed him over. "Such a handsome little man."

"He is." Her voice shook a little as she kissed the top of her baby's head and stood.

"Ready?" Benedict asked as he stood by the door. He'd never pulled the emergency exit on a metro car, never seen it pulled. It was not an experience he'd craved. Particularly with a sick baby.

"Ready or not, we're going." Penny's gaze wandered past his to Cole's mom. "I'll lead, you and Cole in the middle and Benedict… Dr. Denbar in the back. Okay?"

Benedict waited for Cole's mother to acknowledge the plan, then he pulled the emergency release button and pushed open the door. "I'm glad you were on my train this morning, Penny." The words weren't meant to come out, but he couldn't draw them back in now.

And he didn't want to. Benedict didn't know what to do with those thoughts, so he let them slide away as he watched Penny step into the dark tunnel.

A small boy started clapping as they left and soon the whole metro car was clapping. It was a weird and unique way to start his morning shift. One he hoped he never had to repeat.

Though he didn't mind starting the morning with Penny... He let that thought slide away too as he gripped the edge of the railing of the evacuation path. The tunnel was barely lit, not completely dark but close. He was thirty-eight years old and being afraid of the dark was ridiculous, but he'd never been able to banish the fear instilled by his parents' long punishments. The shadows pressing along the side sent worries draping through him. His feet shook as he made his way on the tight path. So he turned his gaze to the leader of their small pack.

Penny's shoulders were straight, her dark hair pulled into a ponytail. So in control of the uncontrollable. It sent a wave of calm through him. He couldn't put words to that either, but he didn't push the thought away this time. Penny was here and he was happy about it. That was enough for now. He'd figure out the emotions later, find a way to categorize them and move past them.

"Your actions today made the news." Alice flipped her laptop around on the kitchen counter with a grin as she held up her glass of wine and winked. "A spokesman for the hospital used it as an opportunity to raise the issues of fundraising for the new wing, since they couldn't comment on the child's condition and you and Dr. Denbar were unavailable for comment."

Penny rolled her eyes as she grabbed a frozen dinner from the freezer and popped it into the microwave. No one had asked them to give a statement, though she would have declined to comment. So it was probably for the best.

They'd been granted a reprieve, for now. But with the fundraising push for the expanded wing so they could offer maternal health support for high-risk pregnancies, she suspected she and Benedict would be trotted out to help with the public relations for the multimillion-dollar project.

Benedict likely wouldn't mind. The maternity wing was his brainchild.

She mentally wished she'd used her day off to meal prep, so she would have had a stash of leftovers in the fridge, as she watched the frozen meal spin in the microwave. But she'd spent the day out at the park, drawing and reading trivia books.

And trying not to think about today.

A year ago today, she'd sold her wedding dress. Sold it on the day she'd expected to tie the knot. Not that she should have expected to walk down the aisle. It had been the third date she and Mitchel had set.

Third date!

Who set three wedding dates? She hated how accommodating she'd been for the first two setbacks. How she'd bought each of his lies, let him smooth away all her worries.

Of course she wanted his mom, whom she'd never met because she was living abroad, to be at the wedding.

If she had a conflict, then rescheduling was the right move.

Her parents were willing to move mountains to be there for their daughters' special events. But not every parent put their child's needs and desires first. Mitchel had said it really mattered to him that she be there. So Penny had called the vendors and moved the date back.

The fact that she'd never met any of his family, even after offering to video call, bothered her. But she'd accepted his statements that his family wasn't close, but he hoped their family would be. The seemingly romantic statement was designed to placate her, and she'd swallowed it every time she'd worried something was off.

The second date had come and gone because he was starting a new job. As a business management consultant, he traveled all over, sometimes gone for three weeks a month. He claimed this new job would give him more time with her, and she'd fallen for that lie too.

Once again, Penny had waved away the sinking feelings in her stomach that something was wrong. She'd ignored the tiny voice screaming that something was off. She'd quieted her fear that he had cold feet. If only it had been so easy.

The third, and final, time she'd canceled everything was because his wife had sent her copies of their marriage certificate and pictures of their two little girls. She'd told her that she was welcome to the cheating bastard. Penny could still feel the embarrassment and shame from those angry missives.

So far from the fairy-tale ending she'd hoped for.

Not that she could blame the woman. Whether Penny had realized it or not, she'd been the other woman. The catalyst for a family breaking down. Objectively she knew Mitchel was completely to blame, but she'd overlooked so many red flags. She'd let him charm away all her worries because she wanted a family. Wanted to replicate the happy home life she and Alice had grown up in, but without having to pack up and leave every few years like when the US Army transferred her parents.

She'd agreed to move to Ohio for Mitchel, but she'd made him promise that it was the only move they'd make, if they could help it. She'd spent her childhood packing her things, never getting too comfortable with friends because she'd have to leave.

She'd wanted a different life for her children. Wanted

them to have friends from grade school that they still chatted with as adults. Wanted them to have the roots to a place they'd grown up in. And he'd agreed with her. Let her plan her dreams on his promises…promises that hadn't been worth anything. At least he'd suggested renting a townhome until they could find the perfect place—which of course never appeared.

It had made it easy-ish for her to move back to DC, to pick back up the life she'd had before. And none of her colleagues had pressed her about her return, or why her ring finger no longer held the fancy bauble Mitchel had purchased.

Fancy. She scoffed as the frozen dinner popped in the microwave. The brilliant diamond she'd showed off to all her friends had been a hunk of cubic zirconia. The pawnshop owner where she'd taken the last evidence of Mitchel's fraud took pity on her sob story and offered her sixty bucks.

And she'd taken it. Not because she needed the money, but because that was all she was going to get from the years of falsehoods she'd been fed. When she started dating again, she wasn't settling for less a second time. She'd get the fairy tale, or she'd move on. No more settling for Penny Greene.

"I'm not surprised people were filming, but it wasn't overly dramatic." Penny shrugged as she pulled the hot veggie lasagna from the microwave. "The baby is being evaluated for epilepsy. Given the family history, and the seizures Benedict and I witnessed today, I suspect that the diagnosis will come from neurology in a day or two. Hopefully they can find an anti-seizure med that helps."

"Benedict. Don't you mean Dr. Denbar?" Alice's tone rippled with a disgust that Penny didn't understand.

"We were friendly colleagues seven years ago,

Alice." Penny lifted her wine glass, enjoying the light tang of citrus as it coated her tongue. Maybe cheap wine and a frozen dinner weren't the hallmark of the family life she'd thought she'd have by her thirties, but they did hit the spot after a long day.

"Friendly colleagues. Please, you had a huge crush on him, and he led you on, then jumped into bed with the next willing nurse or doctor to catch his eye." Her sister shook her head as she crossed her arms. "Playboy Denbar should come with a warning sign."

Penny raised her eyebrow as she met her sister's gaze. That nickname had not been assigned to Benedict when she'd met him, and she didn't think it appropriate now. Yes, the man dated a lot. But that was hardly a crime. He was young, intelligent and hot.

So hot! Just thinking of his soft dark eyes, full lips and toned body was enough to make her knees weak even now. The man was gorgeous. She'd wondered more than once if the world disappeared when he kissed you. Her fingers involuntarily touched her lips, but her sister didn't seem to notice.

Benedict was thoughtful, but a closed book. They'd had a great time at work, but Penny hadn't found out much about his past. Benedict had skirted around the standard "get to know you" questions. But she hadn't minded because they'd talked about everything else. Current affairs, movies, books, the never-ending traffic around DC and their favorite museums, over coffee and night shifts.

The friendship had never progressed outside the hospital, but she'd looked forward to seeing him each shift. Still looked forward to it, if she were honest. Though the woman that had returned to DC was a very different person than the one he'd joked with during their downtime.

Maybe he dated most of the eligible women in the hospital, but he wasn't cruel. And he didn't love them and leave them. No, Benedict was up front. That was one thing he'd made sure everyone understood. He liked his solitary life—or claimed to.

On their late-night shifts, he'd seemed to waver in that belief. Or maybe that was just her heart forcing her brain to remember differently. Wishing that the man she'd seemed to have so much in common with also wanted the life she craved. But he hadn't…and time moved on. Even if her stomach still flipped every once in a while when she saw him.

Maybe she knew he always rode the third train on the Blue subway line when he was on shift at Wald Children's. And yes, it was a little upsetting that she was always a tad crestfallen on the days when the seat where he normally sat was empty. And maybe she'd considered asking if the seat next to him was taken this morning before chickening out…but only because they'd been friends once.

"We were close colleagues, or as close as closed-book Denbar gets, but he didn't want love, marriage and a family, and I do. He was honest and that is a quality severely lacking in some."

Her sister frowned, and Penny hated the look. It was Alice's fixing look. Not that anything in Penny's life needed fixing, but her sister on a mission was a force to be reckoned with. And Penny did not want to be her next project.

Alice was a little less than two years younger than her. They'd been best friends since Alice had learned to toddle after her. Bound together as their family had picked up and moved across the world.

"Say what you want but you pouted around this townhome for months, hoping he might ask you out." Alice huffed as she took a bite of her sandwich.

"I did not pout. At some point, the two of us really need to look into weekly meal planning so we aren't eating such pathetic dinners all the time." Penny stuck out her tongue before grabbing another bite of her frozen lasagna.

"Don't try to change the subject. And I am fine with my dinner. Thank you very much!" Alice took another bite of her sandwich and made sounds best suited to an over-the-top children's cartoon character pretending to enjoy a badly burned dinner his friend had cooked.

She swallowed, then looked directly at Penny, her blue eyes holding hers. "I know what today was supposed to be."

"It's a day like any other day." Penny shrugged, wishing it were the truth.

"So you don't miss Mitchel, the cheating scumbag who should rot for all eternity?"

Penny grinned. Her sister never just called her ex Mitchel, or her ex-fiancé. She always invented some provocative nickname that really got across just how much she hated the man. And if it didn't come out strong enough, Alice just kept adding until she felt there were enough derogatory terms to get her point across.

"No. I do not miss Mitchel." Penny took another sip of wine. She did *not* miss her ex, but she missed the idea of him. The idea of what their life together had seemed. She missed the life path she'd thought she'd been walking. And she hated how much she'd let Mitchel steal from her.

Not her money, though he'd taken plenty of that, always promising to pay his half for things like the move and household expenses. Then coming up short, claiming to have a bad sales month.

Must have been expensive to keep two homes.

Penny hated the bitter thought as it floated through her mind.

It wasn't the man she missed, but the woman she'd been, full of hope and trust. Of course that woman had gotten taken for a ride, so maybe it was a good thing she wasn't her anymore. She knew what she wanted, and she wouldn't settle for less. Her parents had found true love, and she could too. She just had to look and accept the warning signs if she saw them.

"I think you need a rebound." Alice opened the dating app on her phone, flipped it toward Penny and started scrolling through the images of eligible singles…or people claiming to be single.

Would she ever fully trust someone again? She wanted to. She really did.

Her heart flipped as her brain waffled. Her bed was lonely, and on nights when her shift in the NICU was overwhelming, she wished she had someone besides her sister to comfort her. To cradle her to sleep. Intimacy was so much more than a physical connection…though she missed that too.

"I'm not interested in a rebound, Alice." She laughed as an image of a man wearing a Mickey Mouse shirt, holding up a large fish with the caption I'm Your Catch, crossed her sister's phone's screen. "Does that image really work for picking up single woman?"

"We could ask?" Alice wiggled her finger toward the phone.

"Or we could swipe left!"

"Spoilsport." Alice playfully glared at her as she swiped left and held up the next potential match.

He was cute. The profile said he was a broker and into hiking. She looked over the profile, then shook her head. "Nope. He's not a dog person. Who doesn't like dogs?"

Alice looked at the picture, then shook her head. "He's adorable and it doesn't say he doesn't like dogs, just that he prefers cats. You can't look for perfect. Sometimes Mr. Right Now can become Mr. Right… assuming you aren't looking for a real Prince Charming. The secret prince only exists in those cheesy holiday movies we gobble up between Thanksgiving and Christmas every year."

Maybe fairy tales were rare, but they existed—she refused to give up that belief. But she didn't feel like arguing with her sister tonight.

"If you're so interested in the men on that app, maybe we should pick out your date for next Friday." Penny giggled, moving her finger toward the screen as her sister pulled the phone away.

"My dating life is quite healthy, thank you very much. But yours has been dismal since you moved back. You work, read trivia books, watch trivia shows, draw and go to bed. The repetition is even getting to me."

"I wasn't aware my love of trivia bothered you—or maybe it's that I always beat you." Penny chuckled as she held her wine glass in a mock toast to her sister.

"Stop changing the subject." She showed off another eligible bachelor. "The best way to get over someone is to get under someone else, you know." Alice winked as she held her phone up for Penny's inspection, but far enough away that she couldn't actually touch the screen. "He's cute."

The man on the screen was cute. Well built, with a deep smile and eyes that looked kind. But images were easy to fake. Still, as she looked at the smiling man, part of her yearned for a connection. Not with a stranger on a phone app, but a real connection.

Except people formed lasting connections via phone apps these days.

Her heart argued as the walls her brain had raised following Mitchel's betrayal wavered. She was lonely. A date that went wrong wouldn't be the end of the world.

But her confidence had been shattered. And she didn't know how to fix that. Why wasn't there a way for her to practice date? To get her feet wet, so to speak, without worrying about feelings getting tangled.

Ugh! her brain screamed. Pretend dating wasn't an option. She should just pick someone attractive and give it a whirl. So why was she hesitating?

She didn't have to make any choices tonight. "I think we should be discussing the movie we want to watch, not which men are hottest on your app."

"We can do both." Alice swiped right, then left as the images popped up on her phone. "It's fun."

"Alice!" she said before her lonely heart could force her walls down even further.

"Fine," her sister huffed in an indignation that only Alice could manage. "But if you don't want to spend every evening trying to convince Sooty to cuddle, you'll have to jump back in the dating pool at some point."

"At some point," Penny repeated. "But your cat is a good cuddle buddy. He might love me more than you now." Penny chuckled as the black cat slinked across the counter, nudged her wine glass, then glared at her as she pulled it out of the feline terror's reach. Sooty loved Alice, but the cat didn't care for anyone else, and he would never willingly cuddle with Penny.

No, her bed was solitary. But it didn't have to be… She could just swipe right on one of the apps she'd downloaded and never used. She glanced at her phone, pulled up a profile. A handsome man, her age, who claimed to be looking for real love. A Lasting Connection was the title of his profile. Her fingers hovered, then she swiped left.

Coward!

CHAPTER TWO

"I JUST WORRY that if we take her home, then something goes wrong. I… I… We've spent the last one hundred and fifty-seven days hoping, praying, yearning for Hannah to come home. Hoping she'd join the ranks of the NICU graduates. But now that the day is here, I worry we are rushing things. God, that makes me sound like such a terrible mother."

"No." Penny shook her head, making sure Natalie Killson was looking at her as she reinforced the message. "That does not make you a bad mom. It makes you a mother who spent over a hundred days here, watching and worrying. Excitement and fear do not cancel each other out and our brains are able to experience so many emotions at once."

Hannah giggled as she sat in her mother's lap, the tiny tubes that had been attached to her for months finally gone.

"That is the best sound ever." Benedict strode through the door, bent and smiled at Hannah.

The little one laughed again as her fingers reached for Benedict's nose. It took a bit longer for them to connect than an average five-month-old, but preemies took longer to hit their developmental milestones. Though Penny hoped that Hannah's hand-eye coordination would increase fast now that she was going home.

"You got my nose!" Benedict wiggled his face just a little, not enough to make Hannah lose her grip but enough to test her muscle control. The silly game made the baby smile again.

He was an excellent physician. Everyone talked about how he handled stressful situations. Always calm and coordinated to ensure their high-risk patients got the best chance at a normal life. But it was here that Penny thought he truly shined.

When the crisis was over. When their babies were ready to go home. When they were on the safe path, Benedict cooed over them, he played silly games—yes ones designed to help his assessments—but he enjoyed these moments. And that bedside manner was not something all physicians and nurses had.

Particularly in these units.

Treatment capability for preemies and micro-preemies, babies born weighing less than one pound twelve ounces or before twenty-six weeks gestation, had increased their survival rates. But this could still be one of the saddest and most stressful environments in any hospital. Many nurses and physicians kept themselves at a professional distance from the parents and patients to protect their mental health.

Penny understood the inclination. It let them do the best job they could for their patients—and that was what mattered most. But she'd never been able to maintain that blurred line. And neither had Benedict.

It was one of the things that had drawn her to him all those years ago. The reason she'd been so surprised when he'd announced on a late shift that he had no intention of having a family. Of being a father... Because a child should get the privilege of being loved by this man.

But he claimed not to want that. Claimed that he preferred his solitary life. Maybe all his love went to his patients? It was a nice, if lonely, sentiment. But Penny thought there was more to it. Tucked away in the past that he refused to discuss.

"Well, Ms. Hannah. We are going to miss you, but I am also so happy you are going home." Benedict tapped the child's knee, watching her eyes react to the movement, then stood. "She's come so far, Natalie. But we love to keep in touch with our babies. So don't feel like you can't reach back for questions…or to share important milestones."

Natalie's eyes teared up, and Penny passed her a tissue. Days like today were so exciting, and these looked like happy tears. The best kind.

"Thank you." She dabbed her eyes. "I remember the first day I walked through the doors here. The pictures of birthdays for the NICU graduates by the entrance gave me hope."

"That's what it's designed for." Benedict grinned, so proud of his wall of graduates.

"It's why Dr. Denbar petitioned for it to be put up." Penny pursed her lips as his dark eyes floated toward hers. He never boasted of his accomplishments, but Penny wanted Natalie to know that Benedict was the one who'd lobbied so hard for that addition. That his deep conviction in its necessity was what helped provide her peace.

He'd repeated to anyone that would listen that the NICU was scary. That it was the second to last place any parent planning to welcome a child wanted to be. She still remembered his words when the lead hospital human relations representative asked where the last place was. The nurses in attendance had all been stunned into silence, shocked the HR rep couldn't figure it out. But Benedict had kept his eyes locked on the rep as he'd stated, *Planning final arrangements.*

The quiet words had carried over the buzz of electrical equipment and the representative had swallowed before writing a few notes in his electronic tablet. The hospital had approved the wall a week later, and Benedict had come in on his off day to help put it up. Then he'd carefully hung the pictures parents had sent him.

She'd seen more than one parent in distress staring at those images. Reaching for the hope they provided. Praying their babies got to join that wall.

"It's important to know this day can come."

Benedict looked at Hannah, but his eyes seemed far away. There was hurt deep inside him… She'd seen a touch of it years ago. But it radiated from him now before he shifted his position and the self-assured physician returned.

"Well, you are getting all the pictures of her!" Natalie let out a laugh, then a small sob as she nestled her head against her daughter's. "So many pictures." She kissed her cheek. "What else do we need to do?"

"Keep up with the appointments with her regular pediatrician and cardiologist. And Penny will give you her final discharge papers. And enjoy every moment." Benedict offered Hannah and then her mother one more smile, then he turned and met Penny's gaze.

His dark eyes seemed to touch a part of her that had been dormant for so long. Since those late nights in the on-call suite so long ago. A spark blazed between them, and she swallowed as she broke the connection first. This wasn't the time or place for her imagination to wander to unwelcome connections.

"After you finalize the discharge paperwork, can I speak with you for a moment, please?"

"Of course," Penny answered, hating the flutters in her belly. There was *no* need for that. She was just lonely. Clearly too lonely.

Then he was gone, and she was hoping her cheeks didn't look as hot as they felt. She looked at the list of instructions and pulled her thoughts back together. Hannah and her mother were what mattered now.

"For the most part, all you need to do is love on her. I know her cardiologist recommended you have a breathing monitor set up in her crib."

"I got it set up last week. It's set to the most sensitive setting. We won't miss anything." Natalie's fingers tightened just a bit on Hannah's midriff as she bent her head to kiss the child again.

Squatting so she was in line with Natalie, Penny made sure she was looking at her before continuing. "It doesn't need to be on the most sensitive setting. That will set off if she doesn't move in a few seconds. And that will happen nearly every night and make you worry. I promise setting it on the regular setting that the cardiologist suggested is more than enough."

"I… I just don't want to miss anything." Natalie's bottom lip shook as Penny patted her knee.

"I know. But life is going to get even more hectic now." She grinned at Hannah. "This little one will be walking and talking and keeping you on your toes. You need your rest too. Don't discount that.

"Do you have any other questions?" Penny asked as she stood and grabbed the discharge paperwork and passed it over.

"No." Natalie grinned as she stood and started putting Hannah in her car seat. "I'll probably think of twenty as soon as I hit the parking lot."

"Then just give us a call. The nurses' desk will answer anything you need. Hannah may be a NICU graduate as of today, but we are still here to help. Her pediatrician also has a twenty-four-hour nurses' line you can call." Penny grinned as Natalie lifted Hannah's car seat carrier. This was the best moment of her time here. The day she got to see the babies go home. See parents happy to return to a life outside the hospital.

"Thank you." Natalie wrapped her arms through the car seat's handles and bit her bottom lip. "I really can't say thank you enough."

"No need to say thank you. But do send pictures. Bene… Dr. Denbar really does want them for his wall. Hanging them is one of his favorite activities."

Natalie took a deep breath, looked at her daughter and then the door. "Here we go."

Penny beamed as she watched the mother bounce toward the entrance. The happiest walk. A memory she filed away for a tough day. For a day when she needed the reminder that this outcome was possible. Each memory like this was a boost to her soul on those days when the world seemed unfair and dark.

"Penny?" Benedict…no, Dr. Denbar raised his hand as she exited the room.

Why did her brain refuse to think of him as anything besides Benedict? And why did her imagination insist on jumping to thoughts of them alone?

She could also deal without the musings on how he might kiss.

"I'm headed to the cafeteria for a cup of coffee. Care to join me?"

Her brain jumped at the idea of caffeine, but then

it wavered. Coffee sounded lovely but she wasn't sure about going with Benedict. Her lonely soul was clearly reaching for connections. And Benedict was an easy one. A path worn by an old friendship.

But he was also safe. He couldn't trick her into believing he wanted a family with her since she already knew he didn't want those things. Her heart was in no danger of getting attached.

It squeezed a little as she looked at the tall handsome man. *No danger*, she reminded herself.

"So we can discuss yesterday. HR reached out to me this morning, and I suspect they'll want to talk to you later."

"Oh." Penny nodded. Of course this was work-related. *As it should be.* The argument rattling around her brain didn't provide any comfort. "Sure. Though I don't know what HR would want from me. I can give a short statement, but we can't comment on the medical situation."

Benedict let out a low chuckle, and her stomach twisted as the luxurious noise enveloped her. It was a silly thing to hold on to, but Mitchel had rarely laughed. He'd argued that seriousness was the key to success. Though after finding out about his double life, Penny suspected he kept things as level as possible, so he didn't make a misstep and forget which partner had which inside joke.

The door to the elevator opened, and they stepped in. "You've never had to be part of a public relations campaign for a hospital trying to raise significant capital for a new project?"

"No." Penny shook her head. She kept herself inconspicuous whenever human resources went prowling for staff members to participate in their recruitment fairs and videos. But she'd seen Benedict in those videos, delivering his lines in a cool crisp tone.

His tall dark frame looking so elegant in his scrubs and a white lab coat. The perfect doctor image. Though a slightly fabricated one since no one wore lab coats anymore given the studies showing they were a repository for germs. Their babies couldn't afford any wayward germs sneaking in on lab coats, no matter how professional people thought they looked.

"I would have thought you and your sister would be prime targets. Sisters working at one of the top NICUs in the country. I mean the script practically writes itself." Benedict pushed the button for the lowest level and the elevator rattled as it started its descent.

Penny let out a soft laugh. "Alice has been involved, but I generally try to make myself scarce when they come combing for prospects." She didn't have a great reason for it. Alice had pressed her more than once to join her.

Service to others was one of the traits their parents had instilled in their girls. Penny and Alice had each felt called to make a difference in the world. But in civilian careers. In fields where they weren't required to uproot their lives every three to five years.

"Well, our video made quite the stir in social media, and it was a slow news day, so it ran on the six and ten o'clock segments. And somewhere along the line, we became partners."

"Became…?" Penny's voice halted as the true meaning hit. "I see." His dark eyes held hers, and for just a moment she wished it were a true story. Her heart clenched again, and she barely caught the sigh trying to escape her throat.

Maybe she did need more company than Alice and

her sister's grumpy cat. A quick rebound to dust off her dating game before she sought out happily-ever-after. "Is the hospital wanting us to clear it up? I mean colleagues date and there are more than a few married couples working here. It's not exactly scandalous."

"It's not a scandal they are worried about." Benedict gestured for her to exit first. "The story is better if we are a couple. That's all public relations campaigns are really. Stories."

Penny pinched the bridge of her nose. Yesterday they'd helped; that was the important thing. But Benedict was building to something, and she wasn't sure if the nerves twisting through her were warranted or not.

"And they are making a major push for a maternity suite for high-risk pregnancies. It's important that moms not be separated, if possible. Particularly because some of our cases don't go home. They..." He paused, swallowed, then continued. "They deserve all the time we can give them."

Again, Benedict's eyes seemed lost before he collected himself. Her hand itched to reach out to him. To provide comfort for the hurt she saw nestled there. But she didn't know what had caused it, and Benedict didn't seem inclined to elaborate.

Still, she wanted to reach him. To know more about the man than what he presented in the hospital. Such a dangerous desire. And one she didn't plan to give in to.

Penny agreed with the addition of the maternity unit. She'd seen women heartbroken because their babies had been rushed to Wald's while they recovered at separate hospitals. Sometimes they didn't make it to Wald Children's for almost a week. A lifetime. And it forced partners to divide their time between the mother of their child and their fragile newborns. No one should have to make that choice.

"All of that is true but I still don't understand what you're getting at."

"Two NICU professionals helping an infant on their morning commute is a good story. Two NICU professionals who love each other *and* protect babies on their commute is a story that gets a follow-up. That story gets the hospital a fun story to tell for a topic that too often results in tragedy."

She felt her lips fall open, but no words escaped.

Was he really asking her to lie to HR? To claim they were together...in love?

He bit his lip before stepping up to the counter and ordering his coffee. Then Benedict turned and gestured to Penny. "Her coffee is on me."

Penny raised an eyebrow. *"Benedict..."*

"I insist, Penny. Please."

"Large blonde, two sugars and a splash of cream, please." Penny nodded to the barista before turning her attention to Benedict. "So you think coffee is a good bribe to get me to agree to fake a relationship for a series of fundraising events."

He at least had the good sense to look at his shoes. "It's for a good cause."

"Sure, and the fact that Dr. Lioness is retiring, and human resources has made no secret of the fact that all interested internal candidates should expect to attend these fundraising events, isn't driving this request? Even a little?" She'd heard Dr. Cooke, Dr. Webber and Dr. Garcia discussing the request last week. She and the other nurses suspected the doctors were each trying to feel each other out. Trying to determine who might be setting themselves apart with human resources for the head of the department.

If it was just about who was the best doctor, then the man handing her coffee would be the selectee. And everyone knew it. But this world rarely worked like that. Those with the best connections, those who proved they could network for the hospital, who could help raise money for research or facilities would get a leg up.

"I can't say that I don't want that position." Benedict shrugged. "I could help a lot of families."

Penny turned on her heel. She'd been in one fake relationship, one she hadn't known was fake. But still, she would not enter another.

"Penny!" Benedict chased after her as she pressed the button for the elevator. "Please." He sighed as they stepped into the elevator. "I need this maternity ward to work. And if us playing a bit of pretend helps that…"

"Why?"

"What?" Benedict's eyebrows knitted together as he met her gaze.

"*Why* do you need the maternity ward to be funded? It's important to you. I can tell that. And it's more than just it's a good idea that needs funding. It matters to you. So tell me the reason." She paused, then reiterated, "The real reason, unless it really is for the promotion boost. In which case, the answer is no."

Maybe it wasn't fair to press. She'd seen him shut down whenever she broached any topic that revolved around the life he'd had before starting work at Wald Children's. Dr. Benedict Denbar, amazing physician, hard worker, hot doctor…notoriously tight-lipped about anything personal.

"My brother's baby died a little less than twenty-four hours after she was born. Amber, her mother, never made it to the NICU. It…it nearly destroyed her." Benedict sighed. "I've never told anyone here that and I would appreciate…" The elevator shuddered and squealed as it came to a halt.

Penny let out a small cry as the car shook before dropping at least a flight and jerking to a stop. The lights flickered, then shut off completely.

Dear God. The darkness sank around him as Benedict felt his chest heave. As a kid, his parents had locked him and Isiah in a closet as punishment when they misbehaved, or when they tired of them, or just because. They'd hadn't always remembered to let them out.

That had made him uncomfortable in the dark. But he'd dealt with it, mostly.

Until the night Olivia passed.

Even all these years later, he could still remember the inky darkness followed by the squeal of machines until the hospital generator had kicked on. For a short time, he'd believed everything would be okay.

But exactly three hours and twenty-six minutes later, the generator failed. Olivia hadn't been able to survive the second interruption. With the medical training he had now, Benedict understood that Olivia likely wouldn't have survived much longer. But that didn't change the fact that she'd passed in the dark, without her mother.

By the time the kind nurse laid her on his chest, it was too late. So he'd held her and wept in the darkness. Wept for his brother, for the tiny life that hadn't gotten a chance and for her mother who'd never held her. It had taken another hour for the nurses to find enough flashlights to light the hallways and room. But by then his hatred, and fear, of the dark was cemented.

Rationally Benedict knew every room was the same whether the light was on or not, but his brain licked tendrils of fear down his spine whenever his eyes were unable to find a light source. Why hadn't the backup lights switched on? What had happened? When would the door open?

"Benedict?"

Penny's voice slid across the darkness and his chest lightened. He wasn't alone. Penny was here.

Penny.

He'd never spoken to anyone about those awful days following Olivia's passing. Even now they felt like a dream. Like they'd happened to someone else.

When he and Amber had returned to the tiny apartment they'd shared, Benedict had held her as she tried to process losing both her loves in less than six months. He wasn't Olivia's biological father, but he'd done his best to stand in for Isiah. He'd gone to as many appointments as possible, set up a crib and carried bags of clothes and supplies that Amber had purchased from garage sales to give her daughter the best chance, along with the tiny cartoon night-lights she'd purchased for the baby's room.

After Olivia was gone, they went through the motions of their "marriage of convenience" for as long as they could, but it felt hollow. Both Benedict and Amber were locked in their own private spheres of grief—for Isiah, for Olivia, for what could have been.

What should have been…

Amber had been as happy as he had when his acceptance to Oregon State had come through along with a full scholarship. But even now, all these years later, she wasn't interested in ending the union. All for family expectations… Amber's mother didn't mind her having an estranged husband, so long as she wore a ring on her hand.

For a long time, it had suited Benedict too not to face the idea of broken vows, and to keep that link to Isiah, however tenuous it was in reality, but something had changed in him lately.

Penny came back to the hospital.

Benedict tried to shake that thought out of his head but it persisted.

Came back without a ring on her finger. A second chance you never thought you'd have.

Nonsense, he told himself sternly. It was simply time to end a charade that had gone on for far too long.

"Benedict." Penny's hand traced along his jaw. "Breathe with me."

He heard her suck in air and loudly push it back out. Then she repeated the pattern. Benedict did his best to follow her breathing pattern and his heart started to slow. Until it realized that Penny's fingers were stroking his arms.

He knew it was a calming technique. One they used on the tiny infants in their isolettes so they knew they weren't alone. Penny's touch was light, but his body rejoiced at the simple touch.

How long had it been since someone touched him in such a way?

He dated, too often, at least according to some of the whispers he'd overheard. But the touches of the women he dated weren't comforting. They satisfied a need, but when he was hurt, when he was scared, when his heart and brain rehashed past pain, he was alone. No comforting hugs, no soft commands to remember to breathe.

He was lonelier than he'd realized to be reacting to Penny's comfort like this. He didn't want the touches to end but relishing them wasn't a good option either. Reaching for her hand, Benedict gave it a gentle squeeze, then forced himself to let go. "I'm okay."

"Not sure that is the truth." Penny sighed into the dark. "Any idea what we do now?"

As if the universe was answering, the elevator phone rang into the pitch.

"I didn't know those still worked." Benedict let out a nervous chuckle as Penny's warmth evaporated as she started toward the phone. At least his eyes were starting to adjust to the darkness.

"It's federal law that all elevators built since the early 1990s have an emergency call button. Though it would be nice if I could see the button to push to answer."

Of course she would know about elevator codes. She used to spout trivia on long night shifts to help him stay awake. His local pub ran a trivia night every Tuesday and Thursday, and he always thought of her when he stopped in.

Had she ever been? Would she like to go with him?

Benedict filed those questions away. His brain was probably just trying to distract him from the dark. But the idea of spending time with Penny, even in these darkened conditions, sent a thrill through him. That should have terrified him. But he'd examine that feeling later…or perhaps not.

"Success!" Penny shouted as the crackle of the intercom echoed in the elevator. "Hello. This is Penny Greene. Dr. Denbar and I are in here. There are no patients with us."

"Straight to the point." Benedict sighed as he moved closer in case they needed to ask him any questions.

Penny's hip pushed against his, and he nearly lost

his coffee cup. Though the brief connection would be worth a few stained scrubs.

"Good to know. This is Brian Hillion, firefighter with Engine Company Twenty-seven. Are there any injuries?"

"No," Penny responded, before letting out a nervous laugh. "Except my coffee cup. I dropped it when the elevator dropped."

"We'll get you another. I promise, Penny." The voice crackled through the intercom, and Benedict felt a twinge of something he feared was jealousy.

Which was ridiculous. To begin with, the firefighter was probably just trying to make her comfortable. And even if he was flirting with a discombobulated voice, Benedict had no claim on Penny.

Even if he was hoping she'd pretend to love him for a few weeks to benefit the hospital. No, he certainly didn't have a reason for the tingles of jealousy touching his soul.

"I need to hear from Dr. Denbar. Protocol."

"Here." He waited a minute before adding, "It's awful dark. I would have thought the backup lights would have come on."

"The cables snapped and the automatic brakes stopped the car. You're between floors. We'll get you out of the dark as soon as possible. Until then, hang tight. And, Penny, I'll make sure there's a coffee with a splash of cream and two sugars waiting when the door opens."

"Thanks."

"He knows your coffee order? Is that why you hesitated about faking a romance to help boost the fundraising?" The question was out before Benedict could fully process the words. For the first time in his memory, he was grateful for the darkness. At least he couldn't see the likely look of horror on Penny's face at such a rude set of questions.

"He dated Alice a while back." Penny words were crisp and he saw her outline move away.

He hated the distance she put between them but understood.

What had possessed his tongue?

"I am so sorry, Penny. That was beyond rude. I wish I could use hating the darkness as an excuse, but the truth is that was just plain old nosy and self-serving. I am truly sorry." He meant it too. There was no excuse for rudeness, and even less excuse for the evaporating jealousy. It should not make him happy that the man on the other end of the voice box hadn't dated the woman trapped with him.

Penny deserved to be happy. Deserved to find someone that wanted all the same things she did. He'd had a crush on her all those years ago, but it wouldn't have been fair to ask her out, knowing they wanted different things. He'd wanted her to get what she wanted. Still wanted it.

It hurt, more than he wanted to admit, to know that someone else would make her smile and laugh. Would get to see the flash of humor in her eyes when an interesting topic appeared. The woman had a bank of knowledge about so many things. From years of trivia study that she hoped would land her on her favorite quiz show. Then it had been canceled the year she turned twenty-one and was finally old enough to compete.

He'd dated many women but the things those women had enjoyed had exited his memory bank when the connection was severed. Yet Benedict had never forgotten the little things he'd learned through their friendship in those last years of his residency.

"I didn't immediately agree to deceive people because I do not enjoy lying. I've already..." Her breath hitched, and she coughed. "Lying is never the option."

"I could take you out." Another set of words slipped out of his mouth before he could fully process them. Except these ones he didn't really want to draw back in. Maybe it wasn't fair, but Benedict wanted to spend time with her. Wanted to see if her eyes still lit up when she was happy, if the crease just above her nose still appeared when she was thinking hard. Rekindle the friendship that had brought him so much joy.

"Then we wouldn't be lying. It could be real...sort of."

"You're asking me out? To help the hospital?" Penny sighed and he heard her slide down the wall.

Slowly making his way over to her, Benedict slid down beside her, then carefully set his coffee on the other side. "No. I am asking you out because I like your company. I missed you when you were gone." *So much*... He managed to catch those words as he started again, "If it helps the hospital, that would be a bonus. But..." he hesitated "...it feels wrong for me to say I'm glad you're back because I know you left to be with your fiancé. Your ring hand is empty, so I assume that is not a happy story."

He might not like the darkness, but it did make it easier to speak the truth.

"It's not," Penny confirmed, and her head knocked against the elevator. "It's not a happy story at all. You still haven't answered my question. Why is faking a relationship to help public relations for the new maternity unit so important to you? I understand your sister-in-law lost her baby, but given enough time, the funds will come in. The hospital is hosting multiple events over the next few months."

"That won't raise all the money necessary." Benedict's tone was harsher than he'd intended. "And until that unit is in place, we will have mothers who don't make it here to be with their babies before…" The words trailed off, and Penny's hand lay over his before giving it a gentle squeeze.

"There was one last week, and there will be another. It's already heartbreaking. I know we get more NICU graduates than losses. But that doesn't change the fact that if we can have a ward with high-risk patients, it will help them and their babies. Studies have shown how important skin-to-skin contact is, how infants recognize the sound of their mother's voice before they are born. If we can give them the best chance…" He choked up. "I will do anything to make that happen."

And he would. He'd seen the devastation in Amber's life. She'd spent weeks in bed, cried until she couldn't cry anymore and second-guessed everything she'd done, looking for a reason why she'd gone into labor early. He hadn't had the words or knowledge to be much help. But he had that knowledge now. He could help others, do his best to prevent pain.

"And I promise I won't do anything to hurt you," Benedict offered. He didn't know why the promise fell from his lips, but it felt right in the darkened elevator.

A sigh echoed from Penny as she shifted beside him. "That's a sizable promise."

"And one I intend to keep. Promise. I promised myself when we lost little Olivia that I'd do my best to ensure others weren't in the same position. The goal is so close now…waiting…it…"

He choked as the memories invaded his brain. He'd fought with his brother, not knowing he would never get a chance to make it up, then he hadn't been able to protect the woman Isiah loved and the child they'd made. He couldn't change those things, but he could do his best to make sure that history didn't repeat itself for others.

"All right." Penny laid her head against his shoulder, then immediately lifted it back up before squeezing his hand again.

*All right…*was a simple statement with so much meaning. And for just an instant when her head connected with his shoulder, the world had seemed a bit lighter. He understood why she'd yanked it back. But perhaps the dark didn't just affect him.

No, Benedict was not going to go down that slippery path.

"I'll play along for a while. At least through the fund-raising carnival. But I have some ground rules."

"No falling in love. Isn't that what they always say in rom-coms?" Benedict chuckled, though the words felt wrong on his lips. It would be so easy to fall in love with Penny. So easy…

"Of course. But I suspect that won't be a problem for us."

Those words tore through him, and he was again grateful for the darkness so she couldn't see how much the assumption hurt. He should be rejoicing that Penny didn't want to form a more permanent connection. That was what he always said on his dates, and if the woman was interested in long-term, he ended things quickly, before emotions became too deep.

If no one got attached, no one would get hurt. It was lonely, but he'd watched his mother's and father's marriages. Watched how two people could claim to love someone, vow in sickness and health, and then toss it away when things got tough.

"Okay," Benedict chimed in, wishing his voice sounded steadier. "What are the ground rules?"

"No deep conversations. No personal questions. No talk of the past—which shouldn't be hard for you, Mr. Closed Book." Penny sighed. "Whatever we do should be light and fun, and if a few posts make it to the hospital's social media, with a plug for the new maternity ward, then great. If not…"

He felt her shoulder rub his as she shrugged beside him.

"It will make it to social media. One of the videos taken of us on the subway was by the public relations director's grandson. She's already got a whole story outlined—assuming we're dating. It's why I wanted to talk to you before she got to you."

"It all makes sense now." Her shoulder bumped his and she laughed. Though the sound wasn't quite as melodic as he remembered.

They were trapped in an elevator, plotting a fake relationship. Of course it wasn't a true laugh.

Still, Benedict mentally made a note to make Penny laugh, really laugh, as soon as he could. After they got out of the dark.

"I hadn't anticipated this though. I wonder if there'll be someone there with a camera when those doors open."

As if on cue, the door shuddered as it was pried open. A bit of light broke through the sliver. Benedict squinted as it hit his retinas, but he also hated the intrusion. "I really am looking forward to spending time with you."

Penny stood and held out her hand. Benedict grabbed

it as he stood. He expected her to drop it. Instead, she laid her head against his shoulder and squeezed it tightly. "May as well look real if there are pictures." She took a deep breath before adding, "Here we go."

"Here we go," Benedict confirmed.

CHAPTER THREE

"If your frown gets any deeper, Alice, your face might freeze like that." Penny wagged a finger like their mother before she reached for her earrings.

"I didn't believe that hogwash when Mom used to tell it to us, and I have a master's in nursing and am a neonatal nurse practitioner—just like you. Which means I know the muscles of my face are not going to freeze as I *glare* at you. What are you doing?" Alice picked up Sooty and gave him a quick pat before putting him on the bed.

"Going to a trivia night," Penny turned and smiled at her sister. Mostly to annoy her, but she was actually excited. She and Benedict were going on a date. Sort of... Did it count if you knew it was only pretend?

He'd invited her to the trivia night at his local pub. The fact that he'd remembered her love of trivia had excited her...perhaps a tad too much.

Penny loved finding obscure pieces of knowledge. She'd dreamed of being a contestant on the game show *Ask This* and cried when it was canceled shortly after she was finally old enough to compete. The fact that Benedict was taking her to a new trivia hub was exciting.

That was the main reason she was practically bouncing. Not because Benedict would be here in less than twenty minutes. This was just a date so she didn't feel bad at telling Susan Jenkins, the hospital's public relations director, that she could use their dating life as hospital publicity fodder.

It wasn't because of the hot man she was expecting at her door. They'd been such good friends so long ago. She hated that she hadn't sought that connection out when she returned. But that friendship represented the old Penny, and she wasn't really that woman anymore.

Was she?

She swallowed as she looked at herself in the mirror. Was that why she'd held herself back from resuming her friendship with Benedict...or was it because the butterflies had returned to her stomach the moment she'd seen him again? Maybe she should change...

Nope. Tonight she was going to have fun, and look adorable while doing it.

"You don't normally wear earrings to trivia night." Alice crossed her legs as she sat on the bed. "Or that blue dress."

Penny shook her head as she kissed her sister's cheek. "Relax. This is just a date. Or rather a pretend date. Or, well, the point is, you told me to get back out there. Remember showing me the pictures on your phone?"

"I meant you should swipe right and grab a coffee with a cutie! *Not* enter some fake relationship nonsense with Dr. Denbar. I don't want you to get hurt..." Alice wavered, then grabbed her sister's hands "...again."

"I appreciate the concern." Penny meant the words. She really did appreciate it. But the truth was that Benedict and this arrangement were perfect. She could test the dating waters again, without the fear of getting hurt. Like riding a training bike to see if she was ready to step out in the wide scary world again to find her hap-pily-ever-after.

Cuddling with an angry cat for the rest of her days didn't hold much appeal. And she and Benedict had had fun together all those years ago. She'd had so little fun in the last year.

And maybe she would get the butterflies dancing around her stomach to disappear if she spent a little time with him.

She deserved to go out with a hot man, kick butt at trivia and just let the evening happen. Besides, he'd promised he wouldn't hurt her—not that they would get close, but she wanted to believe it. At least a little. Her intuition swore Benedict meant his words…once she'd have believed it. But this particular "trusty" sense had led to the doors of tragedy once already.

The doorbell rang, and Penny grabbed Alice's wrist as she hopped off her bed. "Stay here."

Alice stuck out her tongue but stayed in place as Penny moved toward the door, trying to ignore the dash of hope in the back of her brain. This was just a nice evening, a fun night with Benedict.

It was fake. But that didn't make her less excited to open the door. That was something she should exam-ine after tonight, or maybe it would be better not to. Safer to ignore.

Her knees nearly collapsed as she stared at the fine man before her. His jeans were tight in all the right places and the light blue sweater he wore highlighted his dark eyes. Her mouth watered at the sight of him before they landed on the flowers in his hands.

"Daisies?"

Benedict smiled as he handed her the small bou-quet. "I saw these and thought—" he pushed his hands into his pockets "—you said they were your favorite. Or at least they were all those years ago… I… I just saw them and…"

He repeated the last line and she leaned over and kissed his cheek. "They are still my favorite. Thank you." He'd remembered. She swallowed, trying to force the tiny lump in her throat down as she turned to get a vase.

Mitchel had always said that flowers were a waste. That it was like throwing money down a drain. But Penny loved having fresh flowers on the table. In Ohio, she'd had a small green space where she'd grown a few veggies in pots. She'd mentioned that she wanted some flowers for her birthday and Mitchel had surprised her with rosebushes.

They'd been pretty but when Penny said she didn't know anything about growing roses, Mitchel had snapped and said they were her favorite flower so she should know. She'd reminded him that her favorite flowers were daisies, and he'd blanched. Then recovered by making her believe that she must have said it once. And she'd agreed… That still stung.

That Benedict could remember an offhanded comment all those years ago touched her heart. And the walls she'd built around it shuddered.

Just a bit.

Mentally shaking herself, Penny put the flowers in water. It was a nice gesture. Sweet, even. But that didn't change the fact that this evening was pretend. She needed to remember that.

"Are you ready for trivia night?" Benedict asked as she followed him through the front door.

"Absolutely!" Penny beamed. Tonight was going to be lighthearted and fun. Just what she needed.

* * *

"Who discovered penicillin?"

Benedict popped his hand over the buzzer before Penny got to it, only the second time this evening he'd beaten her to the buzzer and proudly announced, "Who is Alexander Fleming?"

"Yes," the announcer stated as he dropped another point on the board for the Donut Call List team.

"You don't have to answer in the form of a question, Benedict." Penny's foot brushed his calf and his blood heated at the simple touch. Her cheeks were tinged with pink and a touch of salt from her margarita was on the side of her lip.

He reached up and brushed the small crystal away doing his best to ignore the growing bead of desire for the woman across from him. She'd answered nearly every question. They'd only lost points when one of the other teams managed to hit their buzzer before she did.

But she wasn't arrogant or showing off what was a truly impressive body of knowledge on things from the space race to reality television stars. The other teams had grumbled when she took the first three rounds, but those grumbles had turned into looks of awe as she just kept the answers coming.

"I got excited. I knew that one and hit the buzzer first!" Benedict could feel the brilliant smile on his lips. When was the last time he'd had so much fun?

"All right, lightning round time. Not that there is much of a competition." The announcer gestured to the board and the room let out a soft laugh, though there were a few grumbles mixed in.

"Ooh. I love lightning rounds." Penny rubbed her

hands together. Her eyes sparkled as her fingers hovered near the buzzer.

She was gorgeous. And it wasn't just the blue dress that hugged her curves in all the right places, or the blue eyes that seemed to call to him. When he was with her, his body seemed to relax. Tension he never realized he was holding evaporated when she kissed his cheek after he handed her the daisies. *Daisies.*

He'd forgotten that detail, though his brain had clearly filed it away somewhere. When walking past the flower shop on the corner by their townhome, he'd seen the flowers in the window and the memory had switched on.

Penny laughing and saying that daisies were the happiest flowers. That they symbolized purity and innocence in the language of flowers. He hadn't even known that flowers had meanings until he'd met her. But her talking about how she loved their bright yellow centers and white petals had made him smile and so he'd showed up with the bouquet.

To a fake date.

Except it doesn't feel pretend.

That was such a dangerous thought. Such a dangerous longing. He'd promised her nothing deep. No talk of the past. Normally that would suit him perfectly. No chance of getting hurt or hurting others. But he wanted to know Penny.

Wanted to know everything about her. Wanted to wipe away the look of pain he sometimes saw cross her eyes, wanted to see the smiles she'd delivered so easily before return. He just wanted her.

"Are you ready?" Penny tapped his thigh with her hand that wasn't by the buzzer and electricity shot down Benedict's leg.

Maybe he should have told Susan that they were just two colleagues who lived close enough together that they rode the same subway car to work.

That would have been the safer option. But he'd do anything to help raise the funds for the new maternity ward. He'd promised his tiny niece he'd do all he could. At that time, his word was all he had. He would not disappoint her memory.

"Are you going to let me answer any of the questions?" Benedict tapped her hand by the buzzer. The urge to pull her hand into his, to hold it, hold her was nearly overwhelming. But he wouldn't interrupt the lightning round. She deserved to be crowned champion tonight.

"If you hit the buzzer before me." She grinned and the dimple appeared again. A happy Penny was the prettiest thing he'd ever seen.

He laughed and gestured to the button, making a dramatic show of taking second place to her expertise. Though they were technically a team.

"The www stands for this in a website."

Penny hit the buzzer. "World wide web."

"I knew that one." Benedict winked and Penny grinned. This was the best date he'd ever been on.

"Who named the Pacific Ocean?"

"Lots of people." Benedict laughed as Penny playfully glared at him and hit the buzzer.

"Ferdinand Magellan." She nodded as the announcer placed another mark on the board.

"I stand by my answer." Benedict let his finger hover by hers. "Lots of names were probably used for the Pacific. It's just his we know."

"Last question."

"We got this." Penny lifted her shoulders as she looked at him.

"You do." Benedict confirmed as he looked to the announcer.

"In the language of flowers, what is the meaning of a daisy?"

Penny dinged in but before she could answer, Benedict piped up, "Innocence and purity. According to Celtic legend, whenever a child died, God sprinkled the flowers over the earth to cheer up parents. They are sometimes given to mothers, since Nordic mythology says they were Freya's favorite flower."

"We'll accept innocence and purity," the announcer stated as he marked the final points on the board. "Surprising absolutely no one, Donut Call List is the winner tonight. See you all next Tuesday. And maybe study up. Looks like there is a new champ in town."

Benedict clapped with the rest of the room and turned his gaze to Penny. She was sitting nearly still as she stared at him. "Do you know the meanings of many flowers?"

"Only daisies." Benedict shrugged. "I used to get coffee at the hospital coffee bar with a woman who loved them." He winked. "She spent the better part of one shift telling me all about them. There's a Roman myth too, but he interrupted me before I could explain."

Her bottom lip shook as she reached for his hand. "You remembered my whole speech about a flower?"

"It was important to you." Benedict stroked her fingers, loving the simple touch. That felt like so much more.

"Hey, any chance you want to join our team next week?"

Penny blinked as she turned to the man standing next to them. "Join your team?"

"Sure." He smiled and ignored Benedict. "We'd love to have you join us. It would be nice to have a pretty girl to look at while we…" He coughed and pulled at the back of his neck. "Besides, you wiped the floor with everyone tonight, and you were basically a table of one, doll." He leaned over her, his eyes traveling toward her breasts before he ratcheted them back up.

"My boyfriend answered the last question. And did so brilliantly. He was just letting me show off." Penny pulled her hand from Benedict's as she crossed her arms over her chest. "Thanks for the offer but no thanks. Have a nice night."

The man stumbled just a bit and put his hand on the table. "Oh, come on. Don't be like that, cutie. I mean you're smart, sure, but…"

He saw Penny clench her teeth and Benedict stood. "I think Penny eloquently told you no. Go back to your table."

The guy shook his head and threw a look at Penny. "Don't get too attached to this one. I've seen him with a different broad in here every few weeks. Not sure you're the only one using the title *boyfriend* with him."

Benedict felt his mouth fall open as the guy sauntered back to his table. He didn't know what to say. They weren't even really boyfriend and girlfriend. He wasn't sure if Penny had used that term to keep the jerk away or because she was trying to test it in preparation for its use over the next few weeks at the hospital.

He dated regularly. And he brought many of those dates here. It was a quaint local pub that was within walking distance of the National Mall if they wanted to take a stroll in the evening. But hearing it thrown at Penny, used as a weapon, sent a sick feeling through him.

"Are you okay?" Penny's voice was a quiet salve to the unexpected turmoil pulsing through him.

"I feel like I should be asking you that?" Benedict offered a smile that he hoped didn't feel too fake. There were too many emotions tipping through him. Ones that part of him desperately wanted to avoid.

"Not my first time dealing with a jerk at a bar." Penny sighed as she looked up at the board. "When I first started going to trivia nights, I intentionally waited to answer questions, or spaced the right answers out to avoid making other teams—of men—uncomfortable. But Alice told me if they couldn't handle a chick beating the pants off them, that was their problem."

A little of the weight lifted off his shoulders. "Your sister does have a way with words."

Penny laughed, a real laugh, and his heart lifted even further. "She does. And in this case, she was right. Never make yourself sound less intelligent to make others feel more comfortable."

"An excellent plan." Benedict reached for her hand and was glad when she didn't pull it away. "Want to get out of here and go for a walk?"

"Yes." Penny beamed as he gestured for the check. "It's a really nice night."

He nodded. It was a nice night. But the truth was that he wasn't ready to say good night. He'd spend as much time with Penny as she'd allow. Another feeling that should worry him, but with her by his side, worries refused to materialize.

The cool night air wrapped around her, and Penny wished she'd brought a light jacket. Washington, DC, in late March seemed to hover between unseasonably warm days followed by frost warnings. She hadn't considered that when she'd chosen the blue dress, which she knew highlighted her curves and eyes. It was a silly choice for a pretend date, but it had been over a year since she'd been out with someone, and she'd wanted to look cute.

No. She'd wanted to look sexy. Desirable.

"You're cold." Benedict shook his head while he looked around the illuminated National Mall, then lifted his sweater off and handed it to her.

Penny opened her mouth to protest, though her tongue paused as she caught a glimpse of the abs under Benedict's undershirt before he pulled it down. He was gorgeous!

"I insist," Benedict stated before she could force the protest from her lips. "I'm hot-blooded. The chill doesn't bother me. And I am not quite ready to call it a night."

Penny slid the sweater over her shoulders and shivered, warmed by Benedict's heat. His scent wafted over her as Penny hooked her arm through his. Her heart hammered instructions for her to lean her head on his shoulder. But she ignored the impulse. She was already crossing so many lines that she'd mentally set for herself to avoid getting too close to him.

Walking arm and arm was already pushing the boundaries. But the night was too perfect for her to care. Besides, she was using these few weeks as an opportunity to dip her toe back in the dating water. May as well take full advantage.

"I'm not ready to head home either. Tonight was fun. Thanks for taking me to trivia. My schedule is too irregular to join an actual team, and it's not as much fun on your own. Alice prefers dance clubs to trivia night. I think I cramp her style a little with my homebody tendencies. Not that she would complain—well, she would, but not too loudly.

"On this topic," Penny added before chuckling.

"It's nice the two of you are so close," Benedict murmured, and she heard the undertone of pain there.

"Bit of a requirement for military brats. We were the only friend we got to keep. I've always been a little jealous of people that grew up in the same room their whole lives." She pulled her hand away from his. She was enjoying the connection a little too much. "Are you and your brother close?"

It was the wrong question. Penny knew it the instant it left her lips, but there was no way to draw it back in.

"We were," he replied softly. "He died when I was nineteen."

"Oh, Benedict, I'm so sorry." Penny's heart ached for him, but he seemed to barely register her response. He was lost in his memories. Before he could pull too far away from her, Penny grabbed his hands and pulled him toward the reflecting pool.

"Did you know that in 1939 Marian Anderson was prevented from singing at Constitution Hall because of her race? So, Eleanor Roosevelt petitioned her husband to let her sing here. Seventy-five thousand people are said to have listened to her concert here on Easter Sunday."

"Distracting me with interesting facts?" Benedict sighed and dropped one of her hands, but he linked fingers with her other.

It was such a tiny motion, but the feel of his hand in hers touched the lonely part of her soul, banishing it. At least for a little while.

"Maybe. We promised each other nothing serious

over the next few weeks. And I know that your privacy is important to you."

Benedict's free hand traced along her cheek, and she shivered. Though it had nothing to do with the evening chill. "You notice everything, don't you?"

"One of the things that makes me a good nurse, I suppose." Penny's eyes traced the outline of his lips. Did he start his kisses softly, pulling you in until the world melted away? Or in a rush that left you breathless?

"Maybe," Benedict's voice mused as his eyes seemed to drink her in. "But I think it's because you see the truth in people."

She felt her lips dip down. There was a time when she might have boasted that reading people was a skill of hers. That she noticed things no one else did. Then she'd gotten engaged to a married man. Couldn't say you read people well after such a colossal failure.

"Don't say it isn't true." His soft words echoed through her.

She dipped her head, pulling away from his soft touch, though she didn't drop his hand. "I'm not the only one who watches people." That was a safer response, one that kept the talk far away from Mitchel.

"Guess not." Benedict sighed. "Thank you. Not sure I ever said that by the way. I really do appreciate you agreeing to pretend for me."

"Right." *Pretend.* The word caught in her heart. This evening was lovely, but it wasn't anything more. Which was good because she wasn't looking for more from it. This was supposed to be lighthearted, fun. A trial. Nothing serious.

If only she could wall away the romantic nature of her heart.

"It is important. Though I admit that I am using you a bit." Penny shrugged as she pulled her hand from his.

"Using me?" Benedict raised an eyebrow as she stared at him.

"Yep." She tried mimicking the sassy sound she'd heard Alice use when she video-chatted with men from her dating apps. How had she gotten so out of practice with flirting? Not that she'd ever really been a top-notch flirter. But she hadn't been this bad. Maybe it was a good thing she was practicing with Benedict.

"I haven't been on a date since I ended things with my fiancé. These next few weeks are me slowly easing my way into it. Little rusty in the flirtation department. As you can probably tell."

"No, I can't tell. But then I've thought you were smart, adorable and downright gorgeous since about five minutes after I met you."

His smile sent thrills chasing through her. "That is an excellent line, Benedict."

"Not a line." He stepped a little closer. "You are adorable, gorgeous and one of the most intelligent people I have ever had the benefit of knowing."

"If this was a romantic comedy, this is the part of the movie where I jump into your arms and kiss you." Penny raised a brow and leaned a little closer, waiting to see if he'd pull back. When he didn't, Penny decided to let her inhibitions down. What good was pretend-dating Dr. Benedict Denbar if she didn't at least get to see how the man kissed?

"Kiss me." The soft demand left her lips, and if she'd been uncertain, the slow smile spreading across Benedict's lips would have cemented the need in her belly. God, the man was hot.

His lips were soft as they grazed hers. He pulled

her closer, the heat of his body echoing through her. She moved without thinking as she wrapped her hands around the nape of his neck. The world slowed as she relished the feel of his body next to hers.

When he deepened the kiss, her soul exploded. If she was ever given the option to pause time, this was the moment she'd choose to run on a loop.

"Penny."

Her name on his lips reached through her senses as she pulled back. "Wow."

"Wow, indeed," Benedict echoed. "We should probably get you home."

That was the safe answer. The responsible answer. But Penny had spent her life choosing the safe path, looking for the responsible choice. And she was alone. For one night, she wanted to live in the moment. Choose excitement without thinking too much.

"Or you could come home with me." Penny ran her hand along his chin, enjoying the bit of stubble under her fingers. Would it feel as good on her skin if he kissed her again? She hoped so.

"Penny." Benedict dipped his lips to hers, barely connecting before pulling back. "Nothing would make me happier. But…"

She laid her finger over his lips before he could say anything. "We're two single adults, who enjoy each other's company. It doesn't have to change anything."

Benedict kissed her again, not as deeply as before but with a fire that clung to her. He wanted her. Just as she wanted him. It felt amazing, and she wanted to chase the feeling, at least for tonight.

"Alice is probably in her room," Penny whispered as she unlocked her door. "Sleeping," she added, though she doubted her sister was actually asleep. But she did not want her bouncing out to ask about tonight. At least not yet.

"Sleeping?"

Benedict's question hit her back. She heard the doubt, but he didn't press.

She silently closed the door and motioned for him to follow her. The thirty steps to her room never seemed so long. But then she'd never walked them before desperate to kiss the man inches behind her.

Flicking on the light, she closed her bedroom door and turned. Then she carefully lifted his sweater off. "I don't need this anymore." She dropped it on the chair by the small desk.

"No, you don't." Benedict stepped closer and ran his fingers down her arms. "You are so beautiful."

"So are you." Penny smiled as she let her fingers wander to the edge of his shirt before dipping underneath it. His skin was warm, and fire licked up her arm as she ran her hand along his skin.

His head dipped and this time the kiss wasn't soft. The demand of his lips sent pulses of need rippling through her as she let her fingers trace along his stomach grazing the band of his pants before rising.

His hands gripped hers, their fingers tangling together. "If you keep touching me like that, I fear tonight will be over far too fast. And I plan to savor every minute."

"Savor?" Penny whispered as she dropped her lips along the edge of his chin, enjoying the shudder that rippled through him.

"Absolutely," Benedict murmured before he sent his lips to the base of her neck, slowly kissing his way down her collarbone, pulling her dress off one shoulder as his lips caressed her.

She reached for the zipper on the side of her dress, slid it down before pushing the dress to the floor. Cool air hit her skin, and Penny froze. She was really here, with Benedict. Need cascaded through her as the reality stormed across her brain.

"Penny?" Benedict's kisses paused as he put both his large dark hands on the sides of her face, cradling her so carefully. "This stops now, if that's what you want."

She smiled and shook her head. "I want you." She meant the words. She wanted him. *All of him.*

Letting his fingers drip along the top of her breast, Benedict followed the motion with his lips. As her bra fell away, need clawed through her. His touch was too much and not enough at the same time.

The back of her knees hit the bed, and Benedict cradled her as she carefully lay back. Then he dropped his lips to her skin once more. His fingers slid down her thigh, inching ever closer to her core, but never touching her where she needed him.

"Benedict." His name felt like a mantra as it echoed in the room. "Benedict." His lips trailed along the top of her panty line and her breath hitched as he slid her panties to the floor. "Benedict."

"Penny."

Her back arched as his lips traced their way up her thighs. *Dear God.* When his tongue traced the bud at the top of her mound, Penny nearly screamed. Benedict's fingers matched the slow motion of his tongue along her thigh before he pressed a finger inside her. Her body erupted and the night broke around her.

"Benedict." Penny sat up and drew him close, kissing him deeply as she pulled his undershirt off and dropped it to the floor. "It's hardly fair that you've seen me naked, and I've yet to gaze on you."

She loved the smile tracing on his lips before he bent to kiss her. "Then I should oblige."

"You should," Penny chuckled as she undid the button of his pants and slid them and his boxers to the floor as one. Her breath caught as she stared at him. He was magnificent.

She let her fingers trace along the edge of his manhood, enjoying the looks of desire flickering across his eyes. His hands cupped her face again as she stroked him. "I want you." She met his gaze as she reached for the condoms in her top drawer.

"I need you," Benedict whispered as she carefully slid the condom down his length. "Penny." He kissed her and pulled her up before sitting on the bed and pulling her to his lap.

Her breath hitched as she slid down his length and wrapped her legs around his waist. One hand cradled her carefully as she began to move, enjoying the sensation running through her body almost as much as she enjoyed watching the pleasure float along Benedict's face.

His mouth met hers, their tongues dancing as their bodies melded together. Her rhythm picked up. Need driving her ever closer to the edge. When his thumb reached between their bodies, pressing against her, pleasure shot through her and she lost all sense of everything but the man holding her close.

His hips rose to meet hers, driving need through her. "Penny." He sighed as he crested.

Was there a better sound than her name on his lips?

Leaning her head against his chest, Penny felt so many things as he stroked her back and dropped a light kiss along her head. Finally breaking the connection between them, Penny reached for her robe and draped it around herself.

No words came as she watched Benedict dress. Tonight had been so perfect. But asking him to stay seemed like a step too far. She refused to regret what had happened tonight, but she wasn't going to ask him to stay.

No matter how much her heart cried out for it. It needed to put all its romantic leanings aside and just enjoy the moment.

"I had fun tonight." Penny stepped into his arms, inhaling his scent. Desperate to draw this out for a few more minutes.

"Me too." Benedict kissed her lips, holding her tightly, like he wasn't quite ready to say goodbye either. "When are you free again?"

Joy shot through her. Maybe it was silly given that they'd promised to see this through until after the first fundraiser, but she wanted to see him again. "Friday." The answer echoed around her.

"Then it's a date." His eyes lit up as he dropped another kiss against her lips.

She laughed and nodded. "Sure." She walked him to the door. "Good night, Benedict."

He bent to kiss her lips and paused just before they touched.

Penny didn't have to turn to know that Alice was watching him.

He dropped a swift kiss on Penny's lips. "Good night, Penny. Alice." Then he was gone.

"That didn't seem super fake." Alice's words were out before Penny got the door closed.

"But it was fun." Alice's frown wavered at Penny's statement. "Very fun."

"I don't want you to get hurt." Alice hugged her tightly.

"I won't. This is just fun. We both agreed. And I desperately need fun. Promise. This doesn't have a fairytale ending. I know that; so my heart is in no danger." It hammered in her chest, but she ignored it. This was just fun... It was.

Alice pursed her lips, a bit of disbelief hovering in her eyes. But she didn't say anything.

CHAPTER FOUR

"I SAW YOU'RE scheduled to work the go-fish booth at the carnival." Dr. Cooke sighed as he handed over the tablet chart. "I got stuck with the ring toss."

"That should be fun," Benedict offered as he looked over the notes from the previous shift.

"Sure." Dr. Cooke rolled his eyes. "Except, carnivals, fundraising dinners and rubbing elbows with donors were not the main reason I went to med school. But since I don't have a cute nurse to hang on my arm on social media posts, I'm starting at a disadvantage in the competition for Dr. Lioness's position."

The insinuation that the only reason he might be at the top of the promotion pool was because of the recent media attention his and Penny's emergency rescue and relationship had generated rubbed Benedict raw. But not as much as the label of *cute nurse* on Penny. She *was* cute.

Adorable. Intelligent. And sexy. So sexy. His mouth watered at the thought of her, at the memory of the feel of her skin under his fingers.

But she was their colleague and *cute* was the last term Dr. Cooke should be using, particularly with the derision sliding through the man's voice.

A wave of fury rippled through him. As if the nurses

on this floor didn't run this unit like a fine machine. As if he or Dr. Cooke could handle any of their duties without the army of women and men RNs ensuring their patients stayed stable.

"Penny Greene is much more than a cute nurse." He barely kept his tone of voice civil, but if Dr. Cooke heard the anger bubbling under the words, he didn't react to it.

"Is Penny going to help you with the booth?" Dr. Cooke raised a brow, and Benedict pushed his emotions aside. It wouldn't do Penny, or him, any good to argue with one of the physicians. Particularly Dr. Cooke. The man's petty streak would have made his mother proud.

"I haven't asked her." Benedict mentally added that to his to-do list. It would make the Wald's Human Resources Department happy, but that wasn't his main incentive. In fact, if he were to make a list, the attention they might draw to the event was near the bottom. He liked spending time with Penny. Time flew with her. The weight of the past that never seemed to leave him lifted when he was with her.

Laughter was easy. Smiles abundant. It might be a temporary arrangement, but Benedict was going to treasure every moment. "But I plan to."

"Will she come with you to the two fundraising dinners too?"

"I hope so." Benedict regretted the words as soon as they were out of his mouth. They were the truth, but Penny had only agreed to fake date through the first fundraiser. Suddenly the ticking clock she'd set echoed in his heart. One night with Penny wasn't enough.

He wanted…

Again, words failed him.

Holding Penny, watching passion coat her skin, had been one of the best moments of his life. If he concentrated, he could almost feel the ghost of her lips on his. He swallowed as need wrapped around his heart. Maybe he could convince her to stick with him through the first fundraising dinner, and by then maybe whatever burned between them would fizzle out.

His brain laughed as his heart scoffed. He wasn't sure any time would be enough with Penny, but he wasn't going to focus on that now.

"Really going to keep one around for two months then?" Dr. Cooke laughed and looked at his watch. "I'll see you tomorrow." Then he was gone.

But Dr. Cooke's words clung to the air around him.

So what if he didn't do long-term connections? All the women he'd been with had been fine with that arrangement.

But was he?

The air seemed to evaporate from the room as the question reverberated around his skull. He was fine with his life.

He was.

So why was his heart pounding?

Benedict tried to shake the feeling from his soul as he opened the tablet to review the status of his current cases.

Last night he and Penny had given in to the desires coating them. They were both single, enjoyed their evening together. There was nothing wrong with the choice. Countless single people did the same on their dates. It didn't have to mean anything.

Except. Need pooled through him. Except Benedict was already contemplating how to extend this escapade for a couple of months. But that didn't mean he wanted a long connection. He just… Well, he didn't have the time or inclination to think it through now.

"You all right?" Charles, one of the counselors who worked on the floor, asked as he leaned over the nurses' station.

"Yeah." Benedict nodded before adding, "I think so."

Charles put his drink down and looked at Benedict. Really looked.

He barely managed to keep from rocking on his heels under the scrutiny.

"I've asked you that question countless times. You've never answered with anything other than, *yeah, I'm fine* or *yep* in the six years I've known you." Charles's brow furrowed as he slid his tablet under his arm. "Want to talk about it?"

Benedict understood that the counselors were there for the patients, their families and the staff. This was a trying field that had more bad days than good sometimes. But he'd never talked to Charles, or to any of the counselors on staff. He'd seen a therapist for a short while following his brother's and niece's passing, but nothing more.

"It's really nothing." Benedict shrugged. "Just a comment from Dr. Cooke about how much I date."

"I suspect he's just jealous. The man would love to be a playboy like you." Charles smiled. "Jealousy has a way of interfering in most things."

"I'm hardly a playboy." Was this really the reputation he had?

Alice strolled to the nurses' station and shot him a withering glare before dropping her radio in the charging station, grabbing another and heading into the room of Jeremiah Blake.

Charles let out a whistle. "If looks could kill. Did a date with Alice go wrong? Workplace breakups can…"

"No," Benedict interrupted. "I am dating her sister,

Penny." The words were out, and Benedict was struck by how uncomfortable they made him. The relationship wasn't a secret…only the temporariness of it.

HR had posted two pictures of them, one in the unit with the note about the fundraiser and another that showed a headline printed out from a news site regarding their rescue after the metro trains detached. But suddenly part of him wished the rest of the world didn't know.

Not because he wanted to hide Penny. No. Because he wanted to keep her. That terrifying thought stunned him. Each post, each acknowledgment was a reminder that it wasn't more than an act.

"Oh," Charles answered. "Well…" His cheeks heated, and he rubbed the back of his neck. "Sisters can be protective, and the Greene sisters are closer than most."

He paused. "If you need to talk about anything, just know my door is open. Or if you'd prefer we set up a talk with someone outside the hospital, that can be arranged too." He handed Benedict his card, bright yellow with bold letters. He'd handed them to parents hundreds of times. A bright color so it could be spotted in full purses and crammed wallets.

Bright and hard to ignore.

But he was fine. Better than fine. He started to put the card on the desk, then slid it into his pocket as he started his rounds.

"There you go." Penny's voice was soft in Indigo Narvar's barely lit room. The little girl had been born at not quite twenty-seven weeks with underdeveloped lungs. She'd battled a round of pneumonia that had seriously concerned the staff. Her progress over the last three weeks had been slow but steady.

"Are you sure I'm not hurting her?" Piper's worried cry echoed as she gently stroked her daughter's back while she lay on her chest. "I don't want to pull any of her tubes."

"You won't," Penny encouraged as she hovered over the mom and her baby. "Kangaroo care is one of our babies' favorite things. And studies have shown it's good for their heart and breathing. I promise she is doing fine. See." Penny pointed to the monitors and tracking devices on the wall that monitored nearly everything Indigo did. "If anything was wrong, one of these alarms would be going off."

"Nurse Greene is right," Benedict reinforced as he slid to the side and looked at Indigo. She'd weighed less than three pounds when she was born, but after almost five weeks, she was starting to look less fragile. Infants grew at a fast pace but watching the NICU patients put on weight and start to look like all the other happy chunky infants always warmed Benedict's heart.

"You are doing great." He pulled up Indigo's chart and looked over it. "She gained half a pound this week and is using less supplemental oxygen."

Piper closed her eyes before gently laying her lips on her daughter's head. "I love you."

"Why don't we give you a few minutes?" Penny smiled and looked at Benedict as she nodded to the door.

"You won't go far?"

"Nope," Penny assured her. "We'll rush in if there are any problems. But you're doing great, Mom." Her breath hitched a little on the last word.

Benedict pursed his lips as he looked at her. He wasn't sure what had happened with her engagement, wasn't sure how it had affected her, but did she still yearn for a family of her own?

She'd be an excellent mother. Loving, kind, but stern when necessary. A deep well of desire floated across his chest. That life couldn't be his, however much he yearned to have Penny to himself, to cherish her, protect her...

He'd vowed to protect his brother, to come to each of his races, to check his car, to ensure it was ready. Isiah had sworn he was done with illegal races after a friend was seriously injured, then he'd abruptly agreed to one more because of the pregnancy. Without telling Benedict the true reason. He'd been furious.

So, he'd stayed home. And broken his promise...

Benedict bit the inside of his cheek, willing the memories away. Rationally he knew that it wasn't anything with the engine that had caused the crash. Knew that his presence there that day wouldn't have accomplished anything. But if they hadn't been at odds, would Benedict have seen the signs after the injury? He would never forgive himself for not taking better care of his brother. As for Penny, whatever kind of family life was in her future, it would never be with him. He couldn't open himself up to that kind of hurt. Love was dangerous.

"You're frowning." Penny tapped his shoulder.

Such a small connection. Yet his body sang. And begged for more.

Trying to keep the moment light, to ignore the increasing bank of emotions Penny raised in him, Benedict nodded to the nurses' station where Alice was looking over notes. "If glaring were an Olympic sport, I think Alice could win gold."

A quiet chuckle escaped Penny's lips, and she waved as Alice looked up at the noise. "When we were growing up, my mother once told Alice that we were working on tact when she said something lost to the memory of time. Alice promptly responded that maybe the rest of us were, but she had all she needed."

She wrapped her arms around herself as her sister headed into another room. "I learned my parents' lessons well and will always resort to tact and diplomacy. But Alice…" She shrugged. "You always know where you stand with Alice. She doesn't hide anything. There are times I wish I was more like her. Though don't tell her that."

Benedict laughed then. "It was the same with Isiah and me. I think we both coveted something the other had. School came easy for me, but he struggled. But he excelled at making connections, street smarts and reading people. I've gotten better at those things, but as a teenager, I craved the easiness with which he started a conversation. I guess sibling rivalry is universal even if you love them more than anything."

Penny's mouth opened, closed, then opened again. "I like hearing about your brother."

The statement sent a wave of panic through him. What had he done? As a general rule, he didn't talk about his brother but Penny had him opening up in a way that was entirely foreign to him.

An alarm echoed from Indigo's room, and Penny spun on her feet. Benedict was directly behind her.

Indigo's oxygen levels had dropped, and tears were streaming down her mother's face. "She moved and I tried to adjust her like you showed me." Panic laced the frantic words, and she stroked her baby's back. "Indigo, Indigo…"

"Let me." Benedict gently lifted the little one and was glad to see that the oxygen tube was kinked. It was a common enough issue, particularly as their patients got more mobile and pulled at the cords attached to them.

Once it was adjusted, the alarm slowed and finally silenced.

Indigo shifted in Benedict's hands and her eyes fluttered open. She locked eyes with her mother and let out a cooing noise. "I think she's ready for Mom now." Benedict started toward Piper, but the woman held up her hands, her eyes still brimming with tears.

"I shouldn't. I didn't even think about the oxygen cord. I was just so happy she was moving around on my chest like her brother used to do. I'm supposed to protect her, and I failed."

"No, you didn't." Benedict shook his head. He'd watched parents take blame for all sorts of things in the NICU. They worried they were responsible for their child ending up here. Occasionally decisions they made had resulted in a premature birth, but in his experience, that was rare and usually the result of untreated addiction.

But knowing there was nothing you'd done wrong and accepting it were two very different things. As he well knew.

"Your daughter is fine." Penny's kind words carried across the room as she wrapped her arms around Piper. "Even if you had made a mistake, which you didn't, everything is okay."

Piper sniffled. "It wasn't so hard with Larkin. He was born right at forty weeks." She hiccupped, "But I was also in my twenties, not forty-two."

"That isn't an abnormal age to have a baby," Benedict coaxed as he handed Indigo back to her mother. He knew that she and her husband had been shocked by her pregnancy. After years of trying, following their son's birth, they'd given up and had been looking forward to the next phase of life when they'd found out about the pregnancy.

She kissed Indigo's forehead as she carefully cradled her daughter. "Every time I am here, and when I'm at home, in her empty nursery, I keep thinking what-if."

"You can't play that game." Penny offered Piper a smile. "What-ifs get you nowhere."

Penny was right. But Benedict also knew that those words were easily spoken. The action behind them... Well, some people never managed to stop wondering what-if. His throat closed as he pushed his own what-if questions away.

Before he could say anything else, Penny continued, "I know those are easy words for me to say. And I have my own life situations where I still wonder what I could have done better, or different. But all those questions do at night is keep me up. I promise, you did nothing wrong."

Piper bit her lip. "I just worry I'm a bad mom. You know, I wasn't exactly thrilled when I found out I was pregnant." Her shoulders shuddered as a truth Benedict suspected she'd been holding on to for some time slipped into the room.

"Want a little secret all nurses know?" Penny didn't wait for an affirmative answer. "Actual bad parents *do not* worry that they are bad parents."

The tips of Piper's lips rose a bit. Penny had found the perfect words.

"She's right." Benedict nodded. He checked his watch and looked at Penny. "I need to see to another patient. Can you stay with Indigo and Piper for a few more minutes?"

"Of course," Penny answered.

The smile on her face sent another wave of emotions wandering through him. He slipped from the room as Penny helped Indigo and her mother readjust to prepare for breastfeeding. While the NICU substituted formula, when necessary, they encouraged as many mothers as possible to pump breast milk and to try breastfeeding when their babies were medically stable.

As he started for the next patient's room, Penny's words about worries rattled around his brain.

What kept her awake at night? What what-ifs did she replay?

They'd promised that their connection over the next month or so was light, that personal questions were off-limits. It was Penny's rule, but Benedict hadn't minded. But he hated the idea that she lay awake at night wondering what-if. He did the same, far too often.

He knew how sad and lonely that was. It was a state he'd accepted for himself, but the fact that Penny did the same tore through him. She deserved better.

Her feet ached and her body felt heavy as Penny followed her sister down the pavement toward the metro station. The shift had been long and heartbreaking. A micro-preemie who had arrived from Grace Hospital had passed not long after his father had arrived, frantic at leaving his wife but needing to be with their son. The sound of the father's broken sobs was still reverberating around her brain. She needed a shower, a good cry and at least ten hours of uninterrupted sleep.

Two of those things were easy. The third… Penny rolled her shoulders. She'd been honest with Piper. There were questions that kept her up. Everyone had regrets, but on days when her mind was actively trying to avoid thinking of a tragedy at work, it always seemed to wander to Mitchel.

She knew her ex had hidden his life well. But there'd been signs she'd missed. His refusal to talk about the past. The little hints he'd drop about his life before her, or more likely let slip through the cracks by accident, had been nuggets she'd clung to, trying to get to know him better.

But tonight, it wasn't Mitchel her brain wandered to. *Benedict.*

They'd sworn this temporary arrangement was light. Fluffy. Unconnected. It was only meant to be a test before she entered the dating game full-time.

But she wanted to know about Isiah.

In so many of Penny's stories, Alice played a starring role. She smiled as her sister grabbed the rail pull in front of her. "I hear you glared at Benedict today."

Alice stuck out her tongue. "Dr. Denbar is exaggerating, I'm sure. I was nothing but professional."

"I've seen your *only professional* behavior before." Penny leaned against the metro bar. Her body was exhausted, and her soul heavy.

The memory of the father on her shift tonight would not leave her. Torn between his wife and his son, the most terrible day of his life had been made so much worse. And as for the mother who had been separated from her son, who would never get the chance to… Penny's eyes filled with tears. It was the perfect example for why the unit for high-risk mothers was so important. And Penny hated that knowledge. She'd seen it in Benedict's eyes too. The knowledge, and the pain it brought.

"Well, I'm worried about you." Alice closed her eyes as she leaned against the pole opposite Penny. "You trust so easily, and always see the best in people. You want the fairy tale and give your heart too freely."

"Not anymore." Penny sighed. "I learned my lesson." She wanted to believe the words. But she wanted to know the man everyone referred to as *a closed book*. She'd gotten a glimpse at the hidden pages of Benedict, and it wasn't enough.

Such a dangerous desire. She'd spent so long chasing the crumbs Mitchel doled out about his past. She'd promised herself she wouldn't do that again.

Still, her heart ached to know about the brother that still meant so much to Benedict.

"Learned your lesson? So much so that you entered a fake relationship with the hospital playboy so he has a better chance at landing the head of the department job that opens in a month. Sure, sweetie. You keep telling yourself that."

"It's to help with fundraising for the maternity unit."

Alice raised a brow. Penny understood her sister's skepticism. The medical field was full of doctors who went into the position to heal, to make the best of the worst time in people's lives, to help.

But it also had more than its share of social climbers. Men and women who were in the profession for the money and respect it brought. But that wasn't what Benedict was after. She'd never have agreed to the ruse if she thought Benedict was one of those professionals. He truly wanted what was best for his patients. And the high-risk maternity unit was what was best.

"Benedict…"

Butterflies danced across her belly, and she found herself smiling as the man stepped in the metro car just before the doors shut, as if her thoughts of him had conjured him. She was glad he was here. *So glad.*

He tipped his head toward Alice, then moved to stand by Penny. He didn't say anything, but her body felt a little lighter knowing he was so close. It was a silly feeling, especially given the words she'd just spoken to her sister, but Penny didn't care. On days like today, you took whatever comfort you could find.

The metro started up, and she let out a sigh.

"You okay?" Benedict shook his head. "As okay as today allowed anyway."

Penny nodded. She'd spent the first year in the NICU crying herself to sleep after days like today. That didn't happen anymore, but that felt like a loss too. It was important to keep yourself separate from the tragedy.

But what does it mean that I can do that now?

It was a question Penny didn't want to contemplate too closely. At least not today.

"Nothing a hot shower and a mug of tea won't fix." She shrugged, wishing those words weren't the truth. But coping mechanisms were necessary, otherwise she wouldn't be able to help her other patients.

"I usually spend the evening tinkering in my workshop after days like today." Benedict pulled at the back of his neck as the train slowed for the first stop.

"And I go out with friends," Alice added to the conversation before looking from Benedict to Penny. "And I plan to drag my sister with me tonight."

"You do?" Penny felt the words leave her lips before she pursed them and stared at her sister. It was true that on hard days Alice had a few friends that she met up with. They went dancing, and she spun her body around, craving the loud noise, movement and anonymity of the club.

It was not something Penny enjoyed. She always felt out of place, an issue highlighted by the fact that her body did not move to the music the way her sister's did. Alice floated on a dance floor, her body in rhythm to whatever beat played. Penny stomped, against the rhythm, never able to let her body relax despite her sister's coaxing.

"Yes," Alice reiterated. "It will be good for you. Dancing is fun and maybe you'll meet someone." She winked at Penny before turning her attention to her phone.

An uncomfortable silence filled the space between her and Benedict. Their relationship wasn't real. Yes, they were going on dates so she didn't feel like it was truly lying. Yes, they'd spent the night together. They were single and enjoyed each other's company—like countless other singles did.

It didn't matter that, if she closed her eyes, she could still feel his touch on her skin. The memory of his kisses on her body. Her skin heated and she started to lean into him before gripping the bar tighter. She was not going to do that.

"I hope you have fun," Benedict murmured.

Meeting someone shouldn't make her feel like she wasn't being fair to Benedict… So why was her stomach flopping as her cheeks heated?

Penny rolled her eyes before looking down at her shoes. "I'll find a way out of it. I suspect she'll give up when we get to our townhome. She's just…" She let her whispered words die out.

"Protecting you," Benedict filled in the silence. "That's the main role a sibling plays. Or it is supposed to be."

His voice nearly cracked, and she put her hand over his. The connection vibrated between them. She didn't know what he was thinking but she could see the pain radiating behind his eyes. The metro slowed, and she glanced at the stop. Where had the time gone?

"It's our stop." Penny squeezed his hand. "If you ever want to talk…"

"Light and fluffy, remember?" Benedict smiled.

"I know." Penny felt her lips pull to the side, hating the promise she'd dragged from him. But also not wanting to give too much of herself away either. Maybe it wasn't fair to want his secrets when she wasn't willing to give her own. "But the offer still stands."

"Thanks. Enjoy your tea. Or dancing, if Alice holds you to it."

"She won't." Penny patted his hand once more. "She's more bark than bite…though she'd never admit it. Good night, Benedict."

"Night, Penny."

Alice was several feet away when Penny exited the metro car.

"You really want me to go dancing with you?" She moved to her sister's side and matched her quick step.

"No," Alice grumbled. "I mean, you're welcome to, but I know it's not how you process tough days. I just…" She pushed a hand through her hair as she stopped in front of a local restaurant. "I just want you to be happy. If he makes you happy for now—" She held up a hand before Penny could interrupt. "If he makes you happy, then I will keep my thoughts to myself. But your heart is in danger. Whether you want to admit it yet or not."

She huffed out a breath, then tilted her head to the restaurant. "Go on. You'll be much happier with your order of sushi, hot tea and fuzzy slippers than you will be on the dance floor."

Penny kissed her sister's cheek. "I love you, you know that, right?"

"Of course. I'm amazing. And so easy to love." Alice

winked, then tilted her head. "I love you. Always and forever, you and me."

"You and me," Penny agreed.

Her sister waved as she turned on the street that would lead her home. Their bond was for life. And Penny had no idea what she'd do without Alice. It would feel like she'd lost a part of herself.

Was that how Benedict felt?

She pulled her phone out and started to type a message to him before putting it back in her pocket.

They'd all had a rough shift. It happened. And everyone had the way they worked through it. For her, it was hot tea, sweatpants and fuzzy slippers. Benedict would be okay. And it wasn't her responsibility to check in on him.

Except it felt like…

No. She was not going to wander down that path. She was going to get her dinner. Have a quick shower and sit in front of the TV with some show she didn't have to follow while she got all her emotions together. Benedict could handle himself.

He could.

Feel like meeting up?

Penny stared at Benedict's text; it was as if her thoughts of him had conjured the words. Her fingers hesitated for only a moment before she typed back.

Want to meet at the National Mall?

Benedict stared at the text from Penny. He'd sent her a message less than an hour after he'd gotten home, asking if she wanted to meet up. He was surprised he'd lasted that long. After all, his fingers had itched from the moment he hit his front door.

The day sucked. There was no other way to describe the loss of little ones. Comforting parents, dealing with the end was never pleasant. Over his decade in the NICU, he'd watched technology advance. Watched the numbers shift in favor of doctors against the fates that would pull souls to them. But it didn't make them gods. Didn't let him snap his fingers and just make everything okay.

When Penny had laid her hand over his, the storm inside him calmed. He wasn't sure what it was about her touch that made his spirit lift, but it was intoxicating. He craved it.

That should make him call a halt to the ruse they were playing. Should make him shut it down. Tell her they should just be friends...except they were friends. The relationship wasn't real.

There was no need to worry about getting close because it wasn't real. Except it felt... It felt like the beginning of something good. And for the first time in his life, turning away from someone, *from Penny*, didn't seem like an option.

At least not an option he planned to exercise.

His fingers hovered over the screen before he typed.

How about you come here? I have tea.

He held his breath as he pushed Send. As the minutes dragged on with no response, Benedict wished there were a way to recall the message. A way to delete it from the ether. A way to turn back time.

He should have agreed to meet at the National Mall. Or some other neutral space.

I don't have your address.

The words sent an explosion through him. Before he could second-guess the action, he typed out the address and a quick set of directions for how to get to his place from the metro station two blocks away.

See you soon.

He felt the smile pull his lips. A giant grin at odds with the day he'd had. When had that last happened? He smiled, maybe not giant grins, but when had a smile felt like it transported his whole mood?

Benedict didn't want to waste any time on the thought. Instead, he turned on the kettle and grabbed a couple of mugs from the cabinet. All he had was chamomile and English breakfast tea. Not much of a selection to offer a woman who said her coping mechanism was fuzzy slippers and tea.

Glancing at his watch, he shook his head; there wasn't time to run to the grocery on the corner. Even if he did know what to grab, he didn't want to risk missing her arrival. His small stash would simply have to do for now, but he'd make a point to find out if it was better if he stocked something else.

CHAPTER FIVE

THE DOOR TO Benedict's townhome was dark blue. It was the kind of door that screamed for a wreath of colorful flowers to welcome guests, but the door was empty. Not even a welcome mat. None of these thoughts mattered, and for the millionth time since she'd taken the one metro stop from her townhome to his, she wondered what she was doing here.

Her hair was still wet and pulled into a topknot. She had on yoga pants and an athletic top. If she'd had her yoga mat, she'd look just like she did every time she managed to make it to the hot yoga studio.

This wasn't a date. It was... Her mind couldn't find a safe word. It wasn't rational that she was here. She should turn around, go home and make some excuse, but she couldn't force her feet to move.

Her phone buzzed, and her cheeks heated at Benedict's message.

Want me to open the door? Or to pretend I never saw you outside so you can send me a message to say you changed your mind? No pressure either way.

A small giggle escaped her lips before she raised her hand and rapped on the door. She was already here, and already seen. So why not follow through with whatever this was?

The door swung open as soon as she stopped knocking, and she smiled as her body relaxed. "How long have you known I was here?"

Benedict pointed to his doorbell. "It has a camera and sends a notification to my phone. So pretty much the moment you stepped in front of it. But…" he reached for her hand and squeezed it "…you seemed unsure, so…"

"I was wondering if I should have changed, then told myself this wasn't a date, it was just two colleagues meeting up, then told myself that meant I definitely should have changed. I am a champion overthinker!"

"Then you're in good company. I can overthink with the best of them." Benedict started toward the kitchen area of his townhome and pulled up two boxes of tea. "I realized all I had in the townhome was chamomile and English breakfast tea. I contemplated going to the store on the corner at least fifty times, then worried I wouldn't be back in time."

Crossing her arms and shaking her head, Penny let the weight of the worries slide away from her. Any man who'd worry about a tea selection was a person she'd enjoy spending time with. "Chamomile is great. A little late for caffeine for me."

"I am not sure my body reacts to it anymore." Benedict dropped a tea bag into each mug before picking up the kettle. "Sugar?"

"No." Penny playfully covered her mouth in horror as Benedict dropped two large spoonsful of sugar in his own mug. "Alice would appreciate your cup of tea. I swear she prefers tea-flavored sugar water."

Benedict held his mug up to his lips and took a deep sip before making a face. "Too hot."

Gripping her mug, Penny let the heat seep into her. She loved tea, and coffee. Pretty much any hot beverage, but it was this moment she enjoyed most. The warmth of the drink, waiting for it to cool, it calmed her. Stabilized her. She'd never been able to explain the feeling, but it was her happy place.

"That's boiling water for you." She leaned over the counter, still holding her mug, and looked at his lips. So full and close. Swallowing, she pulled back. "Are you okay?"

"Nothing more than my pride injured."

"That's an injury some people aren't able to take." The words flew from her lips, and she saw the flash of curiosity come over Benedict's features.

Why did I say that?

It was true. Pride destroyed so many things. Mitchel had stayed married because he was worried how it would look to the community to divorce his wife. Not that he'd considered how it would look for the world to discover he was keeping a mistress with a fake engagement ring on her hand in Ohio.

Still, it was his pride that had been injured when his wife and Penny sent him on his way. Not a broken heart. Pathetic.

"Well, my pride has taken many hits over the years, and I've always recovered." Benedict nodded to the couch. "Let's have a seat."

"Many hits?" Penny asked as she sat and crossed her legs on the other side of the couch. It was too much space. Space her heart begged her to close, but she was not going to give in to it. "It's hard to believe you've taken a ton of hits to your pride. Have you seen yourself? You're gorgeous."

Her cheeks heated and she raised her mug to cover

her face. *Why the hell did I say that?* Good grief, her tongue had a mind of its own tonight.

At least the statement was true. Benedict was one of the handsomest men she'd ever seen. If he wasn't a physician in the country's top NICU, he could grace the cover of any magazine. It was hard to believe he'd ever felt embarrassed.

"When I was a freshman in high school, the science experiment I'd carefully planned out for advanced chemistry went awry. To this day, I'm not exactly sure what combination of chemicals I mixed wrong. It was supposed to create a rubberlike blue material that expanded and then hardened. I'd done it at home several times perfectly."

He shook his head and raised his mug to his lips. "Instead it made a noxious chemical concoction that forced the school to evacuate, and a hazmat unit was called in. Half the school thought I'd done it on purpose, the other half thought I was a fool. My school record was nearly perfect, so they didn't suspend me, but I spent all summer working at the school to help offset the cost of the cleanup. I was already a gangly nerd. It did not help my reputation."

"Oh, my!" Penny felt her eyes widen. It was hard to imagine the man before her now as an awkward teen but endearing. "That must be quite the story at the high school reunions."

"Maybe."

His gaze shifted and she wondered what he was seeing. What part of the past he was visiting…and if his brother was there?

The moment passed as he looked at her and raised his mug again. "I don't know. I haven't been home since I left for college."

"Not at all?" That knowledge cut a small wound across her heart. She didn't have a place she considered her childhood home. She'd lived in six different states and three different countries before she'd graduated high school. She'd always been jealous of the people she met who slept in their childhood rooms at holiday and family gatherings. She craved the stability that that life represented for her.

"No." Benedict pursed his lips before adding, "Home isn't exactly a happy place."

His body shifted and before he could pull away, she closed the distance between them and laid her head on his shoulder. Whether he wanted to talk about it or not, she was here.

And painfully aware of how fortunate she was. She might not have a specific house to call a home, but whenever she and Alice and their parents were together, it was a home. A wonderful, joyous home.

She hadn't realized how unique that was until she'd moved away to attend college. How many families were hiding their unhappiness and brokenness behind closed doors and smiling family portraits. "I bet you're a legend there and just don't realize it."

Benedict leaned his head against hers but didn't say anything.

They sat like that for several minutes. Just enjoying not being alone after a long day. No words seemed necessary. Sitting in silent comfort, not needing to fill the quiet was a blessing so few understood.

But in the silence, she let her eyes wander. His townhome was large but sparsely furnished. The white walls were devoid of any pictures, and other than the couch they were sitting on, the coffee table and the television, this room was empty.

It was as if he'd just moved in but hadn't had time to decorate. "How long have you lived here?"

"About six years." Benedict set his mug on the little coffee table in front of him and pulled her into his arms. It wasn't sexual but the intimacy of the moment pulled at her. The two of them, dressed casually, just enjoying the other's company after a long day. It felt so much more intimate than the night they'd spent in each other's arms.

Her heart clenched and she briefly wondered if Alice was right. Surely she wasn't actually in danger of losing her heart here. They were just…

Again, her brain refused to provide a word. And she didn't want to dwell on it too much. She was happy and content in his arms. That was enough for today.

"My home growing up never had any decoration." His words were quiet but he kept going. "The walls were the same lemon yellow they were when my parents moved in, though by the time I left they looked more sallow than bright. I guess. So I've never really thought too much about decorating. But it does look a little sad, huh?"

"Not sad," Penny stated, though that wasn't entirely true, but she didn't want to hurt his feelings. Didn't want to push away the small intimate piece of him she was seeing. "If you didn't see decorations growing up, why would you necessarily think of them?"

A slow smile spread across his face. It made her belly twist with an emotion she didn't want to name as she kissed his cheek. The platonic kiss felt so unsatisfying. "Besides, it's an easy enough fix." Penny brightened as she looked around. "We moved every few years with my parents' jobs, but in every rented place, my dad made sure we were allowed to paint."

She smiled as the memories floated through her. "Whenever possible, we'd arrive a few days before the army movers. Mom and Dad let Alice and I pick the colors for our room, and once we were older, it was our job to help turn the rented space into our home. I can still remember the bright pink Alice and I chose for our room when we lived in North Carolina. Our room faced the west with this giant window. It was so bright my parents had to invest in blackout curtains so that we would go to bed."

She giggled. "We could be real pains about bedtime."

"I suspect most kids are that way. Siblings that team up are probably able to leverage more command than those that fight all the time."

"Did you and Isiah fight all the time?"

Benedict's gaze shifted again, and he shook his head. "No, but when we did…" He pursed his lips and looked at her. "What colors would you paint if you lived here?"

Penny patted his hand, aware that she'd touched a painful part of his past. Unintentional or not, it still upset her to cause him pain. And a tiny twist of doubt pushed through her at the knowledge that once again he'd started to open up but then pulled back.

But that was fine, because this was just a light and fluffy fake relationship. Except when she was in his arms…

Her body ached as her soul yearned for more. But she was not going to give in to those feelings.

Instead she swiveled in his lap, desperately aware of the feelings rocking through her as she stared at his kitchen. It was a small open area that led to the living room. He could paint it an accent color and then keep this room neutral with a picture or some plants. If he decided to take this from a hypothetical "change of conversation" topic to the real world. "What's your favorite color, Benedict?"

"Blue."

"Blue." She smiled and gestured with her hand for him to expand. "What kind of blue?"

"Kind of blue?" His dark eyes held hers, and she could see the hint of a smile in the corner of his lips. "Just blue."

Setting her mug down, she playfully hit his shoulder. "There is a whole spectrum of blue. I have a set of pencils that is just shades of blue. Do you mean navy or baby blue? Teal or aqua? The options are endless."

Benedict laughed and wrapped his arms around her, his fingers stroking her back. Did he ache to kiss her as much as she ached to raise her lips to his?

"I have never given blue much thought." He kissed the tip of her nose. "If pressed, I suppose I'd say lighter than navy but darker than baby blue."

"So somewhere around azure or aero would be my guess." Alice kissed his cheek.

"Sure. Aero sounds right." Benedict nodded, playing along, though she knew he didn't actually have any idea what she meant.

"Maybe I should bring my pencils next time. I could show you…" Her mouth dried as she looked at him. "I mean, if you wanted me to come over again." It seemed like such a stupid statement when she was sitting on his lap and discussing paint colors. How quickly she'd lapsed into the idea of this being something more.

"I think I'd really enjoy that." His eyes sparkled with desire.

Before she could overthink it too much, Benedict's lips met hers. The soft brush of them turned demanding as she ran her fingers along the base of his jaw, enjoying the stubble there.

"Penny."

Her name on his lips just after kissing her might be the sweetest sound in the universe. Again, her brain sent a warning shot, but it was easy to ignore when she was in his arms. *Too easy.*

God, Penny. Benedict's mind screamed as his fingers stroked her back. Painfully aware of the thin shirt separating her soft skin from his fingers. He ached for her.

It wasn't where he'd planned this evening to go. When he'd offered her tea, Benedict had truly planned to share a mug and an hour or so of conversation with someone who made it possible for him to forget that the world could be a cruel place. Just some time with a woman who made the hole inside him almost disappear. But as her lips met his again, his body cried out with need.

Her tongue traced his lower lip, and his fingers roamed the top of her waistband.

"Benedict." The softness of his name on her full lips was the most intoxicating thing he'd ever heard.

"Penny." His fingers ran along her chin, enjoying the subtle changes in her blue eyes as they watched him. That color, whatever it was called. Blue with hints of smokiness in the center and a trace of green was his favorite shade of blue. He didn't know if it had a name, but in his mind, it would always be known as Penelope Perfection.

"I want you." Her lips tipped up as her fingers caressed his chest.

"I want you too." *In so many different ways.* He managed to catch those words before he let them loose.

He wanted Penny. But not in just "a few moments of pleasure" way.

That wasn't what they'd promised each other though. He knew she hadn't dated much, maybe at all, since whatever happened with her ex-fiancé. She was using this relationship as a trial before reentering the dating world. A way to get all her nervousness out. He was the rebound with no strings attached.

It was what he'd always wanted. But staring into her eyes, with her in his lap, it didn't seem like nearly enough. This might not be a forever situation, but at least he could relish every minute.

Making sure his grip was secure, Benedict stood, ensuring she stayed in his arms. Her lips traveling across his neck made it difficult to concentrate on keeping his feet steady on the stairs, but he managed to make it to his bedroom. Thrills drifted around his body as he set her on his bed.

"Now I really wish I'd done more than throw my hair in a wet topknot and put on yoga pants." Penny's quiet words rocked the room as she sat on her knees and lifted his shirt over his head.

Before she could do anymore, Benedict caught her hands in one of his and let his other linger on the top of the scoop-neck athletic shirt she had on. "You are gorgeous, Penny. So gorgeous." He swallowed as need raced through him. The urge to rip her clothes off and bury himself deep within her, show her how much she called to him was overwhelming, but he was going to enjoy every moment of Penny in his bed.

"Whether you have a messy topknot, which is adorable by the way." He kissed her, enjoying the sigh caught in the back of her throat as he let his free hand roam her delicious backside. "Or the fanciest hair, ever."

Letting go of her hands, Benedict lifted her shirt, and felt his breath hitch at the sight of rosy desire coating her skin. "Whether you are in an athletic top or the blue dress that made my mouth water, you are stunningly beautiful. And I am weak with need just being in the same room with you."

He twisted his finger through a dark strand that had escaped her bun and let his other hand wander along the edge of her breast, studying which movement made Penny's breath catch. He could easily spend hours discovering every way to make the smoky look come across her face.

Unclasping her bra, Benedict dipped his head to one perky nipple and then moved to another as he let his hands stray into her stretchy yoga pants. His hands fondled her over her cotton panties.

"Benedict…"

The low whimper was music to his ears. He doubted he'd ever tire of hearing his name on her lips as desire surged through him. "Penny," he answered as he lowered her pants and panties. God, she really was gorgeous. And his.

At least for a while.

He pushed that thought aside as his hands roamed the perfection in his bed. He let his lips linger on her breasts before starting to move his way down her body. As he reached her midsection, Penny sat up and grabbed his face, kissing him with such passion it weakened nearly every muscle in his body.

"I want to touch you tonight." Her raspy voice echoed in the quiet room as her hands unbuttoned his pants and slid them with his boxers to the floor.

"Penny…" Before he could utter anymore, she kissed away the statement.

"Tonight I get to watch you writhe with desire. Fair is fair." Her fingers slid along his length and her eyes met his. "Find what turns you on."

Her grin was precious as she stroked him, but the answer was breathtakingly simple.

"You," Benedict murmured as her hands cupped him. "You turn me on."

Her mouth opened, forming a delicious *O* as their gazes locked.

Dipping his head, he kissed her. Not with the fire they'd had only a moment ago. But with the tender reverence calling to him. Her touch shifted from demanding to a sensation that made his heart sing.

The world shifted when Penny was with him. It felt whole, he felt whole when she was in his arms. He wasn't sure what to make of those thoughts but in this instant, he needed her in a way he'd never needed anyone else.

"Penny." Her name felt like a prayer as it hit his lips. "Penny." He dropped kisses along her chin before capturing her mouth with his, drinking her in.

"Benedict." Her tone had shifted too, but it was perfect. "I want you."

Reaching for a condom, he sheathed himself quickly. He bent his head and kissed her as he joined their bodies. She wrapped her legs around his waist, and they lost themselves in these new sensations. The new demands of their bodies.

They crested into oblivion together, and he leaned forward and kissed her forehead. There were no words for what had just occurred between them. It was simply perfection.

Her lips grazed his cheek. "Benedict." Her thumb rubbed his lower lip just before he broke the connection between them. She sighed and then looked at the clock. "I should probably get going."

He pursed his lips as he let his hand run through her dark hair. He wanted to argue. Wanted to beg her to stay. Wanted to explore whatever had just happened between them. Cling to the emotions still pooling within his soul.

But that probably wasn't a good idea. *Light and fluffy.* The reminder did little for his heart as it hammered in his chest.

It took longer than he expected to push those feelings aside. "Just give me a minute and then I'll see you out."

She squeezed his hand and nodded.

"Penny." Benedict gripped her hand as she opened the door to leave.

Was he trying to stall her departure? She didn't want to leave but staying seemed to risk too much. Their joining had felt…different. Not like the desire from the other night, the end of a good date with a hot man. But deeper, so much deeper. And he'd felt it too… She was certain of that.

"I meant to ask this earlier, but do you want to help me with the go-fish booth at the carnival next weekend?" It seemed like such an insignificant question given whatever had just happened between them. But an easier topic to handle. So much easier.

"Of course." She dropped a chaste kiss along his jaw. "I agreed to keep things up at least until the first fundraising dinner." She swallowed and looked at him. "That's what you wanted, right?"

"Right…" Benedict nodded.

It was ridiculous, but for a moment hope had pooled in her that he might say something about tonight. That he'd brave the conversation that seemed to be hovering around them. Ask if she wanted to change the rules.

Did she want to change the rules she'd set? She didn't know. Until she had an answer, maybe it was better that they kept the rules the same. Help the hospital and enjoy each other's company for a month or so. And she'd treasure every memory.

CHAPTER SIX

"You got the go-fish station with Dr. Denbar, and I am stuck in the ring toss with Dr. Cooke." Alice rolled her eyes as she pulled her dark hair into a ponytail.

Penny wrapped her hair in a bun, mostly so there was at least a little difference between the two of them, since the day promised to be too warm to leave it down. Despite the two-year age difference, the Greene girls, as they'd been known in most of the places their parents had landed, looked so much alike that they often got asked if they were twins. A resemblance that had only solidified as they reached adulthood and the shift of their features had slowed.

"The ring toss will be fun," Penny offered as she wrapped a sparkly scrunchie around her bun. It wasn't an accessory she wore outside the hospital, but the kids at Wald Children's always responded to it. And in a children's hospital, finding joy sometimes meant looking for the small things.

"It's not the ring toss that I am complaining about. It's Dr. Cooke." Alice made a face as she clipped a smiley face barrette on the side of her head. It had been a gift from a little boy whose sister had spent nearly one hundred days in the NICU. He'd wanted his sister to always see a smiley face. So, he'd asked Alice, and she'd worn it proudly.

The little girl was now a healthy four-year-old, but they still attended many of the functions at the children's hospital. And Alice did her best to always remember to wear it. Her sister might have a tough outer shell, but she was a softy at heart.

"If I'd known I would be paired with him when I volunteered, I might have thought twice about it."

"No, you would still have volunteered." Penny hit her hip against Alice's as she picked up her lipstick.

Alice huffed before turning out the light in the bathroom and taking her leave.

"Hey!" Penny shouted as she flipped it back on. "I'm still getting ready in here!"

"The kids don't care if you're wearing lipstick." Alice stuck her head back around the doorway and waited until Penny met her gaze. "And I doubt Benedict Denbar does either."

Penny threw a washcloth at her sister as she winked. "Maybe I want to look nice for myself." She chuckled before she carefully lined her lips. It was mostly true. She did want to look nice, not for Benedict, but for herself. But if she enjoyed seeing the look of desire float over his features whenever she walked up...

Well, that was just a bonus. Her confidence was growing with each day. And with each passing day, her heart was crying out for more with Benedict.

After their rendezvous last week, something had shifted. Or at least it felt like it had. They'd shared something so much deeper than desire bubbling over. In that moment the fake relationship seemed to have slipped away, but neither of them had brought it up.

Instead it hovered in the background of everything they did. Begging to be discussed but ignored by both parties.

They'd gone to trivia night again. And won the twenty-five-dollar gift card prize for the top score. And sworn they'd make it back next week, assuming they weren't scheduled at the hospital. It was perfect…or it would be if it were real.

A real relationship with Benedict Denbar…

She swallowed as the desire pooled in her. That was not the ground rule they'd set, and it seemed unfair to demand it now. After all, she'd been the one to set the rules. Light, fluffy, no discussion of the past. No heavy topics. No promises of anything more.

But with each passing day…

She shook her head as she looked at herself in the mirror. This feeling of wanting more, of wanting something real was just proof that she was ready for the dating world. Her heart was healed enough. She was ready for happily-ever-after.

So she'd carry on helping Benedict and Wald's raise money for the new maternity wing for as long as she needed to. By the time the fancy dinners were done, it would be perfectly fine for the illusion to end. Her heart tore a little at the thought.

Losing him completely made her want to weep. Surely they'd remain friendly. They enjoyed each other's company. Besides, men and women could be friends.

But could a man and woman who got lost in their desire for each other whenever they were alone be friends?

She clicked off the bathroom light before wandering down that path. She'd find a way to make friendship work because Benedict Denbar not being in her life wasn't an option.

* * *

Mom is not well. Her beliefs haven't changed and I'm still a disappointment. I just don't want to deal with this right now. It's been seventeen years. What's a few more months?

Benedict wanted to scream at the message. Wanted to throw his phone and pull out his hair. This was beyond ridiculous. He needed this chapter with Amber to be closed, and quickly. Thoughts of Penny crowded his brain.

He knew that their relationship wasn't meant to be forever. But he wasn't ready to say goodbye after the first fundraiser, or even after all the fundraising events were over. And it seemed unfair to her that his divorce wasn't finalized.

It had never felt bad before. His relationships were temporary, so his legal connection to Amber wasn't an issue. But with Penny…so many things felt different. He didn't want to examine those feelings, but after their night together last week, something had changed.

A seed had been planted in his soul and it bloomed whenever he was near her. Not that he'd brought it up with her.

Penny hadn't either. Part of him had hoped she would. Hoped that he wouldn't have to guess if she'd felt the dynamic alter between them.

He didn't know exactly what it meant. Marriage wasn't in his future. If the messages on his phone weren't enough proof that vows of forever were a bad idea, he still had the memories of his parents' loveless marriage and the multitude of others that followed.

And the knowledge that all their relationships started with smiles, laughter and hope. There were pictures in the old photo album of smiling faces from his father's three marriages and his mother's many more. Bright happy grins with people that they thought were forever. But the light of love always extinguished. It was simply too fickle to trust.

But Penny...

His mind twisted as her lovely face materialized. Whether Penny was interested in any kind of relationship with him beyond their arrangement made no difference. It was time to close this chapter of his life.

I need to finalize this, Amber. I am sorry, but according to my lawyer, I can move forward with the divorce without your consent given the time apart. It won't take that much time.

He hoped that was true. His lawyer had said given the length of their separation and separate lives, the court would grant the proceedings quickly, assuming Amber was ready to just sign the papers. If she wasn't, it might take more time, but he hadn't told Benedict how much more time.

He sighed and added more.

You can blame me. Tell your mother I gave you no choice. I don't mind being the bad guy here.

He was done postponing what they should have done years ago. Done living to the standard set by someone else. He hoped that Amber might find a way to find value in herself, even if her family didn't. But it wasn't his responsibility. It had never been. This was a sham, vows or not, and it needed to end.

Have you met someone?

Benedict stared at the message. It wasn't Amber's business. They'd barely been friends when they'd said *I do*. He'd promised Isiah he'd look after Amber if anything happened to him at a race, and when it had, he'd stepped in to make sure she and her baby weren't disowned by her family. If life had been fair, they'd have raised Olivia together. He'd have honored his vows and stayed beside her. But life wasn't fair. He would always mourn his brother and his tiny niece, but time moved on.

Yes.

He typed out the word and stared at it as his finger hovered over the send button. It was the truth. If Penny weren't in the picture, he'd let Amber drag this out. Let her keep up the charade so her horrid mother didn't lament her divorcée status.

Hitting Send, he waited a minute after he saw the Read status pop up. He saw the dots to say she was responding, then they disappeared. He watched them reappear and then disappear several more times.

Okay.

A few more dots appeared as she typed but no further messages came through. On Monday, he'd contact his lawyer to get the process started. Crossing his arms, he let out a sigh as a weight evaporated from his shoulders.

Happy wasn't the right emotion to describe this moment. But Benedict felt hopeful. And hopeful was a feeling he constantly told his patients' parents to hold on to. And for the first time in forever he planned to take his own advice.

His phone pinged. Benedict grabbed it from his back pocket, not really wanting to see anything from Amber, but feeling obligated to follow through.

He felt his lips tip up as Penny's name topped the message.

Alice and I are leaving in twenty minutes. Maybe we'll be on the same metro train.

A smiley face emoji followed next.

Benedict wasn't sure what the emotions dancing through him meant. But he did know that he'd be waiting at the Foggy Bottom metro stop in twenty minutes. Maybe it was silly since he and Penny would be in the booth all afternoon together but getting extra time with the woman was something he craved.

"Well, I think that was successful," Alice chimed as she stepped up to the go-fish booth.

Penny handed Benedict a fishing pole before she grabbed the box of tickets kids had passed her all afternoon. The sun was warm, and her cheeks felt a little burned, but the day had been perfect. "I think so. Look at all these tickets!"

People could purchase five tickets for a dollar or fifty for five dollars. Based on the number of tickets in Penny and Benedict's box, the carnival had raised a sizable amount before even counting the money from the corporate sponsors.

"Yes." Alice waved her hand at the box of tickets. "I'm sure we raised a decent sum for the maternity wing, but I meant it was successful because Dr. Cooke got to live through the afternoon. That man is such an insufferable, whiny brat."

Benedict chuckled as he stepped next to Penny and put his arm around her waist. Penny leaned into him. The social media team had taken their picture a few times over the course of the carnival, but the camera had disappeared an hour ago.

The initial glow of the doctor and the nurse who'd helped a baby on the metro was waning. Their photos were still loaded onto the social media pages, but now there were other stories the team added too. Penny didn't mind. Particularly because Benedict's touches, like this simple one, felt so natural. Like it was just for her. No camera, no team to impress, no ulterior motive they were working toward. And she enjoyed it.

A bit too much.

"I suspect Dr. Cooke is very used to getting his way and when someone challenges that—" Benedict gestured to Alice and nodded "—he acts like a bully or a baby."

"Or both." Alice put her hands on her hips, took a deep breath, and then relaxed a bit. "On the bright side, I've got a date tonight with the photographer who was too focused on the two of you, according to Dr. Cooke. Nice guy. Bet I end up on some of those social media posts."

"You are very photogenic."

"Yes, I am, Dr. Denbar." Alice paused, holding her sister's gaze for just a moment. "Though my sister looks just as good in front of a camera. She's just less likely to step in front of it."

Benedict and Alice's banter caught Penny off guard. She felt her mouth fall open as she looked at her sister's happy face.

He squeezed Penny and kissed the top of her head before, adding, "She is something special."

"Yes. She is," Alice confirmed.

What was going on here?

Penny knew Alice had said she'd not antagonize Benedict or Penny over their... The word for whatever was going on between them failed to materialize. This didn't feel like it had a deadline anymore. But she'd been misled by her emotions before.

Still, watching Alice joke with Benedict warmed her heart. So much hope danced around her belly, mixing with the butterflies that had only intensified the closer she got to the man beside her.

"Wait, your date is tonight?" Alice's words fully registered with Penny. "I thought we were doing dinner and a movie? A nice night in."

They'd talked about it this morning. Or more accurately, Penny had talked about it. Alice had nodded and said very little, though she hadn't actively said no to the idea. But after a long day in the sun, all Penny really wanted to do was curl up on the couch and relax.

Or curl up next to Benedict...

"Want to grab some takeout and curl up on my couch? After the long day, it sounds like a perfect way to spend the evening." Benedict's smile burned through her. "What sounds good? I can order in and have it ready for delivery by the time we get to my place."

"Are you sure? I mean, you just spent most of the day with me." Penny bit her lip and turned to check with Alice, but her sister had disappeared without a trace.

Tricky little sister!

He squeezed her hand as he held up his phone in the other hand. "I am certain. You just pick the place. There is a Thai restaurant on the corner that makes the best pad Thai. Oh, and their red curry is to die for. We could order one of each and share. Or there is a deli with sandwiches."

"Thai sounds great." Penny loved seeing him light up. So he liked spicy food, and she was going to see what kind of movie he preferred tonight. Small windows into the story that was Dr. Benedict Denbar. Maybe it was dangerous to look, and certainly dangerous to cling to small pieces of information like she'd done with Mitchel, but this was just fun.

Besides, she liked learning about the man standing before her. He was interesting and entertaining. And he lit up her insides in ways that hadn't occurred in so long. *If ever.*

After so long second-guessing herself, accepting the quiet loneliness of long distance with her ex and the added pain of rebuilding herself when her plans evaporated, the easy laughter and smiles that Benedict drew from her were a gift that Penny was going to enjoy for as long as possible.

"I have a change of clothes in my bag, in case things got off the hook here." Penny laughed. One never knew when there were so many children around if clothes would survive. Particularly when cotton candy, ice cream and finger-painting stations were involved. "I can use the locker room at the hospital to rinse the heat of the day off and meet you at your place. It did get quite hot today."

"Your nose is a little pink." Benedict ran a thumb along her jaw, and she shivered despite the heat of the day. "I have a perfectly good shower at my place. Why don't we just head there, shower and then order in."

She sucked her bottom lip in as she drank in his dark gaze. Showering here, or even returning home first, then meeting him at his place were the safer options. The ones that kept some semblance of a boundary between them. A boundary they were both failing to keep in place. She should just shower here, but her tongue refused to put those words together.

She didn't want to shower in the locker room. It was clean, but the water was never quite warm enough, and she always felt rushed. And she certainly didn't want to go home. If she went home, she'd probably lose her nerve and text him that she was tired and staying in. And suddenly dinner and movies on her couch—alone—held zero excitement.

"You sure? I can be a hot-water hog. At least according to Alice." Penny leaned her head against his shoulder, enjoying the feel of his arms as he wrapped them around her.

"We could always conserve water. Then you don't have a chance to hog it." Benedict smiled as he dropped a light kiss along her lips. His gaze burned, then shifted as he looked at her. "You got more sun than I realized. Your shoulders are burned too. I've got aloe at home. But we should get you out of the heat."

As his words dropped over her, Penny let her gaze wander to where Benedict was looking. Her shoulders were the color of strawberries. Those were going to hurt, and soon.

"What about you?" Benedict's dark skin wouldn't be as susceptible to burning but they'd been in the sun all afternoon.

"I put on a heavy SPF this morning, and I didn't choose a sleeveless top."

"It seemed like a good idea this morning with the heat." Penny pulled her backpack on and cringed as her pink shoulders rebelled against the touch. "I should have reapplied mine, but it slipped my mind."

"Give me the backpack." Benedict held out his hand. "No need for you to be super uncomfortable on the commute home."

"It's bright pink." Penny pulled it off her shoulders. Even if Benedict didn't carry it, there was no way she could let it rub against her shoulders as they walked to the metro. Just wearing it for those few moments was nearly enough to make tears appear.

"It's hard to miss the color, Penny. Let me carry it." Benedict reached for it and slung it over his shoulders, then pretended to model the accessory.

She let out a laugh at the silliness. And his sweetness. Mitchel would never have carried her bag. He'd have complained that it looked unmanly or too girlie. Or some other nonsense. But Benedict didn't look phased by the brilliant accessory.

Her heart soared at the gesture. How was she ever supposed to let him go?

She swallowed as she looped her arm through his. Light and fluffy... Enjoy the moment for what this was. She was not going to ruin it by worrying about the end. Gesturing to the exit, she smiled. "Where you go, I'll follow." The words settled in her heart as they started toward the metro. It was the phrase her parents always said to each other when transfer orders came in. Their promise that no matter where life led them, they went together. It wasn't accurate for her and Benedict.

But maybe it could be.

"Benedict?" Penny's voice carried through the shower door, and he opened it quickly. He'd said he would stick to their "conserve water" pact, even though she planned to shower in cold water to help with the heat on her shoulders. But she'd told him it wasn't necessary.

They'd had a wonderful day. When he'd mentioned how he loved picking the prizes, Penny had said she'd collect tickets and help the kids with the poles. Benedict had waited for each excited squeal as the prizes he attached to their poles rose over the board painted to look like the ocean. But behind the board, he'd been protected from the UV rays for most of the day. And now Penny was paying the price for staying in the sun.

She was wrapped in one of his blue towels, and if her shoulders weren't the color of candy apples, he'd have pulled it off and worked his way down her body and back up again. But now wasn't the time.

"What's wrong?"

"Any chance you have a tank top I could borrow? I should have worn this shirt today and saved the sleeveless shirt for tonight, but…" She balled up the clean shirt in her hand and threw it back in her bag. "Sorry, maybe I should have headed home. I bet I won't be great company."

"You'll be you. And that means you'll be perfect." Benedict kissed her forehead. It was pink but it was her shoulders that had gotten the worst of the sun.

"You're sweet."

"I am." Benedict laughed as her mouth opened and then she giggled. "Let me grab a tank I use to work out in."

He returned less than a minute later with the white tank and handed it to her.

"Thank you." Penny sighed as she dropped the towel and slid the tank over her head. Then she pulled on a pair of shorts. Her in one of his shirts sent a pang of emotion spooling through him.

No partner had ever grabbed a shirt or pair of boxers from his closet to just hang out in. He liked having her here, liked seeing her in his clothes. Liked the intimacy and the way she made him feel alive, really alive, for the first time in forever.

"What's Cody's Racing?"

The question rammed through his brain, driving away all the happy thoughts. He blinked and looked at her, his brain registering the shirt he'd grabbed. It had sat on the bottom of every workout drawer since he was nineteen. His reminder that he needed to do laundry. He'd been so focused on her he hadn't even noticed what he was grabbing.

He'd placed that shirt in the giveaway pile dozens of times, and always pulled it back out. Cody's Racing was the local place that had sponsored his brother's drag racing dreams… The legal ones at least. And he'd spent more days than he could count in the garage learning everything he could about engines so he could help Isiah.

He'd been there the day another kid's car had come in, so damaged that Benedict hadn't believed Cody when he said the kid had escaped alive. It was that busted wreck that had sent Benedict down the path of research to see how dangerous the sport really was.

Junior Drag Racing used slower racers, half-scale dragsters, but that didn't take out all the risk. And Isiah wasn't just racing on NHRA-approved courses. Not once he learned how much money he could make in the backwoods unregulated matches.

And when Benedict had said he wouldn't help at those races anymore… When he'd broken that vow to his brother. He swallowed as the memories threatened to overwhelm him.

"Do you want me to take the shirt off?"

"No. It's just a shirt." He hated the flinch he saw cross Penny's features.

"Don't lie to me." Penny crossed her arms. "I won't push on this, but don't lie to me."

He nodded, not trusting his ability to spill the entire truth.

"No lies." Penny kissed his cheek. "Promise?"

"Promise." Benedict let his lips wander to hers. That was an easy promise to make. He didn't want to lie to Penny. That didn't mean he was ready to spill all his secrets, but this was a vow that was easy to make.

Penny yawned as the romantic comedy credits started rolling. Tonight had been…nice. That was a word, though not an overly satisfactory one.

Her shoulders still ached. But Benedict's gentle massage with aloe and a couple of pain pills had lessened the pain significantly. By most people's definition, the night was uneventful. They'd eaten Thai, which was excellent, then popped some popcorn and started the movie. She snuggled close to him for most of the night, and he'd been careful not to jar her bright red shoulders.

If they hadn't made a fake-relationship pact a few weeks ago, this might have seemed like a lazy night between boyfriend and girlfriend. Instead…

She ran her fingers on the outline of the racing car on her shirt. She wasn't sure what it was about this shirt that had bothered Benedict so much, though whatever it was, he'd locked it away quickly. Then he'd been her normal, happy Benedict.

But she'd seen the pain. And it had called to her. But she couldn't do anything if he wouldn't talk to her.

And they'd sworn to keep things light. No chance of catching feelings.

Her heart hammered, and she mentally scoffed. She'd caught feelings. *So many feelings.* She wasn't sure what she wanted to do with them yet. But she cared about Dr. Benedict Denbar, and she wasn't going to deny that truth to herself.

Her phone pinged with notifications, and Penny rolled her eyes. "I don't mind being on the hospital social media page, but there was no need for someone to tag me in the pictures."

Benedict chuckled as his lips met hers. "You're the one in most of them. I am behind the pretend ocean mostly. Except for the picture of us together at the booth. Which is an excellent photo."

"It is." That was the truth. The two of them at the beginning of the carnival. His arm wrapped around her waist and her leaning into him just slightly. The smiles on their faces were brilliant.

She looked happy. Truly happy. And she hadn't been faking the feeling, hadn't been putting on a show for the camera. She pulled her lip between her teeth. Benedict looked happy too.

What if she wanted to make this fake relationship real?

Her heart hammered as her brain played the what-if game. She was falling for him. God knew he was easy to fall for.

Mentally shaking away the question for now, Penny sat up. She didn't have to find the answers to right now. "Tonight was lovely. But I should get going before the metro stop closes." She kissed his cheek. Enjoying the pleasantness that was this simple kiss.

Movies made such a big deal out of passion. That

desperate need to claim another, the feel of them deep inside you. But it was these moments she'd missed most. The easy nights, light kisses, the show of affection for affection's sake. Because you cared for the other person, not because you wanted them sexually. Rather, you simply needed them. All of them—the grumpy mornings, late-night desires and everything in between.

"Stay." Benedict's voice coated her heart.

"Stay?" Repeating the word wasn't needed, but the question escaped her lips anyway.

"Just stay with me." His fingers wrapped through hers.

Some other time would be better. Sometime when she had a change of clothes. When she had her toothbrush. When she'd thought through the thoughts rampaging across her brain. When she had a better name for whatever was happening between them.

There were dozens of reasons to say no. And if she did, Benedict would accept it. He'd offer to walk to the metro. In fact she suspected he wouldn't take no for an answer on that, considering it was after ten o'clock. But he wouldn't judge her harshly at all if she left. He'd understand.

But she didn't want to go. She wanted to be here. *With him.*

"Okay." The word spilled from her lips, and she smiled.

"You sure?" His fingers squeezed hers.

This was another shifting point. Holding his gaze, she smiled. "I'm sure."

And she was.

That was the most terrifying thing.

Terrifying…and exciting beyond all measure.

CHAPTER SEVEN

BENEDICT SMILED AS the morning light spilled across Penny's dark hair. He could count on one hand the number of women he'd let spend the night. Exactly one. And the night of simply lying next to her had brought him more fulfillment than any of the other pointless hookups he'd enjoyed in the past.

Who'd have ever thought that her sleeping in his tank top and a pair of his boxers could be so devastatingly sexy?

But with her sunburn, there would be no waking her up by trailing kisses along her body. No matter how much he yearned to. As arousal pushed through him, he kissed her forehead and slid from the bed, careful not to disturb her.

One thing that many people didn't realize was that a sunburn often drained a person's energy. In order to fix the cells damaged by the ultraviolet rays, the body activated the immune system, resulting in a general tiredness feeling the day after a significant burn. Penny needed rest.

Besides, there'd be plenty of time to kiss his way down her body later.

The thought stalled his hands as he reached for the coffee in the kitchen. What was he doing?

The scent of roasted beans filled the kitchen as he stood there. No words or thoughts coming to him.

Actually, there were thoughts.

So many of them. And all of them involved Penny.

And waking next to her often.

His hands shook as he filled a mug of coffee. He'd never had thoughts like this before. Never considered something more permanent. He'd already broken so many of the rules he'd had before Penny.

He set the mug on the counter and rolled his head, trying to gather the emotions and push them behind the walls he'd constructed. But all the feelings dancing around his head didn't vanish into the tomb he'd placed so many in. They wanted to shout with joy. Wanted to relish in the joy they brought. Wanted to claim things he had no business claiming.

He drummed his fingers along the counter for a minute, then he picked up the coffee and headed to the garage. Whenever he was overwhelmed, the garage, his tools and the ability to lose himself in a broken toy or messed-up engine calmed him.

Things that were broken were so easy to put back together. Or at least easier to return to their working condition than people. You diagnosed the issue, then replaced a wire or reattached a broken doll arm or put in a new voice box on a talking toy. It might take him a day or two to calibrate and find the right answer, but he always did.

And then the problem was fixed. The toy worked like new.

If only one could repair the human soul in such a way.

He breathed a sigh of relief as he stepped into the workshop. A broken talking robot sat on his worktable.

Wald Children's had many patients that spent far too much of their childhood in the place. It did it's best to provide some of the standards of childhood. The hospital had a room full of toys for their patients and, in the case of the NICU, for their siblings to play with in the small babysitting facility while parents visited their ill babies.

And since the patients were children, toys ended up broken. *Often.* Benedict had offered to fix a toy car years ago. And then the day-care director had asked if he could look at a light-up toy that had shorted out but was one of the kids' favorites. After those two easy fixes, the director of the day care had let the other units know that he could fix almost anything.

Maybe an overstatement, but he generally found a way to get the toys operational. In the rare instances an item was damaged beyond help, he'd harvest the parts that might be used in the future and then buy a new toy for whichever unit needed it.

He could spend all morning in here. There was a talking doll that needed to be looked at too. Though the pediatric nephrologist had said if the creepy voice didn't return, the doll could just be played with as a regular doll. He understood the nephrologist's dislike of the doll. It was creepy. It was also a favorite in the nephrology department, so Benedict would do his best to get it back to its loveable creepy self.

But the robot was first up. Opening up the back cover, Benedict stared at the wires. One was frayed and disconnected. It just needed to be soldered to complete the electric connection.

It was one of the very first things he'd learned as a young boy fascinated with taking toys apart. He smiled. The very first thing he'd disassembled and attempted to put back together was a toy boom box that played a selection of kid songs. He'd managed to get it to power back on, but it never played songs again. He'd never figured out what he'd broken, no matter how long he tried.

And it had taken Isiah nearly a month to get over it. Even then he'd bring up the boom box when they were teenagers.

If he'd lived, would that have become their inside joke?

He swallowed the sad thought. Penny and Alice had little jokes. Little reminders to just themselves that they were united. The Greene Sisters. He knew they argued, all siblings did.

But Benedict and Isiah's last argument had been a big one. And Benedict had let his anger make him stay away from the drag race. He hadn't been there to inspect the car. To test the engine. To do all the things he'd promised Isiah he'd do.

"Oh, my gosh! This is amazing!" Penny held a mug of coffee and looked around the room with an awe that warmed his soul. "So this is the toy shop?"

"Toy shop?"

"Sure!" She kissed his cheek before leaning over to look at the back of the robot. "Most of the staff know very little about you, but everyone knows you run the hospital toy shop. A toy breaks and Dr. Benedict Denbar comes to the rescue."

He let his fingers wander toward hers. "I don't like talking about the past." The words stunned him as they left his lips. He'd meant to make a joke about the toy shop. Something light and fluffy. Something that fit with them keeping each other in the dark on the important things.

"I know." Her words were so quiet as her hand slipped into his. "It's okay."

But was it?

He was so used to keeping the past buried he'd never questioned it.

Until Penny.

Dipping his lips to hers, Benedict drank in the sensations of a morning with Penny. This was a routine he'd never had. Coffee in his workshop with someone special; he could get used to this.

"Want to fix a robot?" He let go of her hand and held up a soldering unit.

Her eyes widened as she looked at the small machine. "I don't know how to use that."

"It's not hard. I can teach you. What good is a toy shop without an assistant?"

"An assistant?" Her smile brightened the whole room. "I like the sound of that."

"Me too." He grinned, matching hers, and wondered what Alice might think if she saw the two of them together now. Would she really be happy for her sister if this became something longer?

But would he be able to let Penny go if she still really wanted the marriage and family life she'd wanted before?

He'd worry about that later. Right now he just wanted to enjoy having Penny in his shop.

"So a few things to remember." He pointed to the soldering iron, directing her attention to the heating element on the tip. "Never touch this! It heats to around four hundred degrees Celsius. We use tweezers to hold the small wires that need to be soldered back to the element."

He handed her safety goggles and felt his heart skip

as she slid them on. She looked like she belonged here. With him.

Putting on his own goggles, he turned his attention to the robot, pointing to the nickel plate that had come loose from the battery, damaging the wires and creating the need for the repair. He carefully lifted the broken plate and replaced it.

"Now you're up." He flipped the switch on the soldering tool and let it heat up in its charging unit.

"I don't know. What if I break it more?" Penny looked from the tool to the toy. "The kids love these things."

"It would be nearly impossible for you to do that."

"But…"

He kissed the question away. "Then I buy the hospital a new toy robot and we harvest the parts from this one. Which is almost as fun. But you are going to do this perfectly." He grabbed a few wires from the bin where he kept the scraps and a few of the copper and nickel plates. He demonstrated how to solder the wires to the plates, then pushed a few wires toward Penny.

"Now you try."

"All right." She carefully held the iron as she bent her head and practiced on the wires. Her tongue slipped out the left side of her lips. Adorable!

She practiced a few times, then he put the robot in front of her.

She held her breath for a minute, then bent her head again, the tip of her tongue reappearing. It was picture-perfect. He'd seen others do similar things. Mary Stevens, in his high school shop class, had always clucked her tongue when soldering. And Isiah always scrunched his nose…

The memory of his brother's scrunched nose sent an

unexpected wave of nostalgia. The air in the workshop vanished as memories raced through him.

Isiah bent over a workbench. Isiah laughing as Benedict tossed the tool he'd handed him back and demanded the right size of socket wrench. Isiah storming out of the garage, screaming that Benedict was jealous that he had a way out of their tiny town. A way that didn't involve college debt. He said Benedict was jealous that Isiah didn't need him.

Penny's hand slipped into his and he blinked, the memories fading into the recesses of his mind.

He'd been completely lost in the past. He reached for the walls that he always kept the past behind. But they refused to rematerialize.

"You're shaking." She flipped the soldering iron off and then put her hands on both sides of his face. "I'm here."

His heart rate slowed as he leaned his head against hers. Comfort—it was such a small thing that meant so much. "Thank you."

"Anytime." She dropped a soft kiss on his cheek. "What were you thinking about?"

"My brother. He scrunched his nose when he soldered, though he preferred for me to do all the work on the car."

"Car?" Penny picked up her coffee and took a long sip. "So you can fix cars *and* toys?"

Her tone was light, but her eyes held his. The question allowed him to expand on Isiah…or make a joke. She was giving him a choice.

He could fall so easily for her… Part of him already had. A big part.

Pushing a hand through his hair, Benedict took a deep breath. "Isiah raced for Cody's Racing on the Ju-

nior Drag Racing circuit. And I took care of his engine."
The words echoed in the quiet workshop. Words he'd
never spoken aloud to anyone.

"*You* took care of his engine?" Penny's head tilted.
"How? You would have been a teen yourself. At least
based on the little you told me about when your brother
passed."

"I was seventeen when I started helping him. Cody
taught me. I love tinkering with things. I started taking
apart my toys not long after my sixth birthday. Putting
things together, tearing them apart, seeing how they
work. So they taught me, and I sat with the pit crew
during the sanctioned races." His breath caught.

Closing his eyes, he let the pain wash through him.
If Isiah had been happy to only do those races. If he'd
never found out about the illegal races happening in
the rural lands a few miles outside of their small town
and the money he could win. If he'd listened to Benedict's pleas. If Benedict had gone to that last race. So
many what-ifs.

What-ifs didn't get you anywhere, but banishing
them seemed impossible too.

"And during the unsanctioned ones, you took care
of the engine." Penny's hand squeezed his.

Of course she'd guessed. With her trivia skills, she'd
know at least a little about most sports. And it wasn't
a giant leap.

"Except for the last one," Benedict confirmed. "I
saw a wreck the week before. The engine was pushed
into the driver's compartment. The driver nearly had
to have his left foot amputated."

He kept going, his soul needing to get the rest of the
words out. "We argued. I told Isiah that he needed to
stop the backyard races. He agreed...then changed his

mind and refused to tell me why. We argued." A crack had appeared in his dam and some of his past was escaping. Though not all of it. "He told me I was jealous of the attention he was getting."

"Were you?" Penny sipped her coffee, her eyes never leaving his.

"Yes." Benedict shook his head. That was a truth that had taken him a long time to accept. He'd coveted his brother's skill, his ability to try new things, to do things without weighing the risks. But weighing the risks, understanding the odds, that was what kept you from making mistakes. *Fatal mistakes.* "Who says that about their family?"

He closed his eyes, not wanting to see her reaction to a truth he'd hidden from so many.

"Everyone, if they're honest."

His eyes shot open as she offered him a small nod. "We're all human and jealousy comes more naturally than any of us want to admit."

Penny looked at her feet as she continued, "Alice made friends easily in every place we landed. I usually tagged along. It frustrated me to no end. I draw better than her, not that she ever practices, and am more observant. Traits she covets. Again, jealousy is natural. But so is worrying about your brother, and not wanting him to do something dangerous."

She waited a minute, then added, "And sometimes the best way that you can show love to someone is by not supporting the thing they love most if it's dangerous for them."

"Yeah. I know that."

"But you still feel responsible." Penny set her coffee mug to the side and stepped into his arms.

How had this conversation happened? They were

supposed to be fixing a robot. Still, as he stroked her back, breathing in her scent, he felt close to whole for the first time in forever. "I will miss him forever. There's so much I wish I'd done differently."

Wish I'd realized that the glassiness in his eyes hid tragedy, not anger. Wish I'd paid more attention.

But he'd burdened Penny with enough of his past for today.

She squeezed him tightly, not saying anything. No platitudes, no toxic positivity statements that always seemed to make it worse, just her simple presence. It was exactly what he needed.

"Should we see if the robot works?" He winked as she looked into his eyes. Setting the robot upright, he pointed to the button.

Penny pursed her lips and pushed it. The robot lit up and started to walk across the desk. Penny clapped and bounced back and forth on her feet. "Oh! I did that. With your help, but I did it."

This was one of the things he loved about putting things back together. That feeling of accomplishment. The pleasure at seeing something broken fixed. Something made whole.

And for the first time since that awful afternoon he'd argued with Isiah, Benedict wondered if it might be possible for him to be whole again too.

"So you're going to Benedict's tonight to look at colors to paint his kitchen?" Alice handed the tablet chart to Penny.

"He just wants a little help. The whole place still has the plain cream walls it had when he moved in. Not even pictures hanging anywhere. I thought we might go to the street fair next weekend to see if we could find anything he likes. I probably won't be home tonight."

"You haven't slept in your bed all week, Penny, so I wasn't really expecting it."

"I slept there…" Penny's voice died away as her sister raised an eyebrow. She *had* been at Benedict's place all week. It hadn't been intentional. It was just a pattern they'd slipped into after she'd helped him fix the toy robot and heard about his brother.

Another seismic shift had occurred that morning. They hadn't talked about it, but somewhere between getting stuck in the elevator, trivia dates and sunburn, their fake relationship had turned real. It was wonderful, exciting, and in that stage where one waffled between worrying the stability would fall out of it suddenly and hoping the future might be forever blissful.

And it might feel a bit more stable if she broached the topic of the shift in their relationship. But everything seemed so perfect now, and she didn't want to change anything. *Coward!*

"You're happy." Alice patted her hand. "And that makes me happy. And if he hurts you, I will make his life a living hell."

"There is no need for threats, Alice." Penny shook her head as she scrolled through the chart notes. Logan Mitchell's oxygen levels had slipped a little last night. They were still within the range considered normal, but hovering. Her stomach flipped a little as she marked a note in the chart and sent it to Dr. Cooke and Benedict. They might want to ask the pulmonologist to stop by.

"It's not a threat." Her sister winked as she grabbed another chart. "It's a promise."

"So dramatic," Penny chuckled as she started toward Logan's room.

The tiny little man was born at nearly thirty weeks. He'd overcome a serious infection and was starting to put on weight. But the oxygen rate dip concerned her.

He was sleeping and his O2 was steady but still on the low end. It might be nothing, but she'd learned long ago not to discount the tingles her intuition gave her.

"You're concerned too?" Benedict's voice was quiet, but quiet voices carried in the NICU.

"His oxygen is still within normal levels. There isn't a reason to worry." Penny said the words more to comfort herself than because they offered any true insight at the moment. "But something feels off.

"There is no fever. He's still having wet diapers, so no evidence of dehydration. But…" Penny crossed her arms as she stared at the wall of stats tracking Logan's health.

"But something feels off." Benedict nodded. "I have Dr. Huikre coming down to take a look at his lungs. He's already battled one infection. It could be another.

"I sent a message to his parents. I know Jeanne is normally here in the morning. I haven't seen Jack recently." Benedict made a few more notes in the tablet he was carrying.

She was always impressed that he knew not only his patients, but their parents and siblings and the time when they were most likely to be able to visit. One of the sad truths of the NICU was that their babies often stayed for weeks or even months. Most parents couldn't afford to be here every minute.

"You haven't seen Jack because he's with his other fiancée or clearing out of their house since she was as shocked as I by his slimy cheating ways. Maybe the other mistress we found out about took him in." Jeanne's voice caught as she walked into the room. Her eyes were red, and she looked exhausted.

"Other fiancée... I thought..." Benedict caught the words.

They'd been engaged too. Penny had had a few conversations with her about wedding preparations. They'd pushed their date back when she'd gotten pregnant and back again when Logan was born early. Jeanne had been so hopeful he'd be able to be their little ring bearer.

"Yeah. I thought I was the only one too." Jeanne bit her lip as she stepped toward her son. "But that isn't my focus now. What is going on with Logan?"

"I'm not sure." Benedict nodded toward the wall of information the monitors on Logan were producing.

Penny nodded at the answer. She knew parents wanted answers. Doctors and nurses wanted them too. But the truth was that sometimes they didn't know— at least not yet. And she'd seen far too many doctors who had to provide an answer, which sometimes meant changing a diagnosis if they answered too fast.

It just reinforced how suited he was to this career. Why it shouldn't matter who could help the hospital raise the most money. Dr. Benedict Denbar was the best candidate they had for the head of the department position. Though he only wanted it to ensure the maternity wing and other projects he supported had a champion.

Another reason he was perfect for it.

Jeanne slid next to her son and put her hands through the holes on the side of the crib to stroke his cheek. "So what do we do now?"

"I've ordered a consult with Dr. Huikre. She's a top-notch pediatric pulmonologist."

Benedict continued, "If there is an infection in his lungs or something else affecting them, she'll be able to determine what is happening, or if it's just a symptom of being a NICU baby hooked to monitors constantly seeing normal shifts. We'll give you a few minutes with Logan on your own. If you need anything, ring the nurses' station."

"Okay." Jeanne sucked in a breath and laid her head against the isolette. "I'll figure it out. I've messed up a lot lately, but somehow, I'll figure it out. We'll be okay."

The words weren't meant for Penny and Benedict. They'd already turned to go, but the brokenness tore through Penny. She'd felt that pain. That feeling that she'd messed up. The shame that wasn't hers but wouldn't leave her side. She paused, hesitating, then turned back around.

Jeanne's head lay against the isolette and her shoulders shook.

It wasn't her place, but she took a step forward. "Jeanne." Penny reached her hand out and stroked her shoulder.

Tears coated Jeanne's eyes as she rotated her head from looking at Logan to meeting Penny's gaze. Though Penny doubted she could clearly see her through the wall of water.

"If your fiancé hid other women from you, that is not your fault." She kept her voice low. Voices carried in the NICU, and this was not a conversation she suspected Jeanne wanted many people hearing.

"I missed so many things." She hiccupped and looked to the ceiling as she blinked back tears. "No, that isn't true. I ignored the tinges of worry because I didn't want to see what was before my eyes, particularly after I got pregnant. And he was so good at the lies, so convincing. God, I apologized for questioning him so many times."

She sucked in another breath as she turned her head

to her son. "This was already so hard. I… I just wasn't prepared to do it alone."

"You aren't alone. Your sister's been here," Penny offered. "And you said your best friend has been helping you at your house. I know that may not seem like much, but when you get a chance, make a list of everyone you have in your life. I bet it's more than you think."

That was what she'd done, sitting on the floor of her apartment in Ohio. Stared at the empty picture frames, absent of her and Mitchel's smiling faces. She'd felt so stupid and alone. So lost in the world.

She'd pulled out a list and put down everyone she could call right then. And been stunned to see how many names she could add. It had lessened her burden a little in one of her darkest times.

"And *you* are not responsible for his lies. No matter how it feels right now." Penny tapped Jeanne's shoulder one last time.

She turned, surprised to see Benedict still by the doorway. She hadn't said anything about Mitchel. At least not directly, but she'd assumed Benedict had headed to another room. Stupid assumption. Unlike Dr. Cooke, Benedict always made sure his patients and their parents were as comfortable as possible in a truly uncomfortable place.

His eyes held hers for a moment before he stepped to the side and let her pass. Her stomach clinched as the memories of the past pummeled her. She'd meant everything she told Jeanne. She desperately wanted her to believe in herself. To understand that none of it was her fault…even if Penny wasn't sure she'd completely forgiven herself.

Even if she wasn't sure she'd ever fully trust her instincts again.

* * *

Benedict laid out the six different shades of blue that the woman at the hardware store swore were different colors. Laid out end to end, he could tell there were slight differences, but he couldn't imagine it making much of a difference.

But he wanted his townhome to be a home. Wanted it to be a place that Penny wanted to be, a place that was happy. Home meant security and love to Penny, and he wanted his place to mean that to her too.

Because he was falling in love with her. The emotion he never trusted, the one that had driven his parents into the arms of so many people, trying to find happiness. Love, so dangerous. And yet so impossible to avoid with Penny.

Maybe it wasn't fair to make his house feel like a home for her. He wasn't willing to walk down the aisle. To make that vow of forever. But that didn't change the feeling of completeness, the feeling that everything was right in his world that he felt each time he looked at her. Each time he touched her. Each time he thought of her.

He was falling for her…hard. Lying about it to himself wouldn't serve any purpose.

She pushed the swatches around on the counter, but he could tell she wasn't interested in the shades of blue. She'd been a shell of the woman he knew, the woman he loved, since Logan's mother arrived at the hospital. And it didn't take a giant leap for him to guess her fiancé hadn't been faithful.

They'd promised each other light and fluffy. No, she'd made that demand of their relationship, and he'd been happy with it at the time. But not anymore. He wanted to know her, really know her. To give her the comfort she'd given him so many times.

"I want to change the rules of the game." He gathered up the swatches of blue and tossed them in a drawer. They needed to talk and not about the color of the walls in his townhome. But his stomach felt dry as he prepared to finally broach the topic they'd avoided for weeks.

This wasn't fake, at least not for him, and he didn't want to go any longer without acknowledging that.

"If you don't like blue, you could try red or some people really like yellow in the kitchen. I think it's too bright personally." She shrugged and spun the wine glass in front of her.

"Well, then yellow is definitely out." Benedict gripped her hand and let his fingers run along her palm. "Because I want this place to be a place you enjoy."

Her lips opened. "Benedict…"

She looked at him and he could see fear hovering in the blue depths, and he hated it. But there was a tinge of hope, and that was enough to keep him going. "I don't want light and fluffy, Penny. I want you and everything that comes with that."

"I don't want to get hurt again." Penny sucked in a breath. "I know life is hard and know that is such a heavy burden to lay at anyone's feet. But after Mitchel…"

She crossed her arms, and he hated the loss of her touch. The loss of the connection. He needed her. "I promised before that I wouldn't hurt you…"

"That was before we…" Penny met his gaze, then looked away.

Before they'd laughed together, before they'd slept together, before he'd fallen for her. But the promise was still one he planned to keep.

"Doesn't matter to me when it was. I meant it then,

and I mean it now. I promise to do whatever I can to never hurt you." For however long these feelings lasted, Benedict would treasure her. When their feelings inevitably faded, as all feelings did, they'd find a way to part amicably without hurting the other.

"That's a giant promise." Penny kissed his cheek. "I know how important promises are to you. That one..."

"Is easily made." Benedict nodded and pulled her close, enjoying her soft sigh as she leaned her head against his shoulder. "I promise you, Penny Greene. I will do my best to never hurt you. To protect you."

To love you.

He barely caught those words. He'd do that too, but tonight wasn't the right time to make that declaration. "I don't want to put a timeline on whatever is between us, Penny. I want you in my life, but that means I'd like to know why Logan's mother's trials sent you into such a spin. You gave excellent care this afternoon, but your smiles were fake, your tone a little off."

He squeezed her tightly as he heard the soft sob she almost managed to cover. "That is not a criticism. We are entitled to off days, and no one can be perfect and happy every day. Particularly in a NICU.

"If you aren't comfortable telling me..."

"Mitchel had a family. A wife, two kids and a golden retriever." She squeezed him tightly and then stepped back. "He told his wife and me that he was traveling all the time. I was engaged for three years and the whole relationship was a lie."

She started pacing and shaking her head. "Three years, Benedict. Three whole freaking years!" She pushed her hand through her hair before hugging herself. "He was so convincing. I believed he loved me and only me, and I wanted to be settled. To have my place in the world, a place I didn't have to leave. My parents love each other, but even in retirement, the two can't stay in one place for more than three years. They love to move, but I want roots. I thought Mitchel wanted the same."

A huff echoed in the room as she looked at him but didn't quite meet his gaze. "I rescheduled my wedding twice for him. And I never questioned the reasons he gave, which were complete BS. I mean Alice could tell he was human garbage, but I wanted the home, the wedding, the kids in the suburbs."

She sucked in a deep breath as her watery gaze met his. "I wanted the fairy tale. And I silenced the tingles in the back of my brain, screaming that something was wrong."

"There is nothing wrong with wanting a fantasy. A few people even get it." Benedict stepped beside her and wiped a tear from her cheek.

Penny wiped the other tears with the back of her hand. "I know I should be glad that my parents got the happily-ever-after. That Alice and I grew up in a home with so much love. But they made it look easy. And it's just not."

"Do you still want the fantasy?" Benedict's voice was soft. "Because I didn't get to grow up with two happy parents. I grew up with a bitter, angry woman who kept hoping the next relationship would give her what the previous dozen hadn't. No promises of for better or worse were ever kept in my house."

"I want you." Penny sighed. "And I don't want to think of much more than that right now. I want to enjoy whatever we have, without any time limits. I want to know that between the two of us, this is a relationship. A real one."

"It most certainly is." He dipped his head to hers. She

tasted of hope and the future. It was more than he'd allowed himself to hope for in so long. This was perfect.

Except I'm legally married.

The thought thudded through him as he held Penny tightly. Would it matter to her that he and Amber had never even kissed? That he hadn't seen her in years, and had been asking for a divorce since before he and Penny reconnected on the metro? Since she came back into town with no ring on her finger.

He didn't know. He was certain of two things. He loved Penny. And he'd promised her he'd do his best not to hurt her.

Benedict wasn't her ex. He wasn't hiding a family. He just still had an entanglement from the past. A promise to his brother—one he'd kept for too long.

He'd sworn he wouldn't hurt Penny and that vow was just as important as the promise he'd made to his brother to protect Amber if anything happened to him. Isiah, Amber and their daughter were his past. Penny was his future, and he was going to keep his promises to her.

He hadn't heard from Amber since their text exchange. His lawyer had filed the divorce paperwork and everything should be finalized shortly.

As soon as everything was done, he'd explain. When there was no chance of hurting the woman he loved.

Coward.

Benedict breathed her scent and lost himself in Penny's kisses. Everything would be all right. *It would.*

CHAPTER EIGHT

"SNICKERDOODLE COFFEE WITH just a dash of cinnamon."
Benedict laid the cup in front of Penny and her whole
body lit up at his smile, despite her exhaustion at the
hour.

"Night shifts." Benedict winked as he raised his cup
to his lips. "This rotation is always a little difficult to
switch to. Have I thanked you for joining me?"

"Many times." Penny took a deep sip of her coffee,
enjoying the hint of cinnamon. Dr. Kuolon had taken a
position at a hospital in Texas and each of the doctors
vying for Dr. Lioness's position had been assigned a
few turns on the night shift.

There were always open shifts for nurses at night, so
Penny had offered to switch shifts to match Benedict's.
If they were on opposite shifts, the only time they'd see
each other was in the brief moments where the other
was barely awake as they slipped from bed or crashed
into it. And she wanted more time with Benedict. It was
scary to say it, but she'd never been so happy, so content.
They woke together, had a quick dinner—she'd never
managed to eat breakfast food at four in the afternoon.
Then they'd spend an hour together, sometimes just in
silence while she drew or read, and he worked with the

wires or bits of electronics that seemed to accumulate in all his drawers.

People took for granted how nice it was to just exist with someone. How special it was to not *have* to carry a conversation. So often in the newness of a relationship, people talked all the time. But when the initial high wore off, could you just be with them?

She and Mitchel had never really reached that point because of the distance…and the lies between them. But with Benedict, it was different. In fact, in so many ways it felt like they'd been together forever. A few of her outfits had migrated to his closet, and he had a toothbrush at her place. Though they stayed at his place most often.

She yawned as she monitored the stats for their tiny patients at the nurses' station. The NICU was always a quiet place, but at night when the rest of the hospital was less active, it was easy to let your eyes droop while adjusting. Covering her mouth, she yawned again, then took a deep drink, enjoying the heat of the coffee and the promise of the caffeine jolt. Like many new nurses, she'd spent her first few years on night shift, and been grateful when she could move to the day shift.

"Incoming!" The call came over the radio. "Car accident sent mother into preterm labor. Baby delivered at thirty weeks at George Washington. Inbound by helicopter, ETA four minutes."

Adrenaline shot through her system rendering the coffee completely unnecessary. DC traffic was infamous, but the heli was only used for the most serious cases because with the White House less than two miles from the hospital, pilots often had to get extra clearance for takeoff.

DC was one of the few major metropolitan areas to have a medical flight team that specialized in neonates, infants and children. It was a lifesaving service provided by some truly wonderful pilots and specialists. But every time Penny saw the bright red heli in the sky, her heart sank a little.

"Ready?" Benedict asked as he slid the cell phone–looking radio into his pocket.

"As ready as possible," Penny returned. Car crashes with advanced pregnancies were unfortunately not a rare occurrence, but the range of impact it could have on the child varied from minor to tragic.

She hopped from foot to foot as the elevator rose to the rooftop exit. Her stomach slipped as the doors opened. At least Benedict was the primary physician on duty tonight, which gave the little one his or her best chance.

She looked over at him and took a deep breath. They'd handle whatever came their way tonight. Together…as a team.

The wind from the heli pushed against them as they carefully made their way to the helicopter. The pilot nodded through the glass as the flight team stepped out.

"What happened?" Benedict called over the sound of the slowing blades.

"Racers," the flight NICU nurse called back as he shifted the tiny infant in a specialty isolette to the stretcher designed to transport the machine.

"Racing?" She must have misheard. The DC streets were rarely quiet enough for that type of activity. Not that street racing should happen anywhere, but it wasn't nearly as common here as she'd seen in Ohio.

"Unfortunately," the flight nurse stated as he started to move the baby. "Two kids were racing, oblivious to the stoplight cameras that would catch everything and the lone car at the intersection. The delivery happened almost as soon as they got her to the hospital."

"Mother will be fine. Broken clavicle, a few tender ribs and a broken leg from the impact point to the right leg. With the leg injury, she won't be able to make it here for days—at least."

"But she was able to give a thorough history. Preterm contractions started after dinner. She monitored for a while, then decided to head to George Washington for observation." The paramedic shook his head and sighed. "If she'd made it to the hospital, they probably could have stopped the contractions. But…"

He shook his head and passed the papers for transport over.

Preterm labor was common enough. If she'd reached the hospital, they'd have administered a tocolytic to slow or stop the contractions. They would have then given the mother a shot of antenatal corticosteroids, commonly called ACS, to speed up the baby's lung development. Even if the tocolytic was only able to stop the labor for a few days, the ACS could help prevent a number of respiratory disasters.

"Any antibiotics administered to the mother before delivery?" Benedict's question seemed loud in the hallway after the roar of the helicopter's engines.

Penny suspected the answer, but Benedict needed to ask. When the flight nurse shook his head, she could see that Benedict wasn't surprised either. When critical cases occurred, often there just wasn't time. But with no ACS administered and no antibiotics, the little one faced a longer battle. But it was one she and Benedict were here to ensure she won.

"What's the baby's name?" Penny looked in the

transport isolette at the little one covered in sensors that she'd hook up as soon as they reached her room.

"The mother said she was supposed to be named Adeline but after what happened she decided to name her Hope."

Emotion coated the back of her throat as she looked at the little one. Her mother was scared, she'd been through an ordeal and she'd given her daughter the name she needed most. But there wasn't time to give in to the emotion now.

"It's nice to meet you, Hope." Penny stroked the edge of the isolette. It was always hard when the babies arrived without their parents. Hope's mother would not have been a candidate for the maternity ward that Benedict was arguing so hard for. But she ached for its need each time a baby landed here alone.

"Mother plans to pump but asked if there was donor milk available." The flight nurse checked a few more boxes on the tablet before handing it to Benedict to complete the official transfer of Hope's care.

"Of course." Penny was proud that Wald Children's had a bank of breast milk from mothers who had extra or who pumped extra specifically for NICU preemies. Preemies needed nutrients, but some ate as little as an ounce in each feeding. That meant one donation had the potential to do a lot of good.

In fact, many NICU graduate moms pumped and donated milk for the NICU when they got pregnant again and delivered a full-term baby. It was a nice full circle way to help other families in need.

"Good. She is beyond worried with not being able to be here. Her wife is on the West Coast for business. She said she'd take the first available flight out here, but with the three-hour difference, even taking the red-eye, she won't be here until this afternoon."

"If you see Hope's mother when you head back to George Washington, let her know that I promise to be here for her little one until her wife gets here."

It was a nice promise. But one he couldn't keep. They'd be off duty around the time the flight was taking off. Tomorrow was their day off, but he'd be dead on his feet and legally over the time where he could care for the little girl.

The flight nurse didn't say anything as he took the final notes and waved. Penny suspected that he'd heard doctors make boasts like this before. Except Benedict didn't boast. He made promises…and kept them.

As they rolled into the room that would be Hope's for the next few weeks at least, Penny looked at Benedict's shoulders. They were tight, but that could just be because of the check they had to do now.

While doing her rotations in labor and delivery, she'd been taught that there were seven main types of pregnancy injuries from car accidents, one of which had already occurred—the early birth.

Benedict slowly opened the isolette and took a penlight to look at Hope's eyes. The baby let out a soft whimper, and Penny relaxed a little.

Crying was a good sign. A silent NICU baby could spell tragedy. But preemies were sensitive to light. Still, Benedict had to check.

"I'm ordering a CT scan and an MRI. Rush."

Penny put the notes in the tablet and swallowed. "Are there broken blood vessels in her eyes?" The impact of a crash, particularly a mother being caught by the seat belt and held back, had been known to cause a contrecoup injury that mimicked shaken baby syndrome, an incredibly serious condition with lifelong consequences.

"No," Benedict stated. "But we still need to check."

She nodded and added in the additional notes. He was right, but she wasn't sure that a rush order was necessary. Still, on the night shift things seemed to move slower, so ordering it rush wasn't a terrible idea. But something about Benedict's stance worried her.

"What are you thinking?" She opened the notes section of the chart that would grow with Hope.

"That people who race cars are insane. That willfully risking your own life is bad enough but to street race with the possibility of hurting or killing an innocent..." He paused as he looked to the ceiling. "That is indefensible."

"I agree." Penny kept her words even. This was very different than what had occurred with his brother. At least she thought it was. But there were enough similarities that she understood him having issues. "But... I actually meant what do you think about Hope? Are there signs of shaken baby or some other sign of fetal trauma from the injury before she was delivered?"

"No." Benedict let out a soft sigh. "No. She looks like a thirty-week-old premature infant. We will need to monitor her lungs more closely since she wasn't able to receive ACS in utero."

Penny added the note while he finished the final check on their newest patient. She kept her mind focused on the patient...mostly. He still wasn't relaxed, and she could see the worried energy thrumming through him.

The night passed quickly after their new arrival was settled. But the adrenaline crash sent her body straight to an exhaustion that no amount of caffeine could fully overcome. Benedict didn't seem to be coming down from the night's activities though.

He saw all his patients, did his rounds, but she saw him hovering by Hope's door. Looking over the notes he'd made in the tablet. Carefully checking the things he'd added to the notes section of Hope's chart.

He was slightly more relaxed after the mobile CT scan showed no injuries to Hope's body. But she caught him pacing until the mobile MRI confirmed that Hope hadn't suffered brain trauma.

It was good news. Hope was a thirty-week premature infant and that brought with it concerns. But babies born at the thirty-week mark had a 98 percent chance of survival. There'd be hurdles, but hurdles could be overcome.

Every NICU professional knew those odds.

So why wasn't Benedict more relaxed?

She caught another yawn as Alice walked through the front of the NICU. The next shift was here. Like most people, she looked forward to the end of a work-day, but today she was beyond ready to crawl into bed and let the worry of the evening shift fall away.

She wanted to fall into bed, curl into Benedict's arm and let the shift's stresses just fall away. Life seemed simpler in Benedict's arms. She smiled, looking forward to following through with this plan.

After she'd transferred her patient files, Penny went to find Benedict. It didn't take long. He was sitting in the chair next to Hope's isolette. He looked so tired, and she ached to pull him into her arms.

"It's time to go home." Penny kept her voice low. She didn't want to startle Hope, or Benedict.

"I think I am going to stay for a while. See if Hope's

other mom manages to make it." Benedict covered his mouth with the back of his hand as a yawn escaped.

She shifted on her feet and fought against the exhaustion pulling at her. "Benedict, our shift is over and even if the red-eye left right on time, she still won't be here for at least another few hours. We should go home."

"I know. Don't worry. I already clocked out." His fingers clasped hers, grounding her as he looked at her. "I just need to be here." His voice died away before his eyes met hers.

Except Penny was certain it wasn't her but someone or something from his past that he was seeing.

Before she could say anything, he rushed on, "I just want to be able to talk to her mom. Give her some of my notes."

Dr. Cooke could do that. Alice was here along with a whole suite of well-trained nurses. He didn't need to be here.

But she could see the pain echoing under the words. Bending, she kissed his head. She might not understand this need, but she wasn't going to argue. "You know you don't need to stay, right?"

"I know." He kissed her cheek. "But I need this."

"We're going to talk about it later, promise?"

His eyes wavered and she saw him process the words. This wasn't a question she was asking but a promise she was pulling from him. They'd promised this was a real relationship and that meant talking about the hard things.

Benedict pulled his keys from his pocket as he stood. He took a key from the ring and passed it over. "I'll meet you at home."

Her heart exploded at the gesture. The sign that he saw this as something long-term, as someone permanent.

The key weighed nothing…and so much as he laid it in her palm. *Home…* Until this moment she'd have said her home was the townhome she shared with Alice. She let her palm close over the key as she held his gaze. "I'll see you at home."

She tested the word. It felt right. But it wasn't his apartment—it was him. Home meant Benedict. She wasn't sure when that had happened, but it had. *Completely.*

She loved him. The truth settled deep in her as she looked at him.

He kissed her again, a light kiss, one that was friendly enough if someone walked in. But she could feel the heat there, feel the shift between them again, and she smiled. "I'll see you at home, Benedict."

Benedict… Benedict…

Isiah's voice called to him not quite close but not far away. He tried moving toward it, but his feet refused to take any of the cues he gave them.

Benedict…

Madness crept along his skin as he tried desperately to get to his brother. How long had it been since he'd heard his voice? How long since he'd seen his face?

Move.

Giving the order to his feet only served to slow them further. "Isiah!"

"Benedict!"

The voice morphed as the present wrapped its tendrils along his brain. He tried to force his feet to move once more, to reach Isiah. But the fog of the dream was already evaporating.

Penny's hands were warm on the sides of his face as he sat up, the last of the dream leaking from his brain as the on-call lounge, and the woman he loved, came fully into view.

"Benedict?" She smiled as she stroked his chin with her fingers. She looked beautiful, and rested.

Because she'd gone home, while he'd chosen the on-call suite and its uncomfortable beds designed for naps, not restful slumber.

"I'm not sure what captured you in your sleep, but…" She paused and looked at the door. "We can discuss it when we get home."

Home. He loved hearing her refer to his place as home. It lit through his soul, but part of his brain was still trapped in the past. The sound of his brother's voice refusing to relinquish its final hold on him.

"I want nothing more than to go home with you, curl up with an iced tea and watch nonsense on the bed until I fall asleep, but I need to take another quick peek at Hope's charts and check in with her mom." He sat up and stretched; his body screaming as the few hours rest on the on-call bed roosted in his bones— ever the reminder that he wasn't a twenty-something-year-old intern.

"You aren't on the clock, and her mother has already talked to Dr. Cooke. It's time to leave, Benedict."

"I won't be long."

Penny's lips tipped down, and he hated that he'd caused the frown. Hated that she'd gone home without him. Though part of him was more than a little happy that she'd come back for him. That she cared enough to see that he was okay.

That was a treasure he hadn't experienced. *Ever.*

No one looked after Benedict. His parents had always been more focused on themselves and their revolving door of partners. Amber had been understandably focused on her combined grief, and Isiah… Well, he'd been the one to look after Isiah.

"I just need to make sure…" Penny's fingers covered his lips before he could finish the sentence.

"You *just* need to come home and get some rest. Hope is doing well, her O2 levels are good and she took both her feedings this morning. There is nothing more you can add and letting yourself get exhausted won't help you, Hope or your patients on your shift tomorrow."

She pulled him to his feet and kissed his cheek. "I know you want this position. I know you think being here more often will help, but you don't need…"

"It's not about the job." The words left his lips without warning and the look on Penny's face suggested this news didn't surprise her. Of course she would know this was more than the work. More than the hope that if he got Dr. Lioness's position, he'd be better able to advocate for the maternity unit and any other number of things that would help his patients.

This was about Isiah. About the hole that had opened in his soul so long ago.

He swallowed as her eyes held his. She paid attention to him. Noticed the changes…and cared.

There were so many words he wanted to say. So many things he should say, but his tongue felt stiff. He swallowed again, trying to will the words forward.

"Let's talk about it at home. In slippers and comfy clothes after a hot shower. Let me take care of you." She grabbed his hand and started to lead them from the on-call room.

It should have been easy to leave. Every physician cared about their patients…or at least most did. But they were taught to separate those emotions. To wall them off. It gave them a level of mental protection…ever so thin. But he needed to check on Hope.

It wasn't rational. He knew that. But it didn't change the echoes of worry tearing through him.

Car accidents, even minor ones, could spell disaster hours or even days later. And an infant, particularly a preemie, couldn't inform you of their issues. They couldn't say my head is woozy. Or I feel off. Couldn't explain the black dots floating in their eyes.

Even if he'd listened to the signs Isiah had been displaying all those years ago, Benedict wouldn't have recognized the traumatic brain injury. But if he hadn't been so angry with his brother for not listening, and for getting in a wreck—even a supposedly minor one—he would have noticed something was wrong.

Hope had been in utero when the crash had happened. He knew the images from the MRI and CT scans were clear. But drag racing teens could cause so much damage.

Penny turned as she dropped his hand and crossed her arms. She looked like she was preparing for a battle—to make him take care of himself. And she looked formidable as she raised her chin.

"She'll still be here when we're on our shifts tomorrow. Her mother has been through so much. She's splitting her time between this hospital and the one where her wife is recuperating. Give her a little space and trust the facts on this case."

That was the problem. Most of the time he didn't have an issue with reading the charts and forming an opinion based on science. But the drag racing, the car accident, the tiny baby…all of it added up to an itch his brain just couldn't quite scratch.

"And…" she hesitated before straightening her shoulders "…if you can't trust that, trust me. I checked the notes when I arrived. I was by your side last night when the MRI and CT readings came in. I am not a neonatologist, but I have worked in this area for more than a decade. Hope is doing as well as she could be. Trust me."

The intensity in her eyes shook him to his core. He let himself relax for the first time since he'd heard that street racing had caused the issue.

Could he trust her instincts?

Yes. The answer was immediate. He trusted Penny, full stop.

And she was right. He knew that. Knew that he'd done everything he could for Hope. She was at Wald Children's, one of the best hospitals in the country with a level-four NICU that was the best in the country.

He took a deep breath and looked at Penny, soaking in her simple presence. "I love you." This wasn't the right place for those words. Wasn't the best time. But they felt right as they echoed in the small on-call room.

And waiting to say them, waiting until it was the right time—whatever that meant—didn't seem nearly as important as telling her how he felt. He loved her. It was as simple as that.

"I love you too." Penny squeezed his hand. "So let's go home."

He nodded and wrapped an arm around her. "Home sounds perfect."

"The shower was one thing I needed." Benedict dropped his towel into the hamper as he looked at Penny. She was sitting crossed-legged on the bed, her legs wrapped in oversized black yoga pants and her hair in a messy bun on the top of her head.

God, she was gorgeous.

"One thing? What else did you need?" Penny's eyes glittered as they watched him advance. A small grin spread across her face as he bent his head.

He wasn't sure how he'd gone from asking her to fake a relationship to benefit the hospital to having her here all the time. But he'd never been happier. Maybe that was dangerous. If you never let yourself get too happy, to content, then you weren't surprised when life destroyed everything.

But he didn't want to think of those things now. Maybe with Penny he'd never have to consider them again. It was likely wishful thinking, but in this moment he was happy and that was all he was going to focus on.

Finally he dropped his lips to hers and felt the last twenty-four hours' trials fade away. His fingers traced the edge of her jaw as she deepened the kiss.

This was heaven. This was perfection. This was all he'd never been willing to hope for.

Penny leaned back and pulled him onto the bed.

He came willingly, letting her guide his body as she shifted and laid her head on his shoulder. The momentum had shifted from the kiss to an intimacy that felt so much deeper as her fingers ran along his chest.

"Tell me what happened. About the dream and Hope and the feelings you experienced last night." Her fingers continued to stroke his chest, but it was a peaceful connection, a beautiful reminder that after so long he wasn't alone.

"Isiah was in my dream. Or his voice was. Or at least I think it was his voice." He let out a soft sigh. "I should remember my brother's voice. Should be able to recall it, but it disappeared so many years ago. I have a general feeling, a general sense, but the actual tone… That probably sounds ridiculous."

"Not at all." Penny kissed his cheek. "I think most people think of memory as a room full of boxes you can recall at will, but the mind doesn't work that way. It gets rid of things…even things we love and cherish, to make room for new things. It doesn't mean you didn't love your brother, that you don't still love him."

Of course she would say the perfect thing. He squeezed her shoulder and kissed her forehead. "You know he was in an accident, but his car was mostly intact. The other one lit up in flames and they had to race against the clock to get the driver out. But Isiah walked away from his. That's the crazy thing."

He looked at the ceiling as the story tumbled forth. "He was fine, at least physically, for a few hours after the crash. He and Amber were sitting on the couch, talking in low tones. He complained of a headache, but I was so angry that he'd gone to the final race and that he'd crashed."

He pushed air out of his lungs as he let the wash of memories from that fateful day rotate around his brain. Of course he could remember the painful words he'd said, the anger he'd felt, but not the sound of Isiah's voice. Not the look on his face when he grinned. Not the important things.

"Amber said something was wrong." He caught a sob in the back of his throat. "Isiah's eyes were glassy, and he was having trouble remembering the conversation they were having."

"TBI?"

"Yes," Benedict responded. "Traumatic brain injury. We thought maybe he needed sleep, so he went to take a nap. And never woke back up."

"It's why you were so concerned with Hope's MRI

and CT scans." Penny let out a sigh as she grabbed one of his hands and held it in hers.

"The drag racing… I mean who street races in DC? Even at three in the morning, there are people leaving the capital, pedestrians, people just going about their lives that deserve to be able to make it home."

He sucked air into his lungs, hoping to stop the prick of tears he felt building. "Hope couldn't tell us if something was wrong. Isiah didn't have the words to describe what was happening and Amber and I didn't know."

"And your parents?"

"Stopped paying attention to the two of us when we were old enough to heat soup from the pantry in the microwave. I know that wasn't your experience, and I'm so glad it wasn't, but neither of my parents cared what was happening as long as we weren't interrupting their lives. Amber and I looked after him. She and I sat next to him in the hospital over the three days he was there."

Benedict rolled his eyes. "Though to hear my mother tell the story, she labored by his bedside for days, praying, begging, hoping. But it was Amber and me."

"How far along was Amber's pregnancy then?" Penny yawned. "If we lie here much longer, we are going to fall asleep."

"I can think of worse things." Benedict kissed her forehead. "Not quite eight weeks. They were planning to use the money he won in the race to leave town. Her family was, is, very strict in their values."

"It must have been hard after your brother passed for her."

"Yes." Benedict swallowed the feelings those memories dredged up. "She was devastated. Then to lose Olivia. It nearly destroyed her. She's never been the same. She gave in to her mother's demands, and I've always wondered if she's punishing herself for things she couldn't control." He yawned as his body started to lose the fight against his exhaustion.

"I did my best to help. But I wasn't my brother. Wasn't the man she loved and certainly not the one she wanted."

He yawned as his eyes drooped. The night shift and lack of sleep were almost too much for him. His eyes fluttered, and he tried to push them open as Penny's voice caught his attention. "What?"

His brain was foggy but he forced himself to focus as she asked again.

"What did Amber's mother think when she found out she was pregnant? Your brother was gone."

"She told her that there was no room for an unwed mother in their family." He shook his head. "Never will understand why Amber is still so worried about her feelings."

"You're still in touch?"

The question was muffled through his fatigue. This was important. He needed to say something, but the only words that came to his tired brain were, "I love you, Penny."

CHAPTER NINE

PENNY PUT A pod in the coffee machine and tried not to grimace as the ancient machine crackled and hissed before delivering her coffee in a weak and sputtering stream. But beggars couldn't be choosers. At least this was their final night shift.

Benedict walked in the room and held up a trivia pocket notebook. "Not sure I will get any time to look at this on shift but look." He slipped the tiny book into the pocket of his scrubs. "Fits perfectly! I am going to do better the next time we head to trivia night."

"We won Tuesday night." She gripped the sides of the warm cup before taking a deep sip, hoping the caffeine would migrate directly to her bloodstream.

"No, you won." Benedict tapped the book in his pocket as he grinned. "And I love all the knowledge stored in your brain. But it would be nice to feel like more of a team player with you. Don't want you to get embarrassed being seen with me."

He playfully winked and her heart melted. She'd never be embarrassed to be with him, but his desire to learn about something she cared about was the best gift he could have given her.

"I love playing trivia with you. Besides, I didn't

know the answers to the last round of questions." Penny shrugged. "Divorce laws aren't my strong suit."

He put his own pod in the single-serve coffee maker, tapped the top of the machine and the hissing noises ceased before it delivered a strong stream of coffee. "Weird end to the night, that's true. Hopefully the announcer gets some therapy to deal with what he's going through.

"Anyway, my knowledge didn't really help the game. You had us far enough ahead that the final round didn't matter." He took a sip of his coffee, then headed to his rounds.

Penny wanted to follow, but her stomach twisted as she remembered the trivia night…and Benedict's seemingly encyclopedic knowledge of DC's divorce laws.

He was right; she'd had them far enough along that it wouldn't have mattered if they missed each of the questions in that round. But they hadn't missed them. Not a single one. Because Benedict had known every answer.

The announcer had said maybe he needed to talk to Benedict about his upcoming divorce…making it painfully obvious why the awkward subject had been chosen for the night.

It sent a ripple of concern down her spine.

Why did he know so much?

It wasn't a topic that one generally came across in trivia textbooks. Unless it was some obscure law left on the books. Like in the state of Kentucky, it's technically illegal to marry the same person four times.

She wasn't sure why that was a law. Or why the statehouse had decided it was necessary to put it on the books.

But those hadn't been the questions. Instead it had

been about marital property laws in DC and how to file a case if a spouse flees to another state.

The announcer really should have called in sick to work that night.

But why had Benedict known all those answers? And why did it matter to her that he did?

He'd had a life before they'd started dating. But she remembered those early conversations in the on-call room where he'd said he had no plans to marry. He'd certainly never mentioned having been married before.

There was an easy way to find the answer. All she had to do was ask. But each time she'd started to, the words stuck in her throat. They were opening up to each other now. But there were still things that she hadn't told him. Painful pieces of her life with Mitchel that she'd never shared with anyone.

Signs she'd missed. Hunches her mind had desperately tried to warn her about. Times she'd failed to demand better answers. Rationally she knew all the blame lay with Mitchel, but there were some things she didn't want to rehash with anyone. Baggage that continued to haunt her.

Benedict had been a closed book before they started dating. It was the running joke in the office. You knew his name, knew he'd dated a good portion of the eligible women at the hospital—for short periods—knew he cared about his patients and their families, and knew he could fix toys. Outside of that, the rest of his life was a guess.

But she knew him now. *Do you?* That insidious voice haunted her.

She'd thought she'd known Mitchel. Yet he'd been able to hide a family. Hide a marriage. Hide himself.

Penny shook her head and downed the rest of her

coffee. So much pain brought on by Mitchel's lies and gaslighting. He'd made her doubt herself. Made her question the love of the man she was with now.

She might not know everything about Benedict, no one could after only a few weeks of dating, but she knew he loved her. And that promises were important to him. He wouldn't hurt her. She knew that deep down.

She was just letting her past cloud the future.

Grabbing the tablet chart, she shook the final worries from her brain as she walked from the room.

At least most of them.

David Watkins lay in the oversized armchair, gentle snores echoing from him as Benedict looked at his son. Patrick had been born at thirty-four weeks. Not quite full-term, but close enough to thirty-seven weeks, which was considered full-term, that babies didn't typically land in the level-four NICU.

But his mother hadn't survived. The woman had had an undiagnosed heart condition and tragedy had struck. Then in his first twenty-four hours, Patrick's pediatrician had noticed a bluish tint and a murmur when listening to his heart. A cardiology consult had resulted in the diagnosis of pulmonary stenosis, meaning that the valve between Patrick's right ventricle and his pulmonary artery was too small.

So much to handle in a short period for David.

His son had been transported to Wald Children's two days ago and was scheduled for a balloon valvuloplasty on Friday, a procedure that would inflate the valve, letting the heart operate close to average. Though Patrick would have to see a cardiologist for the rest of his life, he'd likely have a nearly normal life.

But all that good news hadn't stopped David from

worrying about his son. Which didn't surprise Benedict. Most parents, even when greeted with good news, worried about their children. His parents had been an exception, and unfortunately he knew how deep the unseen scars that parental behavior caused went.

"He's been here all day according to Alice," Penny whispered as she stepped into the room and held up her tablet chart.

"He's exhausted, but having a newborn is exhausting. Having one with a chronic heart issue—" He looked over at the sleeping man. "At least he's resting now." Benedict quietly opened the isolette to listen to Patrick's heart. He could hear the tiny murmur, but his heart rate was normal. That was good, considering his little heart was having to work harder than most.

"His O2 levels have been good all day. The cardiologist intern saw him earlier, as did Dr. McDougall. The little man is on track for his surgery," Penny recited quietly as Benedict continued his examination.

"Is everything all right?"

Benedict looked up from the baby, and saw Penny turn toward the door as the woman attached to the question entered the room.

"Patrick. Is he okay?" she repeated.

Benedict saw Penny look down at the chart. It confirmed what he already knew. Only David was listed on the child's forms. It was against the law for them to provide information without the consent of the parent.

"Sorry," Penny started, "but who are you? We only have David listed as a parent so we can't…"

"That's Daisy," David interrupted and stretched in the chair as she stood. "You can tell her anything. I'll sign whatever form. She's Patrick's…" He hesitated as he looked from his son to Daisy, tears coating his eyes,

"Aunt, I suppose. The closest thing he will have to a mother." His voice hiccupped as Daisy stepped to his side.

She put her arms around David and squeezed tightly as she looked back at Benedict. "Lori," her voice shook but she swallowed and continued, "Lori and I grew up in the same group home. We may not have been blood, but our bond was as strong as any sisters'. We swore long ago that we'd take care of each other no matter what."

She let her eyes wander to the isolette and the tips of her lips dipped as she looked at the little one. "She was so happy when she found David and so excited to give Patrick the family life we never got."

David yawned as he wiped a tear from his eye. "I don't know what I'd do right now without your support."

"And you don't have to worry about it." Daisy squeezed his shoulders again. "I'm here for you both. Always."

Benedict let out a soft sigh as he looked at the couple. So much grief. His own past sent a wave of sadness followed by the crash of hope. Patrick would be fine. Unlike Amber, David would get to take his son home. Get to watch him grow and thrive.

"Everything has just been so much lately, and I'm exhausted." He stretched, then yawned—again. "You don't realize how much more difficult things are on your own."

"You aren't alone." Daisy placed a platonic kiss on his cheek. "And I'll be able to help with more once we get hitched at city hall."

"You're getting married?" Penny covered her mouth as she looked at the couple, then at her feet.

"I know it's not traditional, but…" David pushed a

hand through his hair. "Daisy, Lori and I were all close. I loved Lori, and she wanted Patrick to have the life she didn't. It was the thing she wanted most, and we… Well, we want to give him that life."

"For Lori." Daisy sighed.

"Oh," Penny stated.

Benedict saw her catch whatever words were buried in the back of her throat. It was an unusual way to handle the loss of love, but Benedict knew it wasn't that unique. His stomach twisted as he saw Penny look at the chart, trying to cover the unintentional judgment and red sheen of embarrassment crawling up her neck.

He understood. It was a lot for people to accept, but people married for all sorts of reasons. And love was only one of them. He wasn't sure it was even the most common one.

"I get talkative when I'm exhausted, clearly," David continued. "Is something wrong with Patrick? That's what we were talking about. What we should talk about."

"No," Benedict answered quickly. He knew from experience that any additional information should be passed after issuing that one single word. Parents listened for confirmation of their worst fears. Even if you had to deliver bad news, delivering it first, then waiting a minute or two before continuing was enough to help people process and hear what followed next.

"Patrick is doing great. And after his heart surgery, the little guy will spend a day or so here and then we'll be able to step him down to the level-three and then the level-two NICU. In a few years, you can send us a fifth birthday pic of him with a fun cake for our graduate wall."

"I'd like that. But with his heart…" David swallowed.

"I want to be optimistic; I do. But…" he wiped away a tear "…honestly, I'm scared. There was no warning with Lori. I found her in the hall of our apartment. We saved Patrick, but she… Well it was too late for Lori." David bit his lip, and Benedict worried he was tasting blood, before continuing. "She was fine when I left for work that morning, then the whole world shifted."

"I am so sorry," Penny murmured. "But with regular cardiology checkups, there is no reason that Patrick shouldn't live a happy and normal life. He'll have to clear sports activities with his cardiologist, but it will be okay."

David nodded, then looked toward his son. Hopefully he'd start believing soon.

"That was a long night. Glad we go back to day shifts next week." She hit his hip with hers as they waited for the subway train to arrive. "I hope your promotion won't mean that for the rest of time I'll be kissing your forehead as you slip into bed and I slide out to make eggs."

He kissed her forehead. "If I get the promotion, I'll have to do a round of night shifts every few months. But I promise to be quiet as I slide into bed."

Penny's eyes brightened as the mention of the future lit across her. He lived for that sign. Lived to see her happy, to know that he'd brought that feeling. It was intoxicating.

And it was easy to talk about the future with her. Easy to see her in his future. He liked that thought.

"What do you think of Daisy and David's agreement?" Penny yawned as she stepped into the train. "Or I guess I should say, what do you think of their marriage?"

"I think whatever works for them is okay." His

stomach twisted as she frowned. He'd done something similar. If Olivia had lived, he would likely still be in Oregon, working in a completely different field and married to Amber without the divorce proceeding that was working its way through the courts now. He'd have done that out of his love for Isiah because he'd promised to take care of Amber if something happened.

A promise was important. If David and Daisy felt compelled to raise Patrick together in matrimony, who was he to judge? It was honestly more sensible than marrying for love.

He loved Penny, but there were no guarantees with the emotion. If his mother made it down the aisle with her newest fiancé, it would be her sixth wedding. His father had elected to stop meeting people at the altar after his third marriage exploded. And divorce was an expensive complication. Better to love someone deeply for as long as you did and then part as amicably as possible.

"I know." Penny nodded as she gripped the handrail. "It's just such a sacrifice for both of them."

"A sacrifice for a lost love and a beloved friend."

Her eyes flashed as the words left his mouth. "Love does not obligate you to a marriage of convenience."

"It's more complicated than that." Benedict felt his nerves shiver as he tried to explain.

His divorce was nearly finalized. According to his lawyer, as soon as Amber signed the papers he'd sent via certified mail to her, the court could finalize the procedure. In DC, the case could be settled without either of them having to set foot in a courtroom since they'd been living apart for more than six months. Over sixteen years more!

It was the right decision to break his vows to her, but it had still taken years, and finding Penny, for him to feel completely okay taking the step. To accept that his promise to never be like his parents would take a hit.

"But love…"

"Is not guaranteed in marriage. It's why the institution itself means so little." They were the wrong words. And he'd said them far too loud as he saw several heads turn his way.

Penny's face was devoid of color, and she refused to meet his gaze as she stared at her shoes.

"Penny," Benedict murmured, "I just meant it's a piece of paper. My mother has signed five marriage certificates so far. My father stopped after three. But people sign that piece of paper all the time without thinking it's forever. They take vows for a host of reasons that aren't based on the fantasy delivered in romantic comedies."

"Except real lasting love exists. People say for better or worse and mean it. I've seen it. Seen what it means for the people lucky enough to find it, and you've seen what it means for those who don't find it. What it can mean for children caught in the middle."

Except his parents had loved each of their partners once. And even though their love had failed, he'd felt hopeful when they'd each found someone else. Until the pattern of love, anger and then hate repeated itself again and again.

"You don't know that Daisy and David will have a bad marriage. Marriage for love is a modern creation. For generations people married for property, as business arrangements or because it made the most sense for their family. And they found love outside of the union." Benedict felt compelled to try to make her understand.

"Let's be honest, Benedict, we aren't really talking about Daisy and David."

And there was the truth bomb. The ticking time bomb in this perfect union. Because despite her saying she wanted fluffy and free, what Penny really wanted in life was the fairy tale. And Benedict didn't believe in the fantasy.

But he knew he loved her. And he'd promised he'd never hurt her. A promise he had every intention of keeping. He didn't know how to explain that, but he could feel the tension bubbling through them. And he knew he didn't want to lose her.

So he said the only thing that he could. "I love you." Benedict ran a hand along her cheek. If only he could stop time, he would let life freeze this moment of love before everything crashed. And he might never unpause it, just enjoying time with Penny.

"And I love you." Penny offered him a smile, but it didn't quite reach her eyes. She reached for his free hand as she leaned against him.

To the rest of the train, it probably looked like two tired professionals in love. And they were.

But…

He buried his head in her hair, desperate to soak her up. To cling to her, to pull at the cords that suddenly looked like they might unravel if he didn't hold on.

Benedict tried to calm his racing heart. Tonight was a blip, a single issue that didn't have to mean so much. They loved each other.

We love each other.

He repeated the words to himself, desperate to calm the worry.

We love each other.

But for the first time since they'd uttered those words, Benedict worried that love wouldn't be enough.

CHAPTER TEN

"I LIKE THAT DRESS." Alice's voice caught Penny by surprise, and she barely caught the navy dress she'd been holding up in the mirror. She hadn't heard her sister come in. Though if she were honest, she'd been lost in her own thoughts.

Lost in her worries.

Since Daisy and David had told Penny and Benedict that they were planning to get married, the reins had loosened on her happiness. It was such a small moment. But she couldn't understand how Benedict could think they were doing the right thing.

No. She was putting words in his mouth, and that wasn't fair. He hadn't said that. What he'd said was he thought that getting married for love wasn't guaranteed, so it made sense to get married for other reasons. When they'd started this relationship, Penny had said she wanted light, fluffy. No strings attached.

She'd lied.

Not intentionally, and mostly to herself. She did want the fantasy. It didn't have to be soon, but what if Benedict never wanted to get married?

Did he want a family? Children? If so, would he want to marry the mother of those children? Or just live together?

Many people did that and were happy. But she always thought her life would include the promise of forever made in front of her family and friends if she fell in love again. It wasn't the marriage certificate itself, but the bond, the vow, the promise represented in taking that step.

Penny took a deep breath. Nothing in her life had seemed right since she'd discovered Mitchel's lies... until she found Benedict. But now doubt was creeping along the edges of what she'd thought she'd been so sure of.

Love. Marriage...

He'd said he didn't want the institution, that he had no intention of ever walking down the aisle. Promises were important to him, but he wouldn't vow until death do us part with someone.

Was she okay never saying I do? Okay being in love with a man who didn't want it because he thought love so fallible? Did that mean he thought their love was so shallow that it would disappear?

She wasn't ready to answer those questions...at least not yet.

"Is that for the fundraising dinner this weekend?" Alice slipped onto Penny's bed and crossed her legs.

"Yep." Penny sighed and laid the navy dress to the side as she picked up the floral one and held it up for inspection in the mirror.

She watched Alice cock her head in the reflection as she pretended to inspect the dress Penny was holding up, though she suspected her sister was scrutinizing Penny's mood. That was one good thing about practically living at Benedict's lately. She hadn't had to see

Alice's inspections, answer any questions that might drive her worry higher.

But being at Benedict's no longer felt comfortable either.

There was a nervous energy humming just on the edge of their love. The sword of Damocles hanging over them. Threatening to slice the happy bubble they'd found.

She wanted to go back to the easiness they'd had before Daisy and David's revelation. The blissful knowledge that she loved him, and he loved her. The simple times of waking together, of not looking to what the future might hold, of just enjoying the present.

But eventually one had to look to the future. Didn't they?

"So what's the playboy done that's got your face so low?"

"You haven't called him a playboy lately, you know." Penny felt her lips tighten as she stared at the floral dress, then threw it aside too. That one wasn't right either.

"Well, lately I haven't seen much evidence of playboy tendencies. I haven't seen much evidence of a *fake* relationship either. I *knew* you couldn't fake a relationship to save your life. To be honest, I want credit for not gloating."

"This feels like gloating," Penny muttered just loud enough for her sister to hear.

"Maybe a little. Little sister prerogative." She winked, looking far too proud of herself. "But he makes you happy. Or at least he did. So, I say again, what happened?"

"Nothing important." That wasn't a lie. They'd had

a couple announce they were getting married for the benefit of the child and his mother's wishes rather than because they loved each other. It was a major occurrence for Daisy and David but a minor thing for Penny and Benedict.

At least it should have been.

But it had raised questions. Questions about the future. Questions about her place in Benedict's life...and his in hers. Questions she didn't want to ask.

Alice stood up and marched out of the room. Penny looked after her, but she didn't feel like chasing her sister down. At least not right now.

"Here!" Alice returned and tossed a pink dress with a slit up the hip that was sexy as hell, but the scoop neck would be acceptable for the fundraising dinner.

The dress was a contradiction, just like her and Benedict's relationship.

"Stop overthinking and put the dress on, Penny."

"I'd tell you that I wasn't overthinking—"

"But you'd be lying. Yeah, yeah, I know. Try on the dress." Her sister pointed to the outfit, then pointed at Penny. "Now."

Penny shot her sister a half-hearted glare and considered ignoring the order. But fighting with Alice was usually a losing battle. So she capitulated, stripping out of her shorts and tank top and sliding the dress over her head.

It was perfect. It hugged her curves in all the right places. The slit only hit mid-thigh. It was sexy but work-function appropriate and the color made her skin shine. She looked great, even without doing her hair. It would make Benedict's mouth water.

That thought sent a shiver of excitement through her.

She could already picture the look of appreciation on his face when he saw it.

"That's the dress." Alice clapped as she moved behind Penny, interrupting her woolgathering. "And you can pull your hair up." She twisted Penny's hair into a knot. "Now the dress is ready, the hair is planned, so all you have to do is figure out how to handle your date."

"Any recommendations?"

Alice wrapped her arms around Penny's shoulders and squeezed. "Figure out what you're willing to sacrifice for love, and what you aren't."

"And if I don't want to sacrifice anything?" Penny bit her lip as the question exited her mouth. She hadn't meant to speak. Hadn't meant to utter the words into the universe and certainly not next to her sister.

Just saying them aloud made her heart heave. Made the conversations that she and Benedict needed to have too real.

Alice leaned her head against Penny's, and she heard her sigh as her sister met her gaze in the mirror. "Love is sacrifice. Everyone gives something. If you're not willing…then…" She shrugged before sitting on the bed. "You guys going to trivia night tonight?"

"Yes." Penny nodded. That was the plan. Benedict said he wanted to see if any of the knowledge he'd gleaned from his trivia books was in the question pool tonight. *Books!* He'd read three trivia books this week. Three that he'd had her quiz him on, and he'd gotten all the questions right. Because he loved her and wanted to do things with her. That was treasure she didn't want to lose.

"Well, I hope you have fun tonight." Alice looked at her sister like there was more she wanted to say but whatever it was, Alice kept it buried. The look sent a shiver down Penny's spine, but she wasn't sure she wanted to know the rest of her sister's thoughts. At least not today.

"I have a date with a handsome spook." And just like that, her sister's playful demeanor was back. The silly Alice that didn't take anything too seriously.

"I don't think members of the intelligence community like being called spooks and there are so many around DC that it's not like they are really hiding." Penny tried to push the tension pooling in her belly away. Focusing on Alice's active and fun dating life lifted her for a moment.

Alice giggled. "That is true. This isn't even the first one I've dated, but they are more fun than politicians. And the only ones worse than politicians are politicians' sons." She playfully rolled her eyes to the ceiling. "But this is the Washington, DC, dating scene, so what is one to do?"

"Somehow you make do." Penny raised a brow as Alice hugged the doorjamb.

"I do…" She paused, and a seriousness hovered in her eyes that Penny rarely saw. "But I know what I'd sacrifice for love. And what I won't."

Then she was gone, and Penny was left staring at an empty hallway. She stood there, unable to move, unable to think…or unwilling to think. Sooty walked by the door, stopped to see that Alice wasn't in the room, then twitched his tail as he left.

That cat was never going to be her friend. But did he have to make it so personal?

And now she was thinking about a cat disliking her rather than what she should be thinking about. Penny smacked her head.

She inhaled deeply and let out a sigh. The world, and

what she wanted, formed in her mind now that there was no reason for her to put off the hard thoughts beating at the invisible wall in her brain. She wanted the fairy tale. She wanted forever, marriage and hopefully a family.

She wanted the forever commitment. She wanted him to believe, really believe, that their love was forever. That saying *I do* meant *I do forever*. That love lasted without growing bitter.

She'd always understood that she wouldn't find that with Benedict…but that was before. Before their fake relationship had turned real. Before they'd said *I love you*. Those words mattered. Those words changed things. Changed lives.

Benedict looked at the clock as he waited for Penny to arrive. She'd slept at her place last night. Not a big deal, except they hadn't slept apart in weeks. They'd slept curled next to each other each night.

He yawned as he looked to the door again, knowing she wasn't there since the doorbell sensor hadn't gone off. Without her in bed next to him, he'd slept poorly. No, that was an understatement. Without Penny, he'd barely slept at all.

His brain had roamed the fretful patterns of what-if, examining the different ways their relationship had changed since Daisy and David had talked about marrying out of loyalty to their lost love. He didn't know if it was right for them, but maybe it was. Who was he to judge?

But that night shift had adjusted the perspective on his and Penny's relationship. It had raised the specter of marriage. She'd been engaged—to a man who'd lied repeatedly. A man she'd loved, at least at some point. Look at the damage he'd done.

His wife, who had loved him once, probably never believed her husband would not only cheat but put a ring on another woman's finger. That he'd promise another that he would walk down the aisle with them. What had marriage vows gotten her? Penny had actually escaped legally unscathed.

Though he knew scars to the heart cut deeper.

He had no intention of meeting anyone at the altar again. His first marriage had been for convenience, born out of a sense of obligation to Isiah. Marriage had killed his parents' happiness, turned the joy they'd once found in each other to a bitterness that led to so much damage in their family. Then they'd played that loop on repeat with other people.

People could be very happy and fulfilled without a piece of paper from the state sanctifying the union. But what if Penny needed that? He felt his brows knit.

Before he could let his mind wander that path too far, his phone pinged. His body relaxed just a little. She was here.

He pulled open the door and smiled. The world was just better when Penny was nearby. It simply was.

"Howdy, stranger."

"Howdy?" Penny raised an eyebrow. "Somehow that is not a greeting I ever expected from you." She kissed his cheek.

"Really?" He kissed her. "You do know that I am from Oregon, right? Small-town boy. Howdy is a word that's used there. At least I think so. It's been so long since I've been back."

"You ever plan to visit?" Penny asked as she took off her coat.

"No." He yawned. There was nothing left for him in Oregon. His mother only sent him news about her impending unions, for reasons he still didn't understand, and his father never reached out. Their sons were accessories to a union they'd hated.

He pushed the unhappy thoughts from his brain. The past was done, and he had no intention of reopening the wounds it offered.

"You're exhausted." She frowned.

"I missed my cuddle buddy." He wrapped his arms around her, inhaling the scent, trying to ground himself. She was here now. The uneasiness he'd felt since that night in the NICU lessened its grip on his heart as he hugged her.

He yawned again. "I'm sure I'll sleep better tonight." If she was by his side, sleep would come easily.

"I vote we stay in tonight." Penny kissed his cheek. "You're exhausted. And if I am being honest, I didn't sleep well either."

"Missed my big bed, right?" Her grin sent a thrill through him as she cocked her head.

"Maybe." She let out a sigh. "Or maybe I just missed the sexy sweetheart in the bed."

"I missed you too." He took a step back but held on to her hands. "Maybe you could stay here…more permanently."

Penny blinked, and he held his breath as the words registered. He hadn't meant to say them, though the thought of her moving in didn't scare him at all. In fact the thought made him ecstatic.

She should be here. Should stay with him. For as long as love pulsed between them.

"That is quite a question." Penny pursed her lips as she looked at him. "I want to say yes."

"Then say yes." Benedict pulled her to him. "Say yes."

Penny put her hands on either side of his cheeks. "I

love you. I'll need to talk to Alice. DC rent is expensive. I don't want to leave her without a roommate to help cover costs. But as soon as she finds one…"

"I love you." He grinned, too happy to say more. Then he let out another yawn.

"Seriously, let's stay in tonight. Order something nice and watch TV. Just relax. Let someone else have a shot at winning trivia at the bar tonight."

He wanted to argue with her. After all, he'd spent the last few weeks reading every trivia book he could easily get a hold of. There were four on hold at the library and two more that he'd downloaded on his tablet. He wanted to rule trivia with her, be the unbeatable couple so he could see her face light up with happiness. But he was exhausted.

"I think staying in might be the best idea. We can put on the channel that runs all the game shows and I can test my trivia knowledge there." He dropped a kiss to her lips, happiness building through him.

"That sounds like an excellent plan."

Benedict didn't know if there was a way to be happier. His belly was full; he'd answered five questions on the last game show they'd watched and Penny was curled in his lap. This was the definition of perfection.

"Up next, four couples try to win their dream wedding by answering trivia questions. Will love survive the heat of the question box?"

"Interesting premise for a game show." Benedict gathered the dishes from the table.

"How so?" Penny grabbed their wine glasses and followed Benedict into the kitchen.

"A game show where you win your dream wedding. How is that a prize?"

Penny's brows knitted as she set the wine glasses in front of him. "Weddings average over thirty-seven thousand dollars in DC. If you get someone else to pay for that by answering questions, why wouldn't you?"

"Thirty-seven thousand dollars, for an institution that is likely to end in divorce and unhappiness." Benedict shook his head. "Some prize." The words left his mouth before he had a chance to think them through.

"Seriously, it's a myth that most marriages end in divorce. A narrative that gets website clicks and generates ad revenue. The truth is always less interesting than a clickbait headline, but the peak for divorces was in the seventies and eighties in the US and as the average age of marriage rose, the divorce rate declined. And continues to decline." Penny raised her chin as he met her gaze.

"Marriage doesn't mean love dies. My parents were proof of that."

She was right. He knew that. But his parents…

"And my parents were proof that marriage can kill love. They've vowed forever too many, and they always end up hating their partner. At least my father gave up after his third failed marriage. My mother seems to be going for some world record of unhappy unions."

"Do you think we could end up hating each other?" Her question was barely audible, but he heard the worry echoing in it. He wanted to dismiss the fear, wanted to push it away. But he remembered his parents laughing together, remembered seeing the pictures of them together in the wedding garb, looking like the world was made for just the two of them.

And he remembered his mother telling his father she hated him. That she wished she'd never married him. And his father screaming back that she was the worst thing to ever happen to him. They'd gone from a happy, blissful young couple to bitter people who could rarely be in the same room together.

"It's hard to imagine that happening." Benedict reached for her hand, grateful when she didn't pull it away from him.

"But you can imagine it." Penny licked her lips.

"Marriage was made for practical reasons for so many years—"

"Yes, you made that argument the night that Daisy and David told us their plans and I was less impressed with the decision than you were," Penny interrupted.

"We don't have to think of this now." He ran a hand along her cheek. "Do we?"

This was a breaking point. He knew it. He knew she knew it. But somehow he hoped he could prolong what felt inevitable from happening. That they could just focus on the love they had between them now.

Two hours ago he'd asked her to move in with him. He still wanted that, but there was a look in her eyes. A look that sent a chill straight to his bones.

Penny wanted the fantasy. And he couldn't promise her that.

"Kiss me." Her words were desperate. "Kiss me, please."

Putting a hand behind her head, he drew her close dropping his lips to hers. She tasted of hope, love, but the hint of loss was already mixed in as she deepened the kiss.

"Penny." Her name echoed in his heart as it fell from his lips.

Her arms wrapped around him. "I need you." Penny trailed her lips down his jaw as her fingers trailed to the top of his pants.

Need crawled through him. He didn't want to think. Didn't want anything more than the woman here with him now. Lifting her into his arms, he carried her to his room.

Tomorrow, with its conversations, would come. But tonight he was simply here with his Penny.

His Penny...

For however long she wanted to kiss him.

CHAPTER ELEVEN

IN THE MORNING light Penny's heart felt even heavier than it had last night. Instead of having the hard conversation, she'd demanded he kiss her. Demanded he take her to bed.

And take her to bed, Benedict had. Despite their exhaustion, they'd spent most of the night making love. Making memories that she feared would have to last them.

She kissed his cheek as she slid from bed.

"Don't go." Benedict's sleepy words reverberated around her heart. There was so much behind the words, a plea for more than her to stay in bed.

She wanted to promise him she wasn't going anywhere, but the words wouldn't come, so instead she said, "Just getting coffee, sleepyhead." She kissed him again, then dropped one of his T-shirts over herself.

"Make enough for two." His tone was a little grumpy, but she was tired too. And dreading the reengagement of their conversation from last night.

She got the coffee started, and picked up her cell. They'd been so focused on each other last night that she'd forgotten to plug hers in and the charge on it was nearly gone. Benedict's phone sat next to hers.

He wasn't on call today, but she knew from experience that that didn't mean the hospital wouldn't call. She grabbed it planning to plug his in too.

The phone lit up and two messages hovered on the screen. The first was from Amber... Isiah's lost love?

Lawyer says our divorce is finalized. Thanks for everything...

She couldn't see the rest of the message, but the text for the other contact sent pain ricocheting around her.

The contact simply said *Lawyer*. The part of the message she could see read:

Divorce finalized. Please call office tomorrow...

Divorce. Benedict was divorced...officially. He'd been married to Amber, the woman he'd said was Isiah's love. Who'd been pregnant when her love died.

His understanding of Daisy and David's choice clicked into place. He'd done the same thing. Taken a chance on forever with someone out of obligation. But not out of love.

"Coffee ready?"

His chipper tone was at such odds with the feelings circulating through her. She felt confused, lost and hurt. *So hurt.*

"Your divorce is finalized." The words slipped between them. She hadn't meant to say them. Hadn't meant to say anything. She handed him his phone. "And you have less than ten percent battery. You need to charge it."

She swallowed, trying to will her feet to move. To carry her away.

"Penny..."

Benedict's fingers gripped her wrists, but she felt nothing. She was numb.

"I can explain. We've been separated for seventeen years. She and Isiah were going to run away together and then…"

"And when he died, you married her because she was pregnant."

"Her mother threatened to throw her out. It may be the twenty-first century, but she is stuck in the past. Then we lost Olivia. Amber's family were all she had left then. I couldn't push for a divorce, and time just passed." He ran a hand through his hair as his dark eyes met hers.

"Did you love her?" She braced herself for the answer, whatever it was.

"No, and she didn't love me." The coffeepot dinged, and Benedict poured a cup.

He held it out to her, but she shook her head. Her hands were too shaky to hold it.

He frowned, then raised the cup to his lips. "We never even slept in the same bed."

Did he think that made it better? That marrying someone and remaining married for so long was better if you never loved them?

"If Olivia hadn't died…" She couldn't quite bring herself to finish the question.

But Benedict didn't seem to need the rest of the words. "I'd probably still be in Oregon, raising Olivia… But life took a different course. I wouldn't wish her gone, ever. But I can't reset the way my life turned out, or how it led me to you." Benedict took a step toward her, but she stepped back.

He frowned but he didn't advance any farther.

"I planned to tell you after everything was finalized. I know it may seem like Mitchel but it's different."

Her eyes met his, and she nodded. She hadn't thought of Mitchel or any of the similarities. It wasn't the lie of omission that was breaking her heart. It was knowing that he'd be willing to spend a lifetime with someone out of obligation but not risk the same thing on their love.

She crossed her arms, trying to ground herself. She was only wearing his T-shirt and a pair of panties—not exactly "storming out the door" clothing.

Why hadn't she gotten dressed this morning?

Because she hadn't wanted to leave.

"You were willing to marry someone for obligation, but the idea of marrying for love…" A sob echoed from her lips, and she gripped herself tighter. "The idea of marrying for love is too much."

"Love." Benedict set the coffee cup down, his eyes searching her face, but she couldn't meet his gaze. "Love doesn't always last."

Penny rubbed her hands along her arms, desperate for warmth as chill stole through her. "So you think what we have won't last?"

He bit his lip, and she could see the truth wrestling within him.

"I don't have the same relationship with the fantasy of happily-ever-after that you do."

"You can just say yes." Penny shook her head. And suddenly it was crystal clear what she'd sacrifice for love and what she wouldn't.

"I love you, Penny. Here and now. Isn't that enough?"

She wanted to say yes. So desperately. But she couldn't live with someone who'd look at her and think that this could be temporary. Who would always wonder if their love would cross the line to hate?

Benedict had said he wouldn't hurt her. That was a promise that had been foolish. She knew that, but she'd believed, really believed, he could find forever with her. That he could believe forever was possible.

She'd misread him, just like she'd misread Mitchel… but in such different ways. However she wasn't going to make the same mistake with Benedict that she'd made before. She wasn't waiting to see if something changed. Wasn't ignoring the red flag this time.

"No." The word was so simple and so final. "I want… I deserve to be with someone who wants to risk the hurt for the chance of finding forever."

As she walked past him, she put her hand on his shoulder. "Your parents' marriages were sad, and I am sure traumatizing, but you're using their mistakes as an excuse to not risk getting hurt." She kissed his cheek. "You stay a closed book, so you don't have to risk everything. If people don't know you, then they can't hurt you. But that is such a lonely way to lead your life."

"And using your perfect childhood as a standard is a bar too high for anyone to meet." He bowed his head and let out a soft sigh.

She knew he was hurting, but the statement cut to her core. Perhaps there was a little too much truth to it. Alice had warned her of that when she was looking at the dating apps. Rather than rise to the statement, she kissed his cheek one more time, knowing it was the last time. Hating the knowledge as her heart tore apart.

"Goodbye, Benedict."

He didn't move as she went to the room they'd shared so many times. She quickly changed and packed up the few belonging she'd accumulated over the last few weeks. When she exited, he was in the same place, the look of devastation so clear on his face.

She wanted to go to him, to hold him, to tell him it would be okay. Tell him they could figure out a way to make it right for both of them. But she'd sacrificed so much of herself for Mitchel. So much of her wants and needs. She couldn't do it again.

Penny walked past him as she exited Patrick's room. The little one had come through his heart surgery perfectly. Today he was stepping down to the less-restrictive NICU. She didn't pause, didn't do more than acknowledge his presence when work required it.

He couldn't blame her. Working with her was torture…and a blessing. The idea of not seeing her every day at least for a few hours, even with minimal contact, was too much to bear.

The last two days had nearly torn his soul apart. He'd lay in bed or pace his townhome, unable to think of anything but her. Even his workshop provided no comfort. There was simply no comfort without Penny. None.

"I can't thank you enough for the care you've given Patrick." David smiled as he looked at his son. "He looks so much like my Lori. Like a little piece of her." The words were sweet, and he didn't tear up as he said them.

"I'm sure she would be so proud of your son, and you. And glad Daisy is staying close and loving her son as she would have."

"Yes. But only as the best aunt this little guy could ever get." David stroked his son's fingers. "We decided to cancel the courthouse visit."

"Oh." Now it was his turn to be surprised by the words. They'd seemed so certain that night in the hospital.

No. They'd seemed lost in grief. Just like he and Amber had been.

He looked up at him and shrugged. "The love I had for Lori, have for Lori, I wouldn't trade that for anything. Despite the pain of raising our son alone. Daisy deserves to find that. Deserves to know the person beside her forever chose her."

"Love is risky." The words left his mouth, and he wished he could pull them back in. This wasn't the time or place for this conversation and certainly not the right person.

But David was too wrapped up with his son to notice the turmoil echoing through him—thank goodness.

"That's true." He nodded. "But love is a precious gift. Dwelling on the risk just means you lose sight of that."

Benedict swallowed the pool of emotions in his throat. The knowledge that he'd let the woman he loved walk out without trying to stop her. That he'd told her he thought their love was destined for failure…even if he hadn't said the words directly.

He carefully controlled the rampaging emotions coursing through him as he looked to the tablet chart in his hand. "The cardiologist is going to check on Patrick once he is transferred, but I meant what I said a few nights ago. Please send us photos of you and Patrick for our wall of graduates. We want to celebrate his milestones."

"Just try and stop me." David laughed, then kissed the top of his son's head. "You and me, buddy. We got this."

Benedict left the room. He wanted to talk to Penny. Needed to. He wasn't sure what the right words were or how to find them. But he needed to see her, ask her to meet him somewhere after work. Beg, if necessary.

She was standing at the nurses' station next to Alice.

She turned her head away as he approached. He tried not to let that hurt. After all, he'd let her walk away.

"Can we go someplace after work to talk?" He kept his voice low, but he saw Alice's eyes widen and a soft smile spread across her face. If Penny's sister didn't think it a completely lost cause, maybe there was hope.

"There's nothing to say." Penny grabbed her tablet and the walkie-talkie they used. "Nothing."

"But what if there was?" Benedict pursed his lips. "What if I realized I made a mistake? Can we at least talk?"

Her eyes watered, and she shook herself. "No. I don't think that is a good idea. We want differ—"

"Penny, Dr. Denbar—just the people I was looking for." Susan, public relations director, smiled at them.

One of the last people Benedict wanted to see right now was the PR director. The only person he wanted to see didn't want to see him and he could barely process that information.

"The fundraiser tomorrow night; we were hoping you two might be willing to talk to the local news station. They wanted a follow-up piece. And I figured, Dr. Denbar, that you could talk about the project and the fundraising status during the evening. I know interviews aren't until next week…but you're a shoo-in for the position. May as well have people get to know you a little."

"I can't make it. Sorry." Then Penny ducked away and headed into a patient's room.

Her words didn't surprise him, and he couldn't keep the look of hurt he felt from crawling across his face. Still, he put on a smile as he looked at Susan. "I'd be happy to talk to whoever you'd like."

Her eyes tracked Penny's retreat, and he barely kept

his composure as he looked at Susan and saw her register what everyone on the floor already knew. He and Penny were no longer together.

The fake relationship that had started to help raise money for the maternity wing, turned into a deep love, had broken and now lay at his feet in a pile of rubble. And he had no one to blame but himself.

"I see. Well, of course we still want you to talk. And I will find another avenue for the local news interview. Thank you, Dr. Denbar."

He nodded, not trusting his voice. He still had six hours left on this shift. Six hours in the same location with the woman he loved. Six hours of hell mixed with sprinkles of heaven.

"You're really not going tonight?" Alice lay the pink dress across the couch and crossed her arms.

Penny set aside the book she'd been pretending to read as she looked at her sister, ignoring the dress she'd fantasized making Benedict's mouth water with just a few days ago.

A lifetime ago.

"There is nothing for me at the fundraising dinner." That wasn't true. She lived for the moments when she and Benedict were in the same room at the hospital. Clung to the tiny clutches of words he spoke to her.

When he'd asked her to go out after their shift, it had taken all her willpower to stand firm. She'd let Mitchel have chance after chance, sacrificed her heart so many times. She wouldn't do that again.

What if I realized I made a mistake?

Benedict's words haunted her. But she'd stood her ground even as her heart shattered. If she were close to him outside the office, she'd lose herself.

"He believes that love is so temporary there is no point in vowing forever to someone. I won't be with someone who waits for everything to fall apart."

"That's fair."

Alice's words shook her. She'd expected her sister to argue with her. "What?"

"That's fair," she repeated. "Provided you're certain that he truly means that. That he isn't just terrified of losing you. Provided you aren't looking so hard for the fairy tale Mom and Dad had that you throw away your own."

"How is it wrong to want the fairy tale?" Penny huffed. "How is that so wrong?"

"Because, as I've told you so many times, it isn't real," Alice stated. "Mom and Dad love each other, but you act like they never fought. Like we didn't spend nearly a year in family counseling after Dad asked for an assignment at the Pentagon without talking to Mom. Their love is real, but it's not perfect. Nothing is."

"I gave Mitchel so many chances, and he didn't deserve any of them." Penny wiped at the tears streaking down her cheeks.

"Agreed. The festering wound of a man who shall not be named ever again deserved no second chances. But just make sure that Benedict doesn't deserve another chance. Or at the least that discussion he asked for. Be sure you are okay with never knowing what he meant when he said he'd made a mistake."

"Eavesdropping isn't a pretty trait, Alice." Penny glared at her sister. She didn't appreciate her sister articulating everything running through her own mind. Didn't appreciate that she was right.

Looking at the clock, Penny slipped from the chair.

"Help me with my hair. And if this goes horribly wrong, I'm blaming you for all eternity."

"Fine. But if it goes right, then I get to say I told you so from here to eternity!" Alice beamed. "Dress on. Let's go!"

The fundraising event was already in full swing when Penny walked in. She looked around for Benedict but didn't see him. Her eyes roamed the faces of the men and women she worked with and the donors whom she'd never met. He had to be here somewhere.

"Thank you so much for coming, and now, ladies and gentlemen, if you'd please give your attention to Dr. Benedict Denbar, the earliest champion of this effort."

Benedict walked onto the stage and her breath caught in her throat. He looked so handsome, but she could see the pain echoing through him too. Pain that she felt so deeply too.

He cleared his throat, grabbed the microphone, then stepped to the side of the podium as a projector screen lowered from the ceiling. "Tonight I want to tell you a little bit about myself. You see around here, I'm known as the closed book by my colleagues."

A few chuckles went up in the audience, and Penny felt her lips tip up slightly too.

Benedict nodded in acknowledgment of the chuckles, then continued, "This is my brother, Isiah." The image popping up on the screen behind him was of a boy who looked nearly identical to the man she loved, just younger. "Isiah lost his life in a racing accident while the love of his young life, Amber, was not quite eight weeks pregnant." The image of Amber holding her belly came up on the screen.

"I promised my brother that I'd take care of Amber—"

the image of the two of them together, her belly slightly larger came up next "—and that meant caring for the daughter he'd never meet too."

The screen went black, and Benedict exhaled a deep sigh. "I don't have any pictures of Olivia. She lived less than twenty-four hours after being born at twenty-six weeks."

The audience let out a gasp, but Benedict kept going. "That was nearly eighteen years ago. And the survival rate for infants born at twenty-six weeks is now almost ninety percent. But not every baby is so fortunate. Amber never got to hold Olivia. She was transferred to an NICU, and we lost her." Benedict closed his eyes.

Penny started toward the front of the room. She wanted him to see her, to know that she was here. This was the most personal thing he'd ever done. Opening himself up to strangers to tell people why this was so important.

He opened his eyes, and they met hers.

She nodded and offered a small smile as a way of encouragement.

"I cannot begin to describe what that loss feels like. And I know these events are meant to be fun as we raise money for good causes, but this is so important to me. I lived it. I saw the damage. If we can keep mothers and their children together when we know the pregnancy is high-risk, we have the chance to make a real difference here. So, I hope you consider donating tonight."

He set the mic down as the room erupted in claps.

"You came." Benedict rocked on his heels as he looked at her. "You came," he repeated as his eyes raked over her.

She nodded, a host of words trapped in the back of

her throat. Taking a deep breath, she reached for his hand. "That was quite the speech. Are you okay?"

"I figured it was time I stopped letting the past drive my present. And the best way to do that is to shine a light on it, let people get to know me and look toward the future with hope instead of worry."

Penny squeezed his hand. "The mistake you realized you made?"

He shook his head. "No. Well, yes. One of the many I made. The biggest mistake was telling you I thought our love might turn to hate. Because I will love you until my last breath, Penelope Greene. I know I messed up but if you'll give me another chance—"

She put a finger over his lips. "I love you too. But I should have given you a chance the other day, should have gone for coffee or whatever you wanted to do. I let my issues with the number of chances I gave Mitchel blind me."

"I can give you the fairy tale."

She smiled at him. "I don't need the fairy tale. I need you and I want so much more. A full life, all the ups and downs and everything in between with you."

"Done." Benedict kissed her cheek.

"Dr. Denbar!" The press of people around them suddenly registered.

He held her hand and she squeezed it. "Go. Speak to the crowd. I'll be here."

"Promise?"

"Promise." Penny beamed.

He dropped a light kiss to her lips. "I love you."

"I love you too." What a thrill those words were.

"And—" he winked "—that dress makes my mouth water."

"I knew it would."

EPILOGUE

"ALL RIGHT! ALL RIGHT!" the announcer called as he rang the bell. "It's the lightning round and for this round, we're going to make it interesting."

Penny raised an eyebrow to Benedict. They'd been coming to trivia most Tuesday nights for months now and the announcer had never said anything like this. He shrugged and smiled. She still got most of the answers right, but his trivia knowledge had expanded exponentially. It was the sweetest thing anyone had ever done for her.

"Since there is no hope of beating the Donut Call List team—" he pointed to their table "—we are going to split them up and make them compete against each other for this round. What do you say, folks?"

The room sent up a cheer, and Penny looked to Benedict. "Are you okay with this?"

"Sure. It'll be fun."

"Okay, but I'm going to beat you."

Benedict leaned across the table and kissed her nose. "Maybe, or maybe I have a surprise up my sleeve."

"Bring it!" Penny laughed.

Another buzzer was set in front of Benedict, and Penny placed her hand over hers.

"First question." The announcer looked to their table.

"What month is the least popular month to get married in?"

Penny struck the bell, and Benedict laughed as she answered, "January."

"Nicely done. Second question. Why is a honeymoon called a honeymoon?"

Again, Penny struck the bell and grinned at Benedict as she answered, "Couples used to drink fermented honey during the first month of their marriage as an aphrodisiac."

"Correct."

The room cheered as another point was added to the scoreboard.

"Final question."

"You ready?" Penny beamed at Benedict as she raised her hand above her buzzer.

"Absolutely."

"Penny Greene, will you marry Benedict Denbar?"

She blinked as the words left the announcer's mouth. Her mouth fell open as Benedict slid to one knee.

"What do you say, Penny? Marry me. Make me the happiest man in the entire world."

"Yes!" she called as the room erupted in cheers. "Yes. Absolutely yes!"

"You may have won the most points, but I got the best prize." Benedict slid the ring on her finger.

"Let's call it a tie." Penny grinned as she kissed him, not caring if the moment was caught on camera phones or anything else. This was her tiny piece of perfect, and she was going to enjoy every moment of it.

"Tie it is."

* * * * *

NEONATAL DOC
ON HER DOORSTEP

SCARLET WILSON

MILLS & BOON

To my partner in crime Juliette Hyland.

Loved writing a duet with you, and thanks for the expert knowledge of Washington and the use of Foggy Bottom, which still makes me laugh!

CHAPTER ONE

ALICE GREENE LET out a sigh as her cat, Sooty, strode purposefully directly across her face for the third time. It was entirely deliberate. As soon as Sooty heard Alice's alarm, he wanted to ensure that Alice remembered to feed him before she left for work for the day.

'Once,' Alice muttered under the covers. 'Just once, I forgot. Do I get this treatment for the rest of my life?'

Sooty, pleased by the attention, let out a loud meow.

Alice sat up, throwing the covers off, and grabbed her clothes for work. She was in and out of the shower in five minutes—watched by Sooty in a lazy kind of way the whole time. 'This isn't a spectator sport,' she said under her breath as she pulled her clothes on and headed into the kitchen.

She pulled the cat food from the cupboard and put a small cup's worth in Sooty's food bowl, refreshing his water too, then giving Sooty an affectionate rub at the back of his neck as he immediately started to eat.

Her little rescue black cat with a smudge of white on his coat was her only company these days. Not that she minded. Her sister, Penny, had found her happy ever after with one of the doctors they worked with at Wald Children's Hospital and Alice was happy for her. She was. Benedict Denbar had made Penny's eyes sparkle in a way that Alice had never seen before. They'd got engaged and Penny had moved in with him, leaving Alice alone in the townhouse they'd shared in Washington.

It was fine. She just needed someone else to cover half the rent, and one of her colleagues from the NICU where she worked, Mariela Martínez, was due to move in.

It would be odd sharing a home with someone other than her sister. They'd shared a room for most of their childhood, moving every three to five years since their parents were in the Army. Alice had always considered Penny her best friend, and had even followed her into nursing.

She smiled as she picked up her backpack and headed to the Metro. Penny was working today. They'd maybe even be able to have breakfast together and catch up.

Her phone buzzed as she took the short walk to the station. Alice read the message via her dating app and shook her head. Nope. Two dates with the guy she'd nicknamed the 'handsome spook' were enough. That was the thing about Washington. There were plenty of men. But the majority of them fell into two categories—members of the intelligence community, or ties with politics. It was all getting boring. The guys who worked for the intelligence agencies seemed to have a permanent level of mistrust about them, and the ones with the political ties all appeared to like talking—mainly about themselves.

Alice wanted someone fun. Someone different. Someone who didn't treat her as if she might look good on their arm. Someone who might look at her the way Benedict looked at her sister.

It was odd. For years she'd been the dating queen.

Never too serious about anyone—always getting out before feelings could be hurt. Or at least she'd tried to.

But around two years ago—right at the time Penny had found out her ex-fiancé actually had a wife and family—Alice had found herself in a sticky situation with a guy she'd dated for around six weeks. After weeks of late-night calls and strange stuff around the townhouse, she'd finally spoken to a friend of hers who was a DC cop. He'd called it stalking, and had a serious conversation with the guy, who'd sworn that Alice had encouraged him and given him a whole host of signals that she wanted the relationship to continue, and to be serious.

She hadn't. But it had made her re-evaluate almost every word she said on a date, and every single text that she sent. She never wanted to be accused of mixed signals again. She hadn't even told Penny about it at the time. She'd been staying in Ohio with her then fiancé and had enough problems of her own without Alice adding to them. And by the time Penny had dumped her ex, and moved back to Washington, everything had been over, so there didn't seem any point in bringing it up. Penny would just have worried anyhow. And at twenty-nine Alice was big enough to look after herself.

It had unsettled her. Her colleagues at work made fun of her dating apps without realising it allowed her to tell others she was looking for love, while keeping all men at a distance.

She sighed as she reached Foggy Bottom station and descended on the escalator to wait for the train. She'd spent the last few days at the NICU looking after twins. Born at twenty-four weeks, and both struggling. Years ago, babies this small wouldn't have stood a chance. But technology and medicine had long since adapted to the special needs of premature babies. Nowadays, chances for babies like these could be good—even if they needed a prolonged stay in NICU until they were ready for discharge. NICU nurses like Alice spent just as much time caring for the parents of her small babies as she did caring for the babies. Most of the parents were unprepared for their early deliveries—or had barely had a few days' notice. Ruby and Ryan's mom was certainly in the unprepared category. Alice was worried about her. She still seemed shell-shocked. It wasn't unusual. But it had been nearly a week now, and Angie still seemed distant. She'd mentioned a type of candy that was her favourite. Maybe Alice could try and pick it up for her at the station near the hospital—maybe even a coffee too. Anything to try and engage with Angie a little more and try to connect with her.

The ringtone of 'The Power of Love' by Huey Lewis sounded and she pulled her phone from her pocket, smiling. Today's tune was from the *Back to the Future* movie. She'd keep it until a workmate could work out what movie it was from, and then change to another. It was like a mini competition and Alice had a world of tunes from eighties movies lined up on her phone. She wrinkled her brow as she saw her workmate Mariela's name light up on her screen. Mariela wasn't working today, and Alice knew her well enough to know she wasn't normally an early riser.

She didn't waste time. 'What's up? Everything okay?'

Mariela's heavily accented voice seemed to rush out a thousand words at once and, coupled with the background noise of the Metro, Alice only caught fragmented parts. 'Mamá…accident…return to Spain…sorry.'

Alice struggled to hear, concentrating as best she

could. Her mind was racing. 'Do you need me to do anything to help you?'

Mariela was clearly understandably upset and Alice hated to hear her friend and workmate like this. Her brain started to claw at another tiny idea, but she pushed it aside to concentrate on what her friend was telling her.

'I think it will be months, not weeks. So I'm sorry to let you down, Alice, but I just don't know if or when I'll get back to Washington—' Her voice broke and Alice broke in.

'Mariela. Don't worry about that. Don't give it a second thought. Save all your energy for getting home and seeing your mamá. That's what matters now. I wish I could come and give you a big hug. I love you, honey. And I'm sending up prayers for you and your family.'

Mariela gave another sob. 'Thank you—and tell my babies that I'm sorry—and all our parents.'

By the time she finished the call, Alice felt wrung out. She stopped on automatic pilot and picked up a coffee for herself, her sister and for Angie, along with a multitude of candy bars for them all. Chocolate was needed at times like this.

Her head was swimming. By the time she reached NICU and stowed her bag and jacket in her locker, she could tell her workmates already knew about Mariela's mother's accident.

Hushed voices were whispering. 'It doesn't sound too good. I hope Mariela is going to be okay.'

'Can we put our heads together and cover all her shifts on a temporary basis? Does anyone mind?'

There were lots of shaking heads.

Alice took a few moments to wash her hands and then go over to Angie, who was sitting in a comfortable chair between the two NICU cribs for her babies.

She looked a little stunned when Alice handed her the coffee and a selection of candy. 'I remembered you said the other day that you liked these.'

Angie's eyes were wide and she nodded at the whispering staff. 'What's wrong? Has something happened to one of the babies?'

Alice quickly put her hand on Angie's. 'No, not at all.' She shouldn't be surprised. The parents who spent a long time in the NICU often picked up on things—and it was only natural for Angie to think the concerns were around a fellow patient.

All staff business was usually kept out of NICU, but the truth was they were all like family in here. Keeping secrets might add to Angie's worry that they were keeping something from her.

Alice shook her head. 'Mariela—the nurse who has worked with Ruby and Ryan?'

Angie nodded.

'She's heading back to Spain. Her mom has been in a road traffic accident and is in hospital. She just phoned to let us all know. The staff are just trying to cover her shifts—and they're worried for her. That's all.'

The sigh of relief was audible to them both, but Angie was instantly embarrassed and started talking quickly. 'She's such a nice girl. Is it serious? It must be if they've called her back to Spain.'

Alice bit her lip. 'We don't know all the details. So, in the meantime, we'll just all cross our fingers.'

It wasn't entirely true. Mariela's mother had sustained a serious head injury and several broken bones. But Alice didn't need to share that.

'She wanted me to tell you that she was sorry she had to leave you, Ruby and Ryan.'

'She did?'

Alice nodded. She could finally start to see some little connections being made with Angie. A quick glance at both babies' charts told her their condition was both steady. Babies in NICU could deteriorate at a moment's notice, so she never took anything for granted.

'Drink your coffee and I'll be back to help you take care of Ruby and Ryan once I've had the handover report.'

Angie gave a nod and settled back in her chair. Her skin was pale and she was clearly tired. Sleeping in a NICU was virtually impossible. It didn't matter that the myriad of beeping monitors were kept at a low level to protect the tiny babies. Parents in here were tuned into the smallest noise, their senses already on overload at being introduced to the scary, unfamiliar environment. It didn't matter that there were plenty of side rooms with proper beds for the parents to sleep in if they chose. Most didn't. And most looked similar to Angie.

Alice made her way over to the nurses' station. Tara, the charge nurse, was talking in a low voice, first running through every patient, stats, test results awaited, then giving any concerns—both about baby and about parents. When she'd finished she nodded at the rota showing on the nearby monitor. 'I've spoken to HR. Mariela will be having two weeks' leave, then will likely go onto unpaid leave for a few months. I'll see if we can get some cover. But you know how hard that is around here.'

They all nodded. Although the unit was generally kept in a quiet and smooth-functioning manner, no one could hide the emotional impact working in a place like this had on staff. Lots of staff only lasted a few years in a place like this. Losing tiny babies was devastating to the staff as well as the parents.

'Just let us know when you need cover.' Penny was at Alice's elbow. 'We can all pitch in,' she said sincerely.

Alice grinned at her. 'Your new fiancé might not like you volunteering to spend extra hours in the NICU.'

Penny shook her head. 'My new fiancé will likely be here himself, so it's fine.'

Benedict was one of the doctors in the NICU and had a strong work ethic, so Alice didn't doubt her sister's words for a second.

He appeared as if by magic behind them. 'Talking about me again?' He smiled. He nudged Alice. 'Watch out, I'll start to think my future sister-in-law might actually like me.'

Alice rolled her eyes, ignoring the buzz from her scrubs. It was likely another notification from the dating app.

'You gonna get that?' Benedict asked.

Alice shook her head. 'I'm on duty. No time for phones. Anyhow, I need to spend the next few hours finding myself a new housemate. Know anyone looking for a place?'

Benedict frowned for a second, then it was almost as if she could see the dots connecting. 'Oh, of course, I hadn't even thought of that.'

Penny reached over and put her hand on her sister's elbow. 'You know I'll help out. I don't want to see you stuck for rent.'

Alice waved her hand. Penny had only just moved in with Benedict—the last thing she wanted to do was spoil her sister's deserved happiness.

She held out her hands. 'This is a giant hospital. There must be someone around here who is looking for a perfectly hospitable, completely house-trained and well-behaved housemate.'

Benedict folded his arms, a look of amusement written all over his face as he exchanged glances with Penny. 'Wow, don't know who they might be, but I'd like to meet them.'

'I'll crack the jokes,' said Alice as she moved off, heading back to Angie and the twins. Her mind was churning. She wasn't exactly penniless. She did have an emergency stash, but she'd rather not dip into it. She'd rather find a housemate. But she wasn't desperate either. Mariela was a friend who she knew well. Agreeing to share with her had been an easy option. She'd heard too many horror tales of unknown housemates with a whole host of weird habits moving into shared properties.

The house that she'd shared with her sister was actually somewhere she loved. When she'd found the townhouse to rent in the Foggy Bottom neighbourhood of Washington she couldn't have been more delighted. The area got its name from the morning mist that rose off its southern boundary at the Potomac River. But the neighbourhood stretched right up to the West End and included the Kennedy Center for Performing Arts, a boat centre, the George Washington University Museum, the gorgeous green space of Rock Creek Park and, of course, the White House. There were a huge array of restaurants, hotels and bars. And, with the university so close, it meant the international students from across the globe lived in the accommodation nearby, giving a real community feel to the neighbourhood. The fact it was in easy walking distance of the Metro made it even better for early-morning starts or late-night finishes.

Her townhouse was bright and airy, with white walls, wooden floors throughout and an open-plan kitchen/living area on one floor. Two bedrooms and two bathrooms upstairs gave her plenty of living space, but she still was uneasy about sharing her space with someone she didn't know.

As she made her way back to Angie she noticed that the young mum was looking a little brighter. Maybe the candy and coffee pick-me-up had been a good idea. Alice would do anything she could to support her patient, hoping that, in turn, it would help Angie relax a little in the unit, and maybe become more attached to her babies.

Alice pushed all thoughts about the townhouse out of her head. Angie, Ruby and Ryan were her priority for the next few hours and they would be getting her complete and undivided attention.

Dougie MacLachlan groaned as he stared at the black door in front of him. 'Could this day get any worse?' He said the words out loud, even though no one else was listening.

He hadn't slept in two days. His first flight from Glasgow to London had been delayed, meaning he'd missed his flight to Washington and had to be rerouted. Then one of the rerouted flights had engine trouble and he'd ended up at a US airport he'd never even heard of, with even more difficulties getting to Washington. Now, it seemed the place he'd rented online had double-booked him and another couple for the same apartment. And they'd arrived first, leaving Dougie with no place to stay in a city that was completely unfamiliar to him.

He'd called the rental agency three times. A 'technical error' had been the first explanation. But when it turned out they couldn't find him another place today he'd used some pretty colourful Scottish language.

He'd dragged two huge suitcases up three flights of

stairs, and now he'd have to drag them back down. The couple who'd reached the apartment before him had been quietly smug. It hadn't helped.

He glanced at his watch. Having lost more than twenty-four hours along this journey, he was due to start work in the next hour.

He ignored his aching shoulders and his rumbling stomach and headed back to the Metro. The job at Wald Children's had come up at just the right time. It was a teaching hospital—just like the one he'd come from in London, and previously in Glasgow, and was considered to be one of the top NICUs in the country.

After a difficult year, he'd jumped at the chance of a change of scenery and a change of faces. But the one thing he wouldn't compromise on was his specialty. Dougie had fallen in love with the idea of working in a NICU before he'd even started as a medical student. Lots of people shied away from delivering specialist care to these tiny patients. But from the first moment he'd stepped inside a NICU he'd known this was where he wanted to work. Everything else had just been a path to his specialty.

He'd grown up in one of the rougher parts of Glasgow. Whilst other people might paint a dark picture of the area, Dougie had been raised in a community where people looked out for each other and walked freely in and out of each other's houses. He'd been bright, and his friends and family had all encouraged him to study. University tuition fees were covered for Scottish students, and medicine had been within his reach.

It had been quite a shock when, the day after he'd celebrated his exam results and acceptance into medical school, his childhood friend Lisa had gone into labour. Her hidden pregnancy and subsequent lack of antenatal care had haunted him ever since, and when she'd delivered her daughter at twenty-eight weeks Dougie had been one of the people who'd sat with her through the last few weeks of the summer in the sweltering NICU.

He'd been fascinated—trying to drink in as much knowledge as possible, while understanding the confusion, guilt and fatigue of his childhood friend. His goddaughter Trixie was now a healthy fourteen-year-old who could literally talk for Scotland and she made every day brighter. She'd made him follow her on all the latest social media channels and regularly filmed clips of herself and her friends dancing in various parts of the city to the latest tunes—usually in some kind of costume. So far they had been clowns, zombies, nuns and priests, rival football teams and finally gangsters. Dougie couldn't keep up. Truth was he was scared to. If he stayed still long enough she might try and drag him into one of those fifteen-second dance clips, and Dougie had as much natural rhythm as a kitten in clogs.

He sighed and started dragging his suitcases down the stairs and back to the Metro, which was more crowded than before. Peak travel time. Great. Just what he needed.

By the time he reached Wald's all he wanted to do was dump his bags and find a corner to crawl into—preferably a corner with food.

But this was his first day in a new job, and Dougie was old enough to know that first impressions counted. He dragged his cases to Admin, then HR, signing everything required and getting a formal ID. If the staff were surprised at his rumpled jeans and T-shirt that he'd travelled in, they were polite enough not to mention it.

Four wrong turns later, he still hadn't found the staff changing room. Worse than that, the smell of cooked food was drifting tantalisingly along a corridor somewhere. Normal people were clearly eating breakfast.

After dragging his cases past the large sign to the NICU for the fifth time, he gave up and used his new ID to scan entry.

Heads looked up as he dragged his cases in behind him and dumped them to the side. Coffee. He could smell coffee somewhere.

A slim nurse with dark hair in a high ponytail and bright pink scrubs moved away from a NICU crib, her head slightly tilted.

'Can I help you?' She was noticeably scanning his body. In his brain-addled confusion he wondered if she was about to say something about his rumpled state or if she was checking him out, before he realised exactly what she was looking for—an ID badge.

He pulled it from the pocket of his jeans. 'Douglas MacLachlan. I'm your new doctor. I was trying to get changed and then report to Benedict Denbar. But someone decided to hide the changing rooms from me.'

There was the hint of a smirk. She gave a nod. 'Alice Greene. NICU nurse.' She raised her eyebrows just a touch. 'Having a bad day?'

He resisted the temptation to snap. He was tired. He was grouchy. He just wanted to get this day started so he could hopefully reach the other end without slumping in a corner. If he ever found the changing rooms in this place, at this rate it was likely to be where he would spend the night.

An older blonde woman appeared with her brow furrowed. 'Alice, it's time for your break. Why don't you try and sort out our new doc?'

Dougie straightened up. 'I've still to report to Benedict Denbar.'

The woman waved her hand. 'Don't worry about that. I'll tell Benedict you're around.' She glanced at the cases. 'And we try not to encourage our staff to move right in.'

As if his humiliation wasn't complete, his stomach gave a loud grumble. He opened his mouth to reply, but Alice had moved next to him and gave him an unexpected nudge. 'Tara's our charge nurse. Her word is law. Let's go.'

As he made a grab for his cases again, Alice held open the door for him. She couldn't hide the amusement on her face as she led him down a corridor that seemed familiar. 'Here—' she pointed '—locker rooms. But I can tell you right now. There's no locker big enough for those cases.'

He sighed, not even wanting to start to explain. 'Thanks. Are there showers in there?'

She nodded. 'Want me to grab you something from the canteen while you shower?'

He hesitated. It was a nice offer. But he'd only just met this nurse. He shook his head. 'Thanks, but no. I'll get showered and changed and head back to the NICU.'

'Do you have your own scrubs?'

It was a completely normal question. A lot of staff who'd worked in NICUs for years wore their own distinctive scrubs. But for some reason it threw him. His mind couldn't quite find the answer.

She gave a little shake of her head. 'No matter, but if you don't, the laundry trolley with towels and fresh scrubs is on the left-hand side of the room.'

Before he had a chance to form words, she strolled down the corridor in the direction of the food he was craving but had been too proud to ask for.

Darn it. Dougie flung the door to the locker room

open, instantly flinching when it banged off the wall behind. He glanced around quickly, relieved to find the room was currently empty. He did have scrubs in one of his cases, but he had no idea which one and he didn't feel inclined to open them and start rifling through them right now.

There was a stack of blue scrubs on the linen trolley that Alice had directed him to, so he grabbed a set, along with a towel, and headed to the showers.

His skin was instantly relieved by the rush of hot water on his skin, and he scrubbed himself briskly with the shower gel on the wall, washing away any aromas or sweat he'd picked up on his long travels. As he washed his face he realised he hadn't had the chance to shave. By the time he'd found his shaving gear and started it would all take far too long. So Dougie just closed off the shower, dried off and pulled on the scrubs. At least he felt a bit more awake and his brain less foggy. He'd needed that.

He put his wallet, passport and other valuables in one of the lockers and walked back out of the room into the bright corridor. It was currently quiet, so for one minute he closed his eyes, put his hands on his hips and arched his back, stretching it out to try and work out all the knots that had formed from sitting in uncomfortable airport seats and cramped plane rows.

'This some kind of pre-match warm-up?' came the amused American voice.

Alice had reappeared and was carrying a brown paper bag and a takeaway cup.

'What?' Not the politest reply, but he was getting tired of being this staff member's entertainment. He hadn't paid much attention earlier, but now they were out of the unit in the bright fresh lights in the corridor Alice Greene was more than a little eye-catching.

Her dark hair swung in a ponytail, held in place by some bright, crinkly thing that would look more appropriate in a disco. She had clear skin, full lips and brown eyes that seemed to have very long eyelashes.

She laughed as she looked at him and pushed the cup and bag towards him. 'Don't you have wrestling in Scotland? You looked like you were doing a pre-match warm-up. Anyhow, I know you said you didn't want anything, but you seemed kinda cranky, so I got you some food.'

As he took the offered items she didn't wait to see what he would say, just kept walking back towards the unit.

'Thank you,' he called after her, a bit later than he should have.

She glanced over her shoulder. 'Try and crack a smile,' she said. 'That cool Scottish accent will only work for so long.'

He breathed, inhaling the coffee and taking a sip. The bag was a different story. He looked cautiously inside. A bagel and cream cheese. Not his first choice. But beggars couldn't be choosers.

What did she mean—'crack a smile'? Was he coming over as grumpy? He wasn't trying to, but the last twenty-four hours had just been one disaster after another. As for the accent comment, he'd have to think about that one later. He watched her swaying hips for a moment before realising what he was doing and gave himself a shake. His stomach gave another growl and he knew it was time to concentrate on the food. He'd taken two bites before he was even near the NICU again and was finished long before he walked through the door.

A tall man with dark skin looked up and gave a beaming smile. 'Dr MacLachlan, come on over.'

It was the first spark of joy that he'd felt since getting here. By this point, Dougie was clearly a bit late—but this guy seemed totally chilled about it. Maybe he'd heard the suitcase story.

They shook hands warmly as Benedict introduced himself. He was clearly as passionate about his role as Dougie was. He showed him around the unit, logged him into the electronic systems and gave him a crash course in ordering tests and reviewing results. He gave him his pager, showed him the on-call rota and introduced him to as many people as possible. Dougie was feeling a bit more awake, and did his best to remember everything he was being told. He'd really have liked to scribble a few notes, but didn't want to seem as if he couldn't remember simple facts.

The NICU layout was familiar, as were most of the protocols and procedures. Once he was finally left to his own devices, Dougie took a bit of time to go through the current patients' records. A few babies in here had reached their hundred-day milestone. Whilst in some ways it was a cause for celebration, it was also a clear indication of how sick some of these babies had been.

Dougie blinked as a woman in patterned scrubs appeared in front of him. 'Pleased to meet you, Dr MacLachlan, I'm Penny Greene.'

The expression on his face must have said it all. At first, he'd thought Alice was joking with him and had just changed scrubs. But after a few seconds he realised this was an entirely different person. The nurse laughed and waved a hand. 'Yes, she's my sister. And yes, some people think we look like twins, but I promise you we are very different.' She leaned over and whispered, 'I'll give you a hint; we have different coloured eyes.'

Dougie reached over and shook her hand, taking in her blue eyes, just as Benedict moved back over and gave her a nudge with his hip. 'Dr MacLachlan's got more pressing worries than telling the two of you apart. I hear he's got house troubles.'

There was something in the way they stood close and looked at each other that told him these two were very familiar with each other.

Penny's eyes widened. 'What do you mean, you've got house trouble?'

Dougie sighed. 'The place I was supposed to be renting was double-booked. My flights were delayed and rerouted, which meant that by the time I arrived the other people had already arrived and had moved in. It seems that finders are keepers.'

Penny shook her head. 'That's ridiculous. Did you contact the rental company?'

He nodded. 'Seems like I've moved to Washington in prime season. They couldn't guarantee they could find me another place.'

'So what are you going to do?' Penny gave a strange glance at Benedict.

'I guess I'll need to find a hotel for the night and try and sort it out in the next few days.' The mere thought of it made him tired. 'Know any hotels close by?'

Alice came over and handed a chart to Benedict, which he glanced at and signed electronically. He could hear the sound of a phone vibrating in her pocket but she ignored it. Dougie shifted uncomfortably, watching as Alice moved to the drug trolley and started drawing up medicine. Things seemed very casual around here.

Penny pressed her lips together. 'I might know somewhere that you could rent at short notice.' She hesitated for a split second. 'As long as you don't mind sharing.'

'My only criteria right now is somewhere that has a bed.'

Penny gave Benedict that look again, then they both turned their heads to Alice, who was locking the drug cupboard with her medicines stored in a disposable tray.

As if she sensed their gazes, she looked up. 'What?'

'Dr MacLachlan is stranded,' said Penny. 'He has nowhere to stay.'

Something flickered behind Alice's eyes. She looked over at Dougie and shook her head. 'No,' she said without thinking. She even took a step back.

Benedict moved over and beamed at her. 'Come on, Alice. It's perfect timing. You need someone to rent a room at your townhouse, and Dr MacLachlan is looking for somewhere to stay.'

'Dougie,' he said automatically. He didn't want everyone to spend all their time calling him Dr MacLachlan. He shifted his shoulders uncomfortably. This was all getting incredibly awkward incredibly quickly.

'He's grumpy,' she went on.

'I'm not grumpy,' he retorted.

Alice waved her hand. 'Well, you were definitely hangry then.'

'I'm not any more, though, thanks to you.'

She stared at him. He stared back.

He wanted to laugh out loud. How on earth had he got himself in this position? He didn't want to share a place with someone from his brand-new NICU.

'I don't even know him. He might have bad habits.'

This was like a playground fight.

'It's fine. I'll find a place to stay. I'm sure it won't take long. The rental agency might come through for me.' He pulled his phone from his pocket, silently praying that he'd missed a call, a text or an email. His phone screen was annoyingly blank.

'Don't give it a thought,' he continued. 'Last place I want to go is someplace that I'm not welcome.'

Alice flinched as if she'd been stung. 'Brutal,' she said quickly.

He had a horrible feeling that as workmates they weren't going to get along at all.

Then she let out a sigh and folded her arms. 'Do you smoke?'

'No.'

'Do you have weird music taste?'

He almost laughed at the bizarre question. 'No.'

'Do you leave everything at your backside?'

This time he did burst out laughing. 'I haven't heard that expression in years! And no, my mother trained me well. I do know how to pick up after myself.'

Alice shrugged and pointed at her chest. 'Army brat. Not many places we haven't lived. I've picked up lots of expressions.'

Her sister moved over next to her. 'Go on, Alice. It will help you out of a bind.'

A look of annoyance flickered over Alice's face.

'I can bake. Red velvet muffins are my speciality,' said Dougie. He was actually enjoying the toing and froing. He got the impression that, although she'd been caught unawares, she wasn't entirely as inhospitable as she was acting. The last thing he'd ever want to do was be an unwelcome guest in someone's home.

Her eyebrows lifted. 'How about banana loaf?'

He nodded. Not entirely sure he could. But anyone could search a recipe.

'Do you like cats?'

This could be a trick question. He wouldn't put it past her. But he pasted a smile on his face because this answer was going to be true. 'I like cats, but cats *adore* me.'

She looked at him suspiciously. 'I'll give you a week's trial.'

A week. That would give him enough time to read the riot act to the rental agency and give them a chance to make up for their mistake. He tried to ignore the fact that they hadn't seemed too bothered at all this morning about their error.

'A week's trial is generous,' he said, not even trying to pretend that every muscle in his body wasn't relaxing at the thought of having somewhere to put his head down tonight. 'Thank you.'

She picked up the drug tray and wagged her finger at him. 'Don't make me regret it.' She moved across the unit and back to the babies in her care.

'Perfect,' Penny said, smiling. She seemed relieved. And Dougie wondered if he should ask why.

Benedict handed him some notes. 'I'd like you to review these patients so we can have a chat about them later at our NICU hub meeting.'

Dougie nodded and took the names of the babies offered. He was used to working this way. It wasn't unusual for staff to gather and review patients together. Often opinions from all staff helped—other NICU specialists, nurses and doctors could give insights and encourage a whole team approach. As Dougie scanned the notes and records the hairs on the back of his neck started to prickle.

No, he told himself. *Stop it*. There was no reason to start with thoughts like that. This was Washington, not London. An entirely new city, and an entirely fresh start.

And he tried to keep that firmly in his head for the rest of the day. He couldn't let the demons of the past destroy his future.

CHAPTER TWO

IT WASN'T UNTIL a few hours later that Dougie finally realised he had no idea what kind of place Alice lived in, how far away it was, how much the rent was, or any of the important things he likely should have asked.

When his shift finished he handed over to the on-call doctor. He felt a little more comfortable now. In the last few hours he'd tried to familiarise himself with as many of the systems and procedures as possible. All while secretly auditing them in his head for any possible flaws. But systems seemed good here. Guidelines and safety signs were visible all around the NICU. The emergency trolley was clearly labelled. All equipment stowed safely, and drug keys kept by the nurse in charge of the unit. He hadn't spotted anything that gave him cause for concern.

When he finally let go of his thoughts, he saw Alice pacing near the door and realised she must be waiting for him. He strode quickly across the unit.

'Sorry, let me just grab my things.'

He felt like a teenager who'd missed their curfew by the look she gave him and hurried to the changing rooms to throw on his clothes and grab his suitcases. The coffee and food throughout the day, as well as the introduction to a new unit, had wakened up his sleep-deprived brain, but as soon as they stepped out into the warm evening air it was like being hit by a tidal wave of jetlag.

Alice gave him a sideways glance. 'Give me one of those cases.'

He shook his head. 'It's fine.'

'It's not fine, Douglas. You look like death warmed over.' Her warm hand reached over, brushing against his, and took it firmly from his hands.

He took a few missteps then shook his head, a tired smile on his face. 'It's not Douglas. It's Dougie.'

Her eyebrows arched. She let out a half-laugh. 'What?'

'It's just the way you say it. It sounds so... Scottish. Doog-hee.' She drew out the sounds.

Dougie shot her an unimpressed glance. 'Maybe it sounds Scottish because it is, and so am I. And it's not Doog-hee. It's Dougie,' he said, knowing it sounded identical to the way she'd just drawled out his name, but entirely ignoring that fact.

'Right.' Alice's one-word answer told him to give up now.

They reached the Metro and he glanced at the stairs. 'It's only a few stops,' Alice said over her shoulder.

He felt around his pockets, praying he could find some change. He'd changed money but had made the mistake of not asking for a mix of notes, meaning most of his cash was in hundred dollar bills.

'I'll get it,' she said. She was beginning to look a little exasperated with him. And he got it. He did. He'd been pushed on her by her sister for reasons unknown to him. But he was too tired and didn't feel as if he should spend the whole time apologising to her.

'Thanks,' he murmured as they headed to a platform,

where the train came along a few moments later. She was true to her word and a few stops later they came out at another station.

Dougie blinked as he looked at the sign. It was as if he'd stepped out into some surreal dream. Maybe he'd fallen asleep on the train? 'You've got be joking?'

'What?' asked Alice as she dragged his suitcase along the platform, the wheels making an unhealthy noise.

'Foggy Bottom?' He couldn't believe he was saying the words. 'This place is called Foggy Bottom?' He started laughing, a belly laugh that bubbled up from deep inside him.

Alice gave a wave of her hand as if she'd heard all this a million times before. 'Yeah, so what? It's famous. Haven't you heard of it?'

But he was still laughing, imagining his childhood friends back in Scotland if they'd known that such a place existed. It didn't matter how juvenile it was. He was always going to find this funny.

He kept staring at the sign as he pulled his other case along, almost running straight into the back of Alice.

'Are you done now?' she asked angrily.

'Probably not,' he admitted. 'This would be hours of fun back in Scotland.'

'I wouldn't come to Scotland and make fun of the places that you live in.'

'Didn't you just make fun of how I say my name?'

There was a few seconds' silence. She blew a piece of hair from her face, looking annoyed. 'Touché,' she finally said, before turning and heading for the exit.

He dragged his case along silently, secretly wanting to ask how far it was to her place, but not wanting to give her the satisfaction.

When she finally stopped at the entrance of a smart townhouse he was pleasantly surprised. Inside, the white walls, wooden floors and open-plan style gave a real sense of space. The kitchen and living areas blended into one, with plenty of windows to let in light. The whole home was clean and comfortable and he sent a silent prayer upwards after his earlier experiences.

'Bedrooms are upstairs,' she said. 'Yours will be the one on the right. It's got its own bathroom, but we need to share the space down here. Do you want something to eat?'

He looked over at her in surprise that she was being hospitable. There had been an uncomfortable edge to Alice ever since she'd agreed to let him stay. Truth was, he still planned on looking for somewhere else.

'You don't need to feed me,' he said, truly not wishing to be any more trouble.

She opened her cupboards and the first thing that struck was how bare they were. 'I'm not really the plan ahead type,' she said. 'I have—' she held up one hand '—noodles or popcorn.' She put down the packets and opened the fridge. 'Or eggs, some salad and strawberries.'

'Eggs and strawberries,' he repeated. 'Interesting combination.'

She gave a shrug. 'It's not like I knew I was about to have a new guest.'

'Someone else from NICU was supposed to be moving in with you?'

'Yeah.' Alice gave a sigh. 'But Mariela is a foodie. She would have moved in with a load of groceries to make great Italian foods. To be honest, I was kinda counting on it.'

He nodded understandingly. 'To be honest too, Alice, I'm knackered. But I'd like to eat something before I go

to bed. How about we pick up some takeaway? I saw
a pizza place just down the street.' He looked down at
his clothes. 'How about we get changed and head out?'

Alice actually looked relieved. 'Sure, give me five
minutes.'

Dougie lifted both cases and carried them up the
stairs. The bedroom was bigger than he'd expected.
It had the same pale wood floor and a large bed with
white bedding that looked good enough just to flop on.
There was plenty of cupboard and drawer space and he
opened his first suitcase and grabbed out some jeans
and a T-shirt. His wash bag was near the top so he carried his things into the en suite bathroom and washed
his face and hands, brushing his teeth and changing his
clothes. It was odd what a relief it was to put his things
somewhere—even if it was temporary.

As he turned around he realised there was a bunch of
bright pink flowers in a short white vase on the window
ledge. Alice must have bought them for her colleague
who should have moved in. It was a nice touch and even
though he sensed she didn't appreciate the situation he
hoped he'd be able to make sure they could be comfortable around each other.

As he looked about the room the door opened slightly
and a black cat with a white smudge wandered in, eyeing him suspiciously. He bent down and gave the cat a
scratch. It kept staring at him with wary eyes but didn't
move away. 'Hi there,' he said softly.

He splashed some water through his hair, dampen-
ing down the slight curl. He'd need to find a barber in
the city at some point.

The cat had now jumped on his bed with an air of
superiority and curled up where his pillow was. Dougie
shook his head and smiled. With one final glance at the
bed, he made his way back downstairs.

* * *

Alice was still questioning all this. She was sure this new Scottish doctor was fine. But she'd wanted to share her place with someone that she knew and trusted. Someone who wouldn't care if they caught her in her underwear or nightclothes walking through the house en route to raid the kitchen. It didn't help that she found the accent sexy, or that she'd noticed just how attractive Douglas—no, Dougie—actually was.

Did he have a girlfriend, a fiancée, a wife? She hadn't noticed a ring but presumed if he were married he might have brought his wife with him.

'Hey.' His footsteps sounded on the stairs and she tried not to notice he'd changed into black jeans and a black T-shirt that showed off his build and made him look like some kind of movie star. Great. 'I met your cat.'

'Sooty. Wondered where he'd gone. Did he scratch you?'

He shook his head. 'Not at all. He's curled up on the bed as if he owns the place.'

'He does…kinda. If he doesn't like you—we'll know soon.'

Dougie gave a maddeningly easy smile. 'I told you. Cats love me.'

She wasn't entirely sure if he was being serious or not. But at the end of the day Sooty would let him know who was boss.

'Let me pick the pizza place,' she said quickly.

'Of course,' he said. 'You know everywhere. And I'll try and pick up some groceries tomorrow.'

She should have planned better. If Mariela had been moving in, they would likely have gone grocery shopping together once Alice had got home from work.

But it hardly seemed like the thing to suggest to a guy who was clearly tired and had two large cases to battle through the Washington Metro.

As they walked along the street it was clear Dougie was taking in all his surroundings. 'Which way to the White House? Where's the George Washington Museum?' The stream of questions was endless. She pointed out a few other places. 'The area down there is mainly full of tourists, the food places overpriced. If you go down that way, there's a wholefoods place and a few market stores, and another block down there's a great place for bread and desserts.

'If you want clothes stores, you'll have to go into the city centre. There's an open-air plaza there with a lot of high-end stores.'

Dougie just gave a nod as he kept looking about. 'Just trying to get my bearings,' he said.

She gave him a sideways glance. 'You said something earlier…knockered?'

He laughed. 'Knackered. Good Scots word. Tired—actually, it really means more than tired. It basically means you could sleep on the edge of a cliff.'

'How come you're so tired?'

He sighed. 'My plane from Scotland was delayed, meaning I missed my flight from London. Then they rerouted me, but that flight had engine trouble and we had to reroute again. I was travelling for more than twenty-four hours. Then, of course—' he gave a wave of his hand '—someone else is staying in the place I was supposed to be renting.'

She blinked. 'Have they given you a refund?'

He jerked a little. The thought had clearly not crossed his mind. 'I haven't even asked,' he admitted. 'I was just so wound up at the time and realised I had to get to the hospital. The agency weren't exactly helpful. Couldn't even promise they'd find me alternative accommodation. I'll get back onto them in the morning.'

She gave him a smile which she hoped didn't show her true feelings. 'It's a bad time of year. This is when most of the international university students move in.'

Dougie groaned. 'Well. You've given me a week's trial. I promise I'll try and find somewhere to go in the next week.' He licked his lips and she tried not to focus on them, keeping her eyes on the rest of the people on the sidewalks. 'I know you feel kind of strong-armed into giving me a place to stay. And I'm sorry about that—but I am grateful. I just want a place to get my head down and get some actual sleep before my shift tomorrow. I hate the foggy feeling in my brain that comes from no sleep. You can't be like that in a NICU. I've always believed it's a place you have to be at over a hundred per cent. Nothing can be missed. Nothing overlooked. The condition of these kids can change in a gust of wind. It's so, so important that I'm on it.'

The skin on her arms prickled. There was something about the way he said those words. She could hear the commitment and passion for his job. Something she knew instantly would be unquestionable. But there was something else in there. Something she couldn't quite put her finger on.

'We're always on it.' The words came out automatically. Defensively. Even though she didn't entirely mean them to. But Dougie shot her what she read as a questioning glance—as if he wasn't quite convinced by what she said. And that *did* make her defensive. She worked in what she considered one of the best NICUs in the country. Dougie was lucky to have got a position there.

'I just need a chance to shake off the jetlag,' he said.

But there was something in his tone she didn't like. She gestured towards the pizza place to their left and tried not to bristle as he automatically held the door open for her. Her grandmother would have called it good old-fashioned manners. But her feminist side wanted to tell him she could hold open her own doors. It didn't help that two servers behind the counter shot each other a completely readable glance. *Hot.* Alice instantly felt their eyes on her, the split-second head-to-toe glance, wondering what Alice had, to have captured the almost movie star in their midst.

As if she were in some kind of B-movie, things happened exactly the way she could have predicted. She was instantly ignored. One of the servers leaned across the counter to talk to Dougie and ask him for his order, then her eyes widened at the accent and both started talking at once. 'Are you from Scotland? Ireland? We love your accent! Say something again? It's fabulous. It's just like Gerard Butler, or James McAvoy.'

Alice moved up to the counter alongside him. She was wearing jeans and a red top. She might not look like a female movie star, but she knew she could scrub up just as well as any of these girls. 'I had you more as a Billy Connolly myself,' she said quietly, referring to the Scottish, much older, comedian.

Dougie let out a laugh, and while he did that she quickly gave her order. It was the first time she'd seen him look truly relaxed. And she hated the way that made her stomach clench with an unwelcome wave of attraction. That was the last thing she needed at work. Her sister might have been happy to date a guy from work and get in a relationship with him, but Alice had always thought that far too messy. She preferred to keep her dating habits well away from the work place.

He gave a nod in agreement with her words. 'I think my friends back home might agree. But you do me too much credit. Nowhere near as talented as him. He's a legend.'

'Well, hopefully, you have an equal level of skill in your own specialty. Because that's where they're needed. Our hospital is renowned for having one of the best NICUs in the country. We need staff who can keep up.'

There. She'd drawn a line in the sand. Maybe this guy was just pushing all the wrong buttons. Maybe it was because she did feel things had kind of slipped out of her control and he'd been foisted on her by her sister without any real discussion. Or maybe she was just feeling conflicted by the fact she might find him a little attractive.

Whatever it was, there was something about Douglas MacLachlan she couldn't quite put her finger on. He wasn't exactly saying anything wrong out loud. But she felt as if there was a deeper meaning behind some of his words. An implication. And she wanted to put her cards completely on the table.

Dougie was leaning on the counter now and he turned back towards her. It was the first time she'd really got a proper look at those bright blue eyes of his. His eyebrows were raised. 'Oh, I think I can keep up. I just like to make sure everything is happening the way it should.'

'And why wouldn't it?' She couldn't help the snappy tone. 'Our NICU functioned well before you got here, and it will function just as well after you leave.'

Maybe it was a bit much. The girls behind the counter took a step back and exchanged glances again—thoughts of flirtation clearly vanishing. Alice frowned, but stood her ground. She'd said it now, and had no plans to back down.

'Safety first, Nurse Greene,' he said in a low voice. 'We have the most vulnerable patients on the planet and it's up to us to protect them.'

Alice swallowed, feeling the steam rapidly rising from her toes all the way up to her ears. She was pretty sure her face was turning the same colour as her shirt. This guy was clearly going to drive her crazy. She had to work with him. But that didn't mean she had to live with him.

Then he gave her a killer smile. But it didn't quite reach his eyes. It was almost as if he'd remembered he was still slightly at her mercy and it wouldn't do to make her mad before he'd finally got the night's sleep that he craved.

She bit her bottom lip. He'd told her a few times he was tired. She'd already seen him a bit cranky earlier today when he hadn't eaten. Alice took a breath and tried to imagine how she might feel in the same circumstances.

Overlong journey. No proper food. Having to turn up at new workplace, dragging her cases behind her, with no real place to stay that night, and completing a shift at work.

Okay. Maybe it was time to give him just the tiniest bit of leeway. But this was a one-off.

'Why did you come to Washington?' she asked. His eyes flashed and that was when she knew she'd hit a nerve with what she thought was a fairly benign question.

'Wanted a change.' The words seemed forced.

'You were in London somewhere, weren't you?'

'St Gabriel's.' The words were still tight. It was clear this was something he didn't want to discuss but all of

Alice's spider senses were tingling. She was curious. She wanted to push. This guy had made a sideways comment about processes being in place.

Just at that moment her phone started to buzz. She pulled it from her pocket. It was an unknown number. 'Hello?'

There was a crackle and feedback at the end of the line. Then…nothing.

Strange. She gave a shrug and put it back in her pocket. One of the girls behind the counter pushed forward two pizza boxes. 'That's your order.'

Dougie reached out and took them both before she had a chance. 'Thanks,' he said, turning around and holding open the door for her—again.

Alice followed him outside and they started back along the street. The smell from the pizza boxes drifted towards her and her stomach growled loudly.

'Hey,' he said over his shoulder, 'you're starting to sound like me.'

She gave a weak smile. 'Maybe. But it's been a long day. I don't have much drinks-wise back at the house. Coffee, some soda, maybe a beer?'

Dougie groaned. 'A beer. A beer would be brilliant.' He closed his eyes, even though they were walking along the street. 'Now, if you had a sports channel that would make the world complete.'

'Ah,' she said, trying to hide the smile on her face. 'I think you'll find I have a cable-wide ban on sports.'

His eyes widened and he turned to her in surprise. 'Really?'

'Absolutely. My house, my rules. Movies or music.'

'That was it.' A huge grin spread across his face. 'I've got it. The ringtone on your phone. It's an oldie.'

She gave him a curious glance. 'It is,' was all she was prepared to give away.

'But I recognised it from a film.'

Her eyebrow arched. 'Really? What film? And be careful here, if you guess wrong you lose.'

'What do I lose?'

'Our NICU game. It's our latest fun. Pick a ringtone from an old movie and you get to keep it until someone guesses correctly.' She patted her pocket. 'I'm kind of fond of this one, so I hope you're about to guess wrong.' She held up her finger. 'And you only get one guess a day. So choose wisely.'

'Maybe I'll save my guess. Give you time to play the tune a bit longer.'

She nodded slowly. 'Interesting tactic. But if you want to guess, know that you have to join the game from that point on. There's no free guesses here. You're either in or you're out.'

She couldn't pretend she wasn't still curious about what had annoyed him earlier. But it seemed to have passed just as quickly as she'd noticed it. When he wanted to be, Dougie MacLachlan could be almost charming.

'Oh, I'm in,' he said without a second's hesitation.

'That was confident. Are you an eighties fan?'

'Seventies, eighties, nineties, and everything else.' He breathed deeply, clearly inhaling the pizza. 'This could be dangerous territory when we get back. If I can't watch some sports, I can challenge you to a movie marathon.'

'You think?'

'Absolutely.'

They'd reached the townhouse again and she pulled out her keys. It only took a few minutes to rearrange the pizza boxes on the small table in the main room in front of the TV. Alice grabbed the two solitary beers that she had in the bottom of the fridge and opened them, carrying them through and lifting the remote control. She flicked the television on and selected a streaming service, where she flicked through some older movies.

'Action, sci-fi, cute, romance...' she started.

'I'd love to go for sci-fi, but let's have something out of season.'

'You want a Christmas movie?'

He shook his head and lifted a finger. 'No, but the ultimate Christmas movie is *Die Hard* and we're not going to fight about that.'

She burst out laughing as she lifted a slice of pizza. 'So what did you have in mind? Something for summer—*Jaws*?'

'No, let's go witches. A bit of *Hocus Pocus*.'

She looked at him in surprise and gave a slow nod. 'Interesting choice.'

'Surprised?'

Intrigued, she wanted to say, but kept it to herself. She found the movie and started playing it, but after a few slices of pizza and half a bottle of beer she could literally see Dougie wilting beside her.

'You should go on up to bed.'

He sighed and nodded. 'You're right. I'm too tired. Sorry, but I need to make sure I feel fine for tomorrow.' He glanced at his watch. It was barely ten o'clock. 'You're twelve hours tomorrow. Maybe you should turn in too.'

And just as she'd thought Dougie MacLachlan might actually be bearable, he'd annoyed her again. She stood up abruptly, lifting the pizza boxes.

'You worry about you, and let me worry about me,' she said smartly.

He looked for a second as if he might answer her back, and she was ready for him. But Dougie gave a nod and headed to the stairs. ''Night,' was the only word he uttered as he went.

And, just like that, Alice Greene knew this was never going to work out.

CHAPTER THREE

DOUGIE WAS FINALLY well rested and feeling wide awake. Alice had been a little off with him last night and things had been a bit awkward on the way to work. But she'd talked him through the subway lines and stops, where to get a ticket that lasted all day or week, and given him a few safety tips.

The route seemed straightforward and he did wonder if he might jog into work and shower and change once there. But that could all be worked out later.

There were fifty-two beds in this state-of-the-art Level IV NICU, with a whole host of specialists and staff on duty at any one time. Dougie was part of a rota of twenty-eight doctors. There was more than three times that number of nursing staff. And a whole load of other specialist paediatric staff—respiratory therapists, pharmacists—who all swiped in and out of the unit throughout the day.

Infection control measures were good—they had to be when the footfall could mean numerous staff required to deliver care to the multiple babies. The noise level was a low persistent hum of quiet conversations and machines working. It was rare to hear anything loud in this environment. All staff were conscious of protecting their vulnerable patients.

Dougie had been given a brief on the patients he was responsible for and was making his way around the unit, introducing himself to each of the parents and chatting through how their baby or babies were doing. He realised quite quickly that two of his patients, Ruby and Ryan, born at twenty-four weeks, were also being cared for by Alice. She was dressed today in pale blue scrubs with teddy bears on them.

He took one glance at the young mum sitting beside the incubators and pulled up a chair. 'Hi, Angie, I'm Dougie MacLachlan. I'm a new neonatologist and will be helping to care for Ruby and Ryan.'

'How long have you been a neonatologist?' came the quick answer. Straight to the point. He could understand that.

'Six years.'

She let out a sigh. He knew immediately it was relief. Most hospitals like this were teaching hospitals. Parents could often meet a whole host of people involved in the care of their baby, and whilst no one liked to object to people learning, parents in NICU were understandably anxious.

'Where are you from?'

'Scotland, but I last worked in London in a NICU there.'

Alice moved over, giving him a nod, and started talking in a low but bright tone to Ruby as she tended to her.

'How do you feel Ruby and Ryan are doing?'

He always started like this. He'd learned it was really important to ascertain what parents understood about their babies, and to get some insight into how they were feeling about things.

Angie blinked back unshed tears. He'd checked her notes and could see that there was no mention of a father and very little family support whilst she'd been in NICU with her babies. 'Ryan is sickest,' she said quickly. 'They put a feeding tube in but he just doesn't seem to have any energy at all. His skin is peeling and I hardly even want to touch him in case I'm hurting him.'

Dougie looked up and Alice's wide brown eyes met his. 'We've talked about this, Angie,' she said reassuringly. 'You know that we want you to have as much contact with Ryan as is safe. His breathing, temperature and blood pressure are still being monitored. As soon as we're sure it will be safe, you'll be able to hold him for yourself for longer times.'

Angie blinked and turned away. 'Is there anyone else we can invite to come into the unit to support you?' Dougie asked.

'No.' It was a definite one-word answer.

Dougie persisted. He sat patiently with Angie and talked her through first Ryan's care, and then Ruby's. Alice was working on both babies as they spoke, and every now and then broke in gently to ask Angie if she wanted to assist with something.

Angie was reluctant, but one glance between him and Alice let him know they were in agreement—this was fear, nothing else.

When it reached a certain time, Alice glanced at the clock on the wall. 'Angie, I'm going to take a break. Would you like to come down to the canteen with me and get something to eat?'

Angie shook her head immediately.

'Dr MacLachlan will stay with the babies,' said Alice. He had a whole host of other things to do, but was quick to offer reassurance.

'I'm happy to,' he said. Anything to try and persuade this frail young woman to get something to eat.

But Angie was determined. 'No, I'm fine.'

Alice gave her a wide smile. 'Well, I'll pick you up something when I'm down there.' She didn't wait for Angie to give her a reply. Just finished up what she was doing, washed her hands and recorded a few things in the electronic record.

Dougie finished a few things himself then followed her down to the canteen since Angie clearly wasn't going to move.

She glanced over her shoulder in surprise when he called her name. Then watched with a smile on her face as he picked up some bacon and made some toast. 'Very British,' she said. 'The bagel and cream cheese didn't work out for you?'

'I was very grateful,' he said carefully as he pressed a button on the coffee machine. 'Can we talk about Angie?'

Alice moved her tray along and added some fruit and yoghurt. 'Sure,' she said as they paid and headed over to a table.

She was interested that he'd followed her down to the canteen to have this conversation.

'What are your thoughts?' he asked.

'Actually,' Alice said carefully, 'I'd like to know what your thoughts are. Your first impressions.'

'Is this a test?'

'You're a new doctor. I like to see how my new colleagues operate.'

He sat back in his chair, his blue eyes watching her carefully. After a thoughtful silence he gave a nod, leaning back and taking a bite of his bacon sandwich. 'She's very young, and very pale. I only have the babies' notes, but I'd be interested to know if she's anaemic, and if she's eating.'

Alice gave a slow nod but didn't say anything.

'I'm also worried about the lack of support. Have you got any idea of her family background? Twins are hard for any mum. But for a new mum, and a young mum, on her own? Particularly now she's had a premature delivery, and we're not quite sure as yet what outcomes these children are going to have, I have a whole host of worries for this family.'

Alice licked her lips. 'Anything else?'

Dougie gave a half smile. 'I guess I'm not quite meeting your standards. But I'm not finished. Ruby seems to be doing well. Ryan is not so good. I'd like to do some more tests on him. His oxygen sats fluctuate, and he gives the appearance of a baby who is dehydrated, even though our fluid charts don't seem to support that. But I've to go with what I see. I'm checking his bloods again when I go back.' He bit his bottom lip, clearly thinking about something else. 'Do you think there's any chance that Angie has an eating disorder? She's hidden under mounds of clothes, so it's hard to tell. Her arms and face are thin. Is there a midwife coming to see her, doing checks? If there is, I'd like to have a chat with her.'

Alice sat back in her seat and looked at him with interest. He'd barely had a chance to read the notes and get to know Angie and her children, but he seemed to already be thinking widely about the situation. She was interested in him telling her that even though fluid charts were telling him Ryan was adequately hydrated, he was more concerned by what he was observing.

The words about Angie were interesting too. Alice had noticed the fact she wasn't really eating much, and had just put it down to her being overwhelmed by her current situation. But it could be something else. And she was glad he'd mentioned it—even if it ended up being something they could rule out.

'Have I passed your test yet?' His eyes had a wicked gleam in them.

She stirred her fruit into her yoghurt. 'Maybe. But I like to take my time over a new colleague before I make any judgement.'

Her phone sounded in her pocket and he laughed. 'Okay, I've definitely won. It's Huey Lewis and the News and it's from *Back to the Future*. Good pick, by the way.'

She gave a sorry nod. 'I was hoping to keep this one for a bit longer. But I guess it's time to find something else. Are you joining in?'

He pulled his own phone from his pocket and pressed a button. A ringtone started and she wrinkled her brow, concentrating. The tune was definitely familiar, but the name of the movie wasn't jumping out at her.

'I've got you.' He smiled. 'That's going to annoy you all day now, isn't it?'

The edges of her mouth hinted at a smile. 'You have no idea.'

'You need to play to win,' he said. 'Don't pick the obvious tracks. Don't pick the one song that was the statement for the film. Pick something else. Something from a key scene. Something that comes on the radio and everyone looks at each other and says—what's that from again?'

Alice narrowed her gaze. This guy was toying with her—deliberately trying to annoy her. But there was a hint of something else. Was he flirting with her? She hadn't even found out if he had any kind of attachment back home. Her stomach gave a little clench. Did she actually want to know?

She tapped her fingers on the table. 'Are you trying to tell me how to play my own game?'

He leaned back a bit further, amusement written all over his face. 'Oh, it's *your* game, is it?'

She could take this. She folded her arms and looked him straight in the eye. 'Yes, it's my game, and I intend to win.' Something sparked in her brain. 'I'm going to put a chart up in the office in NICU. We'll see who can get the most points.'

'Are you going to give me credit for my first point?'

'I get the sense of someone playing to win.'

'Of course. Otherwise, what's the point?'

Just at that, his phone rang for real and both of them jumped and started laughing. Dougie answered quickly. 'Douglas MacLachlan?'

She watched as he nodded and gave short answers. It was clear this was not a call he was happy with. Next came the questions. 'And when will that be? Why can't it be sooner? How much availability? No, that's totally unsuitable. I'm a doctor. I don't have a car. I need to be able to use public transport to get to the hospital.'

The conversation seemed to be going from bad to worse. Deep furrows appeared across his brow and his jaw and mouth were tight. His free hand clenched into a fist and she could see he was starting to get angry. She could partly hear some of the conversation at the other end. Whoever it was clearly didn't have a care in the world, and certainly didn't care that they'd double-booked an apartment and left a doctor without somewhere to stay. Dougie was understandably getting more and more wound up, then suddenly, in a moment that surprised nobody more than Alice herself, she reached over and touched his hand, giving a gentle shake of her head. 'Not worth it,' she mouthed.

She tried to ignore the immediate sensations shooting up her arm as her skin came into contact with his. It was nothing. Nothing at all. But it didn't *feel* like nothing. His gaze met hers and she wondered if he felt it too.

She could see the tension across all his muscle groups, but after a few moments he gave her a small nod and relaxed, asking for some further feedback and ending the call.

He stayed silent for a few moments, eyes fixed on his phone lying on the table. Alice swallowed uncomfortably. She really couldn't get a handle on this guy at all. Sometimes she wanted to give him a sympathy hug, other times he annoyed every cell in her body. Then there was the touch thing that she was currently keeping in the 'ignore' box.

He leaned his head on one hand. 'They've found me a place thirty kilometres away.'

'*What?*'

'Oh, good. So I'm not completely unreasonable then?'

She shook her head. 'No, you're not. They can't expect you to travel that distance when you've no transport and have to rely on public transport. You could get called into the hospital in the middle of the night.'

'Yeah, they don't care about that.' He shook his head and stowed his phone back in his pocket. 'I'll see if they get back to me later.' He pushed his chair back. 'We'd better get back to the unit.'

She picked up the remains of her breakfast and dumped it in the trash, then grabbed another candy bar and coffee for Angie. 'It's not healthy eating at all,' she said. 'But it's the only thing I've seen her eat whilst on the unit. So I'm going to get her some while we have a think about what you said earlier.' As they walked back along the corridor she gave him a sideways glance. 'And, just so you know, you're still on a trial period at my house. I might let you stay—particularly if you do any of the baking you promised.'

He held open the door for her. 'Baking bribery.' He gave a contemplative nod. 'It might be the skill I'll have to use.'

She wagged her finger at him. 'And as for that ringtone. It's giving me ear worm. It keeps playing in my head.'

He tapped his nose. 'Nope. Not giving that one up. You have to play fair and square. And no internet browsing.' He pointed to her head, his finger accidentally brushing a few stray hairs at the side of her brow. 'It has to come from the deep recesses of your brain. Otherwise, it doesn't count.'

'Spoilsport,' she said as she turned and walked over to the sink to wash her hands.

Penny appeared instantly at her elbow. 'You two making friends? That looked cosy.' She had a wide smile on her face, but that only put Alice on edge.

'We're not all playing the romance game. It was a simple conversation. Nothing more, nothing less. He actually annoys me at times.'

Penny gave her a look. 'Benedict used to annoy me at times too,' she said in a tone only a sister could use, before she disappeared across the unit again.

Alice sighed. Dougie had sat back down next to Angie and was talking to her again. She was glad he was taking an interest in their patient. Some neonatologists appeared to focus only on the babies, but Alice appreciated those who spent equal amounts of time with the parents. The psychological aspects of being a parent to an early and sometimes sick baby had only really been understood well in the last few years.

It wasn't unusual for the unit to still get calls from parents whose children had been patients a few years earlier. Even though staff turnover could be high, there were some, like Alice, who had worked here for more than a few years, and there was always someone who would be available to chat with a worried parent.

She watched for a few moments. She still wasn't sure about this guy. From here, as he talked sincerely and then made a few jokes with Angie, he looked like the perfect handsome guy, with a killer accent. But there was something else there. Something else beneath the surface. And she just didn't know what it was.

But Alice, being Alice, would have to find out.

For the first half of the next week, Dougie actually felt quite comfortable finding his feet in the unit. It was hard to keep track of all the staff. In a unit as big as this, he did his best to remember the names of everyone he came into contact with. Angie was still proving to be a little bit of a mystery. He didn't want to put the young mum under any kind of pressure, and he hadn't freely discussed his concerns with any other staff, but he and Alice were doing their best to build a rapport with her and allay her concerns.

He'd also spent a bit of time checking processes within the unit. The fact was, he just couldn't help it. His experience in the last unit in London had scarred him for life, he feared. One newly appointed member of staff, who at first had seemed friendly and well-adjusted, had proved to be much more dangerous. At first, it had just been a few odd words here and there. A few excuses about things not done quite as they should be. Nothing had been risky...nothing had caused any adverse events. Other staff had mentioned, or casually corrected her on a few occasions. But Kayla had a big personality. She was a people person, exceedingly friendly. Inviting people to join her for drinks or dinner. Patients loved her. A bit of a whirlwind, but so nice. And that was it. That was the downfall that Dougie had been swept into, along with others.

There had even been a date that hadn't amounted to anything, even though Kayla had been keen to take things further. And so had Dougie, but something had stopped him. And to this day he didn't know what.

Something had just seemed amiss. Even though he hadn't wanted to, he'd started to watch. He'd mentioned to the charge nurse in the unit—the most switched-on person he'd ever met—a few potential mistakes. She'd been annoyed at first, and talked to him about the seriousness of raising competency issues. But Dougie had been quietly insistent, not making a fuss but ensuring his concerns were noted.

And that was when everything had started to unravel. Staff had talked to each other. Dougie had started to notice quietened voices and suspicious glances towards him—not Kayla. Then someone else had started in a neighbouring ward, someone who'd worked at the same hospital as Kayla before, and she'd made a few comments that resulted in Dougie and the charge nurse taking advice from HR colleagues. When they'd all dug a little deeper it appeared that Kayla had moved quickly from place to place. A few calls had been made to her previous workplaces. Yes, there had been a few incidents. There had been suspicions, but nothing had been proven.

His gut had been telling him something that he had absolutely no proof of.

Finally, on a night he'd never forget, he'd watched her draw up some medicine and stopped her before she'd left the treatment room. The charge nurse was by his side. Although the prescription was correct, the medicine had been wrongly constituted; the incorrect dose was in the syringe. It was a mistake that other people might have made in the past. The dose got absolutely nowhere near the patient it was intended for. But Kayla had been put on supervised practice only and left some time later—entirely her own decision—letting everyone know that Dougie had wrongly accused her of intentional malpractice all because she'd refused to go on a second date with him.

None of this had been true. But he'd noticed that laughter had died around him, and invitations to nights out and get-togethers had dwindled.

When he'd heard that Kayla had been charged nine months later with attempted murder while working somewhere else he'd blamed himself. There had been no trace of where she'd gone; she'd not asked for any references when she'd left. The charge nurse at his NICU had put in an alert to the governing nurse body.

The truth had only been discovered when police came to the unit, asking for statements from staff who'd previously worked with her.

Dougie had been devastated. He should have trusted his gut, but those around him had questioned his motives. He became a person he'd never wanted to be—one who watched everyone around him constantly.

It was a sad fact of life that errors happened every day in hospitals and other care settings. Most were never intentional, and some a result of procedures not being followed, information not updated or pure human error. But Dougie had felt himself becoming obsessed.

It probably didn't help that most of the staff who still worked with him all blamed themselves too for not listening to his initial concerns, and for doubting him. But when he'd started to double-check everything that people were doing, their patience eventually grew thin.

The Head of Department had sat him down and told him, even though he was a wonderful doctor, it was time for a change of scene. He was becoming too wrapped up in what had happened before and how he could prevent it ever happening again that people were spending their lives tiptoeing around him.

He knew that; he could sense it. And when his mentor had told him about the job in Washington Dougie had known it was the right move to make. A new country. New faces. New patients. And no one who would know his past experience.

He was trying his best not to let his past affect him, but he knew that it always would. He could never be comfortable working anywhere until he knew there were protocols and safety checks in place that met the standards in his head. And it wasn't just his work that had been affected; it was his personal life too. He'd been on a date with Kayla. Just one.

But now he was questioning his judgement. He'd allowed himself to be carried along with her warm and friendly manner. It didn't matter that it had only been one date. It had left Kayla with the ammunition to claim that Dougie's questions about her practice were those of a scorned partner. If he'd never gone on that date, that would never have happened. He felt duped. Dating had definitely taken a back seat ever since.

His housing situation had not been resolved in any

way, shape or form. To be honest, he'd thought that the rental company might have taken more responsibility for their mistake. He'd been kidding himself. The fact of the matter was they were indifferent and unapologetic. In their view, they'd made a half-hearted attempt to find alternative accommodation, which was completely unsuitable, and Dougie had turned it down, so they were done.

He hadn't quite mentioned this to Alice yet. But as he went from market place to small store, he knew it was time to try and win favour with his housemate. Baking utensils were hard to come by in the heart of Washington DC. But, thanks to some hints from other work colleagues, he finally had what he needed.

Alice had told him she was going shopping after work, so by the time she got home he'd planned for everything to be ready.

Ovens could be unpredictable for a baker. He'd learned this early on in life. Some ran hotter than the dial, some colder, affecting the length of stay in the oven, and the potential for soggy bottoms or dry overcooked bases or sponges.

Dougie would have preferred a few trial runs, but there just hadn't been time. Red velvet muffins and, her apparent favourite, banana loaf were already cooling on the wire rack under a tea towel. He was currently waiting for the sponges of a chocolate fudge cake to finish in the oven.

The noise of the door opening made him turn around. 'What is that smell?' came the immediate question.

Alice appeared a few moments later in jeans and a yellow top, swinging a bag in her hand. She didn't wait, just moved across the floor and sat at the kitchen table.

'You've finally come good on your early promises,'

she said. 'I was beginning to think you'd just told me
you could bake to try and get a bed for the night.'

'Might have been true,' he admitted.

She stood up and moved to check the trash can. 'Just
making sure there are no bakery store cartons.'

'What a suspicious mind,' he said as he shook his
head.

She grinned. 'Might have done it myself before.'

'Sneaky.'

'Maybe.' Her phone sounded and as she pulled
it from her pocket he turned the vaguely familiar-
sounding tune over in his mind. But the expression on
her face made him pause.

'What's wrong?'

She pulled a face and kept her eyes on the screen before swiping it away. 'Nothing. Just some weird messages.'

'Why would you be getting weird messages?'

She sighed and ran her fingers through her hair as he
sat down opposite her, checking the timer on his own
phone. 'It's just via a dating app that I use sometimes.
Guess I'm attracting the wrong type.'

'You use a dating app?' He couldn't help how surprised he sounded.

He could see her growing instantly defensive.
'What's wrong with a dating app? It's how the modern world works.'

He held up his hands. 'Nothing. Nothing at all. I
guess I just thought a girl like you wouldn't need a
dating app.'

'A girl like me? What does that mean?'

Dougie instantly knew that he'd unwittingly dug a
hole for himself that he was unlikely to climb out of. 'I
mean you're good-looking and you're smart.'

'Like the rest of the world,' she said quickly. 'Good-looking, smart and time-limited. I don't want to spend my life in bars in the random hope of maybe meeting someone. I work long hours. I'm covering for absent colleagues right now. If I want to go on a date—I want to go on a date. Apps work for me. I look for someone who might like some of the same things I do—not too many, though. That could be boring.'

Dougie relaxed a little but reached behind him and grabbed the cooling racks, bringing them to the table and unveiling the red velvet cupcakes and banana loaf.

She inhaled deeply and sighed.

'So, you're not looking for a perfect match then?' he asked.

She shook her head as he grabbed some plates and a knife. 'I guess a perfect match has always sounded a little boring to me.'

He smiled and nodded as he checked through the glass oven door. Another few minutes. 'So, variety is the spice of life?'

She groaned. 'That old one. It always sounds a bit off, doesn't it? What's in the oven?'

She was eyeing the cakes in front of her with a knife in one hand. 'Chocolate sponges,' he said, 'for a chocolate fudge cake. I still have to make the filling and the topping, but they have to cool first. Otherwise, it just ends up a splodgy melted mess.'

She laughed and started cutting a slice of the banana loaf. 'Guess I'll start here then. Any butter?'

Dougie pulled back. 'Whoa. You're going to desecrate my banana loaf with butter?'

'I know how I like it,' she said as she met his gaze. There was an odd moment of silence. Dougie had to remind himself they were talking about cake. He swung his legs around as he laughed, opening the refrigerator and pulling out butter and two beers.

'You shopped?' she said, accepting both the beer and the butter.

'I even bought chicken,' he said. 'Something that might actually be a dinner.'

'This isn't dinner?' She looked up from where she was slathering butter on his banana loaf.

'You know you're ruining it, don't you?'

Her phone sounded again and she frowned.

'The Breakfast Club,' he said instantly, recognising the tune and the movie it came from. 'That one was kind of wasted on me. Simple Minds—Scottish band—always going to recognise them.'

'Took you two listens,' she murmured, her head still over her phone.

'Got a better offer?' He was talking about the ringtone, but realised his words might be misconstrued when she was clearly checking out a message on her dating app.

Even though her hair was partly covering her face, he could see her jaw tighten. With a swish of her fingers the app was deleted. She stood up and disappeared for a few seconds. From the noises he could hear, she was checking the front door.

'Everything okay?' The words came out automatically even though it was clear that everything wasn't okay.

She lifted her head as she climbed up the two steps into the kitchen and shook back her hair. Her cheeks were slightly flushed. There was false bravado on her face and that made his stomach twist in a protective way he didn't expect.

'Fine.' It was one word. But it had a tiny waver to it. 'Plenty more dating apps to use.'

His brain switched gear. 'Anything you need to tell me?' There was much more to this story. But he wasn't sure he had any right to pry. He'd known Alice Greene for less than a week.

She pressed her lips together for a few moments. It was clear she was mulling things over. Dougie knew when to be quiet.

He couldn't really read her yet. If she needed to talk, he could do that. If she needed to be left alone, he could do that too. If she needed distraction, he was the king of that. But sitting here waiting was killing him.

And he couldn't really understand why.

She took a bite of the banana loaf and then a swig from her beer bottle, setting it down on the table firmly.

'Okay,' she said. 'You can stay.'

'What?' It seemed to come out of nowhere. And he was completely aware she'd ignored his earlier question.

She held out one hand. 'You seem relatively clean. You do your own laundry. You don't leave things lying around. I haven't heard you snoring. You buy groceries—and beer. And...you can bake. You can stay.'

It was the best news he'd heard all week.

But he tilted his head to one side. 'I seem *relatively* clean?'

The edges of her lips turned upwards. 'I haven't got that close. And I don't intend to.'

Those final words were probably a bit of an insult that if he'd had a few more beers he might have teased her over. But Dougie knew this wasn't the time.

'Okay. That's great. Thanks. Although I can't promise not to annoy you sometimes, I can at least promise

to try not to annoy you. And to remain relatively clean.'
He took a pointed swig from his own beer bottle.

'The banana loaf is good,' she conceded as she lifted
one of the cupcakes, peeled off the foil wrapper and cut
the cake in half.

As she examined the rich red sponge she kept talking. 'I figure since you're already here and haven't
found someplace else, it makes much more sense if we
just keep this arrangement going. I don't know anyone
else looking for somewhere to rent, and I'd have to advertise and interview people I don't know.' She wrinkled her nose. 'Not really sure I'm up for that right now.'
Her brown eyes met his. 'So far, you seem pretty safe.'

And that was it. She probably didn't even realise that
she'd said it. But Dougie had always been able to pick
up on unconscious cues. It was part of what made him
a good doctor.

Safety was important to Alice Greene right now. And
something about her latest interaction with the dating
app had made her feel unsafe.

Dougie didn't like that. He didn't like it at all. But
he also knew it wasn't his business or place to say anything.

His eyes focused on the digital numbers on his own
phone and he jumped up. 'Darn it!' He pulled the oven
door down and grabbed for the nearby oven mitt, pulling the chocolate sponges from the heat.

'Did you forget about them?'

He grimaced. 'Momentarily distracted.'

She moved over next to him and leaned over the three
sponges. Her arm brushed against his. He knew it was
inadvertent but something stopped him from stepping
away. Her light floral scent drifted around him, mixed
in with the chocolate sponges.

'They aren't burnt,' she said, still staring at them.

He pressed one with a fingertip. It didn't bounce back quite as much as it should have. 'Still a bit overdone.'

She turned around, tilting her chin up to face him. 'But you're going to make that fudge sauce. Who'll notice if the sponges are a bit dry?' This was the closest they had ever been. She suited the yellow shirt. It reflected off her tanned skin and dark hair and eyes. She had a bit of eyeliner on, smudged around her lower lids. And that had to be mascara, because no ordinary person could have lashes that long and perfectly separated. As for her lips?

Dougie blinked. He couldn't remember the last time he'd thought about a woman in detail like this. She was still looking up at him and he grinned. 'I vote that tonight we leave the chicken in the fridge and eat three slightly dry sponges, smothered in chocolate fudge sauce.'

She put her hand to her chest, drawing his eyes now to the skin at the bottom of her throat and the glimpse where two buttons hadn't been fastened. 'It's a sacrifice I think I can make. We could even pick an eighties movie to watch while we do it.'

He licked his lips. His words were a bit hoarser than he liked. 'You're going to sacrifice yourself by eating my cake?'

She raised her eyebrows. 'Someone's gotta do it. You know, take one for the team.'

She laughed, finally stepping back and breaking the weird vibe that had settled around them.

He pulled a saucepan from a drawer and said over his shoulder, 'You have to pick an eighties film we've already used. Would hate to think you were about to try and cheat and find out where my ringtone comes from.'

She shot him a glare. 'It's driving me nuts!'

'Then things are working out perfectly. Hand me over the cooling tray. I have to tip these sponges out.'

She did it, with one hand on her hip. 'It'll have to be *Back to the Future* then. I'm in the mood for some time travel.'

'Whatever you like,' he agreed, wondering what on earth he was getting himself into.

Alice had pulled off her jeans and found some yoga pants. She realised the mistake of not changing her favourite yellow shirt the second Dougie handed her the bowl filled with chocolate sponge and an enormous helping of chocolate fudge sauce. It was still warm and smelt divine. She looked down at the shirt, knowing she could kiss it goodbye with one spilled drop. 'Give me a sec.'

She ran up the stairs, unfastening the shirt as she went, then grabbing an oversized grey T-shirt instead. When she got back down, Dougie had the TV paused at the credits for the movie.

She settled herself cross-legged on the floor between the sofa and the coffee table that held her bowl of cake.

'That can't be comfy,' came the thick Scottish accent.

She waved her spoon as she dived in. 'What won't be comfy is you—if you drop that sauce on my cream sofa. The beauty of a wooden floor is that everything wipes clean.'

Two seconds later he thumped down next to her as he hit play on the remote. She laughed as he tried, and failed, to fold his much longer legs up into the space between the sofa and table. Eventually he gave a sigh and pushed the table a bit further forward.

There was something about being around Douglas

MacLachlan. Maybe it was just his size. His over-six-foot frame and his broad shoulders. Maybe it was just the association with the accent—in every movie she'd ever seen, you didn't mess with a Scotsman.

But right now she felt safe around Dougie.

That last message via the app had been unsettling. The mention of her yellow shirt had freaked her out completely. It wasn't something she was going to tell him—that some random guy who'd liked her via a dating app had sent a few pointed messages in the last few days. But it unnerved her.

So when she'd got home to the smell of home baking, tasted it and then contemplated having to advertise for a roommate, she knew she had to invite Dougie to stay. If he'd told her the rental agency had sorted things out, she might have cried. The thought of even being alone in this place made her distinctly uncomfortable.

Alice Greene was a girl who'd always been comfortable in her own skin. But her bad experience when Penny was in Ohio had unsettled her, and now tonight's message had thrown her.

Pretty shirt. Yellow. Like a sunflower.

It was hardly a threatening message. But that was exactly how it felt. As if someone was watching her. Which made her feel immensely glad to have someone like Dougie around. She didn't know him well at all. But her instincts about him were good.

There was a strong likelihood he might annoy her at work, but as long as she felt safe having him around then she was glad he was here.

Trouble was, having a man with an accent like his, along with leading guy looks, *and* the ability to make chocolate fudge sauce like this—was surely asking for trouble.

For a second when she'd looked up at him in the kitchen, one glimpse of those big blue eyes had swept all the panic she'd felt earlier away. Just the sensation of having him close made her feel protected. Which was ridiculous, and she knew it. Particularly when her eyes had been distracted by those lips...

She was being stupid now. But as she leaned back against the sofa to watch the opening credits of one of her favourite movies, while enjoying all the sensations of the rich cake, she felt strangely happy.

If Penny could see this scene right now she would be asking a million questions. And Alice wasn't sure she could answer any one of them. Best to say nothing. Best to keep things to herself.

Dougie turned his phone around so she could see it. 'Took a selfie outside the White House today.' He looked proud of himself. 'Where else can I go?'

'Wait until you have a few days off. I'll take you to some of the best bits of Washington. There's much more here than you think.'

'Like what?'

'Abe Lincoln's summer cottage, the woods of Theodore Roosevelt Island, the National Museum of Health and Medicine has some exhibits that will make you grue, and then—' she smiled at him '—I've got a special surprise for you at the Botanic Gardens.'

Dougie blinked and looked at her cautiously.

Alice smirked. 'Let's just say it'll be a day you won't forget.'

He shifted, his shoulder brushing against hers. 'And you don't mind?'

She turned her face to him. 'Why would I? My sister is happily in love, one of my best friends is away in Spain to help her family. I have time.'

He nodded slowly. 'Well, thank you. I appreciate it. I like to find out a bit more about wherever I am staying. Plus, I definitely don't know where to shop for groceries. I know you told me some places the first night— but they're lost in a different world for me.' He nodded at the movie. 'Just call me Marty.'

'Okay, Marty.' She took another spoonful of cake. 'But my fees are in cakes.'

'I think I can manage that,' he said, smiling, and she wondered exactly what she was getting into.

CHAPTER FOUR

THERE WAS SOMETHING about a certain time of night in hospitals. It didn't matter whether staff worked in A&E, coronary care, a medical unit or a NICU. That strange hour in the dead of night—the witching hour some called it—usually between three and four a.m., was the time when staff circadian rhythms meant they were most tired, and irony meant that it was usually the time something happened.

'I hate night shift,' said Alice as she poured herself a coffee in the staffroom. 'I would do almost anything to get out of them.'

'Not really a fan myself,' admitted Dougie, 'but it's part of the job. And I usually use the night shift card if people tell me I'm crabbit.'

She smiled at him with her hand on one hip. 'Oh, no, I can't believe anyone would call you crabbit.'

He rolled his eyes. 'I know that's what some of the staff are saying. I just call things like they are. If some people think it's crabbit I can live with that.'

She laughed and shook her head. 'I love the way you say that word and, to be honest, there couldn't be a better description.' She stirred her coffee and then sighed. 'But I also like knackered. I've heard people in here start to say it, and you've only been here two weeks.'

Dougie took a sip of his coffee. 'I'm like a virus. I come somewhere new, start using all my Scottish words and, before you know it, you're all joining in.'

'We should make you a chart,' Alice mused. 'Like the ringtone one. You could introduce a new word every week and see how many people can use it.'

She was trying to ignore the zing she still felt around him whenever they got too close. Even though they still bickered at work sometimes—usually when he was being pedantic about something—they generally got on fine. She might even call her new roommate a friend. And for Alice that was big.

For the last few years, she always joked to Penny that she'd used up her quota of friends and didn't have room for any more. But Dougie was managing to wriggle his way in there.

He'd been true to his word about baking. He was a better grocery shopper than she was—although Alice had been sure to split costs. But most of all it was just knowing there was another presence in the house that gave her some reassurance.

She was never going to admit that when she'd realised he was covering nights this week she'd swapped her shifts so she wouldn't be home alone.

She hadn't told a soul that she'd received another kind of strange message from a different dating app. One word. *Lavender.* Which was growing in a pot at her front door. She was tempted to call her old DC cop friend, just to ask if she was being paranoid. But instead she'd just deleted the app, and swapped shifts.

'My word for this week would be scunner. Usually used by grannies, along with the phrase "you're a wee scunner". I'll let you work out for yourself what you think that means.'

She laughed and pointed at his pocket. 'I've got it.'

'Got what?' He looked down at himself as if he didn't understand what she was saying.

'Your ringtone.'

'You have?' He leaned against the wall, looking interested.

'It's "Oh, Yeah", from *Ferris Bueller's Day Off.*'

'Took you long enough.'

Just as Alice opened her mouth to retort, something started to ping outside.

Their movements were automatic. Both put down their coffee and walked quickly to the incubator where the alarms were sounding. This was a new baby girl, Blossom. Born at twenty-five weeks to a mom with pre-eclampsia. She wasn't breathing on her own, and was already showing signs of jaundice. Right now, her dusky colour was giving cause for concern.

Alice glanced at the monitor and without a word grabbed a very thin suction tube from the wall. She manoeuvred it carefully, trying to remove the blockage from Blossom's airway. After a few moments she shook her head and looked at Dougie. 'It has to be something else. I'm feeling resistance.'

Dougie helped reposition the tiny baby, delicately checking the airway again. 'I think her feeding tube has regurgitated. I'm going to start by taking it out.'

Alice took a deep breath. Putting feeding tubes in babies like this was hard work. Their oesophagi and tracheae were so tiny. Feeding tubes were always X-rayed once in position and prior to any feeding starting, to ensure everything was exactly where it should be. Any mistake could be disastrous.

Dougie removed the tiny tube smoothly and calmly. He then repositioned Blossom. Thankfully, her mom wasn't here right now to see the calamity. Although she had spent some time with her daughter, she was still in Maternity, with her blood pressure being monitored after an earlier seizure. Alice's eyes flitted between the monitor and Blossom, checking her chest and colour.

Although Dougie appeared entirely calm, she could see something in those blue eyes. He put his finger gently on Blossom's hand and talked in a low voice to her. Her heart was racing, and her dusky colour was starting to change a little.

A few other staff had appeared at their sides. 'What's up?' asked the first.

'Airway problems,' said Alice. 'Dougie's just removed the feeding tube. It looks as if she's settling now.'

'Who put the tube in?' Dougie asked.

No one answered. Alice imagined it was because no one knew.

'I need to see Blossom's chart. I want to know when the tube went in. I want to see the X-ray for confirmation of position. And I want to see when the feeds started and what her observations have been since.' His voice was tense, and Alice didn't like it.

She stayed focused on the baby.

Blossom's nurse, Ron, arrived back at the side of the incubator, wide-eyed. 'What's happened?'

He'd only gone on a break fifteen minutes ago, and Alice knew exactly how he was feeling—this had happened to her too. She quickly explained and moved over to let him continue the care of his patient. He knew Blossom better than she did.

She joined Dougie, who was now at the nurses' station, checking the electronic records. The previous X-ray blinked up on the screen. Alice could see instantly the feeding tube with its guidewire still in place, showing it was exactly where it should be—in Blossom's tiny stomach.

She breathed a sigh of relief then was angry at herself. She'd known it would be. But Dougie's reaction had made her second-guess her conscientious colleagues and she hated that.

His eyes were running down her chart. 'Everything is exactly how it should be,' she said, feeling on edge.

'It wasn't when we got to her. Her nasogastric tube had moved and was blocking her airway.'

Alice ground her teeth together. 'Look at when she was last fed. All the checks were done. The amount of visible tube is checked off. No kinking was recorded at the back of the mouth. The aspirate showed a PH below five point five. The tube was in the correct place then.'

But Dougie kept going, looking back through other notes.

After a few minutes Alice could feel herself getting mad. 'Why are you looking for something that isn't there?'

His eyes flashed as he met her gaze. 'We've just treated a baby that couldn't breathe properly. That happened in this unit, on *our* shift. It's our duty to examine every angle of this. To pick it apart, and make sure it doesn't happen again.' He'd pulled the neonatal tube feeding protocol from one of the folders. 'Maybe it's time for this to be reviewed.'

'Maybe it's time to take a breath. Sometimes tubes move. This can't be the first time this has happened to you. There might not be rhyme or reason to it.' She was trying to sound calm and rational but she was still annoyed with him. 'But it doesn't mean that anyone did something wrong.'

He turned around to face her, stopping concentrating on the chart in his lap. 'And if they did?'

'What's that supposed to mean?'

'I mean, if we'd discovered that the tube hadn't been checked, and neither had the aspirate, what then?'

Alice frowned and shifted her feet. 'None of those things happened. So why would you even ask?'

'I just wonder if you'd be willing to overlook failings in your colleagues. Pretend they didn't happen.'

That was it. Red mist descended. 'How dare you? What kind of suggestion is that? I'm a professional, as is everyone else who works in here. We are all human. And even though you might not like it, mistakes can happen. And when and if they do happen we all act appropriately. I would prioritise my patient. I would make sure they were safe. Once I was satisfied with that, I'd report the incident, let it be investigated properly and debrief with my colleagues. We have a procedure for learning incidents in the NICU—like all teaching hospitals. Don't you dare insinuate that anything would be covered up or ignored.' She was furious now. A few colleagues turned their heads and she realised that her voice must have risen.

Dougie should be embarrassed to have even asked that question, but as she stared at him she realised he wasn't embarrassed in the slightest. He was looking at her as though he still had questions.

'Do you think there's something lacking in my nursing skills?' She swung out her arm. 'Or the nursing skills of anyone is this unit? Because if you do I suggest you have a chat with Tara, our charge nurse. You might think you're a brave Scotsman, but I can tell you right now who I'd put my money on in that fight.'

His eyebrows rose and he had the cheek to look the tiniest bit amused.

'Do you think this is funny?' she demanded.

His expression changed completely and he stood up. 'No. I don't think this is funny. But what I do think is that if something goes wrong when I'm the doctor on duty then it's my job to ask questions. It's my job to look at procedures and look at everyone I'm working with.'

Those last words threw her. 'What's that supposed to mean?'

But his gaze had turned steely. 'It means that the lives of these babies are more important than any arguments between us. I can, and will, ask questions if I think they need to be asked. And I will continue to look at all the staff and all the procedures to make sure this place is as safe as it possibly can be.'

He turned and walked away, moving back over to Blossom's incubator. She could tell from the expression on Ron's face that the conversation between them was uncomfortable. Ron was a fine NICU nurse. He'd been here longer than Alice and could recite protocols in his sleep. He wouldn't mess up. She had complete faith in him.

But as she watched him answer Dougie's questions she could almost see him second-guessing himself. She wanted to go and wrap her arm around him.

Alice moved back to the four babies she was looking after. Dougie's words echoed in her head as she checked and double-checked their feeds, urine output, medicines and observations. She could do these things in her sleep, but the latest incident had made her paranoid.

That irritated her. But she wasn't sure quite what irritated most. Was it the fact that Dougie thought that someone in the unit had made a mistake and caused harm to a baby? Or was it the fact that he'd implied that staff covered for their colleagues?

As she tended to her own charges, she tried to downplay things in her head. She was tired. She hated night shift. Might she have overreacted a little? Certain things were true. Any professional should ask questions about anything that went wrong on their watch. So why was she offended by Dougie asking the questions?

As she moved to change one of her babies, she realised exactly why. Because that was the first place he'd gone. There hadn't been room to contemplate if it had just been one of those things that happened. There hadn't been a question about human error. It was as if he had just jumped to the worst possible conclusion. Someone hadn't done their job properly. Someone hadn't recorded properly. The final possibility was just too ridiculous for Alice to even consider, and she certainly hoped it hadn't featured in Dougie's mind—the fact it could have been deliberate.

Totally and utterly ridiculous.

Alice was always meticulous at work. She remembered a time as a student when one of her colleagues in an elderly ward had given the wrong patient an anticoagulant injection. The patient had come to no harm, but the fallout of the situation had terrified Alice about making a mistake at work.

Her colleague had been distraught. She'd got a call on the way into work to say her father had suffered a heart attack. On a normal day, she would have called in sick. But the ward had already been affected by the winter vomiting bug and several staff were already sick. If this colleague had phoned in sick too, staffing levels would have been unsafe. So the colleague had come to work, upset and distracted. She'd done the same medicine round that she'd done many times before as she knew many of the elderly patients. But beds had been swapped around as someone had deteriorated and needed to be moved to a side room. Although she'd checked the patient wrist band, it hadn't clocked in her brain and, before she knew it, she was disposing of a small syringe and realising she'd just given the medicine to the wrong patient.

There had been disciplinary action. And Alice had to give a statement as a member of staff on duty. It didn't matter she hadn't been involved in the medicine round, or that she didn't have responsibility to check the prescription or the patient.

The whole event had stayed with her for years. Even now, thinking about it filled her stomach with hollow dread. Nothing like that had happened tonight on the unit. Not even close. So why was that event now haunting her?

Enough. Alice finished her checks and moved over to talk to Ron. It was clear he was upset.

Alice didn't hesitate to give him her best smile and slip her arm around his shoulder. 'How's your girl doing?'

He sighed. 'She's fine. I just had to phone the nurse on the postnatal ward and ask her to wake up Blossom's mom in the middle of the night to tell her there had been a problem. She's distraught, even though I told her everything is fine now.'

Alice nodded. She understood. They always let patients know if there were any changes in their baby's condition, but she knew that Ron would have felt terrible doing that.

'Why don't you take another picture, and go on down and see her?' It seemed like the most reassuring thing they could do.

Ron sighed. 'I'd love to, but...' he nodded over towards Dougie '...can you imagine what Mr Braveheart might say if I suggested it?'

Alice bit the inside of her cheek, her mind made up in an instant. 'Then let me.'

She walked over to Dougie. 'Ron had to let Blossom's mom know what happened. She's understandably upset, and you'll know she's recovering from a seizure and pre-eclampsia. Stress is the last thing that woman needs.'

Dougie looked at her. For the first time, she could see some empathy on his face.

'We have to keep parents informed—' he started.

'We do,' she said, cutting him off. 'But right now we also have a duty of care to a mother as well as a baby. So either we let Ron go down, take a new picture of Blossom and talk her mother through what happened and reassure her everything's fine—' his brow was already pinched at the suggestion '—or you go down and do that. Or—' she paused '—if Ron goes, you need to sit with Blossom.'

She didn't allow there to be any choice in the matter. After tonight's event, someone would continue to sit with Blossom on a one-to-one basis for the rest of the night. Dougie looked over and she could see him trying to make up his mind.

'I'd suggest you let Ron do it, since he's already met Blossom's mom. Seems better than to send a strange doctor in the middle of the night, doesn't it?'

She was being pointed and she knew it. He could call her out. He could say as doctor on duty everything was his call. But she wanted him to understand they took a team approach here. This wasn't about him, or Ron. This was about the unit team deciding who was best to talk to mom.

He took a deep breath and sighed. 'I'm happy to sit with Blossom. I need to decide the best time to reinsert her feeding tube. I'll let Ron know that if her mum wants to talk to the doctor on duty, I'm happy to go down after he has.'

She could tell that it pained him to say that. Dougie was probably normally the guy who liked to be in charge of everything. But he had to think what was best for the patient.

She watched as he went over and had a discussion with Ron. She could tell instantly that Ron was happy with the decision. He took another instant picture of Blossom, and once Dougie had settled next to the incubator hurried out of the door.

Silence fell over the unit once more. The only noises were the quiet hisses and beeps of pumps, monitors and ventilators.

Alice could sense that Dougie's eyes were on her. But she didn't turn. She didn't look at him. He'd annoyed her tonight, and she wanted him to know it.

So she held her head high and walked back over to the babies in her care and did her job.

CHAPTER FIVE

A WEEK HAD passed and there was still an awkward silence in the townhouse. Alice and Dougie worked around each other with barely a murmur. Alice was still mad, Dougie resolute, both understanding each other a little but determined in their stance.

Dougie was sitting at the table in the kitchen, eating some eggs for breakfast and searching the internet for places to visit in Washington. He had the next couple of days off and wanted to get a better feel for the city. The Lincoln Memorial and Smithsonian were on his radar, but his interest had been piqued by the few different places that Alice had mentioned previously.

She moved silently into the kitchen and picked up the percolator, pouring some coffee into a cup and adding some sweetener. As she toasted some bread, her phone sounded. She'd left it sitting at the edge of the table and Dougie's head lifted automatically. There was a picture on the screen but he couldn't see what it was. Alice continued what she was doing, then turned around and glanced at her phone. He couldn't pretend not to notice how her expression changed. She swiped her screen and shoved the phone into the back pocket of her denim shorts.

'Okay?' He couldn't help himself.

For a few moments all he could see was her back as she put her toast on a plate, then turned and brought it to the table with some butter and jam from the fridge.

It was almost as if something had washed over her, but in a resigned kind of way. 'Just someone thinking they're funny,' was all she said.

As she started eating her toast she looked up at him. 'Where are you going today?' She must have realised he was off.

'Haven't decided yet,' he said. He swung his tablet around. 'Was contemplating a few of these places.'

She looked over and pointed. 'No, not as good as it sounds; this one is interesting—and that one is definitely worth the trip.' After a few seconds she gave a sigh. 'I promised I'd show you around.'

He felt her soften at the edges a little. Dougie didn't mind exploring Washington himself, but having a guide would be much more interesting. 'You did,' he agreed.

She kept eating, clearly thinking carefully. Dougie kept silent.

'I think if we can spend the day not talking about work, this could be fine,' she said. It was as if she were drawing an invisible line in the sand.

'Happy not to talk about work,' he said, lifting his cup and plate and loading them into the dishwasher, before turning around and folding his arms.

He was struck by how attractive she was. Her hair was swept up in a ponytail high on her head but, instead of the regular way she wore it at work, this was much bigger and bouffant. It reminded him of a picture he'd seen years ago of Jackie O. She was wearing a bright orange top that sat just off her shoulders, long gold earrings, her denim shorts that revealed tanned slim legs and a pair of trainers. Deep down, something curled in his stomach, recognising that he was finding Alice attractive.

Alarm bells sounded in his head. There was a reason he didn't date colleagues. He'd learned his lesson the hard way. He couldn't let some casual attraction to a colleague lead to anything that could ruin his six-month placement, and his reputation at Wald. He gave a silent sigh as he tried to rid himself of the weight on his shoulders. All of those things mattered. But he could be friends with his housemate. He could go sightseeing across the city. There was nothing in that—was there?

He made up his mind. 'Where are we going to go?'

She swung her legs out from underneath the table with a smile. 'Oh, you can just wait and see. Let me grab my bag.'

Dougie finished clearing the kitchen and grabbed his wallet. Alice appeared next to him with a small bag at her hip, the long strap across her body, and a pair of sunglasses perched on her head. 'Ready?'

He nodded and locked the door behind them as they headed out onto the street.

He was happy to let her take the lead and, after some subway rides and some walking, she smiled as she waved her hand at a sign for the National Museum of Health and Medicine.

'Isn't this work-related?' he asked as they made their way inside.

'But not specific to our work. Your eyes will boggle at some of the stuff they have in here.'

She wasn't joking. It was like walking through the history of medicine, and Dougie couldn't even try to pretend that he didn't love it. Some of the exhibits were ancient, some from the World Wars. The exhibits of the effects of atomic weapons were heart-wrenching, the research on tuberculosis and the initial discoveries that mosquitoes carried disease were fascinating. Then came the fragments of bullet that had killed Abraham Lincoln, along with pieces of skull. Then there was the malformed megacolon removed from a man with constipation and, last but not least, the completely and utterly hideous stomach-sized hairball from a teenage girl who'd eaten her hair for six years, that left an eye-watering impression.

By the time they got back outside, Dougie was glad to be in fresh air again. 'It's like the exhibits in the Surgeons' Hall Museums back in Edinburgh,' he said to Alice. 'Whilst some of them are fascinating, you've got to question how some of them got here. And how people thought at that time.'

'Makes me glad we've got the technology we have,' she replied. 'So much of this would be discovered early and be able to be treated. The history of medicine and human development is not kind.'

He gave her a sideways glance and a smile. 'Absolutely. Kind of overwhelming. Where to next?'

She gave a thoughtful nod. 'Okay, how about we take a true breather and go somewhere with a spectacular view for lunch, then we could go to the Botanic Gardens? It means a bit of travel. Are you up for it?'

'Sure.' He shrugged. 'Why not?'

They spent the next hour on the subway and got into a good-natured fight about the best ever sci-fi film made, closely followed by the best ever sci-fi series. It was a closely fought battle between *Star Wars* and *The Search for Spock* and *Close Encounters*. Some other people on the subway joined in, all debating the best ever starship captain, with a twelve-year-old girl with thick glasses giving an impassioned debate for Captain

Janeway. Dougie and Alice were still laughing as they emerged from the subway.

'Always Picard,' said Dougie. 'But I didn't want to break her heart.'

His phone sounded and in the blink of an eye Alice groaned. '*Beverly Hills Cop*? You really need to up your game.'

'I'll do my best.' He smiled, pleased that they seemed back on much better terms now. The sun was shining high in the sky, and she'd brought them back out into the middle of the city. 'Where to now?'

She pointed upwards. 'We're going up there. The cafeteria on the sixth floor has floor-to-ceiling windows with spectacular views of the city.'

'Sold,' he said instantly, looking at another sign. 'Thought you were taking me to Library of Congress to see the Gutenberg Bible.'

She waved her hand. 'That's for another day. One where you can give it your full attention. Today's priority is food.'

They took the elevator to the sixth floor and walked out into the wide space of the cafeteria. The food was simple but wide-ranging enough for anyone to find something to their liking. With a hot chicken sandwich for Alice and a Philly cheesesteak sandwich for him, and some diet sodas, they sat down at one of the windows overlooking the city.

'I like it up here,' said Alice. 'Sometimes it can be overrun with school trips. But the food is reasonable, and I've brought a book up here before.'

He looked at her with interest. 'You brought a book to the library?'

'Absolutely,' she said. 'What better place to read? And I'm not the only one who likes to do it. Look around.

Some of these people are staffers from Capitol Hill. There aren't too many places to eat around here. But the rest—the ones who clearly aren't visitors? They're like me. Just here for the view and the food.'

He looked around and she was right. There were a number of people—mainly on their own, sipping coffee or eating a muffin, reading a book.

'Are you really an old soul at heart?'

She wrinkled her brow for a second, then smiled. 'I think I probably am. Penny would probably laugh at that, though. I like a bit of time, a bit of space. But she doesn't always acknowledge that; she still calls me dating central.'

At those words, Dougie gave a swallow and mentioned the subject that had been bothering him. 'Is everything okay with that? I've noted you deleting a few apps.'

She sighed and pressed her lips together. He knew she was trying to figure out what to tell him.

He didn't want to press. And whether Alice did or didn't date was none of his business—something he knew entirely, but strangely annoyed him. He held up one hand. 'Just tell me if there's anything you need to tell me. I'm not being nosey. We're trying to be friends.' Then he said something that worried him most. 'If ever you don't feel safe, you let me know.'

She reached for her soda and there was a slight tremor to her hand. 'Okay.' The word came out much sooner than he'd expected, and with a hint of shakiness.

So now he wanted to know everything. Should he say something to Penny? But no. They were sisters. And they clearly had a bond. Alice spoke to her sister a couple of times a day. Penny would likely know everything about this, and just tell Dougie it was none of his business.

But why did the fact that Alice had fixed her gaze out of the windows and across the city bother him? This whole subject had made her edgy. It shouldn't. She should feel free to date whoever and whenever she pleased.

It suddenly struck him that, even though he'd been here a few weeks now, she'd never mentioned going out on a date. 'You got yoga tonight?' he asked, remembering she sometimes went to a class with a friend.

Alice shook her head. 'Not tonight. Carol has something on with her family. In fact, I was thinking if I haven't killed you by the end of the day, there might be a good place we could go to round off the evening.'

'Do I need to check if you're planning on killing me by exhausting me with our touring around Washington, or if this is just killing me in general?'

She smiled and gathered their plates from lunch. 'Not sure yet. Guess we'll just wait and see how it goes.' There was something teasing in her tone, and the smile she was giving him sent a wave of tingles across his skin. As he stood, she moved alongside him, her arm brushing against his as she pointed at something just a little away from them. 'That's where we're headed next. The Botanic Gardens is only a short walk away.'

As they wandered back outside, the air was still warm. Dougie gave a laugh and made a show of fanning himself. 'Spring in Scotland is usually wind and rain with an occasional bout of sunshine.'

'Well, spring in Washington can equal sweltering days and cooler evenings. This heat isn't unusual at all.'

They walked along the street towards the Botanic Gardens. Alice seemed more relaxed. She hadn't looked at her phone once since they'd left the house. Maybe she'd put it on silent. But whatever had been bothering her before seemed to have been forgotten about now. Dougie was glad. The more time he spent around Alice, the more protective of her he found himself. She was a beautiful woman, with an edge of stubbornness that he actually liked. She could give him a run for his money with an eighties movie marathon, and would probably beat him at any eighties music quiz. He liked the way she was happy to argue with him and stand her ground. It didn't make him shift his position, but that didn't matter. She had an easy way with patients, and clearly adored the babies she cared for. She was intelligent, and gorgeous. Sharing a place with her meant his thoughts occasionally strayed where they shouldn't. But no one knew that but him. There were times when her brown eyes held his gaze for a fraction longer than necessary, or her words had a teasing edge to them. For the first time in a long time it made him wonder about a workmate. He'd never dated anyone from work since Kayla. He had dated other women. Sienna, who worked in cyber security, and then Julie, who was a professional tennis coach in London. But neither relationship had given the same kind of sparks he felt around Alice. He was doing his best to ignore everything about this. But walking with her in the sunshine, playing tourist in her city and being in her company this long—made her hard to ignore.

They entered the beautiful gardens, with paths throughout and a large conservatory in the distance.

'It's nice just to walk, isn't it?' said Alice. Dougie was so easy to be around.

He bent over to take a closer look at one of the flowers. 'Wondered what that one was called,' he murmured.

'You like flowers and plants?'

He waggled one hand from side to side. 'I don't have a garden in London, but the house my mum and dad have in Scotland has an enormous garden. I played in it when I was young. We had brambles, raspberry bushes, apple and pear trees and a whole row of cherry blossom trees.' He glanced around. 'The cherry blossoms around Washington remind me of home.'

Alice stopped for a minute and inhaled deeply, letting the scents wash over her. They were next to a bed of red tulips, each one immaculate. 'We moved around a lot as kids. Most Army houses did have gardens, but we weren't really there long enough to plant and grow plants or trees.' She envied the fact he'd had a large play area at his fingertips.

'What were your favourite flowers?'

He blinked for a minute and she realised it was an unusual question for a man. But Dougie seemed as at ease as ever. 'That's simple. I like colour. Livingstone daisies.'

She wrinkled her nose and he pulled out his phone and typed something in. 'They might have a different name.' He turned the phone around to reveal the pinks, yellows, whites and oranges of the small flowers. 'Yip, one I can't pronounce.'

She touched his screen. 'They're beautiful. I've heard the name, but couldn't remember what they look like.'

She pulled up her own phone. 'That's weird. The one I like best looks like a daisy too. Here—' She swung her phone around to show him the orange gerberas. 'I only have pots at the entrance to the townhouse and have tried a few times to grow them, but my doorstep is directly in the sun and they always seem to die after a few weeks, which is why I've only got lavender right now. I guess I'm just not as green-fingered as I'd like to be.'

They'd walked near to the entrance of the conservatory. She grinned at him. 'Wait until we get inside. But be warned, at one point you might need to hold your nose.'

Dougie frowned. 'What?'

She laughed. 'It's a surprise; come on.'

Alice had been through this conservatory a dozen times already this year, so she knew exactly where she was going. They moved past orchids and ferns before Dougie gave a cough. His nose wrinkled.

'What is that?'

Other people had scarves or masks around their faces. The closer they got, the stronger the smell.

They rounded another corner and Alice pointed to the giant, oddly shaped flower. 'Meet *amorphophallus titanum*,' she said.

Dougie coughed again as he tilted his head to look at the flower. 'Did you just say phallus?'

She laughed. 'I did.'

His eyes darted between her and the giant flower. 'It does look a bit like…' He let his words trail off. 'But the smell…' His hand was up at his nose.

She smiled. 'Yip, when it blooms it smells like rotting flesh. We call it the corpse flower.'

Even though the smell was horrific, there were still a number of curious tourists taking pictures of the burgundy bloom. Alice reached out and grabbed Dougie's hand, pulling him towards the nearest exit. When they got outside she dropped his hand, but was aware of the empty feeling in her palm.

'This is where you bring me?' he asked. 'I get you

to show me the secrets around Washington, and you bring me to a flower that looks like a penis and smells like a rotting corpse.'

As they burst out into the fresh air, Alice doubled over laughing. 'You're a medic. I knew you could take it. Plus, don't let it be said that I don't take you to the best places.'

They were back outside now, surrounded by lush lawns and flower beds filled with rainbows of colour. 'Now this—' Dougie held out his hands '—is beautiful. This is a pleasant walk. A place to get to know someone. Take a seat, while away the day. *That*—' he turned around and pointed '—is a scene from a horror movie. I'm just waiting for the axe-murderer to jump out and chase us.'

He was play-acting, and she knew it. What was more, she liked it. She'd liked being around this guy all day. The work stuff had been pushed to one side, even though she knew it would likely crop up again. For now, she was forgetting about the fact they worked together, forgetting about the complicating factor that they were sharing a place. Right now, she was just concentrating on the chemistry in the air between them.

'Had enough yet?' she teased. 'Or are you brave enough to continue?'

He leaned forward, closer than she expected. 'You have more?'

Part of his dark hair fell across his brow. She resisted the itch in her fingers to reach out and push it back. She focused on his lips. 'I have a lot more.' She couldn't help the way the words came out. She hadn't meant them to sound sexy, but the implication was there before she even really knew it.

Dougie froze. The sides of his mouth lifted slowly.

He didn't pull back, just kept looking at her with those flashing blue eyes. Whether she'd meant the implication or not was irrelevant because it was there, and it seemed as if he'd reached out and grabbed it.

Alice was holding her breath. She was thanking her lucky stars that he hadn't jumped back and laughed it off like some stupid joke. That would have made her feel about two feet tall.

She hadn't misread anything. The looks. The brushed arms and hands.

He kept still. 'Okay then.' His voice was low and husky. He reached out and took her hand. A very deliberate act. She'd grabbed him first. But that had been just to get him through the crowds and to the way out of the conservatory. This was much more.

'Where to?' he asked.

Alice breathed out slowly, her brain misting for a few seconds. Then she instantly remembered her original plan. 'Okay.' She smiled as they started walking. 'We're heading back to Foggy Bottom. I'm going to show the hidden gem we try not to tell others about.'

'Lead the way.'

The subway was busy, and they ended up crushed next to each other. But neither objected. The air between them had changed. Her head was confused. She didn't want to get close to any man. The dating apps allowed her to keep all men at a real distance. After last time, she was scared to let her guard down—scared to trust whether she should allow any man to get close to her. So why on earth was she letting Dougie hold her hand?

She hated being confused like this. She felt safe around Dougie. But what if she'd got that wrong? What if her instincts about him were wrong?

She swallowed and looked down at their joined

hands. Dougie was looking in the other direction, talking freely to another Scot he'd just met on the subway. She took a deep breath, telling herself this was nothing. This was only a first step. She could pull back any time she wanted. Those thoughts washed over her, stopping the rise of panic and giving her the reassurance that she needed.

Alice looked down at her clothes as they left the subway and made a quick call on her phone. It was the first time she'd looked at it all day. She was thankful there was nothing on the screen. 'Maris, it's me. Can I come along in twenty minutes?'

When she heard the news she wanted, she turned back to Dougie. 'Okay, so we're going somewhere a little more upscale. There isn't officially a dress code, but I guess shorts might be pushing it.' She started hurrying along the street towards the townhouse.

Dougie looked curious. 'I need trousers?'

She nodded. 'Yes, pants.'

He shuddered. 'That word means something a whole lot different in Scotland. Trousers. I need trousers.'

'Keep telling yourself that.' She laughed as she opened the front door to the townhouse. 'Now, you need to be ready in ten minutes.'

'I'll beat you,' he said casually as his long legs started to stride up the stairs.

'No way,' she joked as she ran up behind him and ducked into her room.

Less than ten minutes later they were back by the front door. Dougie had changed into black trousers and a black shirt open at the neck. Alice had grabbed the first dress in her closet. It hadn't been out in some time. But the red slash-neck dress with a dipping back had always been easy to wear. She'd slid her feet into black strappy sandals, not too high for the quick walk ahead, and brushed some powder on her face, along with some red lipstick. Her hair had to stick to the same style from earlier today. There was no time for a refresh.

'Are you going to tell me where we're going?'

She shook her head. 'But it's fun. You'll like it. I have a friend who works there.'

'That's who you called earlier?'

She nodded as they walked down the street. 'You have to reserve in advance, but Maris always finds room for me.' She held out her hand. 'Maybe we should have brought jackets. It can get really cool in the evenings.'

'It's not too bad,' started Dougie, then stopped and looked at her. 'Ah, so we'll be outside?'

'Maybe.' They kept walking and she led him into a luxurious hotel.

Dougie gave a low wolf whistle. 'This place is nice.'

The elevator took them to the roof and Alice walked ahead and out to the rooftop bar. 'Now, this is the best kept secret in Foggy Bottom.' She smiled as she held out her arms and spun around to face him.

Dougie's eyes were wide. The bar, based on a balcony, overlooked the Potomac River. There was a collection of low couches and some high tables and chairs. The area was edged by a smoked glass safety barrier that zigzagged around the roof, set with white lights.

'Definitely nice,' he murmured. 'I imagine it looks just as good from the river as it does from here.' His arm slid around Alice's waist.

A woman with blonde hair and a smart black uniform gave Alice a wave and walked over, kissing her on both cheeks. She held out her hand to Dougie. 'Maris Cairns. I know all of Alice's secrets and I can be bought with candy.'

Alice's stomach fluttered. She could tell from the expression on Maris's face that she approved already.

Dougie laughed. 'You're clearly secret twins, since I already know that Alice can be bought with candy too.'

Maris's eyes widened and she gave Alice a gentle slap on the arm. 'Oh, you didn't warn me about the accent. You've got your own Sean Connery.'

Alice met his gaze. *'The Untouchables,'* she said. 'There's an eighties movie we haven't watched yet. We can watch that one later tonight.'

Maris looked at them both with amusement. 'Cosy,' she remarked, before leading them over to a high table next to the glass surround. She handed them drink menus. 'What would you like?'

Alice pondered for a moment. 'It's either white wine or the cocktail of the day.'

Maris smiled. 'It's Sunset Blaze—spiced rum, grenadine, orange juice, club soda and lime.'

'Sold,' said Alice immediately.

'And what about you?' Maris asked Dougie.

'I'll just have a beer, thanks.'

Maris disappeared and they settled on the stools looking over the river. The sun was dipping in the sky, sending purple and orange streaks across the water. 'This is a spectacular view,' said Dougie.

Alice nodded in appreciation. 'This is one of the few places that the locals like to come. Most of the high-end hotels around here only cater for their guests. But this place realised early on it could capture a bit of what was missing for the local residents. Somewhere trendy, not completely out of the price zone and somewhere spectacular to sit.'

'Do you come here a lot?' Dougie asked.

Her skin prickled. Was he asking if she'd brought

other dates here? Because that was what this was—wasn't it? A date?

'If I'm meeting girlfriends, we frequently come here. It's a nice environment.' She pointed to a room through some glass doors. 'There's a whisky lounge through there if the weather is being difficult. But mainly we just like to sit out here, drink wine and cocktails and watch the world on the river.' She licked her lips as she looked around. 'It feels safe here. Obviously Maris is behind the bar tonight, but even when she's not, the staff here are good with locals. They shut down anyone who's getting a bit...forward,' she finished.

Alice was feeling totally relaxed in Dougie's company, so when she was met with silence she realised what she'd just said. Maris appeared and set down their drinks and some nuts before moving away.

Alice took a sip of her cocktail. 'Delicious,' she said. When she looked up, she could see his gaze fixed on her, worry creasing his forehead.

'Safe,' he repeated slowly. 'Are there places around here you don't feel safe?'

'Well, no, but I mean there's always places in every city that aren't too safe...' She was babbling now and she knew it. 'But this place is good like that. I've never felt as if I had anything to worry about when I'm here.'

Darn it. She hadn't really wanted to talk about the fact she'd literally found herself casing every joint she'd walked into since the stalking incident. Looking for anyone out of place, or anyone who could cause trouble. Several times in the last year, she'd encouraged friends to move on from places where there were large groups of rowdy men, or others on their own that stared for too long. All things she would never have considered in the past. She hated that one incident with someone had made her wary of the world.

Dougie's words were measured. 'I get that safety is an issue for everyone these days. And I'm glad you've found a place that you feel safe in. Everyone should have a place like that.' He looked around appreciatively. 'And this is certainly a beautiful place.'

They both watched as some boats and a group of canoes came along the darkening river. Quiet music played in the background, mixing with the conversation around them and the sounds from the river beneath. 'I get why you like this place.'

'See—' smiled Alice '—I saved the best for last.'

'I thought you claimed the corpse flower was the best?'

'I was just keeping you on your toes. There's still plenty more to see around Washington.'

'I think I'm going to stick to the more traditional venues next time. I've still to go to the Lincoln Memorial and the Smithsonian.'

'You'll like them too. I just wanted you to see the quaint and cute. The things you probably wouldn't see on your own.'

As he looked at her, she could sense something change between them again. He reached over and touched her hand. 'I really appreciate what you did today. I've had fun.'

'So have I.' The words came out a little hoarser than she meant them to. But her vocal cords had decided to panic at the way he was looking at her.

It wasn't as if it hadn't happened before. Of course a guy had looked at her before, in a way that meant she knew entirely what might happen next.

She kept her hand exactly where it was. His hand was resting over hers lightly, his thumb tracing circles around the edge of one finger.

'Can we do it again?' he asked.

Every part of her wanted to scream *Yes*—even though she didn't usually get involved with anyone at work. But it had worked for her sister. Penny had met the love of her life at work. Now she and Benedict were happily engaged. And Alice wasn't even considering any of that. All she was contemplating here was a kiss. And kissing Dougie MacLachlan was certainly appealing.

Her throat was dry, her barriers still in place. Moving them even a little lower would be a huge step. Could she trust Dougie? Could she trust his intentions? Could she trust herself?

He'd always made her feel safe. Even though they battled at work, she'd never felt worried around him. It made her realise that she might have more trouble trusting herself than him. She said the words out loud, even though she still had reservations.

'I think that might work,' she said, unable to keep the smile out of her voice.

The connection between them was electric. Both stood at the same time and Dougie pulled her towards him. His hand slipped to her lower back as their mouths connected.

She could taste the cold beer on his lips. Her hands moved, first resting on his shoulders and then sliding around his neck.

She was conscious of where they were—somewhere very public. And the thoughts she was having right now weren't public in the slightest.

She pulled back from him, taking a breath and resting her head against his. 'Whoa,' she said softly.

Dougie didn't say a word, just gave her a slow smile and pulled out his wallet to cover the bill. Then he slid his hand into hers and led her out of the bar.

CHAPTER SIX

DOUGIE WAS SETTLING into the way of things in the NICU in Washington. He'd had time to look at all the protocols and procedures within the unit and had been happy to see that they were regularly updated and reviewed by a multi-disciplinary team.

He'd made a few suggestions to Tara, the charge nurse, about the layout of some of the paper recording sheets kept at the foot of each incubator. She'd listened and taken on board his suggestions, reviewing them alongside the staff and producing some new templates to trial for a month. It had been entirely minor, but he'd noticed a few staff forgot to record some details on the other side of one of the charts. Reviewing the layout and bringing it all onto one page would hopefully stop that happening.

So whilst his work life was going well, his personal life was going even better. But there was no doubt in Dougie's mind that he still had trust issues. Alice was feisty and occasionally lazy. She was meticulous at work at all times. But on her time off she could spend days where she was up early in the morning and keep going until last thing at night, but she also had days where she could drink diet soda, snack on some chocolate and have a giant book or movie binge.

Their first kiss had resulted in a strained farewell on the stairs that night. Since then, they'd become more comfortable around each other in the house. Dougie was careful not to push and let things go at a pace they were both comfortable with. Last night they'd started watching a movie, but then spent most of the night kissing on the sofa. It was amazing how many hours could be spent just concentrating on the perfect kiss—and at this stage he was sure they had aced it.

But it didn't stop the worries circulating in his head. He had doubts. And he hated himself for that. It was as if there was a silent voice always whispering *Are you sure?* in his head. He didn't think Alice was anything like Kayla. But the idea of trusting someone after everything that had happened with her was hard. Really hard.

Today, they were both working again. Both were careful around each other in the workplace. Everyone knew they were living together, but neither felt ready to share that things might be moving on between them and, to be honest, that suited him.

The conversation around this had been easy for them both. 'I don't want anyone at work to know about us,' Alice had said. 'I don't want anyone's opinion or comments.'

'Me neither,' he'd agreed. 'Let's just keep what's happening between us just between us. At least until we know what this is.'

They'd agreed with a kiss. A very long kiss, and that had been fine.

Truth was, Dougie didn't know how things might develop between them. A one-night stand wasn't on the agenda. Something for a few weeks might be fun, or even something for the duration of Dougie's contract, which was six months. But he hadn't even considered what he might do next. His contract had an option to extend, but he wasn't sure if his long-term future would be in the US, as opposed to London, Scotland or anywhere else. And it was clear to him that, after years of being an Army kid, Alice had put down firm roots in Washington. Neither of them was ready for that kind of conversation yet.

He also wondered if his brain would ever stop questioning itself again. The barriers he'd put in place since the incident with Kayla were deeper rooted than he'd ever realised. He'd imagined if he met someone again he'd eventually be able to throw off his trust issues and doubts. But he was struggling to adjust. Maybe it was because he worked with Alice and the added complications would always be there. No matter how comfortable he tried to be in this relationship.

The morning had been relatively calm in the NICU so far. Dougie was just reviewing some charts when the phone rang.

'NICU. Dr MacLachlan.'

'This is Rhonda from the ER. We have a pregnant woman on the way in following an RTA. Paramedics are reporting severe trauma, with the potential for immediate delivery. ETA ten minutes. Can we have a neonatologist and NICU nurse for emergency theatre?'

'Absolutely, be there in a few minutes.'

He replaced the receiver and relayed the message to Tara. She took one look around the unit. 'Take Alice with you and I'll get someone to cover your patients. Let me know how it goes. We have a spot available if required.'

He nodded and hurried over to Alice, touching her elbow and telling her the news. They ran down the corridor and stairs towards the emergency theatre, meeting one of the obstetricians, who was talking into a phone, giving instructions.

Both Dougie and Alice were already wearing scrubs, but dived into the nearest locker room to grab a clean set and pull on surgical hats. They were at sinks scrubbing a few moments later as one of the other staff wheeled an incubator in.

The obstetrician had started scrubbing with the phone tucked between her ear and neck. One of the other staff was tucking her hair under a hat.

'Any more information?' Dougie asked.

The obstetrician finally stopped speaking and turned to face them, her face pale, worry lines deep in her brow. 'Sorry, I'm Val Kearney. Mom is being resuscitated after being cut out the car. It will need to be an immediate Caesarean section. I can't even tell you her gestation right now.'

She took a deep breath and looked around at the staff. 'Everyone please prepare—we have around two minutes. Ambulance is pulling into the ER bay now.'

There was silence. Even though her face was hidden behind a mask, he could see the worry on Alice's face. Staff from NICU could be called at short notice to an emergency delivery. But he didn't know how often she'd been in Theatre and how she would cope with a situation like this.

His own stomach was clenching uncomfortably. No one wanted to hear the news that a pregnant woman was being resuscitated. A door opened and a man, fully gowned and masked, walked through. 'Leo Atwell,' he said. 'General surgeon. I've been asked to assist.' He nodded to the obstetrician. 'Obviously, you go first. But tell me if I can do anything to assist. As soon as baby is out, I'll see if I can do anything to save mom.'

One of the nurses gave a shout. 'We have a positive ID on mom. Lila Higgins, age thirty-four. Hospital records show this is her second pregnancy, nothing untoward noted, expecting a boy and she's thirty-three weeks. She's normally under Dr Amjad.'

There was a nodding of heads. Val moved over to the theatre table. 'Someone let Dr Amjad know the situation with his patient, please.'

For the next few seconds there was silence, with all eyes on the door.

Dougie took a few deep breaths. Calm was what was needed. These people were professionals. They could do this.

The doors burst open. A paramedic was on top doing chest compressions. A doctor was alongside; it was clear he'd got IV access. Another nurse was at the top of the trolley, bagging the patient.

Everyone jumped down and there was a simultaneous movement to slide Lila Higgins onto the theatre trolley. With low voices, everyone did their role. The anaesthetist took over the airway. Theatre nurses cut clothes and attached monitor leads. Dougie and Alice stood back, ready for the next step, waiting to receive the baby.

Lila's stomach was wiped with antiseptic solution as the resus continued. Val Kearney waited for a nod from the anaesthetist and, in what felt like moments, had the little boy out. She placed him into Dougie's waiting hands.

From that point on, all Dougie's and Alice's focus was on the little boy. He was floppy and blue to begin with, but quickly began to pick up. Breathing started with little assistance, oxygen support was given and Alice attached the monitors and read out all of the recordings. A third member of staff charted everything as they talked out loud. Dougie was impressed by how methodical Alice was. She was completely focused and a perfect assistant. As they worked together to establish the condition of the baby, it was as if she read his mind.

They could hear quiet chaos going on behind them, but neither turned around. Once they were happy that their patient was stabilised enough to transfer up to the NICU, Dougie finally looked over his shoulder.

Leo Atwell was working carefully, as units of blood were going in on both sides, and Val was stitching up the uterus. 'Clamp,' he said quietly.

'There's a lot of blood,' whispered Alice.

Dougie nodded. 'It must be her spleen or liver that was damaged in the accident. I hope he can manage to get the bleeding under control.'

Alice fastened the identity band around the tiny wrist. The resuscitation was continuing and tension was mounting. Dougie put his hand on Alice's shoulder. Neither of them had any idea how long the resuscitation had been going before Lila was brought into the theatre.

'Halt,' came the firm voice of Leo Atwell. There was silence for a second, then a slow beep-beep was heard from one of the monitors.

Lila had a heartbeat again. When Dougie looked back over, Val had finished stitching and was round next to Leo, holding a clamp. Dougie couldn't imagine that these two surgeons had ever worked together before, but both were doing their absolute best to give this mum a fighting chance.

As the heartbeat continued, both lifted their heads. 'How's our boy?' asked Val. It was clear that up until this point they'd been just as focused as Dougie and Alice had. Patients always came first.

'Stable enough to transfer up to NICU,' said Dougie.

'Wonderful.' Val nodded. 'Go on up, and we'll let you know how things go with mom.'

Alice moved to a nearby phone on the wall and let Tara know they were coming up. The theatre had a set of elevators exclusively for use for patients and they moved the incubator into one of those. As the doors closed, both pulled off their masks.

Alice moved over and hugged Dougie. It was clear that relief was flooding through both of them. 'Welcome to the world, little guy,' said Dougie, looking down at the baby boy. 'We're hoping your mum or dad will get a chance to give you a name soon.'

Alice wiped her eyes. 'That was horrendous. I feel as if I've gone ten rounds in a boxing ring.' She pulled her watch from her pocket and shook her head. 'It's barely been an hour since we got the initial call.'

Dougie shook his head. 'This little guy was so lucky. He perked up so quickly, and at thirty-three weeks here's hoping we won't have too many complications.'

The hug felt good. It was only for a few moments, but it felt good to have someone to hold onto right now. Lots of staff found it hard to explain the huge adrenaline rushes of reacting to emergencies, followed by the lows that came after. The only people who really understood were those who worked alongside. He put a kiss on her nose, then released Alice before the elevator doors slid back open. Both of them moved instantly back to their positions at the side of the incubator and wheeled it quickly down the corridor to NICU, where their colleagues were waiting.

Tara and a fellow doctor took a handover report and then she gave them both a nod. 'Go and take a break. I know how these things are. I'll see if I can find out any more from the theatre staff.'

Dougie looked reluctantly at the little boy they'd just seen delivered. He wanted to stay. He wanted to make sure everything was done exactly the way he thought it should be, but he knew he had to trust his fellow colleagues. And Tara was right. She wanted to give them both some time to decompress. It was likely that at some point the whole team—ER, theatre, obstetrics and NICU staff—would be asked to get together and learn from today.

Alice came over and gave him a nudge. 'I want some coffee, and some dessert. Let's take five.'

Dougie nodded and grabbed his jacket, ensuring he had his wallet. She looked at him in surprise. 'Let's go a bit further than the canteen.'

She gave a nod. 'Let me get my jacket.' She turned towards Tara to tell her they might be a bit longer, but it seemed that Tara had already guessed as she gave a wave of her hand, telling them to go on.

Dougie walked down the corridor with Alice and as they stepped into the elevator he slipped his hand into hers. She looked up at him in surprise, but didn't pull her hand away. She just moved closer, her shoulder pressing against his. It was a big hospital. Someone might see them together, but equally they might be anonymous to all those around them.

When they reached the ground floor, Dougie walked in long strides across the main foyer and led her out, turning left, then crossing the street to a bakery.

She reached her other hand over and grasped his arm, smiling in delight as they walked through the door and were greeted with the smells of warm bread, sweet cakes and good coffee.

It was a place most of the hospital staff loved but rarely had time to visit during the day. The woman behind the counter gave them a wide smile, clocked their uniforms and nodded to a table. There were other people in the bakery, but the woman came over immediately, as if she realised time would be a priority. 'What can I get you both?'

Alice's eyes looked over at the glass-fronted cabinet. Dougie knew that she'd been in here before and would likely have a favourite dessert. 'Can I have a skinny latte with an extra shot, and a slice of the pecan pie, please?'

'With cream?'

'Oh, go on then,' Alice said, smiling.

'I'll have a cappuccino, and a piece of the apple and caramel pie.' He gave a nod before she asked. 'And yes, with cream, please.'

The bakery owner smiled. 'Be right with you.'

As she walked away Alice reached over and threaded her fingers through Dougie's. 'I'm praying,' she murmured in a low voice. 'Praying for that poor mom, her new baby, her other kid and the poor father, who will be having a heart attack when he hears what's happened to his family.'

Dougie swallowed, his mouth dry. He squeezed her fingers. 'I get that. I've seen a lot of things in my time. But that has to be the most traumatic delivery ever.' He spoke carefully. 'But our little guy? He could be fine. Time will tell. He was flat to begin with, and we don't know if there was a lack of oxygen to him while his mum was being treated. But his recovery was good and he stabilised really quickly. Everything up until that point in the pregnancy seems to have been fine.'

Alice blinked. There were tears pooling in her eyes. 'I hate that bit,' she admitted. 'The part where someone does everything possible to do things right and live a healthy life, then something happens completely out of their control. And that's it. It can mean life or death.'

She looked up as the waitress came back with the coffees and pie. She shook her head as she picked up her fork. 'It's kind of ironic, isn't it, that I'm talking about a healthy lifestyle when I'm about to eat pie.'

'We've had a big morning. We need something to give us a boost. And you are healthy. You're the one with your yoga mat out every other morning, twisting into positions that make my eyes water. You're the one that does those strange noodly vegetable things when you should be using spaghetti.'

She laughed. 'Carrot and courgette is good for you.'

'Not when it's paired with bolognaise.'

She smiled, but they stared at each other for a few moments, then ate some of their pie, still holding hands.

This was something entirely new to Dougie. He'd spent time with colleagues before after a traumatic event. He'd held a crying medical student who'd had to deal with the death of someone her own age. He'd sat next to an older doctor who'd had to debrief a whole team after one of their members of staff had been attacked and seriously injured.

But he hadn't done *this*. He hadn't watched a young mum being resuscitated while her baby was delivered. He hadn't sat later with someone he cared about. Someone he'd thought about during the events and hoped they would be okay.

Alice sipped her coffee and gave him a smile. 'I want you to know that you have permission to make the next few days nice and quiet.'

'I do?'

'Yip. Once we get back upstairs and sort out our boy,

I'm going to spend the rest of the day with the twins. Angie's starting to open up a little now. I'm pretty sure she's been bulimic in the past. She's feeling a lot of guilt about the twins right now, and I'm trying to encourage her to speak to one of the counsellors.'

'She's such a sad girl. So lonely. I hate that she has so little support.'

'I'm trying to strike a balance with her. Angie needs to recognise what she needs and be willing to have it. I don't want to force anything onto her. She's vulnerable enough. I think if I try and push her to attend groups or accept help from different agencies she might withdraw further. I want Angie to feel confident in herself. Confident that she can look after these babies and give them what they need. Of course, I think she needs some assistance, but I want her to feel comfortable enough that when we offer it she doesn't think it's a reflection on her. That will take time.'

'She's lucky to have such a good nurse.' Dougie smiled. He loved the passion that came into Alice's eyes when she talked about one of her patients and her commitment to doing the best job she could.

Alice gave a half-hearted smile. 'I don't get it.'

'Get what?' he asked.

'I know some of our colleagues get a buzz out of emergency situations. The adrenaline, the rush.' She shook her head. 'But just not me. I was terrified in the theatre. And when our little guy came out all limp...' Her voice tailed off.

He gave a slow nod. 'I know. I get it. It was completely and utterly terrifying.'

She lifted her head in surprise. 'You too?'

He smiled at her. 'One hundred per cent. I've looked after a lot of babies born in emergency situations. I've been called to Theatre a lot. But generally it's because the mum or baby have become suddenly unwell during the labour process. I've never had someone brought in who was being resuscitated. I only hope she can't remember a single thing about it—' he squeezed Alice's hand again '—and she wakes up and realises that she has a beautiful son, who is doing fine.'

He knew it was all wishful thinking, but the wonders of modern medicine meant he could actually say those words. There was a chance that both of those things could turn out to be true—her surviving and her baby being fine.

He looked down at their coffee cups and plates. 'We should go back.'

Alice nodded. 'Yeah, we should. I'm kind of scared to find out what happens next.'

Dougie gave a nod as he stood up and left some money for the bill. He paused for a second, then held his hand out towards her.

He thought she might refuse. They might have held hands on the way down, but they'd just both come out of a scary situation. He knew Alice hadn't really wanted anyone in NICU to know about them yet, but something had shifted between them.

She stood up and reached out and took his hand. There was no hesitation. And they walked back into the hospital and up to the unit together.

CHAPTER SEVEN

'WHY DIDN'T YOU tell me?' Penny had the widest smile on her face. It was the next day and it seemed that word had somehow leaked out about her and Dougie.

Alice shifted uncomfortably in the tiny coffee room on the unit. 'Because I wasn't sure if it was going to be something or not.'

'Well, it clearly is.' Penny hadn't stopped smiling.

Alice smiled too. 'Well, yes, maybe.'

Penny leaned against the wall and folded her arms. 'So, tell me more?'

Alice's phone sounded in her pocket and she pulled it out and frowned. Reading the message, she felt her stomach lurch.

'What's wrong?' Penny asked immediately, then pointed at the phone. 'And "King of Wishful Thinking" from *Pretty Woman* is far too easy to guess! And isn't it the nineties?'

Alice nodded automatically at her sister's guess. 'What can I say—I actually like that song. It's kind of catchy.'

'So, are you going to tell me what's wrong?' She should have known her sister wouldn't let it go. Penny was never easily brushed off.

'Promise me you won't flip.'

Penny's face was instantly worried. 'What do you mean?'

Alice sighed as she poured out two coffees. 'Okay, so remember when you moved away for a while?'

'With my disastrous ex-fiancé, yes.' Her brow furrowed. 'Why? What happened that you didn't tell me?'

Alice swallowed uncomfortably. She'd always known the day would come when she'd have to tell her sister what had happened. She never usually kept secrets from her sister and there had just never been a good time to bring this up.

'So, I met a guy on a dating app.'

'Not unusual,' said Penny, clearly wanting Alice to get to the point.

Alice sighed. 'I dated him for around six weeks—but then broke it off. I just got a bad vibe and decided he wasn't for me.'

'So what happened?' Penny's voice had an edge to it. Alice knew she was going to be mad.

'Things got weird. He started turning up places I was. And things happened around the house.'

'What things?'

Alice pulled a face. 'My plant died.'

The furrows in Penny's brow deepened. 'The one at the front door?'

Alice nodded.

'But that's not so unusual.'

Alice sighed again. 'I know. But I bought a new one, and it died. And so did the third. Then I got a note pushed through the door, and a few messages from the same guy.'

'Who was he? Do I know him?'

Alice shook her head. 'I ended up speaking to George about him.'

'Our George?' It was clear Penny was surprised. Their friend George was a DC cop. He was steadfast and eminently sensible. But he wouldn't take crap from anyone.

Alice nodded. 'When I sat down and went over everything and asked for advice he told me it was stalking. He made me fill out an official report and went and had a chat with the guy. Things went quiet after that.'

'And you never told me any of this? Why not? How long did this go on for?'

Alice pushed a cup of coffee into her sister's hand in an effort to stop her waving it around. 'You had enough going on. You'd just found out Mitchel had a wife and kids. Last thing you needed was me giving you any more worries.'

Penny put her free hand on her chest. 'But I'm your sister. This is exactly the kind of stuff you should be telling me. You shouldn't have had to go through that yourself. Who was this guy, anyway?'

Alice shook her head. 'His name was Dave. He worked in IT. I think he probably wasn't well. But he'd misread just about everything between us. Said I'd led him on and encouraged him.'

'What?' Penny looked mad. But something else suddenly occurred to her. 'Idiot. So, what's happening now? Is that him that's just messaged you?'

Alice pulled out her phone and opened it with her fingerprint. 'He can't message me. I blocked him. But I've had some weird messages lately, through a few of the other dating apps.'

Penny swiped her screen. She turned to her sister. 'Where have they all gone?'

'The apps? Every time I get a weird message via one, I just delete it.'

'What kind of weird messages?'

Reuben, one of the doctors, came into the small space to grab a coffee. 'Excuse me,' he said, giving Alice a sideways glance that made her wonder if he'd heard part of their conversation. She waited until he'd left before continuing. She ran her fingers through her hair, untying her ponytail and tidying it up.

Penny pointed. 'You're anxious. You should have spoken to me about this sooner.'

'What?'

'You always do that, when you're anxious about something.' She gave a smile and lifted her eyebrows for a second. 'What's that word Dougie keeps using? Footering? That's what you're doing—footering with your hair.'

'Is that even a word? And I do not.' Alice shot a glare at her sister. She hated it when Penny was right.

'I'm your sister. I know. Now, tell me about these messages.'

Alice closed her eyes for a second. 'I have no idea who they are from—or if they are all from the same person. It's not like I haven't received a weird message before from a dating app. But all of the profiles have been recently formed, all with different photos. One was just quite obscene, so I deleted it and the app. Then another was just quite forward. Naming a place they wanted to take me on a date, and what we could drink.'

'What was wrong with that?'

'The place they named was Roosters, and the drink was Sauvignon Blush.'

Penny's face was serious. 'Your regular bar for dates, and your regular drink?'

She nodded. 'I also got one that mentioned the top I was wearing that day and then another about the plant on my front doorstep.'

Penny put her hand on Alice's arm. 'You have to talk to George again. Have you told Dougie about this? What does he say?'

Alice rolled her eyes. 'No, I haven't told Dougie. This whole thing with him is brand-new. I don't want to tell him I've been registered on around seven different dating apps for the last year and things are catching up with me.'

Penny looked confused for a minute, then her jaw clenched. 'Stop it. You're not doing this. This is not your fault. Don't take the blame for this. You can be registered on as many different dating apps as you darn well please. It's no one's business but your own. And nothing is catching up with you. But this just doesn't seem right. Talking about what you're wearing and what's on your doorstep. That's just plain creepy.'

Hearing her sister say the words out loud let Alice focus. She'd been avoiding this, trying to brush it all off. The truth was, having Dougie in the house with her had made her feel safe. Protected. But that wasn't fair on him. This was her issue. She needed to deal with it herself.

'You're right,' she said. 'I'll talk to George again, and think about mentioning it to Dougie.' She raised a finger. 'But don't you do it. It's up to me.'

'Okay.' Penny nodded. 'But you better do it.' She stopped for a second and put her hands on Alice's shoulders. 'I wish you'd told me. I know I had other stuff happening, but you're still my sister, I still wanted to know.'

Alice's hand closed over her sister's. 'It worked out fine. I knew I needed help and George did that. And I don't want you to worry about any of this other stuff. Go and concentrate on Benedict and be happy.'

Penny looked at her sister again. 'Tell me if you need anything.' She glanced out of the coffee room to the NICU, where Dougie was talking to another doctor. 'And I want all the gossip on your new man.'

Alice took a final drink of coffee and rinsed out her mug, laughing at her sister. 'Absolutely not!'

As she walked out she felt a certain sense of relief that she'd finally filled her sister in on what had happened in the past. She cast her eyes over to where Dougie was standing. He was talking to the doctor who'd been assigned to their emergency delivery.

Alice made her way over. 'Any news on what's happening?'

The other guy, Kabir, gave a nod. 'Mom is in adult intensive care and hasn't regained consciousness yet. Her spleen and part of her liver were removed after the accident. She's had numerous transfusions, and her blood pressure has come up. From what I hear, they're considering reducing her sedation today.'

Dougie turned to face her. 'And our boy has a name. Lyle. Dad apparently was in last night, but is still really upset. Lyle is doing quite well. He's breathing on his own, with some additional oxygen, and although he was tube fed last night because he didn't have much motivation to suck, we're going to try again today.'

'Hello, Lyle.' Alice smiled as she looked down at the baby from yesterday. At thirty-three weeks he was bigger than a lot of the other babies in the unit. 'I'm glad to meet you properly. Yesterday was a big day.'

The nurse who had been looking after Lyle joined them. 'Dad was just in too much shock last night,' she said. 'But...' she smiled down at Lyle too '...hopefully when he comes back in today, we'll see if we can get him to hold you and try feeding you.'

'I'm on call tonight,' said Dougie. 'So, give me a shout if you need anything at all.'

Alice's heart gave a little lurch. 'You covering for someone?' She knew that Dougie wasn't due to be on call.

'Yeah, Lesley Jenkins is feeling under the weather. She asked if I would swap with her.' He glanced at Alice. 'We didn't have plans, did we?'

'No, not at all.' Except she would have liked to be honest with Dougie about the messages. She didn't think for a second he'd react badly. But it would have felt a little bit like a safety net if she'd told him.

She gave him a wave and made her way back to the twins, Ruby and Ryan. Both were doing okay right now. But Angie, their mum, just looked worse and worse.

Alice did all her normal checks on the babies, then sat down with Angie for a while. Angie admitted she hadn't been sleeping at all, and had no appetite. She was feeling guilty because the babies still seemed so detached from her, and she didn't feel like a real mom.

Alice understood. Everyone reacted differently to their baby being in NICU, and Angie had less support than some. She also said that the person she'd found easiest to talk to had been her labour and delivery nurse. It was normal for a patient to form an attachment to the person who'd been there for them during a traumatic time, and Alice wasn't at all upset to hear the person Angie had bonded with best wasn't her. This was about Angie. Alice had been doing this job long enough to know what was important. NICU often worked hand in hand with some of the midwifery or labour and delivery staff and after a quick chat Tara was able to negotiate some time for the nurse to come to the unit.

Things progressed quickly, with Angie agreeing to go out for a walk with the nurse and spend some time away from the unit—only on the proviso that Alice stayed with the babies.

As time moved on, Tara found her again. She gave a sad smile. 'So, Angie's scored highly on the postnatal depression scale, and has admitted to having an eating disorder. She's upset, but recognises she needs some support. The rest of the staff are working with her, but she's insisting you stay with her babies, otherwise she'll come back to the unit.' Tara held out her hands. 'You're due to finish soon and I don't want you to feel pressured into working extra hours if you have plans.'

Alice shook her head. 'I have no plans, and am happy to stay. If me being here is the reassurance that Angie needs, that's fine. I'm just glad she's opened up to someone and hopefully can start to get some help.'

Tara gave a small nod. 'Thanks, Alice.'

The hours passed slowly, but Alice didn't mind. There were other staff on duty in the NICU, but her being there as an extra meant that someone else wasn't assigned to the twins. They were perfect angels with no problems at all, making Alice's job easy.

Dougie was busy. There were a few new admissions and another baby who'd deteriorated and required intubation. There was a quiet hum to the unit for a couple of hours. Staff were efficient and Alice got a chance to sit back and watch for a while. She offered to help out on a few occasions, and to cover breaks, but being an extra pair of hands was odd to Alice and left her a bit restless.

Time was probably not what she needed right now. She had taken screenshots of the messages she'd received via the various apps. As she sat, she flicked through them and let her mind go backwards and forwards. One minute she'd decide they were all related to her previous stalker and things were serious. And then the next minute she decided that it was all just a series of unconnected unfortunate events.

The hours were starting to creep on, and Alice couldn't help how secretly glad she was not to be back at the house by herself. And it wasn't just about being unnerved. It was being around Dougie.

They might not be sitting together or talking, but she could feel his presence in the unit. She kept stealing little glances at him, the way his hair fell over his forehead, the expanse of his shoulders, how meticulous he was at work, when he looked serious, when he smiled and when he was joking with someone.

She was freaking herself out a little by how much she liked being around him and enjoyed his company. Wasn't this supposed to be how things went when you got together with someone?

Every now and then he caught her eye and gave her a smile. She could swear it was only for her.

He was relatively easygoing at home. They'd made a rule not to talk about work, but there was a whole host of other things to talk about. They'd planned some more day trips. He was happy to go for a walk with her around the city, meandering around a few stores, buying a takeout coffee and just wasting a few hours together. Movie marathons were a must, usually followed by an impassioned argument about best/worst movie, character, actor, setting, prop, or a mixture of them all.

She should be happy. She should be over the moon. But still the restlessness was there, the tiny doubts. She didn't know if the spate of messages had just unsettled her again—reminding her not to let down her guard and that appearances could be deceptive.

She looked up as he gave her a wave and made her way over. He was sitting next to Lyle's incubator, and what she hadn't noticed at first was that he had Lyle tucked into the crook of his neck.

She kept her voice to a whisper as she sat down in the chair next to him, before glancing around and putting her tired feet up on another chair. She edged her chair around so she still had a clear view of the twins' monitors. 'What are you doing?'

Dougie shrugged. 'Dad came in. But he only lasted a few minutes holding Lyle. It's all too much for him. He has a two-year-old daughter who keeps asking for her momma and his wife is still sedated in ICU, and the guy was literally just in pieces. I sent him back to ICU because it's clear that's where he needs to be right now.'

'So how come you've got Lyle?'

Dougie smiled down at the little figure, who seemed entirely comfortable. Lyle's face was close to Dougie's neck and his body was resting near the top of his chest over the thin scrubs that he was wearing. Dougie's scrubs meant that the baby had access to some parts of his skin, and one little hand was placed at the bottom of Dougie's throat.

'This little guy decided not to settle after his father held him. I think he liked the human contact. He's been wailing since then, so I decided it was time for a rest break for me and I'd have it holding him.'

'You're supposed to be on a break?'

He nodded but patted Lyle's back. 'This is a break. He's settled. He's happy. He managed to take some milk earlier; his sucking reflex is good.'

'Fabulous.' Alice smiled. It was one of the key steps

for any baby who came into NICU. Sucking and being able to feed was such a crucial skill, and some babies were born too early for that mechanism to have kicked in. But Lyle was thirty-three weeks. He was right on the cusp of being able to suck, and it was good news for him.

Alice shook her head as she rested back in the chair. How could she harbour doubts about a guy like this? Her skin prickled. This was about her. She had to make the step to trust again. She had to stop looking for something, anything, to give her an excuse not to.

'How's Ruby and Ryan?'

She gave a nod; it was a welcome distraction from her own thoughts. 'Really good. Observations stable. Oxygen levels good. No apparent digestion problems so far. They've been perfect tonight.'

She couldn't help but notice how tender he was being with Lyle. Every now and then he tilted his chin downwards and whispered to the little guy while rubbing his back gently.

He could see her watching him. 'You know what I find most fascinating?' he said in a low voice.

'What?'

'How every baby likes to be held differently. I've worked with some real old school staff who maintained there was only one way to hold a baby and they had the precious answer that worked for every baby. And the best of that was—they all said something different.'

Alice smiled and nodded in agreement. 'I've met some of them.'

Dougie lifted his free hand. 'Well, *they* might have had a preferred way to hold a baby. But it doesn't work for every baby. I had this little one every which way. I do believe in skin to skin. But that's primarily for the parent or carer. But isn't it interesting that Lyle has settled best when part of his skin can touch mine— even if it's only a tiny part? And I can feel every breath whilst he's against the top of my chest, just like he can sense mine.'

'You like this, don't you?'

'Doesn't everyone who works in a NICU?'

He had a point. Most staff who worked here were happy to take the time to settle a restless or uncomfortable baby, or to help a parent do the same. There was nothing nicer than seeing a baby sleeping, with their little chest going steadily up and down after a period of unrest.

But what Alice was having most trouble with was watching Dougie up close and personal with a baby. The care. The affection. It was written all over him and it was a side to him she'd never seen before.

She'd known he was a good and competent doctor. She'd known he was particular, with exacting standards. But this was new.

'Have you got young kids in your family?'

He looked at her in surprise. 'No, I'm an only child. But lots of the people I went through medical school with have settled down and have kids. Some of my friends from previous jobs too. I'm godfather to a good friend in Scotland's daughter. She's fourteen now, though, and keeps trying to make me do those fifteen-second dance clips.'

'And you say no?'

'I do the world a favour by saying no, believe me. Anyhow, any time there's any kind of reunion I always end up holding someone's baby, or entertaining the two-year-olds.' He grinned. 'Haven't you found that? Because you work in NICU, other folks think you'll be a natural with children. Then you find yourself surrounded by two-year-olds who seem like giants. Or babies born at a normal gestation and everyone questions you about weaning, or crawling, or immunisations at fifteen months.' He started to laugh. 'And then you want to hold your hands up and say, That's *way* past my area of expertise.'

Alice laughed too. 'We could probably have a competition called *What's That Rash?* How many times have you been sent a photo on your phone saying, Is this meningitis, measles, chickenpox, foot and mouth…?'

Dougie joined in. 'Prickly heat, slapped cheek, ringworm, scarlet fever, hives…' He raised his eyebrows. 'You've got all those photos too.'

She shifted her feet from the chair. 'We could probably write a book.'

'Would it stop the calls or texts?'

'Probably not.'

'Then what's the point?'

'True.' She stood up. 'I'm going back to my little angels. I expect Angie will be back some time soon.'

'Here's hoping she's going to start feeling better soon.'

'I'll let you know how it goes.' She went to move away, but Dougie stopped her.

'Alice?'

She spun back around. 'Yeah?'

'People know about us now.' His voice was steady, but there was a slight question in his tone.

She licked her lips and nodded.

'And you're okay with that?'

'Are you?' Her stomach clenched, wondering if he might not say what she expected.

He shrugged. 'Of course. Just don't want you feeling

uncomfortable at work. You've known these people lon-ger than me.' For just a second, she thought she heard a hint of anxiety in his voice. Something that didn't seem like him. The familiar wave of *Do you know him at all?* swept over her. But she was determined to at least try and push past it.

She pasted a smile on her face. 'Prepare yourself. There might be questions asked. I've never dated any-one from work before.'

'Ah…they'll want to know what my secret is?'

'Maybe.' She shrugged as she walked away.

She kept the smile on her face until she reached the twins again. It was perfect timing; they were due their observations recorded again, and both would likely need their diapers changed.

She washed her hands and glanced at the clock. It was close to eleven. She wasn't quite sure she fancied going home alone on the Metro. Part of her didn't even want Angie to come back because it gave her an excuse to stay longer. But she was sensible enough to realise that she couldn't continue to function as a nurse for any longer. It didn't matter that her area of responsi-bility was much more reduced than normal. She doted on these twins, and wanted to be alert and on the ball if there was even a minuscule deterioration in their condition. They had been great for the whole day, but Alice had worked in NICU too long to take anything for granted.

Just at that the doors hissed open and Angie walked in, the labour and delivery nurse still by her side. They both looked tired, but there was something different on Angie's face, a relaxation that hadn't been there before.

'I'm so sorry, I was away so long, Alice,' she said.

Alice shook her head. 'It's no problem at all. You'll

be pleased to know that Ruby and Ryan are doing fine. How about you?'

Angie glanced at Indira, the labour and delivery nurse, who gave her the tiniest nod. Angie took a deep breath. 'Can you tell me who will be on duty for the rest of the night? I know you need to go home and get some rest.'

One of their colleagues, Matt, came over. 'I'm on duty tonight. Ruby and Ryan will be with me.'

Alice sent a silent prayer upwards. She knew that Angie liked Matt just as much as she liked herself.

Angie nodded. 'In that case, would you mind if I went home and caught up on some sleep, and come back in tomorrow morning? Indira has arranged a cab for me.'

It was a first. And it was huge. They all knew it. Making the decision to trust the staff and to take some time out for herself was such a positive choice for Angie to make.

Matt gave her a broad smile. 'You know you can trust me, Angie. If I was worried about anything I would call you. But it looks like Ruby and Ryan are settled, and I hope that's how they will remain all night. Get some sleep, and you can see them in the morning.'

Angie nodded again, as if she was reassuring herself on the decision she had made. 'You will phone me?' she asked.

'One hundred per cent,' said Matt.

They stepped back and gave Angie a chance to say goodnight to her babies.

'Well done,' whispered Alice to Indira.

'First steps,' Indira whispered back. 'There's a lot to unpick and this will be a journey. But she's finally starting to acknowledge that she has to look at her own health and wellbeing too.'

Once Angie had left, Matt put a hand on Alice's shoulder. 'You too, girl. Hate to say it, but you look tired.'

'I feel tired,' she admitted. 'I was just about to come find you. Just not sure about going home this late at night on the subway.'

He glanced at his watch. 'Think you might just have missed the last one.'

'Darn it.' Her heart sank. She wasn't keen on the idea of a cab and there weren't exactly many comfortable sleeping options around the hospital for her.

'Hey.' Dougie appeared at her side and slid his arm around her shoulders. In his other hand he held out a key. 'Sleep in the on-call room. I'm likely to be up most of the night anyhow.'

Matt tried to hide his smile as he stepped away to deal with Ruby and Ryan.

She met Dougie's gaze. Those blue eyes had a smile in them. He was half teasing her, wondering if she would accept. Knowing it would send a further message to their colleagues. But, instead of being worried at all, it was like wrapping a warm blanket around her heart.

She'd never felt like this before. This was the kind of thing that Penny had tried to get her to understand. The pure elation of being in a relationship with someone you felt deeply for—maybe even loved?

The thought made heat rush into her cheeks and she reached out and grabbed the key. 'Thanks,' she said, her voice steady and sure. Because she wanted to be sure. Sure that this was the right move for her and for her Scotsman.

There were still things to learn about each other. But wasn't that part of the nature of a relationship, anyway? No one got to know someone instantly. There would always be learning, always be growth. She would tell him about her past stalking experience. Maybe he would tell her what was going on when he got that occasionally haunted look in his eyes.

She leaned into him, letting herself press up against the length of his body. 'I'm going to jump in the staff showers and find a new pair of scrubs to sleep in and steal one of the emergency toothbrushes.' She gave him a wink. 'If it's not too busy overnight, I might shift over a little and let you in the tiny bed they have in these on-call rooms.'

'How do you know how small the beds are?' His eyebrows were slightly raised.

'Let's just say that on more than one occasion I've had to wake up a junior that's slept through his page.'

Dougie nodded. 'Been guilty of that a few times in the past.'

He moved and then stopped, and she smiled. Because she knew exactly what he'd been about to do. He'd been about to drop a kiss on her forehead. But work was not the place for that.

A little part inside her was singing, that he felt so comfortable around her that he'd momentarily forgotten where they were.

'See you soon,' he said in a low voice, with a look in his eyes that made her practically skip all the way to the shower and try, once again, to make the effort to trust someone.

It was official. He was part of a couple. It seemed that everyone in the entire hospital knew and Dougie kept getting the odd nod or smile from people he didn't know. When he got to the hospital canteen, he could sense a few nudges and glances from colleagues. And if he and Alice hit the canteen together, he could sense eyes on them everywhere.

Not that he minded as such. Hospitals like this were so big that news was only really news for a short while before it faded, to be replaced by the next thing that people were talking about.

Alice's friend from Spain, Mariela, had put in her official notice as her mother was going to need extensive rehab. Tara had already interviewed and the new member of staff was due to start in the next few days.

Dougie was trying his best to avoid the temptation of overseeing everyone else's work in the unit. The staff were proving capable and competent. One of the more junior doctors had come to speak to him about calculations around doses for one of the medicines, and Dougie had been relieved that the guy had asked rather than just carry on himself. It turned out that the other doctor had done everything completely correctly—but, because it was his first time, wanted to check with someone more senior before writing the prescription and delivering the doses. Next time Dougie saw him he'd had a tiny laminated chart made and slipped it into the pocket of his wallet so he could check again in future.

It was completely understandable. The doctor's last position had been in an adult ward and the doses for these premature babies were minuscule in comparison.

He admired the easy way Alice was at work. Although her actions were precise, her manner with patients and all those around her seemed completely relaxed. She teased him about being uptight, and occasionally rubbed his shoulders on the way past.

They'd had dinner in the past few weeks with her sister, Penny, and her fiancé, Benedict. Since Benedict was partly his boss, Dougie had wondered if it might be a little awkward, but Benedict was great, interested in the places he'd worked and some of the procedures in place in other hospitals. Although Dougie had mentioned the London hospital he'd worked in before Washington, it clearly didn't ring any alarm bells for Benedict, and Dougie had been silently relieved.

Kayla's previous workplaces had been detailed throughout her trial, with mentions of the suspicions raised by another doctor—him. It might only have been in a few newspapers, but he hated the fact that if someone did an internet search for Kayla's name, and his, they were both connected for eternity, along with the fact they had 'dated'. But Benedict didn't even blink when Dougie mentioned his previous workplace.

It turned out they had a mutual colleague who was now working in Australia but was hoping to come back to Washington soon, and it was likely there would be a vacancy due to a retirement in the unit soon. Penny and Alice meantime had been busy talking about plans for Penny and Benedict's upcoming wedding.

Benedict and Penny were also staunch fans of the ringtone game, and when Benedict's phone had started playing Starship's 'Nothing's Gonna Stop Us Now' there had been a few seconds of silence around the table before Dougie, Alice and Penny had all simultaneously shouted, *'Mannequin!'*

Things in the townhouse had heated up accordingly, with them sometimes spending the night in Alice's bed, and sometimes spending the night in Dougie's. He'd noticed that occasionally she seemed on edge, but any time he asked she just shook it off and said nothing was wrong.

It left him slightly uneasy. Nothing about Alice was wrong. She was intelligent, funny, definitely smart-mouthed, gorgeous and a great nurse. But every time he felt as if she was keeping something from him he had flashbacks to London. It didn't matter he'd gone out with Kayla on one date. His radar had been off. He hadn't listened to his gut. Was he doing the same here?

Dougie hated that his thoughts went that way. Alice had done absolutely nothing wrong. He was also conscious that it was more himself he hated, because he still felt as if he should have raised the red flag earlier about Kayla. In some ways, she and Alice were similar—bright, friendly and easy to be around. But that was where the similarities ended. Alice was passionate about the care she delivered to her patients. She was meticulous. Her recording was excellent. Even when practice didn't dictate it, she regularly asked another member of staff to double-check a medicine before she administered it. Kayla had been all gloss on the surface with none of the good practice underneath.

Dougie walked over to the nearest window as he waited for the timer on the oven to sound. Alice was due in from her yoga class at any minute and he had simple oat and raisin cookies in the oven, along with *Raiders of the Lost Ark* lined up on the TV.

He heard her key in the lock and she came in, chatting on the phone to one of her friends. She gave him a wave, then bent down to pick up something lying on the mat at her feet.

She stopped moving for a moment, then stuffed it into her bag, her face pale. As she cut her call, she noticed he was watching her.

'What was that?'

'Nothing.' She waved her hand. 'Just a flyer about an event. I'm going to go upstairs and jump in the shower. Okay?'

He nodded, but it was as if a gust of wind prickled the hairs at the back of his neck.

The alarm sounded and he slid the cookies from the oven, his appetite completely gone. He knew she hadn't been truthful with him. In the UK, everyone had a letterbox on their door, meaning just about anything could be posted through it. But here in the US most people around had a mailbox in front of their house, or a central point where mail was delivered. If someone had stuffed a flyer on the doorframe he would have noticed when he got home earlier. It must just have happened. His mouth was dry. Alice wouldn't get upset about a flyer. But it was clear she wasn't ready to share what was wrong. He started up the stairs to talk to her. The shower was running, but he could hear her on the phone again, even though she'd finished her call downstairs.

He heard the word 'Penny' and turned and left. The last thing he was going to do was listen in to a phone call between sisters. It wasn't his style, and it wasn't his business. He took himself back down the stairs to wait, putting the cookies onto a plate and pouring chilled wine into two glasses.

When Alice came back down the stairs fifteen minutes later, her roughly dried hair was up in a ponytail and she'd put on her pyjamas. The outside edges of her eyes were ever so slightly red. But if he hadn't witnessed her reaction to whatever had been left at the door he would never have noticed.

She smiled when she saw the cookies, the wine and the waiting movie on the screen. 'What more could a girl ask for?' she said as she made her way over to the sofa.

He didn't want to ask more questions. He didn't want to be invasive. It was clear that she wanted him here.

As she snuggled up alongside him, he could smell her orange-scented shampoo. It washed over him in a familiar way.

He liked it. No. He didn't just like it. He didn't just *like* Alice Greene. He was losing his heart to Alice Greene. Every turn of her head, every quip, every wink and every smile made his heartbeat quicken just a little more. When she turned over in the dead of night and flung one leg and arm over him, he didn't wriggle out from under her. He just laughed and pulled her closer. Alice Greene was well and truly under his skin.

He hadn't come here looking for love. He'd come to Washington as a means of escape. A way to start somewhere new, and a place where he could start to have confidence in his judgement again. He could have ended up anywhere. There had been jobs in Boston, New York, Florida, Hawaii, New Zealand and Australia. This had almost been a random pick. Only the pull of the reputation of the NICU and its staff had brought him here.

Dating had been the last thing on his mind. Love had absolutely been the last thing on his mind. But someone, somewhere had flipped a dime and landed him in the NICU at the exact time when Alice had a space to fill in her home. He'd only been supposed to be here for a week and it was coming up to two months.

He'd never been this settled before—not even when he was home in Scotland. He was beginning to understand the old words, *Home is where the heart is*. And Dougie MacLachlan's heart was in Washington. Whether he'd said it out loud or not.

He pushed all the tiny doubts that niggled him out of his mind.

He put one arm around her shoulders and hugged her

closer. Alice made a little noise and put her head halfway on his shoulder and halfway on his chest.

She was munching one of his cookies.

'You know and I know that all those cookie crumbs are going to end up on me instead of you.'

'I guess you need to learn how to make crumb-less cookies.' She sighed. 'I blame the baker.'

'Well, I guess I blame the baker too. Hey, am I still on a trial?' he joked.

'Oh, that boat sailed a long time ago,' she said, then paused for a second and added, 'I don't think I ever told you the trial was over, did I?'

'You did not. That's why I'm still baking. I think I'm still on probation and I'm trying to impress. It's exhausting,' he joked. 'Between that and keeping up with the laundry and cleaning, I'm just about ready to collapse in a heap.'

She turned around onto her back, her head across his lap, and looked up at him. She had a soft smile on her face, but her dark eyes were serious. 'Well, let's just settle this now. Dougie, are you going to stay?'

The question came from left field. But he didn't hesitate in his response because it came from the heart. 'I want to.' He paused for a moment, then asked the question he knew he should. Because he still knew that, deep down, she was hiding something from him. 'Do you want me to?'

She smiled and wound her hands up around his neck, giving a nod towards the TV. 'See that girl in the movie?'

He looked up in time to see Indiana Jones deliver a lecture to his pupils, where one girl was blinking at him. She had 'LOVE YOU' written on her eyelids. He looked back down and put one hand on Alice's stomach. 'Yeah?'

She gave him a big smile. 'Well, that's me. I'm that girl.'

He couldn't even describe the warm sensation that spread over him. He leaned down to kiss her. 'Is that a yes then?' His smile matched hers.

His lips were only millimetres from hers. He could feel her warm breath on his skin, mixing with the smell of soap from her skin. 'That's definitely a yes,' she whispered as her lips met his.

Her hands ran through his hair as they continued to kiss, and his lips moved from her face, to her neck. 'I just want you to know,' he said between kisses, 'that if you were the professor, I'd be the student with "LOVE YOU" on my eyelids.'

Her grin was wider than he could have hoped for. 'You would?' she breathed as he kept kissing the soft skin around her neck.

'Definitely.'

And from that point onwards *Raiders of the Lost Ark* was forgotten.

CHAPTER EIGHT

IT WAS LIKE being in a happy bubble. Alice had always thought she led a happy life. She'd grown up with two loving parents and a fantastic older sister. The Army life had meant that she'd learned how to be adaptable, moving bases every few years, living in different countries and cultures and making new friends.

As an adult, she could see now how that upbringing had shaped her for nursing. She absolutely understood how communication was such a key part of relationships and her working life, so why hadn't she yet let Dougie know that something was wrong in her life?

It was simple. She didn't want the happy bubble to burst.

She was enjoying waking up next to the sometimes grumpy Scotsman. She enjoyed sharing her home with him. Exploring Washington with him had made the whole city fun again for her. She was going back to places she'd visited when she'd first arrived here and never visited again since.

She loved this city. Sure, lots of people moved away from the city centre when they wanted to get married and have a family. But Benedict and Penny had found the perfect place to live, and they planned to bring up a family. There was no reason that Washington couldn't be a for ever home.

She pulled her phone from her pocket and sighed. The flyer last week had really thrown her. All it had said was:

Carol
Yoga Class 7-8 p.m. Tuesdays
Westgrove Center

To anyone else it would simply look like a flyer for a class. But it wasn't that. It was a message. At least that was what Alice thought it was. A message saying that whoever was watching her knew that she went to class every Tuesday night. She'd thought she might be sick and had run up the stairs to speak to Penny. Thank goodness she'd told her sister now, because Penny had talked her down. She'd made Alice take a breath and not panic. Yes, she agreed, it was scary, but it could also be coincidence. And until they knew any different she should keep calm. Dougie was there in the meantime, and Penny had encouraged her to tell him.

She'd wanted to. She was going to tell him when she got back downstairs. But as soon as she'd looked at his face her whole heart had just squeezed. She didn't want Dougie to think about the possibility of his girlfriend being stalked. Part of her still wondered if he'd think she'd encouraged this stranger in any way. But their relationship was evolving every day, and she wanted to keep it like that.

Alice had never truly been serious about anyone before. Things had never lasted more than a few months. They'd either fizzled out naturally or she'd called a halt because she knew she wasn't feeling it. Ever since the stalker incident, she hadn't been able to trust her own judgement. This was the first time she had. *Felt it*. And even though she had a completely adult and rational brain, right now she didn't want anything to destroy her bubble.

But it wasn't just that. There was still something about Dougie she couldn't put her finger on. It was never at home—always at work. Some staff had made remarks that his checks irritated them or made them feel as if they were under the microscope. Another experienced practitioner had given him a curt dismissal when he'd double-checked something with her. All of them now knew that Alice and Dougie were dating. So she was sure if he were annoying her colleagues, most of them wouldn't let her in on the chat. But she just knew there was something else going on. Something else that was making him cautious at work. She wished he'd tell her what it was, but the irony of that struck her hard. They were both keeping secrets from each other. He might be doing what she was right now—wanting to actually talk about it, but just not sure when the right time would be.

Her phone sounded again. An unknown number.

'Hello?'

There was some weird crackling, as if the line hadn't quite connected or there was static somewhere.

'Hello?' she tried again. But there still wasn't anything she could hear properly. After a few moments Alice cut the call. But it left her feeling distinctly uncomfortable. With everything else that had gone on, she hated the thought that someone creepy might have her number. The dating apps didn't give out personal emails or phone numbers. All messaging had to be done via the apps—it was how they made their money.

It was nothing. It was just someone dialling the wrong number by mistake.

She shook off her doubts and got ready for work. Dougie had left earlier but she was doing a favour for a colleague and covering part of their shift so they could take their teenage kid to a recital.

It didn't take long to take the subway into work. Angie was sitting beside the twins and was looking excited. 'Perfect!' she said as Alice strolled in. 'They said I could get to hold them for a while today. I asked if you'd be in, and they said you were in at lunchtime.'

It was honestly the first time that Alice had seen a genuine smile on Angie's face, and it swamped her with relief that she might be turning a corner. She glanced up at Alice. 'Would you mind calling Indira? I'd really like it if she was here too.'

'Absolutely no problem at all. Give me five minutes and I'll be right back,' said Alice as she made her way over to the nurses' station.

Dougie was talking to another doctor, and Tara turned to greet her. 'Oh, hi, Alice. Say hello to our new colleague, Jake. He worked at the NICU in St Gabriel's in London.'

'That's where Dougie worked,' Alice said automatically. 'Did you two know each other?'

She held out her hand to shake the tall black man's hand. Dougie's head shot around. He looked at the new nurse. He gave a minimal shake of his head and also held out his hand.

Jake shook both. 'No, sorry,' he said. 'You must have worked there before me.'

Alice could swear Dougie looked relieved. His smile was broad, but a little forced. 'Did you work with Charles Edwards?'

Jake nodded. 'Loved working with him. His enthusiasm is infectious.'

'Absolutely.'

'Sorry,' said Jake, 'tell me your name again. I'm getting lost in the sea of new names today.'

'Dougie.' He paused, then added his surname. 'Dougie MacLachlan.'

Something flitted across Jake's face. 'Oh, nice to meet you.'

Tara leaned forward. 'Jake's going to be shadowing for his first few days, so he'll be with Lynn for a few hours and then with you, Alice. That okay?'

Alice gave Jake a smile. 'Sure, just come and find me. I'm at Bays Eleven and Twelve, Twenty-Three and Twenty-Four.'

She made the call to Indira, then spent the next few hours watching the pleasure on Angie's face as she got to hold first Ruby and then Ryan. They took lots of photos and encouraged her to just let the babies lie on her skin and rest for a few hours.

Her phone sounded again. Another unknown number, with no real person at the end of the call. Alice ducked into the changing rooms and tried to call George, her friend who was a cop, for some advice. But George didn't answer. After pausing for a few moments she left a message, asking if he could call her back some time. She hated the fact she might be wasting his time.

By the time she finished work it was getting dark. It was only ten o'clock, but Dougie was still caught up with a patient. 'You go on, I'll catch up with you later.'

She was ready to make an excuse, say something so she could just wait for him too. But she was tired and her back was sore. She actually wanted to go home and soak in the bath for an hour and then hopefully be relaxed enough to sit and enjoy some time with Dougie later.

She was fed up with being afraid of something that likely wasn't real. This was *her* city. Her place. She'd gone home alone over a hundred times. She'd travelled the subway at night dozens of times. Why was she even hesitating? Alice picked up her backpack and gave Dougie a wave. 'See you later.'

She changed quickly and caught the line to Foggy Bottom. The subway wasn't busy. She noticed the odd person who was clearly going home from work like herself. A few couples and some groups of friends.

It was dark by the time she emerged from the subway, but the road to the townhouse was clearly lit. It was a warm, muggy kind of evening. Other nights had been slightly colder, but Alice took off her zip-up top and tied it around her waist as she walked home.

She'd been listening to an audio book for the entirety of the journey home. She liked crime thrillers best to listen to, as they seemed to hold her attention better. She turned off the main street, which had been relatively busy, and onto her own road, which was much quieter. There were a few lights at windows and she admired other people's window boxes or potted plants or ferns as she strolled along.

She was so lost in her book that she wasn't really paying much attention to anything else. So as she reached her door she fumbled for her key and dropped it on the ground.

The shove crashed her head into her own front door.

Alice fell to her knees, trying to make sense of what had just happened.

One hand tightened around her backpack and she waited for the tug at her shoulders. She'd never been mugged before, but she expected that was what was happening now.

But the tug never came. Instead, a pair of dark sneakers came into her vision as a force lifted her back up onto her feet. Her key was still somewhere on the ground beneath her.

Alice's immediate thought was to get away. She started struggling, lashing out and kicking. Years before, she'd been taught breakaway training as part of her nurse training, but because she worked in the NICU she hadn't gone to an update for a few years and it hadn't felt like an immediate issue. Right now, she was wishing she'd attended.

There was a yelp from whoever was trying to restrain her, but next thing she was slammed back against the door, with hands at her throat.

Her phone started to ring, but she had no way to get to it. Both of her hands were at her neck, trying to release the clamping feeling at her throat.

Her eyes were wide and a face hissed up next to her. 'Leading someone else on now, Alice?'

Dread flooded through her. She recognised that voice. Dave. The guy who had stalked her. The one who had to be warned off.

'Saw you on the dating apps again. Why didn't you reply to my messages?'

He was hissing up next to her ear. She could feel flecks of his saliva landing on her. But she just couldn't breathe. She tried to form words.

'L-let g-go…'

His hands released her neck slightly.

'You've…been…following me…phoning me,' she said.

Her brain was going crazy. Penny would have no idea

she was in trouble. She hadn't managed to get hold of George. Dougie was still at the hospital. She frantically looked at the other windows in the street. Some homes had their blinds closed. Some were completely dark— as if the residents weren't home at all. Others had lights on, but no one was looking out of their window right now. There was no one to help her.

'Thought you might have learned from last time. Thought you might have stopped leading men on. But that hasn't happened, has it?'

Dave sounded angry, bitter. It had been over two years since they'd dated. She couldn't believe this was happening. She should have made the call to George earlier. She should have trusted her instinct. And she should have told Dougie.

But all that was too late now. Anger surged through her. How dare this guy do this to her?

'Get off me!' she spat.

She lifted one elbow and caught the side of his face. His grip loosened slightly and she took full advantage. She bent double—something he clearly wasn't expecting her to do. But her change of position made his weight adjust. Alice was ignoring the fact that deliberately leaning into the strangle was killing her. She whipped her body back up and caught him under the chin with the back of her head.

She was sure that anyone would tell this was a terrible move—and that she would likely cause more injury to herself than to him. But while she was momentarily stunned Dave had let go and he staggered backwards. Adrenaline was rushing through her now.

'Alice!' The voice came from down the street and she could hear thudding footsteps coming towards her. But her blood was racing now, and she wasn't done yet.

Dave started to straighten; he had pure venom in his face towards her. She didn't hesitate. Not for a second. She lifted her foot and kicked him square in the balls. The move that every teenage girl had been taught by her older sister or cheerleader colleagues as an emergency move.

The yelp echoed around her. She sagged back against the door, conscious that right now she should be grabbing her key and getting behind a closed door, and safety. But those footsteps were almost at her. Dougie launched himself through the air as if he was playing a game of American football and took the guy clean down. There was a short tussle. But Dave was no match for Dougie's muscles, physique or pure Scottish rage. He held the guy down, with one arm pinning him to the ground. Alice was conscious of the fact that moments earlier it had been Dave's hand around her throat.

'Keep him down,' she said with a croaky voice. 'But don't hurt him.'

Dougie changed position as Alice fumbled for her phone. She redialled George.

'Who is this guy?' asked Dougie.

'An ex. One who stalked me and was warned off.'

Her call connected and George's calm voice came on the line. 'Hey, Alice. You okay? What do you need?'

'Help,' she said swiftly. 'I've just been attacked by the guy that stalked me.'

The tone of George's voice changed immediately. 'Where are you?'

'At my front door.'

'Are you safe right now?'

She looked at Dave, pinned on the ground beneath Dougie. He wasn't going anywhere. 'Yes.'

'I'm on my way. I've put a call out for the nearest unit.'

She looked at Dougie. 'Police are on their way.'

Dave started cursing and wriggling under Dougie's grip.

'Don't make me punch you. You've no idea how much I want to right now,' said Dougie, his accent the thickest she'd ever heard it. Something about it seemed to still Dave. Maybe he was having flashbacks to the characters in *Trainspotting*.

Her hands went to her throat. Even though she was free, the feeling of constriction was still there. She started coughing, knowing it was likely a psychological reaction to the event.

'Alice, are you okay?'

She nodded although she was coughing. 'I just need something to drink. Wait until the cops get here.'

Dougie looked down at the guy underneath him in disgust. 'He was stalking you?' His voice was incredulous. 'Why on earth didn't you tell me?'

She felt tears well in her eyes. But the anger was still there. The anger about everything falling down around about her.

'Now's not the time,' she said. She wasn't even sure where to start.

Dougie stayed where he was, keeping Dave away from her until the police arrived, closely followed by George. Everything happened in a blur. She was asked to go downtown and give a statement. When she called Penny to let her know what had happened, Penny was distraught and insisted on coming to meet her. When she was finally finished at the police station, Penny, Benedict and Dougie had all noticed her persistent cough and insisted she get checked out by one of their colleagues.

The last thing Alice wanted to do was end up in the

ER and become the latest gossip, but one of the doctors she knew examined her in a side room. By then, purple bruising had spread across her throat and they all knew what he would say. Her voice was hoarse and the cough annoying. 'You've got definite soft tissue damage. I'd like to keep you in for observation.'

She shook her head.

'There are risks attached to attempted strangulation. Not all injuries are evident straight away. You could have some difficulty breathing if the swelling continues. I need to know straight away if you have problems swallowing, or you have any further voice changes. Headaches or light-headedness are also issues.'

'You should stay,' Penny said automatically. 'Or come home with me.'

Alice wasn't sure how to answer. Dougie would be at her place. But she wasn't sure she could face seeing her own front door right now. Even imagining it in her head was giving her flashbacks.

'Go with Penny and Benedict,' Dougie agreed, and her stomach dropped. He wanted rid of her. He didn't want to be around her.

Penny's face lit up with relief and she wrapped an arm around Alice's shoulders. 'Absolutely. We can sleep in the spare room together. I'll keep an eye on you, and if we need to get back to the hospital quickly we can do that.'

Alice was blinking back tears. 'We're not kids any more, Penny.' She couldn't help but be slightly embarrassed by her older sister.

'When someone's hurt my sister—you better believe I move into big sister mode. I'm in beside you tonight. I'll notice if you start wheezing or anything.' She

squeezed Alice again and set off another coughing fit.
'Oh, no, sorry…sorry.'

Alice shook her head. Dougie had already stood up;
he looked very awkward. There was only one thing she
could read for definite from him right now—he wanted
to get away.

He turned back and reached out and touched her
shoulder. 'Do you need me to get you anything?'

Penny answered for her. 'No, we're the same size.
She can wear my things. And I have everything else
that she needs.'

'Great. Okay then. Give me a text if there's anything
you think of.'

The silence was painful. At least it was to Alice. She
wasn't sure that Penny or Benedict noticed. So she just
gave a nod.

Dougie locked eyes with her for a few seconds and
she caught the confusion and hurt that lingered there.
She wanted to reach out and grab him. Tell him to stay
and say they could talk. But she honestly didn't feel up
to it. She was traumatised. She was exhausted. And
all she wanted to do right now was sleep. Maybe for
a month. So she just licked her lips, gave him a weak
smile and watched him walk away.

CHAPTER NINE

DOUGIE WASN'T QUITE sure what was happening in his life. The person he loved, lived with and slept with had been attacked. He couldn't get the sight out of his head. Every time he closed his eyes he saw Alice pinned to her door, her face red and a look of absolute terror on her face.

What would have happened if he had been five minutes later? The doors had been sliding on the subway as he'd jumped to get in. If they'd slid closed and he'd missed it?

He couldn't bear it. But these were the thoughts that were constantly swimming around in his head. He'd spent the last two nights at home in the townhouse. It was odd without Alice. Sooty definitely missed her, and as soon as he had entered each day the cat was practically attached to his leg.

But the overwhelming thing for Dougie was the fact she hadn't told him. Someone had been stalking his girlfriend—and she had chosen not to share. What did that say about him? Part of him wondered if Alice had realised he hadn't been totally honest himself, and that had made her reluctant to share with him. If that was the reason, then all of this was entirely his fault.

If she'd shared, he would never have let her go home

alone. They could have set up some kind of alert system—anything that might have made her safer. He didn't understand the bond between sisters—because he had no siblings. But he'd seen the look of horror on Penny's face. That was why he'd suggested Alice go back home with her. He'd known that Penny would never have settled without being near her sister. And he didn't want to get in the way of that. He wasn't even sure how Alice might feel about the townhouse now. It was beautiful, a gorgeous home, but would it now be associated with bad memories for Alice?

There was something else too. That little wave of anger that lingered. He was angry with Alice. Angry that she hadn't told him. Every cell in his body told him how inappropriate that was—particularly in his own set of circumstances. But trust felt like the underlying issue here. If she didn't trust him, what else was there?

There had barely been a few texts between them. He'd sent the obligatory How are you feeling? the next day. But the response had been short.

Will be better in a few days.

He wasn't even sure how to read that. Did she want him to visit? Was that a request to give her a bit of space?

He'd been working on autopilot these last two days and that made him mad at himself. As he changed to go into the unit today, he was determined to be back to normal.

The unit was busy. There had been four new admissions overnight. Benedict had been on duty and it was clear from one look that he hadn't got a wink of sleep.

Dougie walked over quickly. 'Give me a handover and go home. You look knackered.'

Benedict smiled at the Scottish word. 'Alice has picked up your words. She called me crabbit the other day.'

Dougie couldn't help the smile. 'How was she last night?'

'Insisting she's coming back to work today.'

'What?'

Benedict took a deep breath. 'I know, I know. Penny kept telling her not to. But she's apparently made an arrangement with Tara to do a half-shift today. Feel free to tell her to go home too.'

Dougie wasn't quite sure what to say. 'I'll talk to her later. Now, give me a handover.'

The handover took much longer than normal. The four babies admitted overnight all had complications; a few were on complicated drug regimes. Two other babies in the unit had deteriorated overnight, and the workload for today was heavy. There were four other doctors working in the unit today, but Dougie was the most senior and the most experienced. He could tell that Benedict was contemplating offering to stay.

'Go home,' he insisted, putting a hand on Benedict's shoulder. 'If things get hectic, I will call you.'

Benedict gave a grateful smile. 'I'm not going to argue. I'm just going to sleep.'

Dougie called the rest of the staff over to discuss the new arrivals and the patients who had deteriorated. He did a ward round, reassessing each patient, writing up new orders and leaving some specific instructions around care. It was complicated and he knew it. Some of the drugs being delivered by syringe pumps were to be amended on an hourly basis, dependent on the baby's observations.

He ordered some new investigations into a few other babies that he felt were deteriorating. He was so busy that it took him to around midday to take some time to take stock of the recent changes.

A horrible sensation drifted across him. A number of the babies who had previously done well in the unit had got worse in the last twenty-four to thirty-six hours. This wasn't unheard of. Any baby in a NICU could become sick at any point. Bleeding disorders, organ damage, breathing difficulties could all occur in premature babies. But the numbers last night just seemed unusual. It was setting off alarm bells in his head that he didn't like.

Dougie sat for a few minutes and tried to rationalise everything in his brain. Ignoring things was the easy option. The quiet option. But it would never be the right option for a practising physician.

He pulled up the rota and scanned it. With so many staff working here it was difficult to pick out any pattern. A few names jumped out at him, but he also wanted to be cautious. He looked across the NICU. A couple of those staff were on duty today.

As the doctor in charge, he could review any baby at any point. So he started doing a walk round. It had been four hours since the ward round and it wasn't unusual to do them more frequently in a unit like this.

The first few babies he reviewed were still very sick. Their medications and observations were all recorded. The next baby he reached was a little late for his observations. But he quickly saw the member of staff, dealing with an upset mother. Dougie checked over the baby himself and recorded the obs, adjusting the syringe driver and marking on the chart. The nurse looked over and gave him a grateful nod.

These kinds of things he understood. This wasn't someone being lazy or sloppy at work. This was a member of staff dealing with a crisis as it arose. He was quite sure that in another few minutes she would have likely asked a colleague to do the checks for her.

The next baby was midway through their checks. The nurse was away to make up a new syringe of medicine. He followed her into the treatment room, where she was on her phone. She had her back to him and clearly hadn't noticed him. She had the medicines in front of her and was reconstituting while she spoke angrily into the phone.

Dougie was instantly unhappy. She was preparing a syringe of diuretics and also a new IV containing fluids with potassium. Two extremely vital medicines that had to be monitored with precision. A wrong button pressed or a wrong calculation could be fatal for a baby.

Two seconds later she was yelling at the person at the end of the phone. As she did so, she pressed some buttons on the IV infusion pump. Dougie knew instantly they were wrong. They might be in the treatment room, not connected yet to any patient, but the apparent mistake was enough to make the red mist descend.

'Nurse Lawson, would you get off your phone, please?'

His voice boomed across the treatment room and the nurse jumped. She spun around, her face reddening as she said a final few words and cut the call.

She started to speak but he held up his hand.

'You know the rules. Phones in the coffee room only.' He held his hand out to the counter and walked over to look at the vial of medicine she'd been reconstituting.

Although she had mixed it, she hadn't yet recorded the date, time or her initials. All of which were an essential part of mixing a medicine.

He held up the vial and pointed to the empty space.

'You interrupted me,' she started angrily, but Dougie wasn't having it.

'I interrupted your call. You'd already reconstituted the medicine. And what about this?' He turned and pointed at the IV infusion pump.

She blinked, indignation on her face. Then looked again, and paled.

'You know that's the wrong rate.'

She didn't speak. Her mouth was slightly open. He could almost see the cogs turning in her brain, wondering why on earth she'd pressed the wrong numbers. He knew this had never been deliberate. But if she'd connected that infusion without changing the rate he didn't even want to contemplate what might have happened.

Alice walked through the door. She'd changed her scrubs three times. Bright pink, purple and then pale pink—all just seemed to emphasise the large purple bruising around her neck. She'd done her best to disguise it in part with foundation. But it was still there— and still visible. So she'd finally settled on a pale blue pair with multicoloured tiny teddy bears all over them in the hope that people's eyes would be drawn to the tiny bears rather than her neck.

She already knew it wouldn't work.

A few of her colleagues literally met her at the door, giving her a hug and all telling her she'd come back to work much too soon. Her stomach was already in knots. Not from being back to work. She felt safe here—and perfectly capable of doing her job. She'd agreed with

Tara only to work four hours today, on the understanding that if she felt unwell at any point she could go home.

But where was home now? She'd spent the last two nights with Penny and Benedict. They'd been perfect hosts but she was invading their privacy and she knew it. Her home was in Foggy Bottom. The townhouse she'd always been so proud of and loved living in. Did she still feel that way? To be honest, she wasn't sure. She wouldn't really know until she went back.

The reason her stomach was in knots was the fact she knew that Dougie was working today. Everything felt up in the air. She'd met a guy she'd worked with, moved in with and fallen in love with, all at breakneck speed. There had been tiny reservations deep down inside. The trust stuff was hard. She'd realised her history had affected her more than she'd ever admitted. But she still had the underlying feeling that Dougie hadn't put all his cards on the table either. He hadn't hesitated for a second when he'd seen her in trouble—she'd known that about him, anyway. But the hurt in his eyes had been evident when he'd realised she hadn't trusted him enough to tell him about her stalker returning. But part of that time she hadn't been sure herself—and if she'd told him she was worried she would just have sounded paranoid.

The last couple of days there had been only a few texts. She didn't want to text him. She wanted to *see* him. *Talk* to him.

And today would be that day. She scanned the unit but couldn't see him. He could be anywhere. He could be away for a break, or called to another part of the hospital if there was an emergency, or in the coffee room or the office.

Jake, the new NICU nurse, came over next to her. 'How are you feeling, Alice? I was shocked when I heard what happened to you.'

He winced as he looked at her neck. 'What is wrong with people?' He shook his head. 'I'm glad that you are safe. I'm covering Ruby and Ryan today. I have a few questions; do you mind?'

She shook her head in relief. 'Not at all,' she said. 'I've been with them since they were admitted, so ask away.'

They moved over to the incubators. Ruby and Ryan both looked well and Angie was sitting in the corner, chatting easily with Indira. Things were obviously working out how everyone had hoped. Jake pulled up the electronic chart, alongside a few tests results.

'Okay,' he said, 'I was just wondering...'

Raised voices were heard from the treatment room and literally everyone in the unit froze. In a place that was normally very quiet they were extremely notice-able and Alice recognised one of the voices immedi-ately—Dougie. He wasn't shouting. But he was telling someone in no uncertain terms that they hadn't fol-lowed procedures.

It took her a few seconds to recognise the other voice. Jill Lawson—she'd worked here for a few months. Alice didn't know her that well, but had always found her fine.

'What on earth is going on?' she asked Jake.

'I have no idea. Sounds like she hasn't done what she should have.' He gave her a sideways glance. 'After what Dr MacLachlan experienced back in London, you can't blame him for being a stickler for details.'

It was like a cold breeze blowing over her skin and making every hair stand on end.

'What do you mean?'

Jake looked confused, his brow furrowed. 'Aren't you two an item?'

'What's that got to do with anything?'

Now Jake looked distinctly uncomfortable. 'Well, surely it's come up?'

'What?' There was a determined edge to Alice's voice. When she was met with silence, she added, 'I suggest you let me know.' She glanced towards the treatment room, where the voices were continuing. 'And quickly.'

Jake ran a hand through his hair. 'It's just…that Dr MacLachlan was the person who first raised suspicions about Kayla Bates—you know the nurse in England who was convicted of trying to deliberately harm her patients.' He closed his eyes for a second, then said, 'Her NICU patients.'

He took another breath. 'Listen, I'm sorry. Because you and he are…you know, dating, I just assumed that this would have been something you'd talked about.'

Alice rocked back on her heels, reaching out and touching the surface nearest to her, which was one of the incubators. Of course she'd heard about the case. It had horrified her. But it had taken place in another country, so she hadn't pored over the details. She just remembered the nurse had gone to prison. She shook her head. 'I didn't think he worked there.'

Jake was quick to clarify, 'Oh, he didn't work at the hospital where the actual events happened. He worked at the one before. And it was him that had flagged her practice before she moved. They unpicked the whole story about her.' He glanced at the treatment room again. 'I worked at the unit after Dr MacLachlan had left. Word on the street was that he'd been really upset about things.' Jake bit his lip. 'I also heard that staff had initially been quite off with him when he'd suggested something might be wrong—though by the time I got there they were all claiming to have noticed things about her.'

Alice straightened her shoulders. She could see people in the unit looking at each other—wondering who should intervene on the raised voices.

'Let me handle this,' she said as she started towards the treatment room.

Jake put a hand gently on her arm. 'Are you sure? I could do this. I might not know Dougie, but I do know the history.'

Alice appreciated the offer. 'You just got here, Jake. Let me sort the trouble out.'

She took some swift steps to the treatment room and walked in just as Jill was clearly about to launch into another diatribe. Her face was red and blotchy, and she was clearly furious. She was also clutching her mobile phone in one hand.

Dougie, in contrast, looked icily calm. Although his voice had been raised it was steady, with a real no-nonsense tone. He wasn't going to let this go.

'Enough.' She raised both hands as she walked in. Both turned at the same time and she could see the simultaneous flinching at the sight of her neck. But Alice had a job to do. 'Your voices can be heard outside. You're disturbing the unit that we strive hard to keep as a calm and peaceful place.' She turned first to Jill. 'Tell me what has happened.'

Dougie tried to talk first, but she kept one hand lifted to him. Jill was clearly worked up and nervous. 'He disturbed me while I was making up a medicine—then complained I hadn't signed and dated it.' She shot him a fierce look. 'Then he said I'd put the wrong number into the IV infusion pump, but I'm nowhere near a patient and it isn't connected. I don't see why any of this is his business.' She folded her arms and tilted her chin up.

Alice turned around to face Dougie. 'Dr MacLachlan, would you like to tell me your side?'

She saw something flash in his eyes. She knew it was her use of his formal title, but in this situation that was entirely correct.

'Nurse Lawson was on her phone while she was in the treatment room. She wasn't paying attention to what she was doing, which is clear by the fact she reconstituted the medicine but didn't initial and date and time it. Then she put the incorrect dosage and rate into the IV infusion pump. It might have not reached a patient, but it was about to. Her mind wasn't on the job. Careless mistakes like this can cost lives.'

There was a tic around his jawline. He was angry. Was it possible he was even angrier than he'd been the other night? This was a whole new side of Dougie she'd never seen.

She was looking at a new man. One with a whole history he hadn't revealed to her. That hurt. She hadn't even had time to process what Jake had told her outside—there would be time for that later.

For Alice this was like playing devil's advocate. Jill started again, but Alice stopped her. 'Enough. Jill. Were you on your phone in the treatment room?'

Jill's face was so red she looked as though she might burst. 'Yes, but—'

'Is there an emergency? Do you need to go home?'

She was being concise and to the point. Jill knew the rules. But Alice had to establish if something unusual had happened that might explain why Jill had taken a call.

Now Jill's jaw was clenched, as if she was contemplating what to answer. She must have known that Alice had just given her a get-out clause. Would she take it?

'No,' she admitted. 'I'm having issues at home and we were having a fight.'

Alice made herself clear. 'Do you need some time out? Is your home life affecting your work life?'

Jill didn't answer, so Alice stepped over and put a hand on Jill's arm. 'Jill, do you feel safe? Is there anything we can do to help you?'

But Jill gave her a grateful smile and shook her head. 'No, it's nothing like that. Thanks for asking.' She looked at Dougie. 'I shouldn't have answered my phone, but I haven't done anything wrong and you've got no right to say I have.'

Alice cut in. 'Actually, Jill, in this unit it's everyone's job to make sure our colleagues are doing things correctly. While we know we are all responsible for our own practice, I would expect any member of staff to question something that they thought was wrong, before there could be a patient incident.'

She moved over and lifted the vial. 'This one isn't signed and dated, so will have to be destroyed. Jill, I want you to record that in the stock items and I'll countersign it with you.'

She still hadn't let Dougie speak. She could sense his eyes on her. But she was doing her best to be fair to both parties. Alice put her hand on the infusion. 'Which patient is this for?'

Jill told her.

'And what's the correct dosage for that patient, based on their weight?'

Dougie rattled it off automatically. Alice knew it too. She'd worked here so long it was practically ingrained in her brain. The current figures on the display were three times the normal dose and it made her feel physically sick.

Alice breathed. She wasn't in charge of this unit. Tara was, and she would report back to Tara later. Right now, she was acting as mediator. But she knew how things should go in this environment. The words 'supportive conversation' circulated in her brain. She couldn't be confrontational.

'Jill, can you tell me what's happened here?'

Jill looked at the figures again. It was clear she was trying to find the words. 'I don't know,' she admitted. 'I don't know why I put that in. I know the correct dosage.'

Alice laid a gentle hand on her arm. 'Okay.' She turned to face Dougie. 'Dr MacLachlan, I understand your concerns and thank you for raising them. If you can leave us alone right now, Jill and I will ensure the medicines are prepared correctly and everything is countersigned and double-checked before it reaches the patient.' She took another breath and kept her voice steady. 'As with any potential errors in NICU, we will record this on the electronic system as a near miss.'

Dougie looked at her. She could tell immediately he wasn't finished and there was so much more simmering beneath the surface. And now she knew and understood what that was. But she had to be fair. She had no reason to suspect anything other than human error. The mistake had been caught and could be remedied with no harm done. Lessons would be learned from today. He continued to stand there.

She lifted her chin. 'Dr MacLachlan, you and I can discuss this later. However, Nurse Lawson and I have a patient to attend to.' She took one step forward and glanced out to the unit. Jake was standing over Jill's current patient, taking a new set of observations. All was well.

Dougie turned on his heel and walked out.

Jill promptly burst into tears. Alice's head was throbbing. But, no matter how unwell she felt right now, she was glad she had come in today. She'd learned something she needed to know. The information hadn't come to her in the way it should have—and it was up to her to deal with it now.

'Do you feel as if you can continue?' Alice asked gently.

Jill was breathing quickly. 'I can't believe I made a mistake like that. What if he hadn't come in? You know I would have checked again before I connected the IV, don't you? Please tell me that you do.'

Alice nodded. 'I understand you were distracted. I understand you were upset. Let's just do everything by the book, get your patient's medicines restarted, then we can sit together and fill in the near miss record. We are all human, Jill. But let's just remember that no harm was done today.'

Jill's breathing steadied and she swallowed and gave a nod. 'Okay. Thank you.' She glanced over her shoulder. 'I just wish Dr MacLachlan would remember that too.'

Alice pressed her lips together. She wanted to say the words—that he was human too.

But right now she just didn't feel she could. It felt disloyal to Jill, and she was trying to hide the fact that she was angry with him for not telling her the truth.

She kept her voice even. 'Okay, let's get this sorted,' she said to Jill, and they started to check the prescriptions again.

* * *

Dougie was pacing. He couldn't help it. He'd done some other checks in the unit and, after a few curious glances from others, had taken himself into the office. Alice seemed to be taking an age. He hated the fact that other concerns were still floating in his head.

He still had questions about the number of kids who'd become sick in the last couple of days, and he knew nothing would satisfy with him without there being some kind of review.

The image that was sticking in his brain right now, though, was the vivid purple around Alice's throat. It was angry, it screamed trauma; he could swear he could see the mark of fingers. It made him feel physically sick that someone had done that to her.

He also knew exactly how brave she was to come back to work and not hide away at home. It was almost like a sign of defiance and that was exactly what he would expect from Alice. She was nobody's victim.

Before he had a chance to think any further she opened the office door and sat down. She was carrying a cup of water and some headache pills in her hand, which she quickly swallowed. 'Why didn't you tell me?' she asked.

He sat back in his chair. 'Why didn't I tell you what?'

'Don't play games with me, Dougie. Why didn't you tell me about your experiences back in London—about that Kayla nurse?'

His throat was dry. Jake must have told her. It was the only thing that made sense right now.

He spoke steadily. 'I didn't tell you because I don't like to talk about it at all. I worked with someone who went on to try and harm children. I raised concerns about her and was made to feel as if I had victimised her. We had no idea where she'd gone, and the first time we found out about everything was when the police turned up to ask questions.'

Alice licked her lips. She kept her brown eyes fixed on his. 'I can't imagine how horrible that was. But that doesn't explain why you didn't trust me enough to tell me. It might have helped me understand why you seemed to double-check what other staff were doing. Everyone had noticed you doing it.'

Dougie closed his eyes for a few seconds and sighed. It didn't matter that he'd tried to temper his instincts. It really hadn't worked.

She continued. 'That with Jill today?'

'She could have done something very wrong,' he interrupted.

'You're right,' she said. 'She could have. But getting into a fight with a member of staff is not how we do things around here. You could have handled things differently.'

'These things have to be handled at the time. We can't just wait and let something happen.'

'I agree,' she said. 'But…' She chose her words carefully in light of what she now knew. 'But we have to assume that a member of staff made a mistake and treat them with compassion and respect. I'm sure that Jill won't sleep a wink tonight. You could have spoken to her differently. I know that you're passionate about this, but not every staff member is trying to do deliberate harm.'

The words came out and hung in the air between them.

Dougie studied her closely. 'And there,' he said after a pause, 'is the elephant in the room.'

* * *

'What do you mean?' Alice snapped. She was getting more irritable. She was tired, her head still ached and all she really wanted to do was go home.

She couldn't understand what was wrong that Dougie couldn't have told her what had happened before. Did she seem judgemental? Or unsympathetic? She wouldn't have thought so, but now she couldn't think straight and felt paranoid.

'You should have told me,' she said, completely exasperated. 'You didn't have faith in me.'

'And you didn't have faith in me.' It was like some weird kind of tit-for-tat.

They sat looking at each other and Alice shifted in her seat. Of course. She hadn't told Dougie about herself; why should he reveal part of himself to her?

'That was different.'

'Why?'

She waved a hand. 'Because it was about life, not work. I thought you might have judged me for being on so many dating apps. And you might have thought I'd done something to encourage him.'

Dougie's brow wrinkled. 'Why on earth would you think that?'

She shook her head. 'Because everything was new between us. It was going so well, and I didn't want anything to spoil it.'

'Ditto,' he said softly.

'What?'

'I came to a new place. Met a new girl—a great girl. I came here with the purpose of leaving the past behind me. I didn't trust my own judgement any more. But you didn't know any of that, and I,' he said slowly, 'didn't want to do anything to spoil it.'

Something pinged in her brain. 'Why didn't you trust your own judgement?'

Dougie leaned forward, clasping his hands over his knees. Now he wasn't looking at her. 'Because before anything happened—' he ran his hands through his hair '—I'd gone on a date with Kayla.'

Oh, dear. Alice's stomach clenched in a horrible, cringing and jealous kind of way.

'You dated her?' She couldn't help the words—it was just a natural reaction.

Dougie looked up at her through his dark hair. 'Once. We went on a date once. And I just had a weird feeling about everything and it never happened again.'

But you still went on a date with her. Alice didn't repeat the words out loud, but they reverberated around her brain.

He shook his head. 'Then everything got horribly complicated. She was very friendly, in everyone's faces. People thought she was great. And when I noticed things at work and mentioned it, people automatically jumped to her defence. Then someone new started at work. And they'd been at the place she'd worked previously. A few questions were asked, and some of the more senior staff took me seriously. Kayla eventually did something wrong and was put on supervised practice. But by that point she was telling people I had a vendetta against her as she'd refused to go on a second date with me.'

'Yikes,' said Alice and she sagged a little in her chair. She bit her lip for a moment. 'You must have been popular.'

He raised his eyebrows, then gave a slow nod. 'You can imagine.' He sat back up properly. 'She left, went to another job, didn't ask for references. Our manager reported her to the nursing governing body, but nine months later the police came visiting because of what had happened at her new post.'

Alice frowned. 'So, why did you leave? Nothing happened on your watch.'

He groaned. 'But it could have. And it made me feel paranoid about everyone around about me. Were they happy and friendly because they were trying to distract from the fact they might be trying to do harm?'

Alice looked at him. 'Is that what you honestly thought about the people you worked with?' She looked out of the office door. 'The people here?' She paused and swallowed, putting her hand on her chest. 'Me?'

Dougie opened his mouth to speak but paused and that made her heart twist inside her chest.

'No…yes…maybe. Not you. Definitely not you. But it made me cautious in general. It made me question everything, particularly my own judgement. After all, I went on a date with her. What does that say about me? And I became really obsessed with procedures and protocols and making sure they were followed correctly.'

Alice's heart was still twisting inside her chest. 'Well, they're there for a reason. We should follow them. I think everyone does.'

'But do you *know*?' The response was instant and if she'd been standing next to him she would have jumped. Dougie sunk his head into his hands. 'My former boss told me I needed a change of scene,' he admitted. He looked back at her. 'He was right. And I thought it would help.'

'But it hasn't?'

His expression was pained. 'When I came in today I noticed that the rate of babies getting sick over the last couple of days is much higher than normal.'

Alice was horrified. She'd been off the last two days, so hadn't noticed. 'You think something is happening here? Is that why you snapped at Jill?'

She couldn't help it. She was automatically defensive of the place she'd worked in and loved for the last five years.

When he didn't say anything it was as if a little part of her died inside.

She took another breath, wondering how to stay calm. But it was clear Dougie had already made a decision.

'Maybe you think it's nothing—and you could be right. But I have to mention this. I have to raise the issue of the number of babies being unwell in such a short space of time.' He put a hand on his chest. 'It could be I'm paranoid. But I've run a few numbers, a few stats, because that's what I do. We are way over the average of where we should be. It could just be an anomaly, and these things happen. But as a professional? I feel responsible to ask Benedict and Tara to sit down and take a look at things. We have to review processes and reach a rational, researched decision that we are confident everything in the unit is working the way it should—and that includes the staff.'

Alice stood up. 'But my sister works here, and Benedict; do you suspect them too? Do you judge everyone by Kayla's standards?'

She couldn't help it. This whole place was family to her, not just Penny and Benedict. It was as if he was finding fault and trying to apportion blame. Her head just couldn't think straight. She put her hand over her heart. 'And what about me, Dougie? Are you investigating me too? Do you wonder if I've done anything? And does what we've had these last few weeks mean noth-

ing to you? Or do you still not trust your judgement?'
It was a low blow, but she couldn't help it.

Dougie looked at her with pained eyes. 'You haven't
been here, Alice. You've been at home. But yes, if you
had been here, then you, as well as me, and every other
member of staff on duty, need to be fed into the details
gathered around the events in the last few days.'

She froze. Hating that was how his brain was working. Tears formed in her eyes. 'This is a good place,'
she whispered.

Dougie held her gaze with his steady blue eyes. 'And
good places are not afraid of reviews. They're not afraid
to cross every t, dot every i, evidence everything to
make sure care is of a consistent high standard.'

He made it all sound so reasonable, so rational—
even though he hadn't been acting that way earlier. But
she couldn't keep her emotions in check. She wished
she hadn't insisted on coming in today. But maybe this
was always meant to happen. Maybe she had to see his
reaction today, and all the events, to understand that
she really didn't know this man at all. What she hadn't
reckoned on was how much it would break her heart.

She'd never really known Dougie at all.

She put her hand on her heart. 'What were we even
doing?' she asked softly.

'What?'

She shook her head. 'Us. This.' She pointed her fingers back and forth between them. 'This isn't about
work. This is about us, and the fact that neither one of
us trusted the other enough to tell them what we should.'

She swallowed, her throat aching. 'I was scared I
would ruin things if I told you about the stalker.' Her
voice was shaky. 'And it sounds like you felt the same
way about revealing your history to me.'

Dougie breathed slowly. 'It's just a horrible story. I came here to get away from that. I came here to start afresh. It's haunted me. It's made me paranoid at work. It's made me not trust my own judgement.'

'And that includes me, doesn't it?'

He opened his mouth to speak and then paused, dipping his head. When he finally raised his gaze he whispered, 'I want to trust you, but I don't even trust myself. How can I really trust anyone again?'

A tear rolled down her cheek. 'I want to shout. I want to scream. But… I get it. Because I couldn't let go the fact that I knew you were keeping something from me. I didn't want to lose my heart to someone I couldn't fully trust. So I always had to hold something back.'

They stared at each other in silence, both realising they'd reached the point of no return. Without trust, there was nothing—no foundation to build on.

'I need to go home.' That was all that could come out right now from Alice.

Dougie's eyes flashed with worry. 'I understand.'

Alice drew herself up as strongly as she could. 'No, you don't.' With every second, she prayed that her voice wouldn't break. 'I need to be alone.'

Dougie blinked; she could see him processing her words.

'I can't be around you. Not while you're thinking like this. Not when you look around and see people who want to do harm, rather than people who are here to do a good job and save lives. You need to talk to someone about this, Dougie. The fact that those thoughts are always in your mind isn't healthy. It makes me think that I never really knew you at all. Just like you didn't know me. We were pretending with each other. We were pretending that we were honest with each other and that we might have a chance at making things work. But all this?' She held out her hands first of all, and then they went almost by compulsion to her neck. She shook her head. 'If we can't be honest with each other, how can we be anything else?' Her voice was deep and scratchy now. 'Please find somewhere else to stay. I think it's for the best.'

He stood there for a moment, not saying anything. Not fighting for her. Not fighting for them. That told her all she really needed to know.

'I'll stay someplace else tonight and arrange to pick up my things tomorrow.'

It came out so matter-of-fact. As if nothing that had just happened had made any impact on him at all.

So Alice turned, left the office, said goodbye to Jake and left the unit. She collected her things from the locker room and made it all the way to the subway before she started sobbing.

CHAPTER TEN

DOUGIE SAT IN the room with Benedict, Tara, the hospital medical director, an independent auditor, a clinical governance expert and someone from another NICU in Washington.

The hospital director started. 'We have agreed to gather here today to review the evidence we have for a one- to two-day period when a number of babies became unexpectedly sick in NICU. We all understand these incidents can happen, due to the vulnerable nature of these patients. However, this was raised by Dr MacLachlan as a potential anomaly—one which we know would have been highlighted at a national level at some point—and we welcome the chance to do a review of the circumstances of each of these patients and take into account all factors which could be an influence.'

Sitting at his left elbow were electronic prescribing records, the staff rota, all tests ordered and reviewed and medical records for every case. 'We have seventeen patients to review. Is everyone agreed with how we will carry out this review, and record and report our findings?'

There was a murmur of assent around the table. Both Benedict and Tara looked worried. But as soon as Dougie had raised concerns about the issue both had agreed the spike in numbers was odd and it would be good to review.

He was feeling strangely acknowledged now, that things weren't just in his head and he hadn't been paranoid and overreacting. But, while that might give some professional reassurance, no one could argue that his personal life wasn't a complete and utter mess.

He'd lost the one true thing he'd finally found. Alice.

His heart felt as if it had been put through a shredder. The look on her face, her upset and confusion haunted him. He'd wanted to text or phone her so many times. But he knew he'd disappointed her.

All he could remember was the vivid purple marks on her throat. At a point in their relationship where he should have been doing everything possible to protect her, love her and reassure her, he'd let her down badly. He had no idea how he could make amends for this. But he knew he wanted to. He'd never been so sure of anything in his life. Alice Greene well and truly had his heart.

He'd spent the first night in one of the on-call rooms. He'd spent the next night at Benedict and Penny's. If he'd ever wanted to experience the complete and utter loyalty between sisters he'd been introduced to it by Penny's wall of icy silence.

It was clear that Benedict hadn't thought before offering him a bed for the night. Or maybe he was trying to play devil's advocate. Whatever it was, he'd slept one night in a comfortable bed but knew he had to find something else. Last thing he wanted to do was cause an argument between two people he respected and liked.

Some of the staff at work had been a little frosty.

Others had been fine. One of the more junior staff had asked if they could look at some data for the review. It turned out he was a bit of a data geek and wanted to do some stats. It was an idea Dougie would have liked to embrace but he didn't want to overstep, so he'd just mentioned the offer to Benedict.

As he sat, the hospital director pushed around some files and once he opened them and saw the charts he tried not to smile. It seemed that Benedict had taken up the offer and before them was a clear table for each child with times, medicines, interventions and observations charted. There was further work with timelines running over each other to show if there were any correlations when babies had started to deteriorate. It was actually a remarkable piece of work.

The director gave a nod. 'This is only preliminary data to give us a starting point for our review. If we decide we need to investigate further, then we can ask an independent advisor to do that work for us.'

Dougie was already scanning and his heart was lightening. They'd be here for hours, but he already got a sense that there was no glaring causal factor. He couldn't begin to say how good that felt. These were people he'd got to know and really like over the last couple of months. He didn't want to think ill of anyone, but he had a responsibility as a neonatologist to always put his patients first. He just hoped others would understand that.

Particularly Alice. He wanted to let his mind drift. He wanted to imagine all the ways he could try to say sorry. Let her know that he still loved her. More than anything he wanted a chance for them to be together again. What he didn't know was how Alice might respond.

But, here and now, he had to concentrate. He had to see through this investigation and accept whatever the results were.

Then he could start trying to rebuild his life again.

CHAPTER ELEVEN

ALICE WAS MISERABLE. It had been three days since her heartbreaking conversation with Dougie and she'd taken some emergency annual leave. Tara had been wonderful—even though Alice appreciated that she must be under a whole host of stress herself. Tara was supporting Jill through the near miss, and also attempting to run a unit where all members of staff knew that questions were being asked and an investigation was pending.

Sooty gave a loud meow and padded over Alice's face again. Anything for attention. She wasn't quite sure what the cat wanted. As soon as Sooty had realised that Dougie hadn't come home the last few nights it was as if it was entirely her fault.

He'd hissed at her earlier when she'd been a little late filling the food bowl. When Alice had come up the stairs earlier, Sooty was lying at the entrance of what had originally been Dougie's room, with an expression on his face that could freeze over a blazing fire. She definitely wasn't popular, even in her own house!

Alice stood up and walked through to the bathroom. The purple had faded slightly and now had streaks of yellow. She hated it. George had phoned yesterday and let her know that, after her ex was arrested, he was subsequently detained, charged and refused bail, due to three other women coming forward with a range of complaints. Now, they just had to wait for his trial.

Alice walked back down the stairs and took up position on the sofa again. There was a dent in the sofa next to her where Dougie had started to leave an imprint with his larger frame.

Most of his things were still upstairs. It was clear he hadn't found somewhere permanent to stay yet, and she hated the way that made her heart happy. When she walked past his room she could still smell remnants of his aftershave.

The last three nights had been hard. At first she'd thought it was because she was in the house by herself. But the noises and creaks had been comforting rather than alarming. Maybe it was because she knew Dave was safely behind bars that she wasn't nervous in the way she'd been before. But having her own feeling of security left her with a huge Dougie-shaped hole in her life.

A tiny part of her had wondered if she'd been clinging onto Dougie for the wrong reasons—because she was nervous and felt threatened and didn't want to be home alone. Yes, Dougie had certainly made her feel safe and secure. But if she didn't need that now, if she wasn't scared any more, why did she still miss those, as well as other aspects of him being around?

Alice sighed as Sooty gave her another disgusted glance before strutting away with his tail in the air. She missed Dougie because she loved him. She loved all aspects of him—his baking, the way he hugged her, the way he made her laugh, his accent, even his slightly crabbit nature. All those little pieces built up the man she'd unexpectedly grown to love.

She hadn't been looking for any of this and it had just landed on her lap out of the blue. And she'd let it slip through her fingers.

She'd spent the last few days picking apart those few hours in the unit. Every bone in her body knew he'd been right to raise flags. Her colleague had done something wrong, not followed protocol and could have accidentally harmed a baby. Even though Alice liked Jill, she always knew that if Dougie hadn't intervened, Jill could have gone ahead and connected the IV pump without rechecking the rate because she'd been distracted—it didn't even bear thinking about. Jill could never have lived with a mistake like that. It would have destroyed her. So Dougie's actions had not only saved a baby, they had likely saved Jill too.

Alice had been full of emotion and reacted defensively around Dougie. She wished she'd paused. She wished she'd taken more time to think things through—maybe even discussed it with Penny before telling him he had to move out.

She might as well have wrenched her own heart clean out of her chest. Because when it came down to the bones of it, they just hadn't trusted each other enough. She felt to blame—even though she knew the blame was equal.

Why had she let Dave impact her life so much? Why couldn't she have had enough assurance and confidence to write him off as the bad guy he'd been? She'd put barriers in place that were tough to try and shift. Would she ever get the chance again, and learn to trust someone?

She also knew that Dougie was currently assisting with the investigation. Benedict and Penny had both mentioned how worried they were. They all knew that a rapid rise in stats for their unit should be picked apart to make sure everything was functioning as it should.

Alice had been sending up silent prayers for the last few nights that, even though it would be unusual, all of these anomalies were merely coincidence.

She loved her unit; she was proud of it. Dougie had fitted in well. For a time he'd appeared to thrive, working alongside her. He was a good doctor. He was quick to spot any deterioration in their tiny patients and put plans in place. Being thorough was never a bad thing, and now it felt as if she'd judged him too harshly.

Her doorbell rang and she jumped in surprise. She wasn't expecting anyone. She pushed away the few milliseconds of panic and relaxed her shoulders and walked to the door, glancing through the peephole.

All she could see was orange.

She pulled back, blinked and looked again. Yip, orange.

She opened the door.

Dougie, with the biggest bunch of orange gerberas that she'd ever seen.

He looked nervous. He was wearing a leather jacket and jeans. 'Can we talk?'

She was still stunned that he was there and as she stood in silence he pushed the flowers towards her. She took them and gave a delayed nod, standing aside to let him come in.

He paced for a few moments before she said, 'Sit down,' trying to keep her face blank as he immediately sat in the Dougie-sized space on her sofa. He couldn't know that she'd sat with her hand on that space last night.

She grabbed a vase from under the sink, filled it with water and put the orange gerberas in the vase.

He'd remembered. He'd remembered what she'd told him was her favourite flower. She had no idea where he'd got them in the city, but she was still struck by his thoughtfulness.

'How was the investigation?'

He leaned forward, resting his elbows on his knees. 'It was…good. All the data was examined. We are officially a statistical anomaly.'

'We are?' She was smiling now as relief surrounded her like a giant cloak.

He nodded. 'We are. There were a few tiny things picked up—but nothing that could have contributed to a deterioration in any child's condition.'

Alice sat down next to him. 'What things?'

He shook his head. 'Late recording of observations on occasions, late administration of medicines. A test being delayed. A blood result not being available because a sample was mislabelled.'

Alice nodded. She knew there were lots of reasons all of these things could happen. The unit was a busy place and if there was an immediate emergency—such as a cardiac arrest or intubation required—that had to take priority.

She breathed slowly. 'Anything else?'

He shook his head. What struck Alice most was how completely and utterly relieved Dougie was. He'd never wanted anything to be wrong at her unit.

'I know you had to raise your concerns,' she said slowly. 'And I was upset about it. I hated the fact that something might have been wrong in the place I loved and worked, and I couldn't be rational about it.'

'I know that,' he said easily. 'But our issues were never really to do with this.'

She looked at him steadily as he continued. 'I was

angry that you didn't tell me about being stalked. I was annoyed you didn't trust me—even though I didn't really trust myself either. It seems ridiculous I could be upset about it.' He licked his lips and kept talking. 'And when you agreed to go home with Penny after being attacked… I just felt so useless.'

He held up a hand. 'I get she's your sister and you're close. I get you were attacked outside your house and it was perfectly natural to want to get some space. And when I say this out loud it seems entirely rational.' He gave a gentle smile. 'But I guess I just can't be rational when it comes to you, Alice.' He shook his head. 'I wanted to protect you. I wanted to look after you. Now I feel like a Neanderthal man saying that out loud. You hadn't told me about Dave, you just wanted to get away from me, and I just thought…I'd imagined what I thought we had together.'

Alice could hardly breathe. She reached out and touched his hand. 'When you encouraged me to go with Penny I thought you didn't really love me. I knew you would be angry I hadn't told you about Dave, and it felt like you weren't prepared to fight for me. Then, after our words in the unit when I found out all about what happened back in England, I just couldn't make sense of what we were to each other. How can we be anything to each other if neither of us knows how to trust?'

He looked down at her hand, then back up into her eyes. 'I made a mistake. I should have trusted you from the start and told you about England. And not fighting for you? Alice, I wanted to fight the world for you. But you'd just been through a traumatic experience and your sister clearly thought the best place for you was with her. You were vulnerable enough. And yes I was angry, but not really at you—at myself mainly for not being there when he attacked you. I wanted to respect the fact you might have needed space and some time with your sister to feel safe. I wanted to argue—but I thought that made me some kind of selfish monster.' His blue eyes fixed on hers. 'I'll never be that man. I love you, Alice. I want this to work between us. Tell me what I can do to fix it.'

She swallowed slowly and looked him in the eye. 'Anything?'

He didn't hesitate. 'Anything.'

She didn't hesitate either. 'Go to counselling. Talk through what happened and how it has made you wary of people—how at times you mistrust your colleagues without even wanting to. I know counselling might not be for a big Scottish guy like you. But I want you to try it. I want you to see if it can't take you out of that mindset.'

He gave her a soft smile and pulled a card from his pocket. She looked at the name of the private counsellor, frowning in surprise. 'Where did you get this?'

'Indira. She was in with Angie again, came over, had a quiet word and gave me a recommendation.' He sighed. 'I was touched. And yes, my immediate response was to say no, but I took it, thanked her and made an appointment for next week.'

'You have?'

'I have.'

She squeezed his fingers tighter. 'You thought I wanted to be with my sister to feel safe. Penny will always be my confidante, my partner in crime and my best friend. But you're the one that I love, Dougie. You're the one that makes my heart sing, then break a moment later. You're the one that I want to wake up next to in the morning. You're the one that makes me feel safe.' She gave him a small smile. 'You're my happy ever after.' She put her other hand over their two clasping hands. 'I think we need to work at this together. I didn't tell you about Dave because I felt partly to blame—even though I wasn't. Then I felt as if I was imagining things.' She lifted her head and looked up. 'I guess I did what a lot of women do without realising it. I became a victim of myself. I shouldn't have doubted. I should have told you everything straight away. I have some work to do myself—' she put her hand on her chest '—because I don't want to feel like this, I shouldn't feel like this, but I let it happen.' She gave a slow nod. 'I won't let it happen again. Give me that card. I think I need it too. And if this person comes with Indira's recommendation, then that's good enough for me.'

He reached a hand over and cupped her cheek. 'Can we do this, Alice? Can we really do this, and make this work between us? Because you are the only thing in this world that I want.'

She moved closer to him as Sooty appeared, meowing loudly and winding his way around Dougie's legs. They both laughed as Alice wrapped her hands around the back of Dougie's neck. 'Looks like I'm going to have to share you.'

'It's a lot to ask,' he said in the gruff Scottish accent she loved so much. 'But I guess I can make the sacrifice.' His lips hovered millimetres away from hers.

'I love you,' she whispered.

'I love you too.' Just as their lips were about to touch, a corny song started playing loudly from his pocket.

Laughter erupted. 'I know it!' squealed Alice. 'Miami Sound Machine. "Bad Boy" from *Three Men and a*

Baby. I was always going to get that one. You got to play tougher than that.'

Dougie tossed his phone over his shoulder as it continued to play, and proceeded to pull her down onto the sofa to show her just how bad he could be.

EPILOGUE

BENEDICT AND PENNY had chosen the perfect setting. The hotel was on the outskirts of Washington, with beautiful gardens, chairs set on the lawn and a decorated floral archway where the registrant stood waiting.

Alice was more nervous than Penny. It was a relatively quiet wedding as Benedict didn't have a large family. Alice and Penny's mom and dad were there, along with many of the couple's friends from the hospital.

Alice stared out of the window of the large room above the gardens where Penny's hair was just getting some final touches. Benedict and Dougie, who was his best man, were already waiting under the archway, both dressed in smart suits.

'Come on, Penny,' said Alice nervously. 'Your groom is waiting.'

'All ready,' Penny said, smiling, the calmest woman in the room. She stood up in her slim gold dress and picked up her ivory flowers with a few gold ribbons.

Alice gave a little gasp. 'You look perfect,' she sighed, air-kissing her sister's cheek so she didn't spoil her make-up.

Penny gave a nervous laugh. 'Let's hope Benedict thinks so.'

A few moments later Alice walked down the aisle first in her coral dress, smiling as Dougie winked at her.

Penny followed on their father's arm, beaming the whole way. The sun shone brightly as they recited vows that they had written for each other, and their friends all cheered loudly as the registrant finally said the words, 'And now you may kiss the bride.'

Benedict didn't need to be told twice.

The relaxed feel of the wedding continued into the evening. Dougie held Alice's hand whenever one of them wasn't called to other duties.

The meal was finished, speeches completed and cake cut when Penny gave her friends a shout.

'Before myself and my husband—' there was a loud cheer and she smiled '—have our first dance, there's another tradition I want to fulfil. Come on over, ladies.'

Alice frowned. She hadn't remembered this part, but as Penny stood in front of her friends, then spun around with her back to them, clutching her bouquet, Alice quickly caught on.

'One...' She started swinging her arms with the bouquet.

'Two!' shouted her friends.

By the time they reached three, the whole room had joined in.

But Penny stopped. She spun around again, a knowing smile on her face as she walked over to her sister and deliberately handed her the bouquet. Alice didn't understand until the woman next to her gasped and nudged her side.

She looked behind her. Dougie was down on one knee, looking entirely nervous. Her mom and dad stood smiling, arm in arm and clearly in on the surprise. Penny and Benedict came alongside her too.

Dougie let out a slow breath and held up the black box he had in one hand. 'Alice Greene, the woman I love and trust with my entire heart and every single cell in my body, will you do me the honour of being my wife?'

He lifted his other hand, which held a single orange gerbera.

She leaned forward and whispered in his ear, 'I think you're supposed to open the box when you ask,' she teased.

'Darn it,' said Dougie in his thick Scottish accent, flicking the box open with his thumb.

The truth was, Alice wouldn't have cared if it had been a jelly ring in the box, but the square-cut emerald with a diamond on either side was stunning.

She wrapped her arms around his neck. 'Get up, dummy,' she said, grinning. 'Of course the answer is yes.'

The crowd let out a cheer around her as Dougie picked her up and swung her around.

Alice let out a squeal of delight, catching glimpses of Penny and Benedict, and her mom and dad, who had all clearly plotted with Dougie.

Their relationship had grown stronger and stronger in the last few months. Both of them had seen the counsellor and learned to unpick their deep-rooted feelings of mistrust. It had taken a little time, but they'd finally and joyously got there.

'Hey—' she grinned as he set her down '—does this mean I get to see you in a kilt and find out if the stories about Scotsmen are true?'

He kissed her thoroughly. 'Absolutely,' he said in a voice only for her. 'How about I hire a kilt and start practising?'

Her smile widened. 'You know what they say…practice makes perfect.' And she laughed as he picked her up and spun her around again.

* * * * *

COMING SOON!

We really hope you enjoyed reading this book.
If you're looking for more romance, be sure to
head to the shops when new books are
available on

Thursday 28th April

To see which titles are coming soon, please visit

millsandboon.co.uk/nextmonth

MILLS & BOON

MILLS & BOON®

Coming next month

SHOCK BABY FOR THE DOCTOR
Charlotte Hawkes

'First, however, we're going for a scan.'

Fear rose in Sienna's chest.

'We most certainly are not. I told you, I don't want the entire hospital gossiping about me, which will be inevitable if they know I'm pregnant. Let alone if you're the one accompanying me. I've had a scan. Everything was fine. I am definitely not going for another with you.'

He cast her a cool look.

'Are you quite finished with your rant?'

'I'm not being that conversion nurse who got pregnant with Bas Jensen's baby.'

'You will have that scan, Sienna. And I will be with you.' He folded his arms again, and this time she was struck by quite how authoritative the man was. How had she failed to appreciate quite what power looked like on a man? He didn't just bear the Jensen name, rather he epitomised everything it represented.

She glowered at him, but it seemed to bounce off his solid chest without making a dent.

'So you're…what? Taking charge now?' The idea of it should baulk more. So why didn't it? 'I told you, I don't need your help, I'm perfectly used to taking care of myself.'

'And I'm beginning to think you tell me a few too

many things whilst you aren't as keen to listen. But I suspect that part of the reason for telling me now is because this is beginning to overwhelm you.'

'You're deluded.'

'No, I'm not, but I think you are,' his voice dropped to a sudden, quiet hum. 'I suspect that whether you want to admit it or not, deep down, you don't want to be the one taking care of everything. You want someone to take the reins for once.'

And it was odd but it was still there, that lethal air, swirling beneath the surface like a rip-tide, just waiting to drag her under. But he was controlling it with a fierceness that struck an unexpected cord in her.

As though by controlling that, he could control some dark secret of his own. As if a man like him had dark secrets at all.

Continue reading
SHOCK BABY FOR THE DOCTOR
Charlotte Hawkes

Available next month
www.millsandboon.co.uk

Copyright © 2022 Charlotte Hawkes

MILLS & BOON

THE HEART OF ROMANCE

A ROMANCE FOR EVERY READER

MODERN

Prepare to be swept off your feet by sophisticated, sexy and seductive heroes, in some of the world's most glamourous and romantic locations, where power and passion collide.

HISTORICAL

Escape with historical heroes from time gone by. Whether your passion is for wicked Regency Rakes, muscled Vikings or rugged Highlanders, awaken the romance of the past.

MEDICAL

Set your pulse racing with dedicated, delectable doctors in the high-pressure world of medicine, where emotions run high and passion, comfort and love are the best medicine.

True Love

Celebrate true love with tender stories of heartfelt romance, from the rush of falling in love to the joy a new baby can bring, and a focus on the emotional heart of a relationship.

Desire

Indulge in secrets and scandal, intense drama and plenty of sizzling hot action with powerful and passionate heroes who have it all: wealth, status, good looks…everything but the right woman.

HEROES

Experience all the excitement of a gripping thriller, with an intense romance at its heart. Resourceful, true-to-life women and strong, fearless men face danger and desire - a killer combination!

To see which titles are coming soon, please visit

millsandboon.co.uk/nextmonth

JOIN US ON SOCIAL MEDIA!

Stay up to date with our latest releases, author
news and gossip, special offers and discounts, and
all the behind-the-scenes action
from Mills & Boon...

 millsandboon

 millsandboonuk

 millsandboon

It might just be true love...